SERRA ROSE

Death's Shadow

First published by Serra Rose 2024

Copyright © 2024 by Serra Rose

First published in 2024 by Serra Rose in Melbourne, Australia.

Editing: Ellen Klowden

Cover design by Miblart

For permissions, inquiries, or further information, please contact through:

www.serrarosewrites.com

First edition

ISBN (paperback): 978-0-9756102-2-0
ISBN (hardcover): 978-0-9756102-7-5

This book was professionally typeset on Reedsy.
Find out more at reedsy.com

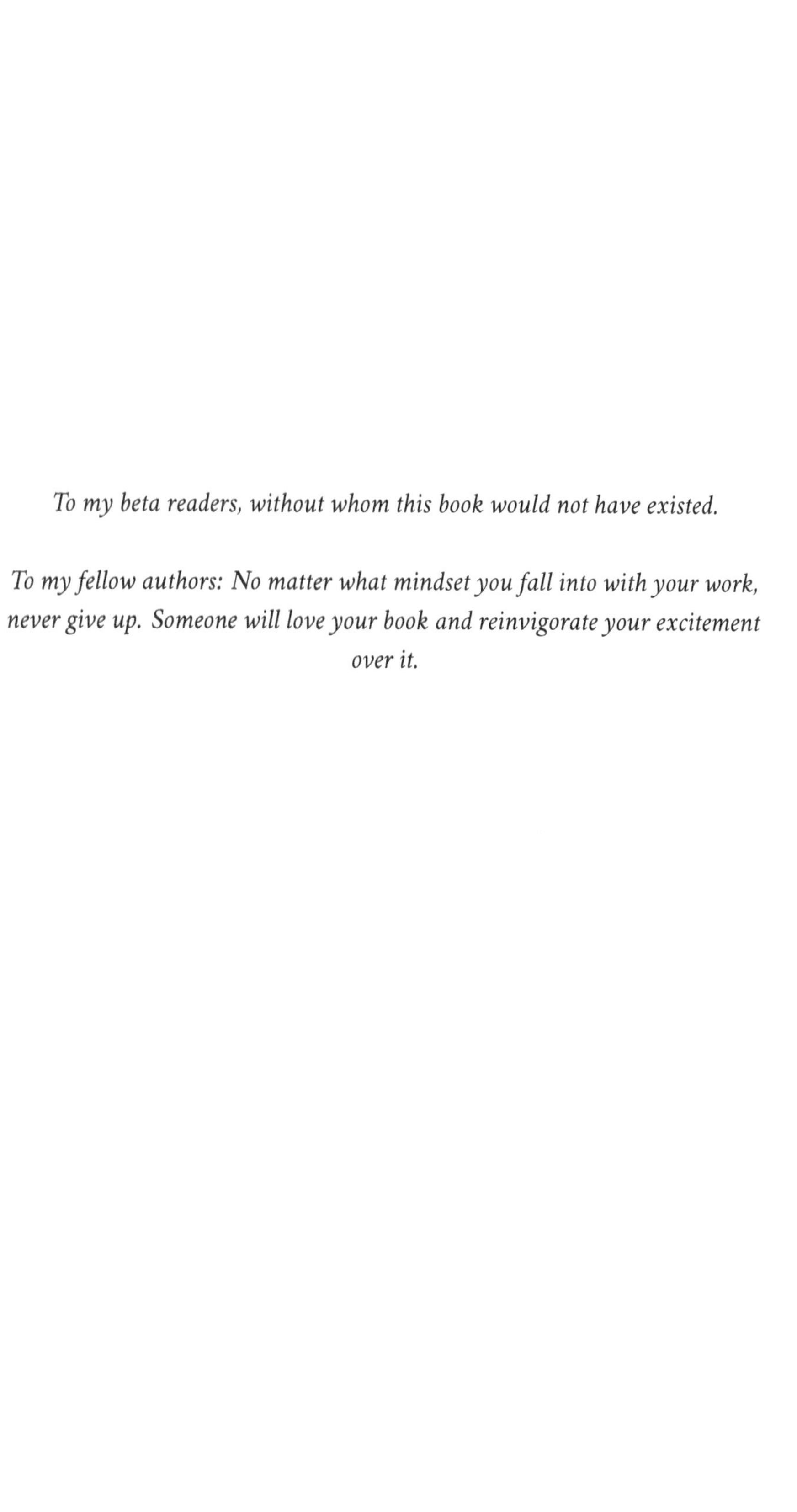

To my beta readers, without whom this book would not have existed.

To my fellow authors: No matter what mindset you fall into with your work, never give up. Someone will love your book and reinvigorate your excitement over it.

Contents

A note to my readers

To my readers:

Thank you for giving this book a chance, I hope you enjoy it as much as I enjoyed writing it. The journey has been full of obstacles, but finally, here they are. From me to you.

To my American readers.

This story is situated in Medieval England, and to stay faithful to my characters and the world they inhabit, I've written the book in British English rather than American English. You may notice words like "colour," "honour," and "realise." These are not errors but reflect the unique English of a different time and place.

Content Warning

This story contains some heavy themes that may trigger some readers. These include but are not limited to:

Abandonment
Anxiety
Trauma
PTSD
Abuse
Loss of loved ones
Talk of child loss.
Violence
Mental torment
War trauma
Acts of war
Forced exile
Razing of buildings and loss of home and property
While this isn't a romance, there is spice.

Remember, always be kind to yourself. Your mental health matters.

Death's Shadow has been read by a sensitivity reader.

Previously in The Shadow Within

Thomas Blake returns from the war in France, to his wife, Emma and their son, Isaac.

Mysterious murders result in Thomas being summoned as an Enforcer to hunt down the killer known as The Shadow of Death.

During his duty as an Enforcer, Thomas struggles to be the father, husband, and brother he was unable to be during his time at war. His wife and daughter die in childbirth. Given that his own mother died giving birth to him, Thomas focuses on being the father his son, Isaac, deserves.

Clues soon point to Graeme, Thomas's twin brother, who has dark dreams and creates a list of people already killed, and others about to die at the hands of The Shadow of Death. There is a darkness inside Graeme that Thomas has known about their entire lives.

Thomas discovers that his son's name is on that list, and he decides to do all he can to protect both his son and his brother, fearing that it will be Graeme from whom he'll have to protect Isaac.

The twins' father, Ethan, falls sick with the Black Death, and he is soon visited by The Shadow of Death.

Graeme is seen standing over the body of the latest victim. Thomas tells him to run. The Enforcers and the Lord of the Manor attempt to hunt him. Thomas is arrested for his actions. Graeme is soon captured, too, and the brothers escape, becoming wanted fugitives.

It is soon revealed that Thomas is the killer; he is unaware that his actions at war had created The Shadow: a physical manifestation of the Darkness within him.

After having killed Graeme, Thomas gives in to the Darkness completely. Graeme's spirit has returned, speaking to Thomas from The Shadow Realm.

Thomas was arrested, but before he can be executed, he is hit by lightning, and dark energy explodes from him, killing all those around him, including Lord Samson and his son, Isaac.

Graeme and Thomas have become one being. *Death.*

Chapter 1

Kempschester - 1348

Alone and scared, Isaac cried out for Father. Enforcers and Lord Samson had told him terrible things, calling his father a murderer. A monster. They'd locked him in a room and left him there. His screams had gone unheard. He sat in the corner, wrapping his arms around his knees. Two swords hung on the wall, and a fire crackled and hissed in the fireplace. The heat of the room did nothing to warm him. He didn't know how to get out. Last he'd seen, Father was locked in a cage in chains.

"Bring the boy out," a voice rumbled from the other side of the door. "Lord Samson wants him to watch."

Isaac jumped to his feet, searching the room. They were coming to get him, and he had a chance to run as soon as the door opened. He could find Father. Nearby, a leather journal lay on the table, alongside a dagger. He grabbed the dagger, hands shaking. The leather handle was easier to hold than when he'd tried to lift Father's sword.

Not so long ago, he had run around in the snow as Father gave chase, the two of them laughing on the cold ground, water seeping into their clothes as Hunter ran after them. That man couldn't be as bad as they claimed. That man only made Isaac feel safe, loved. After Mother died, they had shared sadness in their loss, as Father tried to be the man Isaac had heard so much about.

The door opened, and Isaac ran for freedom, only to be stopped. Three Enforcers stood in his way. He held the dagger up, yelling.

"Lord Samson left a dagger in there with him?" an Enforcer asked.

"He's as feral as his father," someone laughed and took the dagger from him. "There's no point trying to escape, boy; you're in servitude now!"

Arms wrapped around him. "Let me go!" he growled, squirming.

"Stop struggling," an Enforcer commanded him.

Arms wrapped around him, pinning his arms to his side. They walked him past a bedroom. Inside, a woman hummed as she rocked a boy in her arms. She looked up but said nothing.

"Let me go!" Isaac squirmed and kicked. His foot made contact and the Enforcer grunted, dropping him.

Not waiting, he ran towards the room. The woman's eyes widened. Arms wrapped around him again.

"Sorry to disturb you, Lady Vivienne," an Enforcer said.

"Who's child is that?" Lady Vivienne asked.

"I'm Isaac Blake!" Isaac said. "Help me!"

Her eyebrows drew together. "Is that his son? Why is he in here? Shouldn't he be in the servant quarters?"

"Nothing to worry about. We have him under control." They left the woman.

"Stop squirming, you little animal," a voice grunted in his ear. "Or I'll throw you in a cell."

The idea of being chained to the wall was enough to make him stop.

The Enforcers walked into a courtyard filled with people, leading him through the angry crowd. It was morning, but the sky was dark, with a cold wind pulling at his tunic and cloak. A drop of rain fell on his cheek. Everyone in the courtyard faced a wooden tower in front of him.

Chains rattled as they marched Father out, heavily shackled and escorted by Enforcers. Isaac whimpered. As their eyes met through the crowd, Father's warmth was gone. The eyes of a stranger stared back, as if Father didn't recognise him.

"Father!" he cried out in desperation.

Isaac broke free of the Enforcer's grip and ran. Father would protect him. He had fought in battles; he would be strong enough to take on the Enforcers, and they could leave. But Father only watched as the Enforcers caught him easily. He screamed. *Why isn't he protecting me? What is wrong with him?*

Voices around him rose, the angry buzz deafening.

"Your father is going to burn," his captor whispered in his ear.

Tears streamed down his face as men tied his father to a post. Crying, he closed his eyes. *They cannot make me watch!* They had set his house on fire and torn him from Aunt Amelia. Now, he was to live in this strange place without his family.

"Ruuuun!" A voice boomed in his head.

Isaac turned at the voice. *Uncle Graeme!* He searched the crowd, but people towered above him. Uncle Graeme was dead, but it was his voice.

"Uncle Graeme?" he called out, his voice drowned by the noise.

"Kill them," Graeme's voice echoed in his head. **"Kill them all."**

Lightning struck and darkness enveloped Isaac.

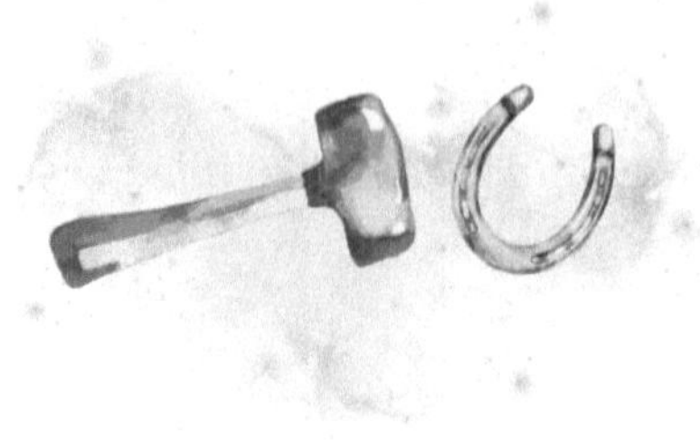

The grip around Isaac was gone, as was the courtyard. It was dark and foggy but no longer cold.

"**Isaac,**" a voice called to him that sounded like Mother's.

"Mother?" His own voice echoed in the silence.

"**Isaac, where are you?**"

He took a step towards the voice, then stopped as people in flames approached him. Scared, he tried to back away. There were faces in the flames. Grandfather's. Mother's.

"Mother?" He gasped with the joy of glimpsing her welcoming face. He reached out. *She's come back for me!*

Her eyes bore into his, but she didn't seek to comfort him. Instead, as she neared, a deep fear ran down the back of Isaac's skull. Mother was gone, lost to him, vacant. He tried to run from the people in the red flames. Their whispers followed him. Terrified, Isaac called out for Father, his voice echoing in the emptiness. But as he ran, he started to fade. Red flames began to climb around his body, burning away his fear. He stopped, trying to remember why he was running or who he was looking for. Only nothingness awaited him.

"Isaac." The voice was familiar. It called deep within him, waking him again as he remembered who he was. *Father! He's come to take me home! I knew he wouldn't leave me.* Isaac ran towards the voice.

CHAPTER 1

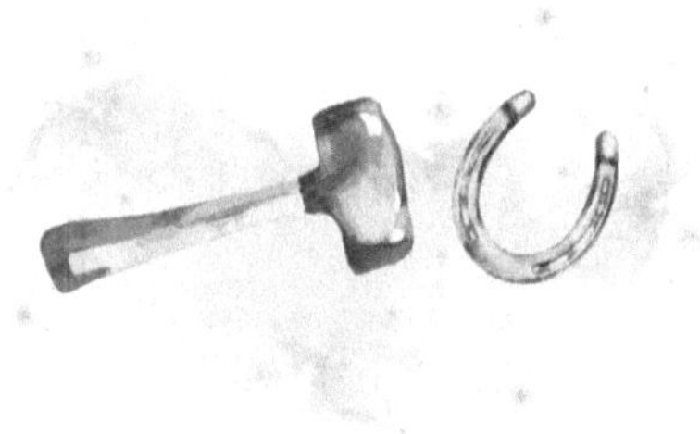

Back in the courtyard, everyone who had been shouting before lay on the ground around him, sleeping. A figure knelt over him, looking away from him. *Father*? But before he could say anything, something inside held him silent. It was not his father, but someone else. Something dark. One eye white, one black. Dark lines marked one side of his face and neck, and dark fog seemed to come from his body.

"Thomas?" Aunt Amelia called out.

Father stood, moving towards her.

"I saw what happened; how are you alive?" she asked.

She spoke in a low, but audible voice amidst the eerie silence of the courtyard.

"Amelia." Father's voice was equally low.

"Lightning hit you in the chest. No one survives that. You should be dead." She looked around at the bodies. "*I* should be dead. How did I know to run from this?"

"Graeme told you to," Father said.

"That was him? I thought I was hearing things."

"You were not." Father confirmed.

"Where is he?" She looked around again. "Thomas, you killed everyone in this courtyard."

He killed them?

Father walked away.

"Thomas and Graeme Blake are no more," he said.

No more? Father is gone? Isaac's eyes stung.

"Then who are you?" Aunt Amelia asked.

Father looked down at the ground.

"I am Death," he revealed. "Live a long, happy life, far away from here. Do not return to Riverwick. Go back to Willowdale. Forget about Graeme and all that happened here. Know that he loved you."

She reached for him. "Wait."

Father changed shape. A shadowy figure stood where Father had a moment before. Aunt Amelia stepped back, her mouth open. It was not Father, but a monster.

"I said leave!" the thing said.

It walked into the stable, before riding Father's horse out, a man again. As he approached the archway, something black appeared in his hand. A scythe.

Hunter ran towards Father with a low growl. Shadows or fog curled around them, and they disappeared.

"Father?" Isaac looked to where they had been. "Don't leave me!"

"Isaac?" Aunt Amelia called out. "You were here when…" she rushed towards him. "You're alive?" Her arms wrapped around him. "Oh, you sweet boy. You're safe now."

"What happened to my father?" Isaac asked. "Will he come back?" He was trying not to be scared, not to cry, but his efforts were overcome by the idea of his father leaving him. He didn't want to be alone.

Aunt Amelia pulled away, meeting his eyes. "I don't know, but he's gone now. They're both gone." A tear slid down her cheek as she lifted his chin, examining his face. "Oh, little darling, does it hurt?"

"Gone? Gone where?" His voice broke. His own tears fell freely.

"I don't know." She glanced around. "We should leave; you shouldn't have to see this."

"They were going to burn him," he told her. "They wanted me to watch." Lightning had come out of nowhere, and those who'd wanted Father to burn were dead.

Aunt Amelia seemed at a loss for words, instead pulling him to her again. In her arms, he felt safe, as he had when Father had embraced him.

"Uncle Graeme was here," he said. "I heard him shouting, but in my head."

"You heard him, too?" Aunt Amelia's voice rose.

"I did, right before the lightning hit; and then I was in the dark place, but Father called me back. I heard his voice."

"The dark place?" Aunt Amelia's voice shook. "What are you talking about, Isaac?"

"There was fog, and there were strange people there, *on fire*. I saw my mother, but something was wrong with her. She didn't know me. Then Father whispered my name, and I was back here." He peered up at his Aunt.

Screams rang out from the town. Many screams, a sound that sent chills through Isaac. "What's that?" he asked.

"We have to go," Aunt Amelia said.

"Our house burned down. Where do we go?" Isaac asked.

"I don't know. Perhaps James can help us," she said.

Mother was gone, as was Father, but he had Aunt Amelia. She picked him up and carried him to the stable.

They fled from a sight that Isaac knew he would never forget. People running, and screaming, chased by a man on a horse. Father's horse, Guinevere. Nightmares had become real as the man swung a scythe, and flames burned around them. Now, Isaac sat at the front of a horse with Aunt Amelia behind him, her cloak wrapped around him but unable to stop his shaking. Cold and scared, he understood his life would never return to as it was, but he wasn't ready to give up on it yet. As they neared Riverwick, a heavy black smoke rose above the village. A thick, burning smell stuck to the back of his throat. It reminded him of the day the church burned down and of watching his own house in flames.

Aunt Amelia stopped the horse. "The village is on fire." Screams reached them, and Aunt Amelia covered his ears, pulling the cloak over his face.

Isaac pulled himself free of the cloak. "Uncle James? What if he needs help? And John."

"I'm not sure we should be here. Something bad happened, Isaac."

"I'm not afraid," he lied, his voice shaking.

"*Run!*" A voice warned them, and Leo rode into view, with a quick glance over his shoulder. "Save yourselves; he will come for you!"

"Who?" Aunt Amelia asked.

"Thomas. He's not human!" Leo said.

"Thomas did this?" Aunt Amelia questioned him.

"I thought you said my father was gone?" Isaac said to Aunt Amelia, twisting around to look up at her.

Aunt Amelia followed Leo. "Please, stop. Tell me what happened?"

"He burned the village to the ground and is slaughtering any survivors with a scythe, telling them it is their time." Leo's eyes were wide as they darted to Isaac's face. "His father's evil has spread to him. Leave him and flee, far from here."

"Where's James?" Aunt Amelia demanded.

"He's dead. *Everyone's* dead." Leo turned from them, riding away.

Three villagers ran towards them. "He's coming! The Shadow of Death is coming!"

Aunt Amelia kicked the side of the brown horse and they fled. Isaac looked back at Riverwick, and a figure emerged through the smoke. Empty eyes met his. Father was not gone, after all, yet he was almost unrecognisable. There was no warmth in the smile he gave before turning back towards the village. Cold, Isaac leaned against Aunt Amelia, wrapping his arms around her, the cloak dropping over him as they escaped.

"You're safe now, Isaac. We'll go somewhere he cannot find us," Aunt Amelia whispered.

Chapter 2

O*akborough - 1368*

Raven's skin crawled.

The sensation of being watched had returned, and she suppressed a shiver. She turned in the saddle to scan her surroundings. The busy street showed no one to be looking at her. A shadow moved in her peripheral vision, and dread crept up her spine. A sense of urgency had brought her into town to see Zac, more brother than cousin, and she hurried the rest of the way to his smithy. Dark dreams leading to sleepless nights had left her exhausted.

A picture of a hammer and a sword hung above the shop, with *Dale*

Smithy written underneath on a wooden sign. It swung in the breeze, the metal hinges creaking. The need to talk to her cousin about her worries overwhelmed her as she dismounted the horse. In front of the shop, a man and a woman were locked in an intimate embrace, kissing. The man's hands drifted down the woman's body.

"The street isn't the place for that. Perhaps you should keep that in the bedroom," she said.

The woman pulled away, red-faced as she stared at Raven in embarrassment. With hazel eyes and brown hair, she was a small woman with a round face. The man's eyes met her own, one brown, the other smoky grey, hair as black as her own, and a full beard. He murmured something to the woman, caressing her cheek. She pulled away completely, casting one more look at Raven before saying something and walking away. The man closed his eyes and took in a deep breath with a small smile. Then he opened them, annoyance clear on his face as he breathed out.

"Thank you for that, Raven," Zac said in a low voice, eyes still on the woman.

"No, thank you, now I have to scrub my eyes," she retorted. "You have a bed, why must you do that outside?"

"We were kissing, it's hardly cause for your alarm…or judgement." He glared at her. "Is there a reason for your poorly timed visit, little sister?"

Despite the fact that they were cousins, he always called her 'little sister'. Before she could answer, a woman with long, white hair caught her attention. The woman's ice-blue eyes were wide, staring. *She's looking at me.* A shiver ran down her spine.

"Don't look at her. She'll offer to read your palm, or look into your future or something," Zac warned. "Then she'll want money."

"Darkness," the woman declared, her voice a whisper as she stared at Zac. Her eyes shifted back to Raven. "And Death. His shadow follows you."

"Vera, go away." Zac ordered. "We don't want to hear it."

Raven walked past him, stepping into his smithy. The forge burned, and the smell of hot metal filled the air. He followed her in, and he moved an unfinished sword into the flames.

"I came to talk to you," she said. "I can't tell Mother; it would only worry her."

He pointed, directing her to take a seat in a chair near his workbench. "What is it?" His tone changed, softening.

"I've been having dreams," she revealed. "And they scare me."

He sat opposite her, his face unreadable. "What kind of dreams?"

"We're surrounded by shadows, and someone is watching us," she whispered. "I can feel his stare before I see him, a man in a black cloak with the hood over his head. There is nothing but emptiness in his eyes, and he reaches out for me, but you step forward. Darkness surrounds you, and you're taken."

"Taken where?" he asked.

Raven's stomach churned just talking about the dream. The overwhelming fear of losing him, that it was a warning, hadn't faded as the sun rose.

"I don't know," she admitted. "I woke up calling your name, terrified that you were really gone." She took a breath and let it out. "Something is coming."

"Something?" he pressed.

"Something dark," she replied.

Zachary's gaze never left her face. "Do you think there's anything to your dream? Or is this your fear of the darkness of your father?"

I think we should all be running, far from here. She didn't say it, afraid to put words to such dread.

"I see. I can see why you don't want to tell Aunt Amelia. With all she has gone through, I'm not sure she'd respond to that very well," he commented.

"What if the Darkness has caught up to us? Their Darkness," she asked.

He leaned forward, his hand on hers for comfort. "I know you're afraid of succumbing to—"

"With good reason," she cut him off. "I'm having dark dreams, just as he did."

"He wasn't always bad." Zac sat back with a sigh. "All you know is what Aunt Amelia told you of him. The bad things. I never told you what I remembered of him. She'd asked me not to. She thought it best to leave him in the past."

"You told me he was like a second father when yours was away at war," Raven said.

Zac nodded thoughtfully. "I have memories of him making a wooden sword for me. He taught me to draw, and to ride a horse. The man I remember was kind. I know Aunt Amelia loved him. She tried to forget him, the good and the bad. She cried a lot after everything happened."

"Kind? Until he gave in to darkness and killed people?" She looked away from Zac. "Mother told me about the dreams he had. Now *I'm* having them."

"Raven, you are *not* like your father," he consoled her. "Any more than I'm like mine."

"But we are still their children. Do you not fear what dark inheritance lies within our blood?" she asked. "What if he's the one watching me?"

He frowned. "This really worries you."

"It does. The feeling of being watched, even now, by something menacing, makes this room cold," she confessed.

"Raven, how do I ease your mind? There is only you and me in this room; no one is watching us," he asked.

His words did little to ease the feeling of being watched.

"I know you're filled with fear. I wish I could remove it for you," he said. "You're safe, Raven."

She sighed, the weight of disappointment on her. "I'm not sure that we are."

"I'll always protect you." He moved towards the forge. "We cannot let what our minds show us while we sleep, feed into our fear." He gave her his tools. "Here, pull the sword from the forge, will you?"

She feared that there was already Darkness in her.

The fire cast warmth over her as she carried the sword to the anvil, and out of habit, she started beating the metal. The sword seemed a little on the small side. This type of work had always been relaxing for her, and it was no different now. Her cousin watched her with a smile on his face.

"You did this to calm me." She cast him an accusatory glance.

"It usually works." He watched her. "Are you sure you don't want to work here with me?"

"And walk in on you and whichever woman takes your fancy?" She rolled her eyes. "No thank you. Besides, when Lucian and I marry, I'll live with him. I won't have time to come to Oakborough."

He laughed, then reached out for his tools. She handed them over and moved towards the workbench, glancing at papers covering the top.

At the top was a drawing of a sword, a scythe drawn on the blade, *Kempschester* written across the top.

"What is this?" she asked, picking up the page that contained the sword.

He barely glanced at it. "You're not the only one haunted by dreams," he admitted.

"You weren't going to say anything?" she demanded.

"I didn't think it was anything." He shrugged.

Her hand shook as she glanced at the drawing. "Why do you draw this sword? What are your dreams about?"

He hesitated. "Kempschester."

"You've been dreaming of Kempschester?" her voice rose.

Zac gave her a tight lipped smile. "Calm yourself, Raven, it's no different to when I was a child."

"So you're having nightmares again, of the shadow being?" Raven asked.

"No…but it is connected to the shadow. To my father," he told her.

She waited for him to finish.

"In a bedroom of the estate, I see a leather journal. They showed me, told me it was Uncle Graeme's," he said.

Ice crawled down her spine. "No, that would have burned."

Zac let out a sigh. "I know, but I can't stop dreaming about it, and about the sword. My father's sword."

Raven studied his face. "Why? What answers do you hope to find from a monster?"

"He's a monster to you through stories. He's my father. I still have hope."

We're going to drown in darkness. She shuddered, hoping she was wrong. "He left you, Zac; you need to stop trying to hold onto a young boy's desperation for what was lost. There is no hope, only nightmares."

"He brought me back. I was in The Dark Place, and his voice called me back," Zac said.

She put a hand to his arm. "Yet he has never sought you out as you seek him. Please stop; don't bring that into our lives."

He frowned at her words. "The sword is my last connection to him."

"You *have* a family, Zac; why must you seek one who abandoned you and left you for dead?"

He said nothing as the hammer hit metal.

"Your obsession with your father isn't going to end well. Darkness took much from you, and from my mother. Don't let it take you, too," she warned. "I cannot lose you, Zac."

He put the hot blade into water, and a hiss of steam rose. "You won't lose me. I'm right here."

She had come there about her own dreams, but now it was his that caused the most worry. Zac had always provided a sense of comfort, ready to protect her. His presence gave her hope that the darkness she feared was nothing but just that. Fear. For that reason she had come there, hopeful that he'd console her, convince her that she had nothing to worry about. But as she stared at the drawing of the sword, uneasiness constricted in her chest. She hoped she was wrong, that she wouldn't be left to face the darkness alone.

Chapter 3

Zachary rode under the archway, entering what used to be the main street of Kempschester. The early autumn sun warmed his back through his tunic. He rode through empty streets of what was once a thriving town. Now silent as a grave, piles of bone, of those who'd died twenty years before, remained. The Estate of Lord Samson was still mostly intact. It had not been destroyed by fire, as much of Kempschester had been, but it nonetheless had blackened walls that stood high, a remnant of the past. *Every time I come here, it only seems to grow more eerie.* It was his third time there in as many years, and it still cast chills down his spine.

That day, twenty years before, was firmly cast in his mind. The town burned, with a heavy scent of charred flesh and the sight of a dark figure pursuing people. But before that, he'd seen a leather journal in the Lord's room. Hopeful that it was still here, he had come a long way. For the past few months, recurring dreams of sword, journal, and Kempschester had brought him back there, hoping it would put a stop to the dreams. Raven's warning to not return echoed in his mind. *Is she right? Should I have stayed far away from here?* She had an annoying habit of being right, sometimes, with her warnings. But he needed to know, to see if his dreams held anything. *Are they still here, after all these years?*

Lance's hooves resounded sharply on the cobblestones as Zachary made his way towards the Estate. To be back there after all those years still stirred memories of a life he had refused to let go of, despite Aunt Amelia's insistence. The loss of his parents had never left him, and that his father wasn't truly dead only made it worse. He was sure his own death had occurred here. His father's voice still echoed in his mind, calling him back from a place of shadows and fog. A place that felt as real as this world.

His own reflection was a greater reminder of the father he sought. He'd taken to growing a beard, the only difference between his face, and what he remembered of his father's was that his eyes were brown, not blue. His hair sat at his shoulders, longer than his father's had been. The smokey grey eye was a constant reminder of that day, but none more so than his own reflection. On that day, black lines had covered half of his face, only to disappear a few days later. Only he still saw them, like a shadow under his skin. A reminder.

A stone archway leading into the courtyard was blackened, half of it crumbled. In the courtyard, no one had removed any debris; the skeletal remains of the dead remained scattered around the yard. *It could have been me lying here among them.* A chill passed through Zachary as he climbed off his horse. "Stay here," he told Lance, rubbing the horse's neck.

Stepping around the bones, he moved towards the stable. As he entered, a large black bird took flight towards him, its raspy croak breaking the silence. Heart pounding, he ducked out of the way. The cage in which he had seen his father still remained, door wide open, one hinge gone.

"**Runnn!**" Zachary turned at the voice, a mere echo of the past. A voice both he and Amelia shared memories of hearing.

"**Kill them,**" he heard Uncle's voice again, filled with Darkness, commanding. "**Kill them all**." And his father had. The Darkness that followed, however short, felt like a lifetime. He had started to disappear, red flames engulfing him, before his father's voice brought him back. Aunt Amelia had later told him of Uncle Graeme's talk of lost souls. Had he become a lost soul, he might still have been in that place.

But some part of him still felt that moment, where he had left the living; his heart had stopped. It had left a void in his chest. He had awoken, only for his father to walk away. Overwhelmed with grief, he glanced at where his father had been as Lord Samson and an Enforcer had approached with torches, ready to kill him. To burn him. It could only be their remains that lay closest to the rubble that had been the pyre.

Finally, he moved towards the stone building. A tunnel was completely caved in. He had walked that tunnel once, leading to underground cells. A grate in the ground shone light into a cell under his feet. He hoped no one had been down there when it caved in.

As the stone building pulled at him, he couldn't hold back the memories. Lord Samson had dragged him in there on that last day. With his father caged in the stable, the Lord had sat him down, pointing at a journal, with drawings and words that he couldn't read. He had told Zachary that his father and Uncle Graeme were murderers. That his father had killed people on that list, and he was going to pay for his crime. Lord Samson had then said that Zachary would be a servant for the rest of his life, as people would be fearful of the son of a killer.

An Enforcer had entered, whispering to the Lord. The book landed on a small table with a soft thump before the Enforcer left. He had found himself locked in the room, as Lord Samson ordered someone to guard the door.

Before he could stop himself, he moved towards the building. *If that journal is still in one piece...* Uncle Graeme had been as much a father figure, in the years his father had been away at war. A raven, possibly the same one as before, sat above the doorway. He took a step through and into the building.

Stone walls and marble floors were scorched by the flames. The further he walked, the black scorching faded, and his footsteps echoed. The walls were covered in paintings and tapestries. As he made his way towards the room in which Lord Samson had held him, the hairs on the back of his neck stood up. Unease followed him. *Why am I digging up the past?* Aunt Amelia had told him *never* to look back, or return. To live his life for the future and let go of the pain of the past. Unable to, he kept returning, in hopes for some sign that his father remained here.

Raven's presence had been a ray of light for the both of them, but it didn't chase away the shadows in his mind. The fears and grief of a child still gripped him, even now as he walked through empty halls. The cold of twenty years ago remained.

In a doorway to a bedroom, his fear suffocated him. Forcing it down, he stepped into the room and his eyes fell to the book, in the same place Lord Samson had thrown it twenty years prior. Zachary reached for it, his fingers closing around the leather. Opening it, the pages were yellowed, ink faded yet still readable. He recalled seeing Uncle Graeme writing in the journal, hunched over his desk. A memory forced its way up, one he must have buried. Watching Uncle Graeme from the doorway, and his uncle staring at him with black eyes.

The journal slipped from his fingers, hitting the floor with a dull thump, landing open. Names jumped out at him. Lord Samson's was one he recognised. Then a name he hadn't been able to use in years. *Isaac Blake.* The name had died with his father and Uncle Graeme, and he'd become Zachary Dale. Aunt Amelia had also changed her name, to disconnect them all from any link to the Blake twins. Word of The Shadow of Death had spread across the country. Mothers told their children stories of the shadow that would find them. But no one knew of the family that remained.

With a shaking hand, he picked up the journal again, heart loud enough to wake the dead. Flicking the pages back, he read through the other names. Ethan Blake, his grandfather's name, and others that he didn't recognise. Heat spread through his face as he returned to the last page, staring at his *own* name again. Aunt Amelia had told him the names were of people whose deaths Graeme had foreseen.

"He saw my death?" Fear prickled his skull. "Was I supposed to die?"

Chapter 4

Raven stood in front of the closed blacksmith. Worry churned in her stomach. It wasn't like Zachary to close his shop. She'd come here after a night of dark dreams, in which a deep sense of foreboding had driven her back to Oakborough, only to find his smithy closed.

She knocked on the door with urgency. It was normal that he detached from the world for days at a time to lose himself in work. Just as likely, he was wrapped in the arms of a woman, drawn to what many called 'the Zachary Dale charm'. But this time, something told her it wasn't either.

"Zac!" When he didn't answer, she knocked louder with her fist on the wooden door. "Zac, it's me. Open up, or I'll let myself in. If anyone's in there with you, this is your warning."

"He's not here," a voice behind her said.

One she recognised.

Startled, she turned around, standing almost face to face with a tall man dressed in finery. He had brown hair and kind grey eyes.

She lowered her head in respect. "Lord Gerard!" She tried to hide her panic from him. "Do you know where he is?"

"One of my Enforcers saw him leaving this morning. He was heading west." His eyes studied her face. "I've never noticed how the two of you resemble each other."

Heading west. Zac, what are you doing? Their conversation from a few days before hung over her. His mentions of Kempschester. Of the sword and the journal. *Why can't you leave it alone?*

"I have a key; I'm going to let myself in," she said.

Lord Gerard nodded and left her alone in front of the shop. She pulled out the key Zac had given to her, pushing it into the lock.

The door closed behind her, shutting out the sunlight. Inside, her eyes adjusted to the dim room; the forge that he always kept hot was out. The sweet scent of red-hot iron lingered. She cast a look over his work bench, searching for the drawings. It felt wrong to go through his belongings while he wasn't here, but she had a sense that they wouldn't be there.

Orders for swords and armour littered the bench, for soldiers and Enforcers. Her own name jumped out at her. Raven picked up the pages and felt a warm glow. There were drawings of armour and a sword. The armour was for a metal breastplate, the blade a smaller one than what the soldiers and Enforcers carried. Casting her eyes around the workshop, she found the sword. The very same sword she had seen only days ago.

Lifting the weapon, she swung it around. it was a perfect weight, and well balanced in her grip. Instead of excitement, though, she just felt dread. Zac's absence only added to it. Her jaw ached as she bit down in frustration at her brother's actions. *Why can't you just let go of the idea you'll have a happy reunion with your father?* She sighed.

A knock on the door made her jump. Raven opened the door to find a blond man in the doorway, wearing the brown cloak and chain mail of Enforcers. His tanned face held a stern expression, with a hard glint in his blue eyes. He had a few days of growth lining his jaw, and his shoulders were broad. He pushed his way past her.

"Who are you?" he demanded, glancing around. "I've never seen you before, Where's the blacksmith?"

"He's out of town," she said, not liking his tone. "Who are you?"

"If he's out of town, why are you here?" He cast a look towards the door to Zac's bedroom in the back corner of the shop. A smirk crossed his face. "Are you one of his women? Should you be here without him?" He pointed to the sword in her hand. "You could hurt yourself."

Raven threw back her head and laughed, unable to help herself. It only angered the Enforcer.

"What's so amusing?" he demanded.

"One of his women?" she repeated through tears. "I'm his cousin, you blind oaf!"

"Careful," he warned. "I'm an Enforcer."

"I don't care who or what you are; you walked into Zac's workshop and made an assumption you had no place making."

She moved towards the door, holding it open to make him leave and caught his eyes darting down the length of her body.

She frowned. "Like what you see, do you?" she snapped, and his eyes quickly lifted to hers.

The Enforcer met her gaze without flinching. "What if I do?" he asked with a smirk.

His words only enraged her more. "You're lucky he isn't here. Enforcer or not, he would have had a sword on you for that. We may be cousins, but to him, I'm his little sister."

"What can a blacksmith do to an Enforcer?" He laughed. "He wouldn't risk being thrown in a cell because I looked at his cousin the wrong way."

He cast his eyes over her again, smirking at her discomfort. She closed the gap between them, pressing her sword to his throat, choking on her own rage.

The Enforcer's eyes widened. Raven enjoyed a flicker of joy within her rage.

"I am betrothed to another; you have no place eyeing me like that," she declared.

"I'll have you in chains for this!" His eyes glinted dangerously.

"On your knees," she ordered, pressing the blade in, feeling movement as he swallowed.

His resistance lost out to the fear of what she might do, and the Enforcer sank to his knees. He glared up at her, eyes lit with a mixture of anger, humiliation, and a spark of intrigue. He had the authority to arrest her, and the idea should have scared her.

A voice in the back of her head told her to stop. Threatening the Enforcer was stupid, and it would get back to Zac. That's if Lord Gerard didn't have her arrested first. But she was enjoying the moment.

"Give me your sword," she demanded.

He didn't move, so she reached for his sword, holding that on him, too.

"I will arrest you," he glared. "I hope you like dark cells."

She chuckled. "You're going to tell Lord Gerard, or your captain, that you were disarmed and forced to your knees by a woman?"

His nostrils flared, face reddening.

"I thought not." Raven smiled coldly at him.

"Now what?" he challenged, his eyes hardening as he scowled up at her. "You don't strike me as a killer, so what's your next move?"

She pressed the blade in a little harder, drawing blood. Fear glinted in his eyes. Satisfied he'd received her warning, she held his sword towards him, offering it up. "You should leave."

Fury blazed in his eyes as he pulled the sword from her hand and rose to his feet. "I'll not forget this," he grunted as he re-sheathed his sword.

"I'll not forget your lack of manners," she returned, her own anger a storm within. She caught the humiliation under his rage. "Looks like I struck a nerve. Perhaps next time you'll think twice before staring at someone in such an unwelcome way. Next time it won't be me with a sword to your throat. It will be Zac. Now get out."

"There's something wrong with you," he accused, storming out.

The door slammed behind him.

Raven put down her sword, fear crushing her chest as the feeling of being watched returned. She turned, her eyes darting around the workshop, but no one was there.

"There's no argument there," she murmured in response to the Enforcer, suppressing a shiver.

Chapter 5

With the journal grasped tight, Zachary left the building to find Lance still waiting for him. He rubbed the steed's muzzle and put the book in a leather saddlebag, leading the horse from the estate. He knew where he would find the sword; his dreams had told him as much. Passing houses that could only have belonged to nobility, they were almost as untouched as part of Lord Samson's. He stopped. The flames barely touched this house, just as he'd seen in his dreams. This was where the sword would be. A connection that he had sought since the day they ran from Riverwick. Once finished here, he would ride to the village that had been his home. It was always a comfort to return, regardless of what remained.

He left Lance behind, approaching the house. The door hung from one hinge, and the smell of rotten wood stuck to the house. He stirred up ash, and a startled rat ran past him. Zachary found the sword on a table. He knew this sword all too well. His father had sat next to him, explaining the meaning of the scythe engraved in the blade. With the sword gripped tight in his hand, he stared at the scythe. *It's his! Just like I dreamed.* A mixture of joy and pain washed over Zachary. He had come here looking for the only connection to his father that still remained. His father had gone everywhere with this.

Leaving the town on the back of his horse, he caught sight of the familiar empty plains and bridge. By now he knew the way by heart. But every time he crossed the bridge, the thud of hooves brought back their escape from the horrors of Kempschester. Below, the hiss of the river was louder after recent rains. The walls of Hazelbury were visible as he rode, his mother's town. Pain squeezed in his chest as he gazed at it, a soft, comforting voice humming rose up from his memories. Her eyes filled with warmth. Her arms around him. *She rests in Riverwick.*

He left the bridge, following the path away from Hazelbury. Squeaky wheels drew his attention. A man with a cart approached, heading in the direction of Hazelbury, recognition in his eyes at the sight of Zachary. Recognition quickly became fear. Up until now, Zachary had avoided being noticed, aware of how much like his father he looked.

"You've returned?" The farmer asked in shock, looking at the town behind. "Please, don't hurt me, I'm just a farmer. I wasn't there that night." His voice trembled. He had clearly mistaken Zachary for his father.

For a warm day, the chill that passed through Zachary went deep. The sun shone, but it was as if a cloud had passed overhead.

"I'm not here to hurt you," he said. "Why didn't they rebuild Kempschester?"

"Because you haunt it. The town is cursed," came the Farmer's reply.

Zachary frowned. This was exactly what he'd hoped to avoid. "I'm sorry, you have mistaken me."

"I don't think so. I know who you are. I ask that you spare me. I have a wife, children."

Zachary said nothing and turned his focus on the path.

"You're him, aren't you?" another peasant approached, a woman. "It's not the Shadow of Death, it's his son. Look, his face is unmarked." She cast a wary look over Zachary. "You look just like him. I've seen you ride into Kempschester. You were there that night, weren't you?"

"I was." He nodded to acknowledge her recognition of him.

"You poor child," she said. "To witness that of your own father, and have to run from him along with the rest of us."

"Tell me about him," he said to the man. "He was once a farmer, like you. Did you know him?"

The farmer looked around fearfully, as if afraid The Shadow of Death would appear before them. "We traded often with your father and uncle. Such a shame, what happened to him." He shook his head sadly. "I wasn't there that night, but I knew people who were. Lord Samson tried to kill him. Everyone celebrated that The Shadow of Death had been captured. Instead, he killed everyone who showed up to watch. Then he burned down the entire town and ran everyone down with a black scythe from the back of a horse. Everyone in his path fell. Very few escaped to tell their story. People still see him, and the dead walk the streets at night, crying to be freed, tormented."

"I remember the hunt for The Shadow of Death," the woman said. "He... your father was in charge of hunting him. No one saw the darkness that lay in him. He continues to haunt all of Kempshire. Now he just calls himself Death."

"He's been seen?" Hope flared in Zachary. "Recently?"

They both stared at him, a glint of terror and pity in their eyes.

The man spoke up. "Why do you come back here? I don't know how you escaped. You should have stayed, where-ever you ran to. You'll only be met by fear in this place. He and his twin brother were well known, and your face will hold no comfort. Not while he still haunts us. What is it you seek? Why did you return?"

"Because he was my father, and unlike everyone else, I have mostly happy memories of the man. And my uncle."

"You want to find him?" the woman asked with wide eyes. "Knowing what he did, what he continues to do, and you still want to find him?" She backed away.

"I do," he confirmed.

The man shook his head in disbelief. "If your father wanted to be found, especially by you, do you not think he would have sought you out? He burned everything that connected him to his life as Thomas Blake. Now he's barely a man any more. He's been seen kneeling over the dead; and some say that if you see him, it's because you're next. You're only asking for trouble in seeking him out."

Zachary had heard this from Raven and Aunt Amelia for years. To hear it from a stranger wasn't going to stop him on his search.

"Go back to wherever it is you ran to," the woman said. "You'll be better off. His name has left a curse in his wake. You'll not find what you're looking for here. Kempshire will fear your name and face as they fear his."

They spoke in hushed tones, shooting him fearful looks. Zachary knew any further attempt to converse with the pair would be wasted, so he resumed his ride towards Riverwick.

The woman called out to him. "Those who knew him most, were first to fall by his blade. His own village didn't survive him."

He said nothing in response, leaving them and their fear behind. This was the closest he had gotten to any sign of his father, and it was likely he still remained in the area. The desire to see his home, regardless of its condition, was too much.

He followed the only road to his village, and soon reached a split in the road. Signs pointed to Riverwick, Kempschester, and Ashvale. As he started to follow the road to Riverwick, the chill from that day gripped his insides. A deep fear that had him trembling and cold, clinging to his aunt under her cloak years before.

Turn back.

There were no spoken words, and he *felt* them more than heard them. Lance had stopped, Zachary frozen in the saddle. Paralysed by dread, he considered going home. Back to Oakborough, to his life as a blacksmith. Where he could convince himself there weren't things in the world that people liked to ignore. Where his life would always feel like he didn't belong. As that settled down around him, he broke through the dread.

I need to keep going. I'll always wonder if I should have kept going, if I go home now.

Riverwick came into view, the familiar sight of more remains scattered around the village. Houses were almost nothing but large piles of blackened wood. A burned sign lay on the ground in halves. A sharp weapon had sliced through it, the letters *Leo's* across the wood barely visible. A memory from deep inside told him this had been a tavern. A warm room flashed into his mind, an older, dark-skinned man and crinkled eyes smiling at him. That smile turned to fear as he rode from the burning village towards them. Zachary climbed off his horse and knelt over the sign, running his hand across the flaking surface.

"Wherever you went, I hope you made it," he murmured. Leo had seemed a happy man, friendly to all.

He followed the road to the centre of the village. The only thing left standing was a graveyard next to what should have been a church. He approached and dropped the leader rope to find his way to a grave he knew. Even without a headstone, he still knew where she lay. Aunt Amelia had brought him here in the days following her death, as had his father when he wasn't working in Kempschester. He fell to one knee, hands over the ground.

"Hello, Mother and Sister," he whispered with a break in his voice. "I'm back."

Chest aching, Zachary closed his eyes, head bowed. Her face in his mind was still as clear as it always had been. A gentle smile and warm hugs. Her comfort after his nightmares about Enforcers, whispering 'You're safe, my little boy.' Her telling him stories about his father, and the man he was, fighting in a war in France. His excitement every time she told him about Thomas Blake, imagining a brave warrior fighting to get home to them.

Tears streamed down his face as grief for his mother and father engulfed him, as fresh as it had been twenty years before. "I was only a child, but I still miss you," he murmured as if his mother could hear him. "And Father. I wonder if you were still here, he would be too, instead of whatever it is he's become now. I don't know what happened to him, but I'm going to find out. For such a short time, we were a happy family. The three of us, with Aunt Amelia and Uncle Graeme." He let go of a shaky breath. "I never forgot you. I never got to meet my little sister, but I was gifted with another. She's my cousin, but that doesn't matter. I wish you could have met Raven; she has Uncle Graeme's eyes, and black hair, and there's a little of him in her, but there's more Aunt Amelia than you would believe. I think you would have liked her. I taught her to fight with a sword."

Zachary stayed where he was, not knowing how much time had passed. A part of him felt like he had come *home*. But unease remained, panic threatening to overwhelm him, as if it had dug its claws in, refusing to let go. A light touch brushed the back of his neck. On his feet, sword drawn, nothing was there. A shadow hung above Riverwick, again nudging him to leave. Nearby, a headstone had been smashed entirely, stone crumbled, only able to make out the letters I, S and O.

Blackened trees stood where pears and apples had once grown. He found the broken skeletal remains of three together where they had fallen. Only the stable remained untouched. Finally, he turned towards what used to be his house. It had burned down beforehand; he recalled the flames licking at the building as Enforcers gripped him tight, the heat uncomfortable. The worst night of his life. Home gone, father arrested, and uncle dead.

Unsure why he continued to come here, his shoulders slumped, weighed down by disappointment. No life remained here, not even his father.

Chapter 6

Not wanting to wake her mother, Raven shut the door quietly. She needed fresh air, and to clear her head. Dark dreams continued to plague her, and she needed to shake off the feeling of being watched. She peered into the night. No dark shadow figure jumped out at her. Nearby, voices of the neighbours were barely audible as she tried to listen for any hint of someone watching her.

She couldn't tell her mother; it would only worry her. For the past few years, dreams had been filled with someone watching her from the shadows, a cloaked figure hidden in fog. Tonight was no different. She lay on the cool ground, gazing up at the star-filled sky.

"Please don't let me be like my father," she pleaded to the stars. "I don't want to be haunted by the same Darkness he was."

The talk with Zac about it had helped a little. He knew that she held fear of the Darkness of her father, and her terror that it was inside her. She imagined it close by, waiting to claim her. Now, outside in pitch black with warm tears on her face, Raven forced in a deep breath.

I'm not my father, she told herself over and over again. *I'm not my father.*

But the feeling of being watched didn't go away. Something hidden in the dark, not ready to reveal itself to her yet. She sat up.

"Hello?" The shaky word came out before she could stop it.

The silence that answered her was no comfort. The idea that Zac had returned to Kempschester had left dread following her in the days that followed.

A shadow moved, and Raven climbed to her feet. Another, then a third. Moving in a way that reminded her of soldiers. Every time she turned towards the movement, there was nothing.

She couldn't hold back the shiver.

Raven.

Her name was whispered, the voice softer than an echo on the wind.

"Who's there?" Her voice trembled. "Show yourself."

The village around her vanished, replaced by black fog, a blue moon, and a shadowed figure in front of her. She stepped back.

"You're the one watching me," she whispered.

Before she could react, the village returned.

What just happened? Raven reeled from the experience, casting her eyes for the shadow figure. Unsure it was real, she quickly made her way back to the house.

Returning to her bed, Raven couldn't sleep, her eyes glued to the ceiling. Dread pressed down on her, the shadows she'd seen outside the sign of something to come.

"What's wrong with me?" she whispered, fearful of the answer.

"Raven?" Her mother's voice broke the silence. "Are you awake?"

"I am," she confirmed, sitting up.

The door opened; a yellow flame reflected on her mother's face. In this light her blonde hair appeared almost silver. "I heard you go outside. What's wrong?"

"I..." she hesitated. "I feel like something awful is on its way," she admitted. "Something is going to happen."

Mother sat on her bed. "Are you having dreams? Nightmares?"

"No. A feeling." Raven was not ready to admit to her dreams. Her mother had always asked her to say anything about unusual dreams, but Raven didn't want to put that worry on her. Her father's dreams had shown him death; she didn't want to admit hers could lead to the same. "Maybe I'm just tired," she said. "Fearing things in the dark that aren't there."

She had heard stories from her mother and Zac her entire life. Her mother still woke up screaming every now and again, crying over the loss of her husband, and terrified at the idea that Uncle Thomas would come after her. According to her mother, the twins had somehow become one being. Zac's insistence that he could find his father and everything would be alright was something that he had never grown out of. He had seen the horrific actions and still refused to believe the man was a monster. Their father's shadow had followed them all.

"That must be it," her mother's voice interrupted her thoughts. Raven could tell by the rising pitch that her mother was worried, though. "How is Zachary?"

"He's busy," Raven said quickly.

"Perhaps you should invite him for dinner next week. It will be good to have dinner as a family again," her mother commented.

One last dinner before she became part of another family. She would move in with her fiancé. It would be *his* family that surrounded her every day, until they had a home of their own.

"I'll make sure to invite him," Raven said. "You know what he's like though, he gets lost in his work."

Crinkles showed at the corner of her mother's eyes as she let out a low laugh. "Is he still training you?" she asked.

"Not for a few weeks, but I've been practising," Raven said proudly.

"I don't like your interest in swords and all that, but with the rate the

French have been invading recently, it gives me peace of mind that you can at least protect yourself. Make sure you always carry your dagger, no matter where in the village you go."

"I will. I do," she agreed.

"Get some sleep. We have breakfast tomorrow with Lucian's family," her mother instructed her and took the candle with her.

Once more in the dark, Raven watched for any shadows again. Uneasiness hung over her, making breathing difficult. "Something terrible is going to happen," she murmured and closed her eyes.

Raven awoke early and picked out her favourite dress, a pale yellow one. Without a cloud in the sky, it was difficult to feel the gloom from last night, and she was excited for breakfast with Lucian and his family. She had hoped to have some alone time with Lucian and wanted to look good for him.

Brushing her hair, she stared at her reflection. She hadn't slept well, and the shadows under her eyes were evident.

"Here, let me." Her mother walked in, taking the hairbrush from her.

"You haven't done that in a few years," Raven noted.

"We had our best conversations when I brushed your hair." Mother smiled at her in the mirror.

Raven sat in the chair, the hairbrush running through her hair relaxing, until it stopped. When she glanced up at her mother's reflection, she caught her wiping a tear away. Twisting in her seat, she raised her eyebrow.

"I'm sorry, my little Raven. Your father used to brush my hair as a way to spend time with me." Her mother started brushing again. "He would stare at me in the mirror with such a look of awe on his face."

Raven hated speaking of her father, but knew her mother needed to.

"You've been thinking about him a lot lately," Raven acknowledged.

Her mother was silent for a moment, a wistful expression on her face. "Your betrothal just reminds me of my own. It was long before I knew of any darkness that resided in him."

Raven reached up, grabbing the hairbrush, turning in her seat. "Do you regret it? Marrying him?"

Her mother's eyes were wide with shock. "Oh no! Not at all. I loved your father. It took a while to get to know him, but he was very welcoming. He was busy with work around the farm, but he always made sure to check whether I lacked anything. He was a little awkward, not always sensitive, but he genuinely cared, and that's how I grew to love him." Her mother squeezed her arm. "To regret my marriage, would mean to regret you. You're my little miracle."

"Mother, I'm nineteen, almost twenty. I'm not so little any more," Raven laughed.

"Indeed. You've grown into a beautiful, strong young woman, and I am *so* proud of you. He would have been, too. I see such a bright future ahead of you. I hope you are as happy in your marriage as I was in mine." Her mother wiped a tear from her eye.

"Is that why you never remarried?" Raven asked.

Her mother started brushing her hair again. "I almost did," she said, her eyes with a faraway look in them.

This was something Raven hadn't heard before. "When?"

"Not long after you were born." Mother gave her a small smile.

Curious, she turned in her seat. "Is it someone I know?"

"Actually, yes," came the answer. "Hector."

"Our neighbour?" Raven almost squealed. "You have to tell me about this!"

"I was an unmarried woman with two children, so I didn't think I'd attract anyone's attention. Zachary wouldn't let anyone near him, only wanted his father. He spent hours crying. Hector had a way with him. He was very gentle and understood that we had suffered, even if he didn't know more than that. He arranged for the blacksmith apprenticeship for Zachary and told me that training in sword fighting might calm him," her mother told her.

"That's when Hector took him on as a student?" she asked.

"That's right." Her mother nodded. "He found solace in training, and he soon calmed down. Hector and I became very close."

"What happened?" Raven was curious now.

"He backed off." The hurt in her mother's voice was clear. "Not long after that, he married Maria."

"Oh, I'm so sorry." She gave her mother a sympathetic smile.

"I did alright. I had the two of you and built a successful bakery business. Now it's time to watch my daughter get married,"her mother said, her voice breaking.

"I'm a little nervous," Raven admitted.

"About what? Lucian will make a wonderful husband for you," her mother told her.

Raven bowed her head to hide her embarrassment.

"I only want you to be happy. Do you not want to marry him?" her mother asked.

She met her mother's eyes in the mirror. "Oh, I do! It's not that! I just..." she stopped. *Can I talk about this? Should I?*

Her mothers laugh startled her. "I know what you fear."

"You do?" She raised her eyebrows.

"You worry that you will not satisfy him, and he'll seek that pleasure elsewhere," she laughed again. "I had the same worry about Graeme. Until he met Emma, Thomas was well known for...well, Zachary takes after his father in favouring the women." She started brushing again. "I was fearful

Graeme would be the same. Worry not, sweet Raven, Lucian will crawl into your bed every night yearning for you."

"No!" Raven said, uncomfortable with the topic. "That's not it. What if he doesn't satisfy me?" She let out a sigh. "It's different if it is like that, he will seek pleasure elsewhere, and no one cares. It's not like I can do that. I'd be branded a harlot."

Her mother was silent, a small smile on her face.

"What?" Raven asked.

"If a man cannot satisfy you, then you'll just have to do it yourself."

"Mother!" Ravens cheeks heated. "Stop! I can't hear that from you!"

"I'm sorry, I did go too far, didn't I. How do you want your hair?" Her mother laughed.

"A crown braid," Raven confirmed.

"Don't you want to wear it out today? Beautiful black waves to frame your face. It makes your eyes stand out." Her mother smiled.

"No, Lucian likes it with braids." She smiled back.

Her mother had a knowing expression on her face as she worked on Raven's hair.

"I hope your cousin can get to the wedding," her mother said, braiding Raven's hair. "I'll be so disappointed in him if he doesn't. When was the last time he came home?"

"He lives in Oakborough now, in his shop," Raven reminded her.

"That's not his home, though," her mother disagreed.

Raven met her mother's eyes. "I think he considers it so."

"He needs to find a wife. Whatever happened to that young one he was with a few years ago?" Mother asked. "The one with the curly hair. He brought her here once. They seemed to care about each other."

"She left him," Raven said sadly.

"Why?"

"To this day, he still doesn't know," Raven admitted.

"Finished." Her mother stepped back. "Are you ready? We should go. We don't want to be late." She glanced over Raven. "You do look beautiful, sweet girl; he won't be able to keep his eyes off you."

Raven opened the jar of perfume, the sweet floral scent of lavender filling the air. "That's the intention." Raven grinned.

Chapter 7

Zachary left Lance with a stable hand to wash down and feed. Few people in town owned horses, and those who did, left them in one of three stables around Oakborough. He rented a stall nearest to his shop and knew the horse was in good hands. With the leather saddlebags in his arms, he hurried home, wanting to get Raven's armour finished in time for the wedding. He had little time left and couldn't go empty handed.

No sooner had he reached the door to his smithy than an Enforcer arrived. A blond bearded man with blue eyes and a tanned face. Hoping to get rid of him, Zachary forced a smile.

"I have your sword," he said, struggling to remember the Enforcer's name. This one was new, and had arrived three years before, in Oakborough with his father.

"I met your cousin while you were out of town," the Enforcer told him.

Raven was here? Damn! Did she see my wedding gift for her? Irritated at himself for not being more careful, he unlocked his door.

"You met Raven?" He opened the door, greeted by the smell of hot metal.

"She's, uhhhh...." The Enforcer looked down, embarrassed. "She's a very angry woman. Unpleasant."

"That's my cousin you're talking about." He walked inside. "Unpleasant? Did something happen?"

The Enforcer followed Zachary into the shop. "Does she often attack your customers?"

"She attacked you? Why?" Zachary glared. "What did you do?"

"You're blaming me?" The Enforcer glared back.

"I am." Zachary replied. "She has a quick temper, but you had to have done something to offend her first. What did you do?"

"I'm not here to talk about your cousin." The Enforcer glanced around the shop. "I have an order for new armour, too. Lord Gerard wants us in metal."

Zachary dropped his bags and pointed to the Enforcer's chain mail. "You're wearing metal."

"Metal *plate*. There are reports that more French soldiers have started attacking port-side villages. The Lord wants us well prepared in case they come further inland."

"This doesn't give me a lot of time. If they come inland, they're only half a day's ride from here. I can't make thirty Enforcers' armour that fast."

"You better get started then. Tomorrow—" the Enforcer started.

Zachary cut him off. "No, not tomorrow, I'm closed."

"Closed? Why would you be closed? You were just gone for days, now you're closing up again?" The Enforcer gave him a look of confusion, eyebrows drawn together.

Zachary glanced down at the order. *Markus. That's right.* The papers on his bench had been moved, drawings of his work for Raven not where he left them.

"My cousin's wedding." Zachary eyed Markus. "You changed the subject, which makes me think you're trying to hide something. What did you do to Raven?"

Markus avoided his eyes. "I offended her."

Zachary crossed his arms, waiting.

"I thought she was one of your…" Markus's eyes darted towards the door at the back of his shop - Zachary's bedroom.

Zachary's shoulders shook. "You…No, you…" tears of laughter streamed from his eyes. Markus's eyes narrowed. Zachary held a hand up. "Sorry, but you what?"

"I thought she was one of your…. It's no secret that the women like you. When I walked in to find her holding a sword…" Markus pointed at the sword Zachary had been working on for Raven.

Damn, she did find it.

Zachary shook his head. "That wouldn't have angered her. She would have laughed at your stupidity."

Markus let out a huff of impatience. "Is this important?"

"Yes, the fact that you're trying to avoid this discussion only makes me more curious." Zachary advanced on Markus. "So I will ask again. What did you do?"

"She caught me looking at her," Markus admitted.

Protectiveness shot through Zachary. "Looking at her?"

Markus shrugged but took a step away from him. "I saw a beautiful woman. Do you not look when you see—"

Zachary fought back the temptation to punch the Enforcer. "Again, that's my cousin!" He took a deep breath.." You said she attacked you, what did she do?"

The Enforcer stared, clearly not wanting to tell him, backing away again.

"You brought it up. Now you tell me, or I'll force it out of you." Zachary threatened.

"She held a sword on me, forced me to my knees and disarmed me," the Enforcer confessed through clenched teeth.

"She disarmed you?" Zachary burst out laughing. "You're an Enforcer, how did you let a woman get the best of you?" Pride burst within.

"I did not expect her to hold a blade to my throat." Markus muttered.

Zachary crossed his arms over his chest. "Well, can you blame her? She's due to be married, not for the likes of you to look at."

"I wasn't to know that, was I?" Markus snapped.

"Well, now you know; and if I catch you looking at her again, I'll burn your eyes out of your head. Her betrothed is like a brother to me." Zachary threatened.

"Need I remind you that I'm an Enforcer?" Markus declared. "I can have the both of you arrested for threatening me."

"But you won't," Zachary grinned. "This isn't something you want public. You'd never live that humiliation down. Lord Gerard wouldn't want an Enforcer who allowed himself to be disarmed or bested by a woman."

"Can I have my sword now?" Markus demanded.

Zachary grabbed a sword from the workbench and pushed it towards him. "Take it and get out of my shop."

He lit the forge, and the smell of smoke and coal filled the room, flames emitting heat.

"About the armour." Markus reminded him.

"I already told you; I'm closed tomorrow," he said without looking up.

Zachary pulled the blanket from the armour he'd started on for Raven, moving it to his work bench to inspect it. The shoulder guards and bracers were all he needed to finish it. Staring at the plate, he got an idea regarding what to engrave in the middle.

"Lord Gerard—" Markus said.

"Why are you still here? GET OUT!" Zachary shouted.

The door shut behind him, and Zachary set to working on the rest of Raven's armour. He couldn't wait to give it to her, even if she had come in and ruined the surprise.

Sweating from the heat of his forge, Zachary opened the door, propping it open again. Before he returned to his work, he drew his father's sword. With a smile creeping across his face, Zachary swung the sword, stepping into moves he'd learned years before. Imagining himself to be fighting in France, a man trying to get home to his family. Zachary swung at and blocked imaginary enemies. He was a boy again, only instead of the wooden sword Uncle Graeme had made him, he held his father's. Laughter bubbled up from inside.

Someone cleared their throat, and he almost dropped the sword. The man that stood before him was dark brown, with short black hair. Well dressed and flanked by a servant and a guard, Tobias was one of the richest of Oakborough.

"Tobias." Zachary noted, embarrassed.

"Have I come at a bad time?" the noble asked.

"No, not at all." Zachary put on his best smile. "I was...training."

"Of course. There's a tournament next month. You should enter; I'd like to see you in action." Tobias smiled.

Zachary shook his head. "I don't know if Lord Gerard allows—"

Tobias laughed. "Let me handle Lord Gerard. You showed some good moves, for a peasant."

Hating the reference to his status, he forced down the rising annoyance.

"I had a good teacher," he said, eyeing Tobias. "Don't you have enough elites to fight against?

Tobias sighed. "I grow weary of the same predictable fights. We need new blood, which makes it more exciting when you can't predict your opponent's moves. I would love to see women fight, too; they can be ferocious." Tobias gave him a smile. "I need five new swords by next month. Can you fit that in?"

Zachary started writing a new order, glancing at his other requests. "I can. Delivery?"

"Of course." Tobias agreed.

"This is smaller than your usual order, Tobias. You wouldn't be doing business with another blacksmith, would you?"

Tobias smiled again. It was warm. "And break our deal? We have a good thing here; do you not trust me?"

Zachary glared.

"What can I say? It's what was asked of me." Tobias admitted.

"Is your brother shopping elsewhere?" Zachary demanded.

"Soldiers get a Dale blade before they go now. They've worked out it's cheaper to get it from you directly. Your business is booming and it's hurting me, but you're complaining?"

Zachary scoffed. "I'm sure it's hurting you."

Tobias shrugged. "Why live this close to the war if you can't make a little coin from it?"

"Maybe that's why they're coming to me directly, instead of adding more gold to your pockets. No one likes giving their hard-earned gold to the likes of you."

The servant beside Tobias gasped. Zachary had been in business with Tobias for five years and had grown comfortable in their conversations. It occurred to him that peasants didn't usually talk to the nobles so boldly.

Tobias raised his eyebrows. "I didn't see you complaining about it at the time. In fact, if I recall, it was your idea."

Zachary shrugged. "I was broke, and saw an opportunity; you're well known for your service to the war efforts."

"Well, you're not short of money now, are you?" Tobias winked. "Or women."

His chest ached. Raven was about to get married, and he couldn't ignore the bitterness or feelings of failure that he was still unmarried with no children of his own. At his age, Father had already fathered him, with a second on the way. "Women, but no wife."

"You're a slave to your own desires," Tobias grinned. "When you're ready for a family, you'll find her. If you don't already have one you don't know about."

The thought had occurred to Zachary; he hoped anyone would feel comfortable telling him. His business with Tobias, taking on students, and the fights he had taken part in meant he had more than enough money stashed away to support any children he may have fathered.

Tobias threw a leather pouch of coins at Zachary. The coins inside jingled as he caught it one-handed. The nobleman left, the servant and guard with him.

In his bedroom, Zachary unbolted the cupboard and unlocked a wooden chest in the bottom, filled with coins and leather pouches; he added to his collection. He had more than he knew what to do with, and it bothered him that he couldn't live more comfortably. For a peasant to suddenly display or flaunt wealth would raise suspicion and create more trouble than he wanted. *One day I'll have a family and won't have to hide this. We can live anywhere and have a nice house for children.* Such dreams only seemed to get more out of his reach.

He returned to the shop, and a sword on the counter drew his attention. One had been waiting to be picked up since before he went to Kempschester. Gideon was late in picking up. It was likely Gideon expected him to deliver, despite not having paid for it. Either that or dead. Finally, Zachary returned to Raven's armour. He'd had enough interruptions and needed to finish.

Chapter 8

Lucian's sister Rosamund basked in the sunshine at a table outside the front of the house. Raven's eyes slid over Lucian, taking in his rich brown colouring, his black, curly hair, and the dark stubble lining his narrow jaw. With high cheekbones and a beautiful smile that he now gave her, heat flamed in her cheeks. She loved his eyes, a deep brown, that always seemed to light up when he saw her. He reached for her hands. Raven let all her fears and worries fall away as she greeted her fiancé. She just wanted to focus on today and enjoy Lucian's company. *I'm about to marry him.* An excited tingle set off flutters inside her stomach. She wished she could have time with just him. He kissed her on the cheek.

"Raven, you're always a refreshing sight," he said. "While we wait for breakfast, we'll leave your mother with my sister and go for a walk. Enjoy the sunshine, and each other's company."

Delighted at the idea of having time with him, in which they wouldn't be watched, she smiled up at him. "I'd love that."

"Don't go too far," Rosamund called out. "We'll start without you."

"No, you won't," he laughed over his shoulder. "We are the guests; you cannot start until we sit down."

He took her arm in his and they walked away. With each step, she leaned more into him, the tension in her shoulders easing.

"Thank you," she said. "Your sister was staring."

"She has listened to my rambling about you for the last few months," he chuckled. "But I did want to get you to myself before we sat down with our families."

"You did?" she asked.

"Of course. I hate the necessity of formality in front of them. Until we're married, I feel so awkward. I like it when it's just the two of us."

She couldn't hold back the smile. "I do, too," she confessed. "Your household is very busy; I hope we can enjoy each other's company like this more often."

He laughed. "So, what you mean is, you want me to yourself, without my family around."

Raven's cheeks were warm. "Am I that predictable?"

"No, I want the same. They can be a little...crowding at times. Rosamund and Noah are overwhelming to me at the best of times. I can't blame you for wanting time away from them." He stopped and turned to face her. "I want you to feel welcome. This will be your home, too, Raven. If they crowd you, make it known to them. They will give you space if you ask for it."

His gaze grew intense as he smiled down at her. Raven's stomach flipped. They'd stolen kisses in the past, and he'd always hesitated. He'd told her respecting her honour was important.

"Tomorrow we will be wed; you will have no need to hesitate when I am your wife. You have no need to waver now. I know what you desire, and I want it, too," she reminded him.

She wanted the kiss as much as he did. His hesitation made her impatient. She grabbed the front of his tunic, pulling him towards her. His surprise soon faded as he yielded to her, one arm slipping around her lower back, the other cupping her cheek.

The closeness thrilled her, sending shivers throughout. Her cheeks heated as they pulled away.

"You are a forceful woman," he beamed at her. "I cannot wait to get more of that!"

"Nor I," she said.

He stroked a thumb across her cheek. "You're blushing."

"Your lips lit a fire within," she murmured.

"Can I make you blush again?" He smirked.

She caught the wicked gleam in his eyes and opened her mouth to remind him he need not ask. Before a word left her lips, he pulled her into another kiss, deeper than before. Pleasure crawled through her, their kiss sending sparks of desire within her stomach. He pulled away. Disappointed, she looked up at him. He pressed his forehead to hers, fingers under her chin. "I would take you to my bed right now if we were married," His voice had grown husky, his breathing quick.

"Then perhaps we should return to our families," she said, her breathing matching his. "Desire burns through me. If you were to take me to your bed, I would not resist."

She had known Lucian all her life, and this was an unexpected side to him.

"Not yet," he said. "I want to show you something." He took her arm again and led her through the village.

They walked arm in arm, and Raven enjoyed the silence, not feeling the need to fill it with conversation. Many villagers smiled at them as they passed by.

They stopped at the church. Inside, it had been decorated for their big day. Yellow and white roses lined an archway placed before the door.

"Your mother told me those were your favourites," he said.

"It's beautiful," she gushed, leaning over a rose to breathe in its sweet scent, the petals soft in her fingers.

He led her towards the front of the church. There sat a large chest, which Lucian opened. Inside lay swords.

"You've already shown me these," she said.

"Villagers are going to hold swords up as you walk into the church," he grinned at her.

He had brought her here once before, as a warning when they'd heard the French were attacking villages.

He'd shown her the chest of weaponry, and a door in the floor that led to a cellar under the church.

"We've built this in the event that the French soldiers get too close. Our village is unprotected, but there's a soldier's outpost nearby. If we get raided, you run here, and take a weapon. I will find my way to you. Help people into the cellar while you wait for me."

She frowned. "Lucian..."

"I know, you can fight, I've seen you practise with Zac. It's what drew me to you. But if the alarm is raised, I will know where to find you."

"I will come here," she promised. "If the French invade our village, they will find themselves up against my fury if I cannot find you though."

"We really should go back," Lucian said, breaking her from her thoughts. "Before my mother and yours send out a search party."

Lucian escorted her from the church.

"It's such a beautiful day," she murmured. "I hope this continues tomorrow."

"Rain or shine, our wedding will be one to remember," he told her as they arrived back at his home. "All of Eskham will be there."

"Finally!" Lucian's younger brother of seventeen, Noah, declared. A younger version of Lucian, he was well known for his mischief. "Lucian, you make us wait on you to take your bride for alone time. Meanwhile, we're starving!" He winked at Raven.

"Poor Noah. I'm sure you could manage," Lucian laughed. "I'm surprised you held out so long."

"He didn't," Lucian's mother, Elaine said. "He stole some bread while I wasn't looking."

Noah widened his eyes at his mother. "I did nothing of the sort."

Elaine leaned towards her younger son. "Then why do you still have breadcrumbs on the front of your tunic?"

Noah looked down, which set off Rosamund's laughter.

Lucian shook his head as he pulled out the chair for Raven. "You should know better than to fall for that."

Taking the seat, she smiled around at everyone. Her fiancé took the chair next to hers. She caught a glint of amusement in his mother's eyes, and her cheeks heated again.

Chapter 9

Zachary awoke to warmth pressed against him. Her head on his shoulder, arm across his torso. Smiling, he wrapped his arm around her bare shoulder.

"Julianna," he murmured into her ear, satisfied at the shiver that passed through her.

"Mmm, Good morning," she whispered, lifting her head, chin on his chest as she gazed into his eyes. "Do you have work soon?"

Zachary gave her a slight squeeze. "I do. But work is less appealing than the warmth of you."

She beamed at him. "I have heard how charming you were with your words."

"Is it my words or my tongue that please you?" he pressed.

Her cheeks reddened.

He raised his hand to lift her chin. She shifted, getting close enough to kiss him.

"Is that what you have heard?" He gave her his slow smile, knowing its effect would melt her. "Is that all?"

Her eyes closed, her lips curving upwards. "I have heard many things, and you do not fail to provide the satisfactions spoken of."

"Satisfaction?" He laughed. "You call my words charming, when yours are sweet." He kissed her again. "As are your lips."

Rolling them both over, he pinned her body under his and lowered his face to whisper in her ear. "Are you ready to go again?" One hand lowered between her legs, fingers probing, and she let out a soft whimper.

He breathed in her scent, sweet, floral, before pressing his mouth hard against hers, and she dug her nails into his back. Her lips were soft, yielding and she pressed herself against his erection. When he pulled back, desire sparked in her eyes.

"Yes," she whispered. "Zachary…"

Heat rose in his groin, and he ran his hands across her body, and took a nipple in his mouth while cupping her other breast. Pressed against her, he resisted thrusting in, her impatience showing as she rose up to meet him.

Pulling himself out of reach as she squirmed, he gave her a grin, gripping her chin. "You don't hurry me," he reminded her. "The more impatient you are, the longer you will wait." She stopped, instead rubbing her hands from his torso to his chest. "Good, that's better." His lips brushed across her jaw as he lowered himself. Not moving, he looked into her eyes. She let out a moan, her body against his, trembling. "Am I living up to my reputation, then?" he asked.

"Yes," she breathed, and tried again to press against him.

"I don't think you're listening to me," he said. "You're being impatient again."

The sound she made was halfway between a laugh and a groan. "Zachary, please."

The word 'please' tugged at him, and he relented, burying himself in her.

He started slow, his thrusts gentle. His movements elicited heavy moans from her, only adding to his pleasure, her fingers digging into his back. Her own hips rose up hard, matching his momentum as they increased in pace. He slid in and out, tension building. He drove harder, chasing pleasure, and her moans grew louder. His name fell from her lips.

She squirmed under him as she neared climax. His own hit him moments before hers. Satisfied, he collapsed on top of her, catching his breath. Julianna's fingers ran up his back, and down again, a motion she repeated.

Her heart drummed against his ear. *This was a wonderful way to start my day.* He pulled out of her, kissing her again before starting to rise. She reached for him, but he pulled away.

"I have work." Leaving his bed, he cast a look over her naked body, glistening with sweat. "I'm not ready to leave," she complained, sitting up.

"Good, stay," he commanded her. "Be here for me throughout the day whenever I have need of you."

A slow smile crawled over her face. "But anyone can walk in."

He pulled trousers on and returned to her side. "Let them."

"What if I have things to do?" she asked, a gleam in her eyes as they ran up his body.

"You don't," he told her.

"You're going to make me stay?" she teased.

He motioned to the door. "You want to leave?" His own smile widened as she glanced at the door, making no move towards it. "I thought not."

She reached for her dress. "No." He pulled it away from her. "No clothes."

"What if I get hungry?"

He gave her a kiss again. "Then I will bring you food." He nudged her on to her back, pulling the blanket over her. "Today, I shall think of you in here and be warmed by your presence."

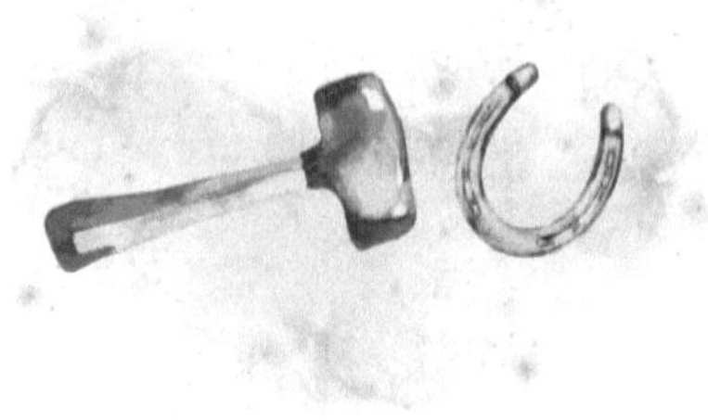

As Zachary covered Raven's armour with a blanket, he heard Julianna moving around in his bedroom. "Julianna, bed," he called out with a grin. The idea of her being naked in his bedroom made him want to go back in there.

He pounded on the sword before him. Working metal always gave him calm. The world faded away and it was just him and the blade and hammer. This was to be a new sword for himself, inspired by the one he'd pulled from Kempschester. He had made swords for himself before, but this would be his pride.

"Have you finished my sword yet?" A loud voice boomed at him. Gideon. Zachary clenched his teeth together.

"I finished it on time. You're a week late," he grumbled.

"Then why didn't you bring it to me? You know where I live," Gideon spoke harshly.

Zachary glared. Gideon was a few years younger than him, with brown hair and grey eyes. A soldier on his way to the war in France. One of many demanding his services before they left. One of many who would take his blades to battle and likely never return. *A damn waste of a good sword.*

"You want a sword delivered; you pay for delivery," Zachary retorted. "You didn't pay for delivery, so you pick it up. Preferably on time."

Gideon stepped towards him as if to attempt to be intimidating, but his size didn't match Zachary's "I'm here now, where is it?"

Zachary nodded towards the bench at the front of his shop. "There," he put down the tools, following Gideon to the bench.

"What's this?" Gideon reached for his father's sword.

"*Not* yours." Zachary pulled it from Gideon's grasp. "*That* one's yours." He pointed.

"What's that etched on the blade?"

Zachary held the sword before him, inspecting the engraving at the top of the blade. "It's a scythe," he said.

"You engraved a scythe on a sword? Like that killer, what was his name? The Shadow of Death? Did someone ask for that? How do I get one like that?"

People hadn't engraved symbols onto swords for a good ten years, so Gideon's question was a stupid one. Gideon's use of the name by which Zachary's father was known sent a painful twinge through him.

"This was my father's sword. The scythe is to honour his family. They were farmers. He died when I was young." He hated telling that lie.

Gideon's eyes glazed over. "I don't care about your father or his family."

Zachary pointed again. "Take your sword and go, I have work to do." Zachary turned his back on Gideon.

"I want that one," Gideon declared.

Zachary's shoulders tensed. "It's not for sale. If it were, you couldn't afford it. You could barely afford the one you paid for."

"You're very unwelcoming," Gideon laughed. "Give me your sword. It's not like you're using it. You've probably never swung a sword in your life. You only make them for those who can."

The tip of a blade pressed into his back. He clenched his hand around the leather hilt, roaring in his ears.

Zachary turned, raising his own and deflected Gideon's sword down and away before knocking it away. It clattered on the ground. He held the blade against Gideon's throat. "You can't have this sword. If you want to test whether I know how to use this, then go right ahead."

The slight widening of Gideon's eyes gave him satisfaction.

A hint of lavender announced her arrival. "He doesn't like to share,"

Raven's voice interrupted the moment. "Gideon, maybe you should take the sword you paid for. Enforcers value his work and would not favour you in this. Neither would Lord Gerard."

Gideon grumbled under his breath as he left. Zachary turned towards Raven, meeting her piercing blue eyes. She wore a pale-yellow dress, her black hair split into braids, wrapping around the crown of her head.

"Did you have to bring the Enforcers into it?" he asked but gave her a smile. She was hard to be moody at.

Raven's eyes lit up as she smiled back at him. "It worked, didn't it? He couldn't escape fast enough." She glanced back at the door. "It's not as if I wasn't speaking the truth. You've made swords for most of the Enforcers here. They have respect for you, for your work."

That was something he hadn't considered. "I don't care about their respect, only their money. They pay well." He frowned at Raven.

"These aren't the Enforcers of Kempschester; you don't have to hate them." Raven noted.

"They're still Enforcers. Speaking of which, I heard what you did to Markus," he said.

Her face went blank. "Who?"

"Markus, the Enforcer you had on his knees," he reminded her.

Sheer joy lit across her face. "Is that what his name was? I never bothered to ask."

"It's not that funny." It was amusing, but he had to have this conversation with her. He kept his expression stern.

Her eyes narrowed. "He offended me! If you were here, you would have—"

"Raven, threatening my customers is bad for business," he said.

Her smile vanished. "So, you're alright with him looking at me? Lucian would have defended me."

He hated that she was bringing up Lucian's name, comparing him to his friend awoke a familiar need to compete.

"I've already told him that if he does it again, I will burn out his eyes. But it's my business, and my customers will listen to me, just as Lucian would see. You can't do that again."

She gave in with a nod. "You're in a bad mood today. More so than usual. What's wrong?"

He had started the day in a good mood. "That idiot tried to steal from me, using a sword I made for him, on me."

Her eyes dropped to the sword. "I see you went to Kempschester. Again. Why must you go digging up the past?"

Zachary said nothing in response. He had dreamed of nothing else but the sword and the journal, and those dreams had stopped since his return.

"He's a murderer, Zac; you would invite that into your life? Into ours?" Her voice was tinged with fear.

Zachary laid the sword on the bench and returned to his work. "His voice called me back from the other realm. I'm here because of him."

Raven touched his arm. "Have you given thought to my mother if you do find him? She still has nightmares and is in hiding because of him. Because of both of them." Her refusal to mention her father was unmistakable. "What will you do if you find what you're looking for? He killed a lot of people, including his own brother. Are you certain there is anything left of the man you knew as your father? He's never sought you out."

People keep saying that. Zachary returned to his workbench, pulling the blade back into flame. "I'm not trying to upset Aunt Amelia. You only know what you've been told about him. And Uncle Graeme. I knew him. I remember him, both of them."

"So does she. You're holding onto a ghost. Your father is gone. It's time to let him go."

Frustration rose in Zachary as he scowled at Raven. She glared back at him, unflinching.

"If you're here just to argue with me, then go home, Raven," he snapped.

Hurt glinted in her eyes. "No, believe it or not, I'm here to invite you to dinner. I'm getting married tomorrow, and I want to have one last dinner with my family before I join another. Do you think you can tear yourself away from your work long enough for that?"

Zachary put down his tools again, anger melting. "Of course I'll be there.

It'll be good to see you and Aunt Amelia again." He gave her a wide grin. "I'm closing the shop tomorrow; you know I wouldn't miss your wedding for anything. I'm going to have a drink to celebrate with Lucian tonight."

Her eyes lit up again, eerily similar to those of her father's. "Good. I need you there."

Zachary wrapped her in a hug. "I still can't believe you're getting married. You really convinced Lucian to take on the burden—"

Raven pulled away and hit him playfully. "Zac!"

He laughed, holding his hands up. "How was breakfast? That was today, wasn't it?"

Her cheeks turned red, as a gleam of joy shone from her eyes.

"That good, was it?" He laughed.

She was beaming and lowered her gaze. "We kissed," she murmured.

"You've kissed before," he said.

"Not like this." Her eyes lit up again.

He grinned at her. "Some pre-wedding passion between the betrothed?" Laughter burst from him.

Raven had gone bright red.

He grinned at her reaction. "It looks like it was a pleasing experience, then."

"Oh, it was." Her eyes twinkled, and he wasn't sure her smile could get any bigger.

"Well, I suppose there will be tension at the wedding tomorrow," he commented.

"Tension?" Raven looked baffled.

"You've both had a taste of that; you'll be wanting to tear each other's clothes off. Just no sneaking off until the wedding is over and everyone has left. People will come looking for the married couple. You do not want them to find you in the throes of—"

"Zac, stop!" Raven pleaded.

"You're the one who told me you had a passionate kiss," he reminded her. "Did you think after hearing that I wouldn't say anything? I'm certainly going to bring this up with Lucian."

Her eyes widened in horror. "Please, don't."

"What are you afraid of?" he asked. "He'll be thinking about that as much as you are. Unlike you, he'll give me all the details."

"Stop!" Raven shook her head. "I have to go. Mother sent me in to see you. I get the feeling she wanted me out of the house."

"Very well. I'll let you go, then," he relented

Raven turned to leave. "Please don't be late." She pointed at his father's sword. "Don't bring that. If she finds out you were in Kempschester..."

"The sword stays at home," he reassured her.

She left, and he returned to the sword he was working on. Then he glanced towards his bedroom door.

Chapter 10

The journey home was quick. Eskham was a small, quiet village of about a hundred people, most of whom travelled to Oakborough for the markets. They were close enough to the sea for some to work in the port. Villagers waved as she passed by.

Her home was welcoming, while reminding her that she would be moving to a new home after the wedding. She was looking forward to quiet time with her mother before Zac's arrival. It was her last night of it just being the two of them in their quiet house, and she would miss their talks and her mother's reassuring presence. The warm aroma of fresh bread meant that her mother had been baking again.

Her relief at returning home was shadowed by the feeling of being watched again. Casting eyes around her, a shadowed figure at the corner of her eye was gone before she could get a proper look. Raven climbed from her horse and glanced around again.

"Are you alright, Raven?" Her mother's voice drew her back. "Did you do everything you needed to in Oakborough?"

Her mother's blonde hair was a mess, with flour over her face and front. Her blue eyes twinkled at Raven.

"You have flour everywhere." Raven laughed.

Her mother wiped her hands down her apron, and pushed stray hair from her face, casting flour in her hair.

"I had some orders for bread," her mother said.

"I hope you have an extra loaf; Zac's joining us for dinner," she said with excitement.

Her mother looked pleased. "He is? Oh good, it's been too long since he stopped by."

Raven needed to cover for Zac. "You know what he's like: He gets caught up in his work. Once he starts a sword, the world just ceases to exist for him."

Her mother pressed her lips together.

Raven narrowed her eyes. "What?"

"Nothing." Her mother averted her gaze.

She put her hand to her mother's arm. "No, I know that look, what is it?"

"I heard from one of the villagers that his shop was closed for a few days. I worry about that boy." Her mother sighed.

This time, it was Raven who looked away. "Maybe he needed time off?"

"You do exactly what your father did when he was hiding something. Look at me."

Raven raised her eyes; her mother's hands were on her hips. *Uh oh.* As she met her mother's glare, she squirmed. It was as if she was a child again, being scolded.

"I knew it. He's been looking for his father again, hasn't he?" her mother demanded.

"I ..." She hated lying. Especially to her mother.

"Raven Dale, don't you lie to me," her mother ordered. "The two of you are just as bad as they were, protecting each other. For my sake, be honest with me."

"Yes," she confirmed, lowering her head.

Amelia looked around them, as if expecting Thomas to appear right then, her chin quivering. "Where did he go?"

Not wanting to get Zac into any more trouble, Raven shook her head. "Perhaps you should talk with him. I've said enough; this is between you and Zac."

Her mother narrowed her eyes at Raven, but finally relaxed, hands dropping from her hips. "I'll get it out of him," she said and put on a smile. "Your dress arrived while you were in town. It's in your bedroom."

Raven started towards the house and again, fingers of ice on the back of her neck sent a chill through her. *Something is watching me.* She glanced around, rubbing her arm.

"Are you cold?" her mother asked.

"No," she lied.

Her mother said nothing, watching her.

"It's nothing, just wedding nerves." Raven forced a smile.

"That's what made you shiver?" Her mother wasn't letting this go. "The air is not cold enough for that yet."

Damn, she misses nothing. "Yes."

"What is it honey? You can talk to me," her mother reassured her.

Raven wasn't sure she wanted to talk about this. "What makes you think something is wrong?"

Her mother frowned. "You shivered, rubbed your arm, and looked around, biting your lip."

Did I bite my lip? Raven met a steely gaze.

"I keep feeling like someone is watching me," she said at last.

Panic crossed her mother's face as her eyes darted around. "And you feel it now?"

"Yes. It's nothing," she repeated. "As I said, wedding nerves."

"Thomas?" her mother called out; her voice cold. "Is that you?"

The hairs on Raven's arms stood on end. "What are you doing?" Her voice came out a whisper.

Her mother didn't move as she eyed the village, her face hardening. "Get inside, Raven."

"There's no one there," Raven argued.

"Graeme?" her mother whispered, the cold tone in her voice softening. "Is it you watching her?"

Ice crawled up Raven's spine, and the hair on her arms stood up.

Silence.

"I told you, there's no one there," Raven said again.

"How long have you felt it?" her mother asked.

"Only for a couple of days," she lied. "If someone was watching me, I'm sure we'd see them."

Mother let out a deep sigh. "Not if he's watching from The Shadow Realm."

Hairs on her arms rose. "What? You think—?"

"I want you to tell me if you feel it again." her mother instructed her.

"I will." Raven wished she hadn't said anything.

"Let's go inside." With one last look around, her mother led her into the house.

Raven went to her bedroom, eager to see the dress. As she caught sight of it, warmth spread out from her chest. A deep blue skirt, the bodice and sleeves yellow.

"It's beautiful," she whispered, running her hand over the material. "This must have been expensive."

"Elaine helped pay for it. She already thinks of you as a daughter."

"Thank you. It's perfect." Raven gushed.

"So are you. You're a true gift, Raven, one that I had prayed for." A tear slid down her mother's cheek. "Your father would have…" She stopped, shaking her head and exhaling. "Tomorrow you'll be a wife, I'm going to miss you."

The mention of her father made Raven uncomfortable. Despite everything, the fear and horror her mother felt, he was a man she had loved. His death had left a void in her heart, and Raven could see the raw grief, even after all these years, and through her fear.

"I'll still be here. Just not in this house." Raven hugged her. "You won't be alone, you know."

"Zachary lives in town, and you…" her mother didn't finish her sentence.

Raven put a hand over her mothers. "If you get lonely, why don't you visit him? It would make his day."

"You're right. It will be nice to get out," her mother agreed.

Raven smiled. "In the meantime, we should prepare dinner in time for Zac. No point inviting him to eat otherwise. It'll be like it always was. Just the two of us, while we wait for him."

"Did I tell you Zac designed me a sword and armour?" Raven asked as they prepared food.

"You may have mentioned it, once or twice," her mother laughed. "But you can tell me again."

"He's already forged the sword, and it's so easy to hold. I've held swords, but this one is lighter, more suited for me. The armour looks like it will fit me perfectly." Raven realised she was talking fast. She glanced up to find her mother watching her with pride.

"You're a strong young woman, and I couldn't be prouder. God help anyone that faces you. You'd be a force to be reckoned with in any fight."

Raven beamed. "That's a reputation I'd be proud of."

Her mother laughed. "alright, my little Raven, get the cooking pot."

"I'm not such a little Raven any more." Raven squirmed at her mother's nickname for her.

Her mother squeezed her chin. "No, but you'll always be my little Raven," she started to move the food into a ceramic cooking pot, singing as she did.

The sound was a comfort, bringing up memories of being held when she was young, the singing filling her with warmth. "I love you," she murmured. "I'll miss this."

She realised she would miss her mother. She had reassured her that she would still be in the village, but it wouldn't be the same. Seeing her mother every day, listening to her singing, spending time with her, everything was about to change.

Her mother wrapped her arms around Raven. "Please don't be like Zachary and forget me. Your poor old mother will be all alone."

"Zac didn't forget about you…he just gets lost in his own world. Business for him is really good at the moment." Raven embraced her mother. "He loves you as his own mother, and he'll be here tonight."

Her mother stiffened. Raven pulled away.

"What's wrong?" Raven asked.

"Zachary's mother…Emma," her mother replied. "Somehow I still miss her, after all these years."

"So does he," Raven said. "He doesn't talk about her in front of you, but he still remembers her. He said you used to take him to her grave. It helped him in a time when he just wanted his father around."

"He was so lost." Her mother's sadness shone through. "She and I were like sisters." She seemed lost in the memories. "Emma's buried in Riverwick, with no one to visit her. I do miss that place."

Raven held her mother's hand. "I want you to stop living in fear; I worry for you. Your fear of the past - of him - keeps you prisoner. I only want you to be happy."

Her mother patted her hand. "Don't worry about me. Your mother will be alright." she wiped away the tear. "Let's get this done."

Chapter 11

Eyeing his father's sword, Zachary picked it up. Memories rushed him. Sitting, as his father explained the meaning of the scythe. His father returning from war, and the way his mother had rushed to him. Standing over her grave as his father hugged him from behind, the two of them needing each other in their grief. Walking into a cell where his father was heavily shackled to the wall and running to him. He had so few memories of his father, but he clung to them.

Tears streamed down Zachary's face, his chest aching. The yearning for his parents had never ceased. "I don't care what you are, what you did," he whispered to no one. "I miss my father. Why did you walk away from me? I'd already lost my mother; you were supposed to protect me." He choked on grief, hurt, and anger.

Zachary tightened his hand around the hilt and swung the sword. The blade hissed through the air. He hadn't made this sword, but he liked its feel and weight. He started to lower it into his belt. Raven was right: He couldn't take that with him. Aunt Amelia would take one look at it and know where he had gotten it from. She had the uncanny ability to get the truth out of him and Raven, so it was best not to risk that. He couldn't explain to her his visit to Kempschester and digging through the ruins. Or his dreams that had started a few weeks before.

With no more pick-ups for the day, he moved towards his bedroom.

"Julianna," he said. "You'd better be naked in there. I'm coming in."

"I am," she called out.

As he turned to lock the front door, a shadow caught his eye and he sighed at the sight of someone standing at his door.

A strong horse smell came from The Enforcer.

"I'm closed." He glanced down at Markus's feet. "Did you step in horse faeces? You're not setting foot in my shop like that."

The Enforcer's eyes focused behind Zachary, as if looking for someone. Zachary glanced behind him to make sure Julianna wasn't there.

"She's not here," Zachary said.

Relief crossed Markus's features.

"I meant what I said, Markus. You don't look at her," Zachary commanded.

"Hot blade, eyes, I heard you. I was just making sure she wasn't here. She's very unpleasant." Markus laughed but stopped at Zachary's hand tightening around the sword hilt.

"You say that because she humiliated you. I taught her that move, and she is a fine swordswoman. You're lucky she didn't do more."

"Lord Gerard has asked to see you.," Markus said, composing himself.

"He can wait. I have company," Zachary declared.

Markus smirked, his gaze shifting towards the door. "He's on his way here."

Zachary froze. "Now? What does he want?"

"That's between you and him," Markus said. "My job was to inform you he was coming to see you; I've done that."

"I don't have time for this," Zachary grumbled.

"That's not my problem." Markus said.

"I know you're not from this town," Zachary said. "And you're a new Enforcer, trying to prove yourself, just not in my shop. Not with me. I won't tolerate that from any Enforcers."

Markus eyed him up and down. "You don't like Enforcers very much, do you?"

"*No one* likes Enforcers," Zachary pointed out.

Markus shook his head. "No, this is personal to you."

The sharp echo of a horse's hooves announced the Lord's arrival. Lord Gerard sat on a black horse. "If you must know, I don't have the greatest experience with them," he told Markus. "Where I come from, they were known for their cruelty."

"I've heard that they are in the bigger towns," Markus said.

Zachary frowned. "I didn't say I was from a bigger town."

Before he could say anything else, Lord Gerard entered his workshop. "Zachary."

"My Lord?" Zachary bowed his head in respect.

"Are you looking for an apprentice?" Lord Gerard asked.

An apprentice? He hadn't considered that. "I don't know, sir. I hadn't given it much thought," he admitted.

"I want you to consider taking on my son," Lord Gerard proposed. "He's of age for that. Maybe teach him how to use a sword, too."

This took Zachary by surprise. "You want me to train him to fight?"

"I do. I know you were involved in the street fights, and that you're good with the sword." He shook his head. "Better than some of my Enforcers."

"I had a good teacher," he said.

Lord Gerard eyed him. "Word has it that you had students in secret, too."

Zachary kept his face blank, careful not to allow the annoyance to show. If the Lord knew of that, someone had broken their silence on his private lessons. "No, my Lord."

"No, you didn't have students?" Lord Gerard raised an eyebrow.

"Not in secret. Not if word got back to you," Zachary affirmed.

Lord Gerard smiled. "I heard good things. How long have you had this smithy now?"

"Five years, my Lord." Zachary shifted from one foot to the other, forcing his impatience down. This was poor timing, and Julianna would probably come out to see where he was.

"I'm surprised you didn't already take on an apprentice," Lord Gerard said.

He smirked at the Lord. "I did, it just wasn't known."

"You have an apprentice already?" Lord Gerard asked.

Zachary hesitated. "Not any more, I guess you could say she graduated."

Lord Gerard looked impressed. "She? Your cousin?"

"That's right," he confirmed.

Lord Gerard laughed. "Then I pity anyone who picks up weapons against her."

Markus's eyes widened.

"So, will you consider it?" Lord Gerard glanced around the shop.

"I will. Just not right now; I must be somewhere." Zachary struggled with his impatience.

"Your cousin is getting married tomorrow, is she not?" Lord Gerard asked.

This young Lord was one who took the time to know his people, and knowing that Raven's wedding was tomorrow was just another way to show he cared. It was all the news of Eskham, and he had taken notice.

"She is. To Lucian Carter," Zachary agreed.

"Oh yes, Young Lucian, he is a good man." The Lord gave a small smile. "Give them my congratulations."

Zachary turned his gaze back to the bedroom door again.

"Is there somewhere else you want to be?" Lord Gerard asked, with a gleam of amusement in his eyes.

Zachary couldn't find a response.

The Lord gave a low chuckle. "I will leave you to your....business," he said in amusement. "I will bring my son over in two days. I trust that you won't be too intoxicated from the wedding?"

Zachary grinned. "Maybe three days, my Lord; it is a big celebration. All the village will be there. The tavern owner has been buying ale and wine just for the event."

Lord Gerard slapped him on the back "Of course! I'll see you when you get back."

The Lord started towards the door and stopped. "I don't know why you didn't join my Enforcers. You have the skills. I would welcome you in without hesitation."

Zachary's chest tightened. "No thank you, sir, I'd much rather make swords for them."

Lord Gerard nodded. "I need you to design new armour for them."

Zachary's eyes darted to Markus. "I've been told." He met Lord Gerard's gaze. "I'm not sure I can get them in the time you need them. Do you have a design in mind?"

"I can get that to you when I bring my son. Get them in the time *you* need." He paused. "A hundred coins a piece should be enough to cover it."

Zachary caught slight movement from Markus and couldn't blame the look of shock. "You are very generous, Lord Gerard. I'll get started on that next week," Zachary promised.

The Lord left, and Markus followed. A dark-skinned woman with curly hair walked past, and his heart skipped a beat. *Delia.* He stepped back into the shop, his own heartbreak sweeping over him. A woman he'd lain with for two years, the sight of her a reminder that he'd given in to feelings for her. He'd thought to take her as his wife, only for her to refuse to see him one day.

Regret still haunted him that he hadn't fought for her. Instead, he'd respected her wishes, letting her go. As pain gripped his heart, he considered calling out to her. Unable to find words, he hid, as he did every time he caught sight of her. *Coward.* Even after five years, her leaving him without a word still hurt. Zachary locked the door. Julianna was waiting, and he would need to leave soon to make it to dinner in time with

Raven and Aunt Amelia.

Chapter 12

Raven smiled at her mother's singing behind her as she left the house, chewing on the warm, seasoned piece of chicken she'd stolen. Zachary would be there soon, and she wanted to pick up a blueberry tart to go with dinner. Her friend Anne made the best in Eskham. She stopped to admire the red and orange as day became dusk.

A footstep sounded off to one side and a large hand enclosed hers, pulling Raven in the other direction than where she needed to go. A warm body pressed against her; his lips curved into a small smile. She fell into the brown eyes. Lucian's other hand rested against her cheek, warm and calming.

"Lucian, you scared me." Her heart had taken fright, pounding hard.

He smiled down at her. "Sorry, that was not my intention."

This close he smelled earthy, and of wood smoke. She breathed it in, wanting to rest her head against his chest. To feel his strong arms wrapped around her.

"Is something wrong? What are you doing here?" she asked.

"I'm sorry, I had to see you. I've been thinking about this all day," he said.

His finger crooked under her chin, bringing it up, and his mouth found hers.

Raven's heart skipped, his lips soft, gentle, with his stubble rough against her chin. *Oh...* Her stomach flipped, and she offered no resistance, returning the kiss, just as eager. She grasped the back of his head, her fingers tangled in his hair. Desire raced down her spine as their kiss grew hungry, ravenous. His hand let go of hers, moving to her hip, sliding up her back, pulling her hard against him. His touch set off shivers, and her body responded to their closeness. Hot with lust, she pressed herself into the bulge in his trousers.

Raven let out a soft moan against his mouth, yearning for more. She wanted to rip his tunic off him, to run her hands over his body, imagining the firmness of his abdomen beneath the clothes.

He pulled back, his hands on her arms. "Perhaps we should stop before we get carried away."

Raven struggled to catch her breath, her arms around him. "One more day," she breathed and rested her head against his chest. His arms slid around her, and she was engulfed by warmth. Neither of them moved, their breathing filling the silence. Convinced the entire village could hear her heartbeat, she tried to calm herself.

"Lucian?" she whispered.

"Mmm?" He didn't move.

She forced the words out. "If we don't separate, I am going to tear that tunic to get it off you."

He sucked in a breath, but said nothing, as if hoping she would. His embrace tightened almost painfully.

"I'm supposed to get dessert," she said. "Zac will be here soon."

"Tomorrow night I'll have you all to myself," he said. "But the day will be torment, to have you so close and not able to…" He kissed her again, this time a short kiss. "I will see you tomorrow, my beautiful wife."

My wife. Two words had never sounded so joyous. Reluctantly, Raven let him go. She still had to get the blueberry tart. Tonight was her last as an unwed woman, and her future with Lucian was something to look forward to.

With the blueberry tart in hand, Raven bid farewell to Anne. She lifted the dessert, breathing it in. Tangy and sweet, it made her mouth water. It was a brief walk home, the village darkening. Zac would be there by now, and probably getting impatient. Raven chuckled at the idea, then froze as shadows moved in the darkness. *No, it's just like the other night. There's nothing there.*

A voice behind her filled Raven with terror, the French unmistakable. *A Frenchman, here?!* She ran, but rough hands grabbed her. Forced around, she faced her attacker. Other soldiers slipped past, spreading throughout the village.

"English whore," he spoke with a thick accent, holding a dagger to her throat. "Where are soldiers?"

With the blade against her throat, Raven struggled against her anger. *You dare threaten me?* She spat in his face. "We don't need soldiers for the likes of you," she hissed through her teeth.

"Your Lord no protect you?" He spoke in broken English.

The smile in his voice gave her regret for her words spoken in haste. Waves of anger battered her, his hand tight on her arm.

Having his hand grip her arm, with metal pressed in against her throat, wasn't helping her temper. Raising her knee, she made contact between his legs. A grunt escaped his lips. It was enough for his grip to loosen, and she ran, throwing the blueberry tart to the ground.

Her feet took her towards the church. "French!" she shouted. "We're under attack!" She pulled her dagger from its sheath at her hip. "French soldiers are here!"

The man caught up with Raven and grabbed a fistful of hair and pulled her back. He threw her to the ground, standing over her, drawing his sword. She hit the ground hard, and a wave of dizziness passed over her. Voices echoed around her. Alarm had been raised, the village alert, responding to the attack. But it was too late for her.

"You'll die for that," he growled.

Her eyes stung as she gazed up at the full moon, waiting for her death. Her mother, Zac, and Lucian would find her body and grieve her. Tomorrow there would be a funeral instead of a wedding. *I'm sorry Lucian. Zac, Mother...* Tears spilled over. Instead of praying for a quick release, she reached out to whatever would listen. *May his death be as painful as mine. May he suffer.*

The howl of a dog made the hairs on her arms stand up. A sound that pierced her very soul. Staring up at the French soldier, Raven gasped. It seemed as if a dark shape stood over him. The form towered over her attacker, and a blade pierced the French man's torso from behind. Blood splashed onto her. His body hit the ground with a thump. Raven couldn't look away as the dark shape moved towards her, taking the shape of a man, kneeling beside her.

"Raven." His voice was strange, as if two people spoke at once.

"Zac?" she frowned. "I think I hit my head. You sound strange."

"Isaac is here," he said. "But I am not him."

She sat up, reaching for his arm. "What are you talking about? Why are you using the name Isaac, you know you're not sup—"

As her hand made contact, she froze, fighting against rising panic set off by a deep cold that spread from where she touched him. *That's not Zac.* Darkness stretched out and showed her burning houses, Zac kneeling over someone, two men fighting, silhouetted against flames. Pain punched into her chest before the vision changed, revealing the man that knelt before her, reaching for her mother. "It is your time." His voice echoed in her head.

Once again the vision changed to herself locked in battle, pain and terror on her face. *What is this?* Then it was Zac, on his knees before the same shadowed figure.

She gasped, pulling her hand away from him, the Darkness receding.

He's the death of us all.

"You saw something," he noted.

"Please don't kill me," she whimpered.

Everything went dark.

Chapter 13

The setting sun painted the sky with fire as Zachary walked into Aunt Amelia's house, greeted by her singing. He was looking forward to a meal cooked by his aunt. His intake of food in town did not compare to what Aunt Amelia made. It had been a long time since he had enjoyed a family meal. He breathed in deep, the aroma of hot food making his stomach growl.

Aunt Amelia stopped singing. "Zachary, is that you?"

"What gave it away?" he asked.

"Your heavy steps." She beamed as he entered the kitchen. "And your stomach. Welcome home."

He wrapped arms around her in a quick hug. "Where's Raven?"

She pulled away from him with a smile."She's gone to Anne's for a blueberry tart. She won't be long."

He couldn't hold back his own grin. "Good. Come with me, I have her wedding gift."

Aunt Amelia followed him outside. He led her to Lance, waiting with a cart.

"Let me see it, then," Aunt Amelia said.

He lifted the cover off, showing her his masterpiece.

"It's beautiful." Aunt Amelia gushed. "She'll love it. The raven on the chest is a nice touch."

"Is that Zachary Dale?" A voice behind him growled.

Lucian.

Zachary spun around.

Lucian's face split into a smile. "Zac, it's been too long! You've been living large in town, avoiding the people who know you best." He winked. "Are you married yet, or still drawing the women to your bed?"

Zachary shook his head with a chuckle. "What brings you here?"

Lucian's head jerked towards Amelia, and he said nothing. Zachary shook with laughter. "Still trying to sneak in those moments?" he queried.

"Is this the armour?" Lucian changed the subject.

"How do you know about the armour?" Zachary asked.

Lucian wrapped his arm around Zachary's neck. "I know everything!" he teased. "You can't hide anything from me, Zac!"

"Is there anyone Raven didn't tell when she was sneaking around my shop in my absence?" Zachary grumbled as he struggled to pull from Lucian's grip. "Was this a discussion during breakfast, or after you kissed her?"

"You should be more careful with where you leave things," Lucian gloated.

Lucian had always been shorter than him but now towered over Zachary. "When did you get so tall?" he joked.

Lucian let him go. "You're the short one now, my friend."

"I can still beat you in a fight," he boasted.

Their friendship had started out badly, with fights between the two. As a boy, anger had been hard to contain. But over time they had grown close, their fights less serious, but just as rough. It surprised everyone.

Lucian raised his fists. "What are you waiting for, then?"

Zachary raised his own.

Aunt Amelia stepped in. "No! You two are trouble. Before you start your usual rough play, Raven will be back soon. Lucian, you should not be bruised on your wedding day."

Lucian frowned. "Who says I'll be the one—"

"Have you forgotten the damage I did last time?" Zachary gave Lucian a playful punch on the shoulder. "Your eye and cheek? It took forever for that swelling to go down. She's right. Probably best you don't look like that tomorrow."

"Lucian, perhaps you can help Zachary get this inside?" Amelia prompted.

Lucian nodded, his respect for Amelia clear. Zachary handed him the sword and lifted the armour.

"Are you sure you can manage that?" Lucian asked. "Perhaps you take the sword?"

"Just get inside," Zachary said, rolling his eyes as he lifted Raven's armour.

He followed Aunt Amelia and Lucian inside.

"Smells delicious," Lucian said, bending over the fire where dinner was simmering.

"Go." Amelia said to Lucian. "If you're still here when Raven gets back, we'll never get our family dinner."

"I'll be back," Zachary called over his shoulder, following Lucian out.

"I know it means a lot to Raven that you're here," his friend said. "I'm glad you're here, too."

"Where is it?" Zachary asked once they were outside. "I know you brought it. You said you and I would have that drink the night before your wedding."

Lucian retrieved a bottle from the corner of the house and held it out to Zachary. "We don't have long, though; I really should leave before Raven returns. It was difficult enough to let her go once tonight."

Zachary opened the bottle. "She told me what the two of you did today. You came back for more, didn't you?"

Lucian laughed. "I couldn't resist. She's a very bold woman. I couldn't stop thinking about her all day."

"I knew someone like that a few years ago. Delia," Zachary admitted.

Lucian nodded. "I remember her. You said she was really something."

His smile faded. "She was. Until she wouldn't have anything to do with me any more."

"Pity. I'd really hoped she would be enough to make you a family man." Lucian said.

"So did I." Zachary drank. The wine was rich and flavoured heavily with honey and other flavours he couldn't name. "Where's this from?" he asked. "This isn't your usual stock."

"It's from a village called Willowdale," Lucian admitted.

"Willowdale?" Zachary passed the bottle back, trying to hide his shock.

"You've never heard of Willowdale wine? My father claims it's among the best in the country. To come out of such a small village is surprising. I wanted to get some good wine; Raven doesn't like ale."

Zachary passed the bottle back to Lucian. "I'm glad she has you," he said. "There's no possibility that I'd approve of anyone else."

"The seal of approval." Lucian's shoulders shook. "I'm lucky we're friends."

Zachary shook his head in amusement. "Would you rather I threaten you? Tell you to be good to her, or I'll slit your throat?"

"You know I will, Zac. Raven will be happy with me, I promise you." Lucian assured him.

"I know." Zachary agreed. "She holds her own heart in her hands for all to see. I can see how she feels about you. I am happy for you both."

"I feel the same for her. I will protect her heart." Lucian took a swig of wine. "I should go. I will greet you all at the church in the morning."

"Let me have one more sip of that wine." Zachary held his hand out.

"It grows on you, doesn't it?" Lucian asked.

Zachary took a deep gulp of the wine and handed back the bottle. He turned and went back inside.

Aunt Amelia was serving up their dinner when he walked into the kitchen.

His stomach rumbled again.

"I wish Raven would hurry up," he complained.

"She has been gone awhile," Aunt Amelia agreed with a worried tone.

"I can look for her if you want," he offered.

"I'm sure I'm worrying about nothing." Aunt Amelia contemplated.

"I'll go," he told her. "I'm sure she's just looking at the stars or something."

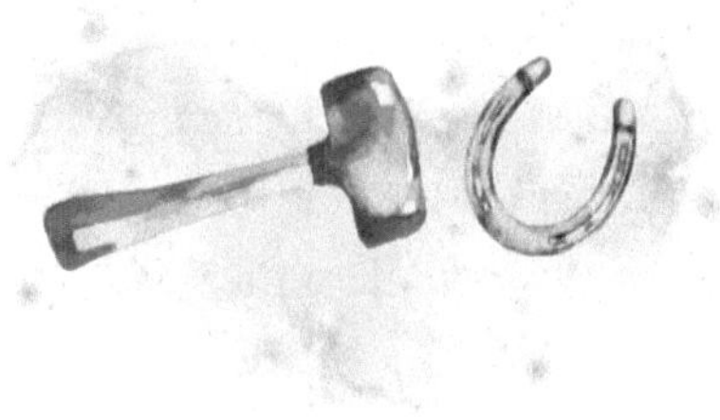

Zachary wandered through the village, hoping he had taken the route Raven had. He didn't see any sign of her or Lucian, so chances were she was just talking to her friend.

The howl of a dog nearby raised the hairs on the back of his neck. A cold, prickling sensation crawled over his back and arms. Shouts started to spread as villagers took on the call. Alarms had been raised; they were under attack.

"Raven, where are you?" he muttered and ran towards where Raven should be. "Please be alright."

A French soldier set a house on fire, the flames lighting up the village around him, its heat already scorching against his skin. Bodies on the ground caught his attention and filled him with dread. Zachary ran, his heart racing. One was a French soldier, the other, Raven, not moving.

"Raven?!" Zachary skidded to the ground. The house that burned behind him cast an orange glow over her. There was blood on Raven, and her dagger lay nearby.

"No, not tonight of all nights," he exclaimed. "Raven!"

Fear gripped tight as he took in the sight of his little sister. Her hand was cold, her stillness spreading panic. *She's dead. That's a lot of blood.* Villagers ran past him, swords in hands, seeking out their attackers. Metal struck metal; cries rang out around him. But all that filled his attention was the sight of Raven. "Please wake up," he whispered. "You can't be …"

"Is she dead?" a voice brought relief to Zachary. His former mentor always had a calming effect on him. A man stood over him, with dark brown skin and a shorn head, with a greying beard. His sword was already bloodied as he stood over Zachary.

"Master Hector." His own fear was suffocating. "She's not moving. There's a lot of blood."

"Get her to Amelia's quickly. We need you, little Zac. Defend our home. This is what I trained you for."

"Yes, Master Hector."

Hector ran. "Make sure Maria goes to the cellar," he called over his shoulder.

Zachary grabbed her dagger, and gently lifted Raven, and she groaned. Relief soared, and for a moment he thought he was going to be sick. He had to get her to Aunt Amelia's so he could help the people of Eskham.

Chapter 14

She was moving; no, someone was carrying her. Raven opened her eyes, groaning.

"Raven, shh, you're safe." The familiar voice of her cousin broke through.

She glanced around them. "Zac, that man, he…"

"I know. I'm sorry I was late. I got distracted," he apologised.

They arrived at Raven's house, and he lowered her to her feet. "He looked just like you."

"I see you used your dagger," he said, handing it to her.

She shook her head. "No, that wasn't me. He killed him."

"You found her!" Her mother ran over.

Raven turned, meeting her mother's panicked eyes.

"She's alright. I don't think it's her blood," Zac said.

She recognised the quiet rasp of a sword being drawn.

"The French are going to regret attacking this village," he swore.

"Zac, you have no armour." Raven grabbed his arm.

He pulled his arm away. "No one does. We don't have time for that. We're under attack. Both of you, get to the church."

Before she could say more, Zac ran off, other men running in the same direction, shouting.

Raven met her mother's worried eyes. "I have to help them."

"I know." Her mother didn't look happy about it, but at least she wasn't arguing.

The church. "Get everyone to the church," Raven said. "To the cellar."

Screams filled the air, and the roar of fire as more houses burned. Gagging on the smell, Raven and Amelia ran towards the church. The metal of swords clashing mixed with cries of anger and pain. French and English. A nearby house burned, flames engulfing the building. Heat pressed at her as she ran past. She checked over her shoulder, relieved that her mother was only steps behind.

Running into the church, she could already tell Lucian was not there. Villagers were reaching for swords and spears from the chest. One of the men handed her one, the blacksmith who had taken Zac as an apprentice. He was older, with dark blond but greying hair. He had battle scars from the French war, with a noticeable limp. His grey eyes bored into hers.

"Fight with everything. Take them down quickly; don't let them draw it out," he told her. "They won't be accustomed to women who fight back. Use that to your advantage."

"Raven." a voice called out to her. Lucian's mother, Elaine.

"Where is he?" she asked.

"Our house is on fire," Rosamund said in shock. "He was right behind us. I couldn't find Noah."

"Get down there," Raven instructed. "I'll find them."

"I'll come with you," Rosamund said, grabbing a sword from the blacksmith.

Elaine grasped their arms. "Please be careful," she said. "Both of you."

"Help the others. I'll find him," Raven promised. "Noah, too."

As she made her way towards Lucian's house with Rosamund, a soldier ran at her. She lost sight of Lucian's sister as she fought. Meeting his blade, she gritted her teeth as she blocked the blow. He towered over her, orange flickering over his face. Before he could swing again, she buried her dagger into his thigh, slicing down. He immediately fell.

Leaving him bleeding in the dirt, Raven ran. Fog wafted around her. It was a clear night; her burst of energy after fighting must be making her see things. She blinked and it was gone. A deep dread, like a punch to the chest, winded her as she ran for Lucian's. Overwhelmed by urgency, something deep within told her she was running towards disaster. A shadow moved in front of her as another soldier attacked. This time another villager took on the fight.

She finally caught sight of his house. Flames leapt towards the sky with a thunderous roar.. Smoke stung her eyes and throat. Two silhouettes fought in front of the inferno. The house caved in with a loud crash. No sooner had she identified Lucian's shape, than he fell under the sword of his opponent. Eyes on Lucian, a cry tore from her, a sound she never thought she could make. The French soldier turned to her. Firelight reflected off the side of his face as he faced her, his blade red. Raven raised her own sword, ready, as fury burned through her.

There was no fear as she ran at him, letting calm overtake her. He swung his weapon at her, and as she blocked it, the contact was jarring. She forced it all from her mind. To let grief weigh her down was a distraction that would cost her greatly. With sword in one hand, dagger in the other, she struck hard with the larger of the blades, her blow deflected. Before he could return a swing, she slashed across with her dagger. He grunted in pain as the blade cut across his chest. A shallow cut.

A shadow behind him should have distracted her, but she didn't let it. She had seen it before, killing the soldier that attacked her. "No!" she growled out. "This one is mine!" Her words confused her, but she continued to match the soldier blow for blow. He was strong, and every time his sword met hers, it jarred through her hand. Flames roared behind her as she felt herself tiring.

Zachary's training washed over her. 'Don't let tiredness make you desperate.' She clenched her jaw as fear made its way in. His blade sliced across her shoulder, pain radiating from the wound.

What she'd seen earlier was coming to pass. *I'm going to die.*

Chapter 15

The English soldiers had arrived. Bloodied, Zachary caught his breath, a burst of pride as he grinned. The people of Eskham had held their own. The roar of houses on fire and orange glow showed much had been lost. He needed to find Raven and Aunt Amelia, to make sure they were safe. To lose them would be unthinkable. He forced down the rising fear.

"Zachary! My husband, he's been wounded!" a woman called out to him. Maria was light brown, but her face took on an orange glow, reflecting the firelight. She had black hair styled into a braid down the length of her back. He ran to her, sheathing his sword. Maria led him back to Hector. He appeared in bad shape, his midsection showing blood.

"He was protecting me," Maria said. "I didn't go to the church when I was supposed to."

Zachary knelt beside Hector, holding the man's trembling hand in comfort.

"Is Raven…?" Hector choked.

"She is," Zachary said. "She's with my Aunt. I know they would have gone to the church."

"Maria." Hector's eyes widened.

"Your wife is safe," he said. "Soldiers have arrived from the outpost." The sounds of English soldiers pushing back the French clamoured around him.

Hector eyed his wife over Zachary's shoulder, gasping in pain. Zachary's stomach twisted for his former mentor.

"You'll be alright," Zachary whispered.

"Don't lie to me, little Zac." Hector choked out, using the nickname he'd given Zachary years ago. "I trained you better than that. I'm dying. Denying the fact won't change anything."

Zachary swallowed back his anguish. "You're right," he said and squeezed Hector's hand. "I owe you more respect than that." The man was fading, his breathing shallow.

Zachary half-turned, reaching for Maria with bloodied hands. "Hold his hand," he said. "You'll be the last thing he sees."

Maria knelt opposite him, following his encouragement to hold Hector's hand. She murmured to Hector, her cheeks wet in the orange glow.

Hector's breathing slowed, eyes wide and staring at Zachary. "Will it hurt?" his voice was barely audible.

He's asking me if it will hurt to die? Zachary swallowed, unsure how to answer that question. "I don't know," he said truthfully. "But the pain will soon end. Maria will be alright."

"I'm sorry, Maria." The deep regret reflected in Hector's voice.

"You fought well, my master." He gave the elder man a gentle smile, gripping his other hand. "You can rest now. Be at peace. Your fight is over."

Something in him responded to the words, awakening, like a jolt of lightning, sending sparks through his entire being. Zachary shook his head, taking it to be weariness from the battle.

Zachary and Maria knelt on either side of Hector as life left him. A sob escaped Maria. Zachary suppressed his own. Hector had been very fatherly to him, the elder man's gentleness enough to get through Zac's rage. Despite his best effort, a tear escaped, leaving a hot trail down his cheek. *Hector...master.*

"Zachary?" Aunt Amelia called out. He heard the twinge of fear in her voice.

"Aunt Amelia! I'm here!" he answered.

Aunt Amelia found him. "Hector?"

"He's gone," Maria told her.

"Oh, Maria." Amelia pulled the other woman to her feet, hugging her. Over Maria's shoulder, a tear slid down Aunt's cheek, her eyes on Hector.

The two women pulled apart. "Let me help you home," Amelia offered.

Maria shook her head. "I cannot leave him."

"Help her," Amelia said to villagers who had caught sight of Hector. "Take them to the church."

"Where's Raven?" Zachary asked, standing as Hector was carried away, with Maria following. "Did she get to the church, to Lucian?"

"He wasn't at the church; she went looking for him." Aunt Amelia gasped. "What if..."

"No, don't think that way. I've seen her in training; she has fire and fury." He comforted her.

Aunt Amelia's eyes narrowed. "You mean she has her father's rage."

Zachary didn't know what to say. He knew it worried Aunt Amelia that Raven had her father in her. That Uncle Graeme's Darkness would follow Raven. When he was a boy, he often found Aunt Amelia watching Raven, looking for signs that she would fall to Darkness.

"We'll find her," he said and led Aunt Amelia to the other side of the village.

Lucian's house had crumbled, flames still licking at what was left. For a moment he was a boy, back in Riverwick, his own house on fire, and he couldn't breathe. Panic jolted through him, and he froze.

"Zachary." Aunt Amelia's urgency brought him back.

Two silhouettes were in a fight to the death. One of them, Raven. The way she moved, exactly as he'd taught her. Pride surged. *My little sister, the fighter.* Swords clanged; Raven raged as she fought. But he recognised signs of her tiring.

Before Zachary could move to help her, he noticed a heap on the ground. Reflected in the firelight, Lucian's face was visible. "Lucian!" Zachary ran forward, Aunt Amelia behind him. Lucian's eyes were open, unblinking, sword still gripped in his hand. Zachary choked on sorrow. *My closest friend.* Aunt Amelia's hand on his shoulder was a comfort. He had been overjoyed when the betrothal of Lucian and Raven had been announced, happy for both of them. To see his friend dead, not that long after they'd shared a drink, set off a pain in Zachary that pierced him to the core. First Hector, now Lucian.

"Oh, no." Aunt Amelia pointed. "Noah."

Not far away, Lucian's younger brother Noah lay, throat gaping, sword still sheathed. "He didn't have time to fight back," he murmured. Noah was a boy known for mischief. For him to die so young was a deep loss that hit Zachary equally hard. The family had lost both their sons.

Raven's cry drew his attention.

"Help her," Aunt Amelia pleaded.

Overcome by rage and grief, Zachary ran towards where Raven fought the French soldier. He had never experienced the desire to kill someone as much as that moment. A scream bubbled up. He looked into Raven's eyes. Dark fury lurked within, and a spark of fear.

Chapter 16

People moved around her, voices low. She recognised that of Zac. For the second time that night, she faced her own death. The soldier knew she was losing strength as he drove forward harder. All her training, and she was about to die. *If Zac sees me fall, will he avenge me, and Lucian?* She struggled to keep her mind clear, fear crowding in. A spark had grown into an inferno, burning through her.

Raven, fight. He leaves his throat unprotected when he attacks.

Unsure where the words came from, she dug deep. Sure enough, every time he struck, there was free space where a spare blade could find its way into his throat. She took the opportunity presented to her, slicing deep. Just as she did, movement caught her eye: Zac's eyes blazing with madness as he ran forward. But she had already claimed her kill, and as the soldier dropped, she and Zac were left staring at each other, her blade glistening in the firelight. She breathed hard, shoulders heaving as it dawned on her that she had escaped death once again.

Then her legs gave out.

Zac stopped her from falling. "You did it." There was no hiding the pride in his voice.

"He's dead." She could barely talk.

"Are you hurt?" he asked. "Let me check."

"Only my shoulder," she murmured. "He's dead, Zac." The crushing grief that she had forced away came rushing back. "I was too late, I saw him die." *I knew he would die.* "Help me to him." He supported her as she struggled to Lucian's side. Every muscle in her body ached from the fight, tremors spreading out. She fell to Lucian's side, eyes on his face. A sob tore from her. "Lucian, you were supposed to come to the church to find me." She clung to him, sobbing. His scent already faint, his still body would soon grow cold.

Zac knelt beside her. "Raven." His hand touched her arm.

With hot tears on her cheeks, and raw grief piercing her heart, she turned to him. "Tomorrow *was* our wedding day."

"I know." He wrapped his arms around her.

She continued to cry into his shoulder, and arms encircled them both. Her mother's soothing presence was as much a comfort as Zac's.

"I'm sorry, my little Raven," her mother whispered.

"I killed him." She turned her gaze to the soldier on the ground. "Does this make me a killer?" her voice trembled. "I've never taken a life before."

"No! You defended the village. I'm proud of you," Zac said.

"You both did," her mother said. "Blakes, through and through."

Raven lifted her eyes to Zac's. It was the first time her mother had referred to them as Blakes.

"I can't escape the fact that you're their children. You fight hard to protect those you care about, and this village is your home. The men they were before...before everything...they would both be incredibly proud of the two of you."

"We have to find Elaine," Zac said. "To lose both her sons in one night. This will devastate her and Charles."

"She told me to find him. Both of them." Raven mumbled. "Rosamund, too; I don't know where she went."

He gave her a squeeze.

"Hector's gone, too," he murmured.

Hector, the whole village would feel that as much as Lucian's death.

"We should go," her mother said, rising. "Everyone will be looking for us."

"No," Raven said. "I'm not leaving him."

He's gone. The voice that had told her to fight sent chills through her.

"Did you hear that?" Zac asked.

"Hear what?" Her mother looked around.

The cold from earlier that night filled her. "Something's coming," she whispered. *It's him, from earlier.* They stood as the presence grew closer. "Something dark. It's what's been watching me."

A gasp came from her mother, and Raven stepped back as a dark figure appeared in front of her. The dark shape of a man formed from shadows, soon taking on a human appearance.

The same one that had helped her earlier, his resemblance to Zac uncanny. His strange eyes were just as empty as they had been before. Black lines stretched across one side of his face. A large grey dog stood at his side and let out a low growl.

Her mother shook her head, eyes wide, focused on the figure before her, shaking. *She's terrified!*

She touched her mother's arm, but got no response, so she looked at Zac, a look of wonder on his face.

"Thomas," her mother breathed, taking a step back.

"This is your father?" Raven whispered to Zac.

"Not exactly." The voice of two men, filled with Darkness, echoed as the strange eyes remained on her mother. "I am Death." He gave a small smile. "But I will show you the face that brings you comfort." His voice changed, losing its echo.

"Graeme," her mother said, her voice barely audible. "Oh, Graeme."

Zac broke out of his trance and touched Raven's arm. "No, that's yours."

"I am not the man you once knew. You were right to mourn me." His voice still reflected Darkness. "You will not find your husband in me."

My father? Unable to look away, Raven's intrigue horrified her. His eyes shifted to her with an unwavering gaze that sent a chill through her. His very presence, shrouded with Darkness, pierced her soul, and ice clawed its way to her heart.

"Hello, Raven." His voice spoke to terror deep within her.

"Why are you here?" her mother asked.

"Amelia," he whispered, finally shifting his gaze. He held his hand out. "It is your time."

"You're here for me?" her mother asked without surprise. It was as if she had expected it.

Raven moved to stand in front of her mother, and Zac did the same. Death frowned at them as if they were an inconvenience.

"It is your time," he repeated. "You knew this day would come. You cannot run from it any more. Nor hide behind my children."

"No," her mother sighed. "I'm not ready to leave them," she whispered. "Please, Graeme, not yet."

"No one is ever ready," he told her. "Do not plead with me. You cannot appeal to humanity that isn't there. It hasn't been there for twenty years. I am not the Thomas, or the Graeme you knew then, but I have chosen to show you the face you know, one that soothes you. The face of your husband, to comfort you. You have seen my other face. I can make this unpleasant if you fight me."

Raven raised her sword. "You get away from my mother!"

"Raven, stop," her mother pleaded. "You don't know what you're doing."

Piercing blue eyes met her own, cold emptiness within their depths. His mouth curved into a menacing smile, and she caught a glimpse of a man filled with nothing but Darkness. She fought against the urge to run, her instincts screaming at her that she was staring into the face of her own end.

She recalled the visions from earlier when she touched his arm.

"I've been watching you. You have spirit. It makes a father proud." He stepped towards her. "What did you see earlier?" He pointed to the body of Lucian. "You saw that, didn't you? Or felt it."

How did he know?

"Why are you watching my daughter?" her mother demanded, in an attempt to hide her fear.

"*Our* daughter," Death smiled. "She is as much mine as she is yours. In a moment before death, she sought her attacker to suffer. I heard her. She *is* my daughter, and I have felt her dark presence since she took her first breath."

Dark presence? So there is *Darkness in me!* Horror gripped her throat tight.

Raven rushed forward, raising the sword. Before she reached him, he took a step towards her and vanished, only to reappear inside her reach, hand closing around her wrist. She let out a groan as his grip became painful. Her sword dropped from her fingers.

"Raven!" Zac called out, stepping forward.

"Please, Graeme, don't hurt her." her mother's voice trembled.

Death held his hand out to her mother again.

"You knew about her?" her mother took a step towards him.

"She could sense my presence, too. I knew there would be a day I would reveal myself to her," he confirmed.

Raven suppressed a shudder. All the times she had known she was being watched. "It was you watching me," she murmured.

Death nodded. "It was. Your gift has awakened, hasn't it?"

"My gift?" She was confused.

"You saw this when we first met. Your eyes were black." His own changed colour, dark as the night around them, reflecting flames of the fire.

She said nothing.

"She is the reason you heard me telling you to run," he said to her mother.

"I heard you," Zac murmured.

Death's eyes shifted to her cousin. "Isaac." He smiled. it was a terrifying smile, and Raven backed up again.

"His name is Zac." Her retort was met by a brief glance toward her.

"You came back. I knew you would." Zac said.

Death took awhile to respond. "You were unexpected. I was certain you were gone."

"Your voice...I heard you. You called me back. I'm alive because of you," Zac said.

Death genuinely seemed surprised, his eyes on Zac. "You didn't come back quite yourself, though, did you? Your time in The Shadow Realm affected you. I can see the Darkness beneath your skin, faded from mortal eyes but not invisible. Lines just like the ones on my own face."

"I'm not a killer," Zac insisted.

"But you *are,*" Death disagreed. "I saw what you did tonight. You took a life with the Touch of Death."

"The Touch of Death?" Zac's shoulders stiffened.

Death held his hand up, and for the first time, Raven noticed dark lines traced around his fingers up his arms. Just like the ones on his face. "A part of me that you seem to have inherited somehow."

"No. Soldiers attacked us. You would have done the same to protect Riverwick," Zac said.

Death raised his eyebrows at the mention of Riverwick, a small smile on his lips. "You expect much from me, but you will be disappointed. You saw what I did to Riverwick. But I do not mean the soldiers. Hector. You held his hand; your touch parted him from this world."

Zac shook his head. "No!"

"You told him his fight was over. To rest and be at peace," Death affirmed.

Zac shook his head again. "No, that was to comfort him. He was dying, and afraid."

"It does not change that you eased him into the next world. Unfortunately, without guidance to where he belongs, he is stuck in The Shadow Realm, and strangely enough, I cannot release him." Death lost his smile and turned back to Amelia, holding his hand out to her again. "Time to go."

Raven retrieved her sword from the ground and stepped in the way. "No, you're not taking her."

Death laughed, a chilling sound, and a black scythe appeared in his hand. The face of Graeme shifted, becoming a shadow once again. "**You would challenge me?**"

"I would," Raven said, surprised at the strength of her voice.

"**Did I not already best you?**" He laughed.

"Then fight me without your tricks," she demanded.

"Raven, what are you doing?" Zac asked. "You cannot beat him."

"I've just lost Lucian, you've lost Hector, I'm not letting him take my mother from us, too," she snapped.

Death's laugh raised the hairs on her arms. "You sacrifice yourself for your mother. Moments after you've already fought, do you have the strength for another fight?"

She wasn't sure she did, but she wouldn't admit that.

"You cannot fight him any more than you can fight fate," her mother spoke up. "Please Raven, don't do this."

"No! I'm not letting him take you." Raven raised her sword again, wavering slightly with exhaustion.

"**You know who you face?**" Death demanded. "**Listen to your mother and cousin. You cannot beat me.**"

"Then what are you afraid of?" she challenged..

"**Afraid?**" Amusement shone through. "**Very well.**" A black sword appeared in his hand and he returned to his human form. "So be it. A fight to the death, between father and daughter to save the life of your mother."

Her vision of earlier flashed before her eyes, herself locked in a battle. Not that of her fight against the French soldier, but against Death himself.

Chapter 17

Something in his being spoke to a deep part of him. He couldn't let Raven fight her father. *Their* father. Their fathers.

"It has been a long time." Death said in Uncle Graeme's voice, swinging the black sword. "I will enjoy the fight."

He would willingly fight his daughter to the death? Horrified, Zachary found himself stepping forward, drawing his own sword.

Cold laughter burst out from the man before him. "My own sword. You are your father's son," he spoke as if impressed.

"Back off, Zac," Raven ordered him. "This is my fight."

"No. You think I'm going to just stand here and watch that?" Surely, so soon after a fight, she didn't have the strength she needed.

Sparks rose into the air from what remained of Lucian's house.

"You're fighting over who will die," Uncle Graeme noted in amusement. "But this is Raven's choice. Hers was the challenge that initiated this."

"Graeme, please. I cannot lose my daughter," Aunt Amelia pleaded.

"The two of you will stand back. Raven has made her choice," Uncle Graeme said, casting a look to Raven. "I accept your terms."

Something about the words felt final. "What terms?" Zachary asked.

"Stop stalling, Isaac," his uncle demanded.

Stop calling me Isaac. "You agree to terms, but we've heard none," he stated.

"Very well," Uncle Graeme said. "If you win, what do you ask of me?"

Raven turned her gaze to Aunt Amelia."That my mother lives. You leave her be." She glanced down at Lucian's body. Hope flickered in Zachary as he realised what she was about to ask for. All that she had lost, could be returned. Just as he had been. "Bring Lucian back. And his brother."

"I cannot bring back those who have crossed over. Your fiancé is gone, as is his brother. You must accept that." A chilling smile crossed Uncle Graeme's face. "However, I *do* agree to your first condition. And when you fail?"

Sympathy flooded through Zachary as the words took their impact on Raven. Her shoulders slumped, and a tear slid down her cheek.

"Well, if I fail, I can't stop you from taking her, can I?" Raven pointed out, her voice breaking.

His smile changed, resembling that of Zachary's father and Uncle Graeme's, more than the one before it had. "You have courage, I will give you that. Ready?" Without warning, he moved fast, striking hard.

Raven barely had time to raise her sword in defence. Instead of metal clashing, it was a dull thud. Zachary's hand twitched, wanting to step in. He had trained Raven, but Death moved without hesitance. Another blow followed, and another, giving Raven no chance to return strike, only defend.

"Zachary," Aunt Amelia whispered. "He's going to kill her."

Her words rang true, and the two of them were helpless to do anything but watch it happen. Death's blows were powerful and quick. Every time he moved his blade, Zachary's whole body tensed. A sliver of cold fear ran down his back.

"Push back, Raven," he muttered. "Just like I taught you, don't let him control the fight."

As if she heard his words, Raven finally moved her sword to strike, only for it to be deflected. She moved again, mirroring Death's actions by not allowing him to return swing. She pushed forward, her movements hesitant. She let out a cry and swung hard. Her footing unstable, her swing left her open.

Oh no, he's drawing her into this. Fear gripped Zachary, and he could do nothing.

Without warning, the dark blade pressed to her chest. "Drop your sword," Uncle Graeme commanded.

Raven's weapon hit the ground.

"You took the only opportunity I gave you," Uncle Graeme said. "You would let an opponent force your hand like that? You dropped your guard the moment you thought you could best me. You were never going to win, but I admire you for trying."

"You were playing me," she glared.

Uncle Graeme raised an eyebrow. "You were the foolish one who challenged Death, what did you expect?"

"Are you going to kill me?" Strong defiance in her voice would have made Zachary proud if the situation weren't so dire.

"It was a fight to the death," Uncle Graeme said.

Zachary did step forward then, only to have a blade at his own throat. "She's only nineteen," he pleaded. "Let her live."

"She is old enough to raise a sword in challenge; as such, she shall suffer the consequences of her defeat." Uncle Graeme raised his eyes to Aunt Amelia. "I am tired of this. I have elsewhere to be." He held his free hand out to her. "Amelia."

Aunt Amelia stepped forward and Uncle Graeme's hand wrapped around hers. Zachary stopped her. "No," he said. "Please, let her go. Both of them. Take me instead."

"What?" Uncle Graeme, Aunt Amelia, and Raven said in unison.

"Leave my aunt, and Raven. I will go in their place." Zachary offered.

Uncle Graeme's eyes bored into his. "You would sacrifice yourself?"

Zachary took in the sight of Aunt Amelia, ready to accept her death. Raven with the tip of a blade still held to her chest. *I cannot lose them, and at least in my death, they will have each other.* "I would. Let them live, let them have the second chance that I was given."

"Zac, what are you doing?" Raven's voice rose, revealing her fear.

"Protecting you," he told her. "As is my job."

"I once said the same thing about my brother." Uncle Graeme's voice changed, and Zachary recognised that of his father. "Until I killed him by mistake." The black sword disappeared. "But you cannot change that it is Amelia's time, and she is ready. You speak of second chances, but to live past her time will have an effect on her."

"Then release her from whatever fate you've set, and take me," Zachary sank to his knees. "Please Father, Uncle, leave her. I will go willingly. I will not fight you. Just leave them."

His father seemed to consider his offer.

"Zac?" Raven's voice shook. "You can't go, I'll never see you again."

Zachary locked eyes with her. "I'm sorry, little sister."

"I accept," his father said finally, releasing Amelia's hand. "Say your goodbyes."

Zachary lifted his head, meeting Raven's eyes, and Aunt Amelia's. *How can I say goodbye? They're all I've known, for years.* He rose to his feet. Aunt Amelia ran to him. He embraced his aunt and watched Raven. She wouldn't move.

"Raven..." Zachary moved towards her.

"You can't take him," Raven pleaded. "I challenged you, I lost."

"He has made his choice. I have accepted," his father said.

"Why did you have to come on this night? Have we not lost enough? He's just lost his closest friend, and the man who trained him to fight. Hector was a father to him." Her voice shook.

"Raven, it's alright," Zachary told her and wrapped his arms around her. "I'm doing this for you."

“No, it’s not. You have to be here to bury Lucian and Hector.” She pulled away from him and planted herself in front of him, blocking his father from him.

His father eyed Zachary. “Calm her down before I decide to take all three of you.”

Zachary put his hand on Raven’s shoulder. “Stand aside, Raven.”

“No. I can’t lose you. too.” Her voice broke.

“You have to look after my smithy,” he whispered in her ear.

“What?” She glared.

“You spent time learning from me, you were my apprentice. You know the craft.” He turned to face the figure before him. “I’m ready,” he said with false courage and gave Aunt Amelia a smile.

His father’s bony hand grasped his arm, and a shock passed through Zachary. Cold. Dark. Fog swirled around him. The village was gone. A blue moon cast its glow over the world, and red lightning flashed across the sky..

“I’ve been here,” he murmured as father removed his hand. “I know this place.”

“And you will stay here.” His father’s eyes bored into him. “Welcome home, to The Shadow Realm Isaac Blake, son of Death.”

Chapter 18

Zachary was gone. "What do we do now?" Her question erupted from her before she could hold it back. Her mother's silence was unlike her. "Mother?"

"He's gone." her mother said, unblinking, her voice strangely calm.

"He is." The loss of her cousin, right after she had lost Lucian, only added to the weight she bore. *I failed, I can't protect anyone.* Tears finally fell, and she fought against the urge to collapse. Now wasn't the time.

"I was supposed to go with him," her mother said.

Raven pulled her mother into a hug. "No, you weren't. I don't care what he said; it was not your time." As she said the words, they felt like a lie. *I saw all of this, but how?* Her eyes fell once more to Lucian's body, and Noah's.

Villagers ran towards her. She recognised the four men who arrived to help; they worked in the fields. One man looked at her shoulder. "Are you injured?"

"Nothing too deep," Raven murmured, glancing down at her shoulder. "Lucian and Noah are dead, though. Please help me; I need to bring them to Elaine and Charles."

As the men carried her fiancé and his brother through the village, a sense of loss greeted them as they passed others. Each step felt as though the ground would open at any moment. Part of her wanted it to, so she could fall into the void and not feel like she was suffocating. Once again, hot tears streamed down her cheeks, as guilt and anguish raged within.

Raven caught sight of bodies in front of the church. As she approached, Elaine ran through the door, kneeling over one with an agonising scream. "Rosamund!"

The name pierced Raven as Charles ran to his wife, pulling her into his arms. *How can she be dead, too? I saw her as we left the church.* She swayed as her world shifted.

"Elaine," she called out.

The woman turned at the sound of her voice. "Oh Raven, I'm so glad to see you alive." She smiled sadly at Raven's mother. "You are blessed this night, Amelia. Our daughter, Rosamund, has been taken from us. Lucian will be devastated."

"Not as much as Noah," Charles said. "Did you find them?"

Raven's heart broke for the pain she was about to cause. Elaine and Charles were good, kind people. She was about to tear their world apart and leave their hearts in pieces.

"I did," she could barely speak the words, and her emotion choked her, preventing more from tumbling forth.

She didn't need to say anything as Elaine's eyes fell to her sons. A long, pained wail ripped free. "My sons! Not my sons!" Held up only by Charles, the woman's cry tore at Raven as she rushed to embrace her fiancé's mother.

"I was too late," she whispered. "I'm so sorry, Elaine, I saw him fall."

Charles's arm wrapped around her, and they were crowded as others came from the church. Cries of grief and surprise filled the air.

"Noah, my youngest, not quite a man," Charles's voice was pained. "Lucian, to be wed. It should not have been this way." He lifted his head, looking around them. "Where is Zachary?"

"He's gone," her mother's voice added to Raven's pain.

"Oh, Raven, why didn't you say anything?" Elaine's teary eyes met hers. "To lose them both."

"My pain is no greater than yours," she said. "We have all suffered loss tonight."

"It was supposed to be me," her mother rambled. "They took him."

Raven sighed. "Mother, no, it wasn't."

"What is she talking about?" Elaine pulled away, moving towards Raven's mother. "Amelia, who took him?"

"My husband," her mother whispered.

A shocked silence passed over them all. "Amelia?" Elaine turned back to Raven. "I thought your father was dead."

"He is," her mother smiled. "But he came for me."

"Florence, honey, take Amelia inside. I think she needs to sit down," Elaine said to a villager. "Get her some water."

"Where is Zachary's body?" Charles asked.

How can I explain that there is no body?

"They took him," her mother said as she was led to the church.

"Mother, please stop." Raven begged.

Elaine's hand grabbed her own. They both clung to each other in their grief. "Is she trying to say the French took him?" Elaine asked.

It was the only answer that would make sense. "Yes," she whispered.

Elaine pulled her towards the church. "Come, tonight has been emotional, let us go inside."

She allowed herself to be led towards the church. Many were filling in. Her village coming together in such a tragedy was only to be expected.

A villager spoke to Charles. "Thirteen?" His raised voice stopped them.

"Thirteen what?" Elaine asked.

"Thirteen dead." his voice broke. "Eight homes lost. Many are putting the fires out now." He shook his head in disbelief. "Some families have lost everything." His eyes darted back to where his children's bodies lay.

"At least we have each other, and a home." Elaine's arms tightened around Raven.

"Your home is gone," she said.

"No, Raven. Eskham is our home. They can never take that from us. We can rebuild a house. It is the people that make this village our home." She cast a look back to the pile of bodies now including her sons. "We've lost all three of our children." Her voice broke.

Inside the church, candles had been lit for those lost, placed in the front. Elaine and Raven moved towards where Maria lit one.

"I light this to guide Hector home. May he find his peace." Maria prayed..

Raven picked up a candle when Elaine did.

"I light this for my eldest son, Lucian," Elaine said. "May he know that he is loved by us all. My son, I hope to hold you in my arms again. Until then, look after Noah and Rosamund."

Raven watched as Elaine lit the candle from Maria's.

Raven stared at her candle as Elaine held hers forward. *He took him. Does that mean he's dead?*

"Why don't you light a candle? It won't hurt. If we get him back, we will welcome him home with open arms." Elaine's voice was gentle.

He's not coming back. The sight of him again, on his knees, before both he and Death disappeared made her want to weep. She had lost her cousin, and now she had to mourn for him under a false pretence.

She lifted her candle to Elaine's.

"I light this..." She took a deep breath, trying to steady her voice. "I light this for Zac," speaking the words only tightened the pressure on her chest. *He's gone because of me. I challenged Death; this is my punishment.* Her eyes stung."You've always been like a brother. I'm not ready for you to be gone from my life. I'm sorry."

"Raven, do you wish to have him included when we bury the rest?" Charles asked her.

"What?" She turned towards Charles. "Included in what?"

"We will hold thirteen funerals, and bury thirteen bodies," he explained. "Zachary makes fourteen, but without a body, we cannot lay him to rest."

"I…" Unsure what to say, she shook her head. "I don't know."

"Charles, we do not know if he's dead yet," Elaine said.

"If the French took him, I do not believe they would keep him alive for long."

Despite her best efforts, a sob escaped.

"I don't think she's ready to make such a decision. She's only nineteen," Elaine explained.

He nodded at Raven's mother, who sat in the front pew, staring into nothing. "I'm not sure Amelia can, either."

"Perhaps we should try to provide hope." Elaine's voice was gentle, but Raven could tell she was being firm.

"He's not dead," her mother's voice rang out through the church. "They took him. He's not dead."

"Amelia, it's alright," Charles knelt in front of her mother. "We'll do everything we can to get him back if we can."

"His father has him," her mother insisted.

Elaine guided Raven to sit next to her mother.

"She was traumatised when she first arrived here; something had given both her and young Zachary fright," Elaine whispered to her husband. "The poor boy kept insisting his father was alive, and that he would come back. Amelia explained that both their fathers died in the War. His mother had died in childbirth recently."

"That explains his anger; he was confused and hurting." Charles cast a look of sympathy over Raven and her mother. "If they kill him, we can only hope it's quick. He doesn't deserve to suffer."

"Charles, *shhh*, don't speak like that." Elaine said.

"Do we hold a funeral for him?" Charles asked.

"Why don't we give Amelia some time to accept what has happened," Elaine suggested. "Raven, you'll want to go to his smithy, won't you?"

His last words to me. "Yes," she said, numb.

"We'll hold the funerals tomorrow," Charles declared.

Chapter 19

I *need to get out of here.* Zachary was alone in the dark. Last time he had been here, people in red flames had circled him. His mother had been here. Convinced that something moved in the shadows, he spun around, but no one was there. Yet a presence watched him. His instincts told him it wasn't human, and to be afraid. Unsure if it was his father, but it was made of the same Darkness that had claimed him. He didn't know how he knew, just that it was. It spoke to something within his soul and whispered his name from the void.

He had shouted himself hoarse, and now panic started to set in. Fear choked him, and finally he slumped. There were no bars in this prison, yet he stood more of a chance getting out of a locked cell than this place. Just endless shadows, fog, and nothing. Despite his terror, his heart was still. The absence of the familiar beating was a strange sensation.

"Please, Father," he begged, his voice raspy. "Let me go."

But his father had left him here, and calling for a man without humanity would have no effect. Angry at his own stupidity, the years of wanting his father back. He should have known that his father wasn't as he had been. He should have appreciated the family he had. Aunt Amelia had taken care of him, loved him. A frightened little boy who had lost both his parents. She had been there, loving him as her own. When Raven had been born, he had taken on the role of the big brother, for his little cousin. But he had still sought answers about his father.

"You betrayed me!" he shouted into the dark. "You abandoned me." His voice echoed back at him. "My father would never have abandoned me like this. I don't know who you are, but you're not him!"

Unsure if he would ever see Raven and Aunt Amelia again, he already missed them. Aunt Amelia, the mother in the absence of his own. Raven, following him around when she was young, begging him to teach her to fight, just as he had once begged his father.

"Aunt Amelia, Raven, I'm sorry," he whispered. "I cannot be there to protect you any more."

Lucian and Hector had died; likely others, too. He would miss their funerals. *How will Raven and Aunt Amelia explain my absence? My closest friend and mentor, I should be there.*

Town folk knew he was closing for Raven's wedding, but before long someone would notice his smithy was still closed. He had told Raven to watch the shop, and he hoped she would and that he wasn't expecting too much of her.

He wandered around The Shadow Realm again. It had felt like an eternity in the dark, and the ability to measure time was not there. No day, just endless night.

"Father!" he resumed shouting. "Let me out of here! Please, I have a family who need me!"

"Zac?" a familiar voice spoke behind him.

He spun around, meeting the eyes of his master. "Hector?"

He's dead. If he's here, and I'm here, does that mean I'm dead, too? The last time he had come here, he had been.

"How did you get here?" he asked.

"I don't remember. I remember you talking to me, and Maria. You told me to find peace, and I wanted to. But this isn't peace," Hector stated. "Am I in hell?"

"How do you remember who you are?" he asked. Last time, the familiar faces had not known him. He had started to forget himself.

Hector frowned. "Am I not supposed to?"

"I don't know," he admitted.

"Are you dead, too?" Hector gave him a sympathetic look. "I'm sorry, Amelia and Raven must be devastated.

"I don't know," he repeated.

Hector's presence made him uneasy, and he wondered if this was his father's doing. Another way to torment him, as if leaving him here wasn't bad enough.

"You're supposed to help me," Hector informed him.

He frowned. "Excuse me?"

"The man who looks like you told me that you were the only one who could release me from here." Hector replied.

"My father." Zachary groaned.

"He looked different from the last time I saw him." Hector noted.

"You've seen him before?" Hector had Zachary's full attention now.

"Yes. It was an unpleasant meeting. Last time he was just blue-eyed, like Raven's eyes. Not the black I saw this time." His eyes glazed over as he recalled. "He warned me to stay away from Amelia. Threatened to open my throat if I continued to pursue her." Hector paled. "Then a black scythe appeared in his hand. It was the single most terrifying moment of my life."

"*That's* why you pulled away from her," Zachary murmured. "Then you married Maria."

"That's right." Hector gave him a thoughtful look. "I thought your father was dead."

"He was..*is*." Zachary paused. *Is he dead if he's Death?* He didn't understand it himself. *How do I explain that to Hector?* "That man you saw, though, who he appeared to you as, it wasn't my father, but Raven's."

Hector gasped. "Amelia's husband? I thought he died, too."

"He's not dead the way you are, but not living either. Something in between." He had no other way to explain it. "After all these years, they are still married, I suppose. She still loves him very much, but he's not the man he once was. He and my father are brutal murderers, without humanity."

Hector stared at him. "What curse did you bring down on our village?"

"We ran to escape it," Zachary explained in desperation. "We thought we'd eluded him."

"You didn't. How do I get out of here? Maria needs me, and I have to protect her from whatever your father is," Hector said.

"I don't know." Zachary glanced around.

Hector moved closer. "He told me you *do*. Take me back to Maria. Please."

Zachary frowned. "I can't do that, Master Hector. Even if I knew how, you're dead. They've probably buried you by now."

"Please, Zachary, help me. I cannot stay here; the shadows talk to me."

Zachary cast his eyes around, the whispers getting harder to ignore. "I hear them, too. If I figure it out, I'll let you know."

"Why did you do this to me, and keep me here?" Hector demanded.

He left Hector, not wanting to look the man in the eye. If he had been the one to end the man's life, he had not been aware of doing so. Looking down at his hands again, he sighed. Father had called it *the Touch of Death*.

"Whatever it is, take it back," he muttered. "Of all the things to inherit from you, that is an unwanted burden."

Fog rolled towards him, wrapping around his body. "**Isaac.**" A voice called to him from the dark. One that he knew.

"Mother?" He turned towards it. "Mother, I'm here!"

"**Isaac.**"

He followed her voice. "Where are you?"

"**Isaac.**"

He ran into the dark.

Chapter 20

Raven had never been so exhausted in her life. Every time she'd fallen asleep, the night's events pulled her back, screaming. Lucian's arms around her, his kisses, and his fall. The sight had awoken her many times.

Death's presence had followed soon after, trying to take her mother, fighting her, before taking Zac. Her mother's absence, when she would usually rush to comfort Raven, was all too noticeable. The house was too quiet.

She chose clothes for the funeral with a heavy heart. As the fiancé of Lucian, she was supposed to stand with his family. She opened the shutter at her window, sunlight filling her room. The blackened ruins of a neighbour's house made last night's events that much more devastating in the light of day. Grateful her home still stood, she watched people move past her window. The mood was somewhat sombre, as people were coming to terms with their losses. Conversations and cries drifted towards her.

"Raven, my dear girl, how are you?" Maria asked from outside the window, shadows under her eyes.

It had been a long night, many huddled together in the church, both in mourning, and in fear of the French returning. "Tired," she replied. "I didn't sleep very much."

Maria reached through the window, taking her hand. "I do not think anyone did. We have faced no night like we did on this one. I do hope your cousin is alright. He's a good young man, and I would have liked to thank him for what he did for me and Hector last night."

Her words were like a punch to the chest, reminding Raven that Zac meant a lot to many others too. "What did he do?"

"He held Hector's hand, and mine. Because of him, Hector didn't die alone." Maria glanced around and leaned in to whisper. "But then I did have dreams of him calling my name, surrounded by fog. I couldn't find him."

"You dreamed of…." She stopped. She'd had the same dream of Zac. Of him begging her to help him, a voice in the dark, and no matter how much she tried, she couldn't reach him.

Maria turned her head, as if listening. "I must go. I'll see you and Amelia at the church. I do hope she has had better sleep than you and I." She hurried away.

Raven moved towards the kitchen "We should prepare to go to the funeral soo—" The kitchen was empty, cold. "Mother?"

Met only by silence, dread churned in her stomach. She lit the fire to heat water. With the filled pot in place, she made her way to her mother's bedroom, finding her on the bed, still wearing last night's clothes. Eyes open, staring at the ceiling, there was no movement as Raven approached. In the low light, her mother's hair appeared more silver, as if she had aged a decade, not a night. She took her mother's hand in hers, surprised to find it freezing. "Mother?" she whispered.

Her eyes remained blank, but flickered towards her. "Raven?"

Raven took a step forward. "What are you doing? We have the funerals today. You need to get ready."

"I have to wait for him; he's coming back," her mother said in a strange tone.

Her bizarre behaviour has worsened.

"Who?" She asked.

"Isaac."

She never uses the name Isaac. "He's Zachary, remember? His father took him; I don't think he's coming back." Pain squeezed her chest as she sat on the side of the bed. *She is not alright.* Her shoulders tensed with worry. "Get your dress. I am to bathe, I know you'll want to, too. I won't be long."

As Raven started to move away, her mother's hands tightened on hers. "You shouldn't have stopped him," she murmured.

"Don't say that," Raven pleaded. "I couldn't let him take you. I know you would have done the same for me."

"What if he'd killed you?" Those blue eyes finally showed something, only a spark, but it was something. They filled with tears. "I don't want you to leave."

A flash of hurt rose to her chest. "But you would have left me!" she cried. "Mother, you were ready to leave with him, to take his hand and I would never have seen you again. But you tell me I shouldn't have stopped him? Are you saying you *wanted* to go?"

"Hush, Raven. Go, take your bath." her mother instructed.

Her mother seemed herself again, putting a stop to Raven's outburst. She paused at the door to glance back, not wanting to leave, worried that she would return to an empty room.

After having prepared the bath, Raven lowered herself into the hot water, sighing in relief. She closed her eyes and leaned back. After last night, her entire body hurt. Heat from the water seeped in, soothing aches. She pulled back the dressing over her shoulder. The soldier's blade had not cut deep, but deep enough that it stung as she cleaned it in the water.

Her thoughts turned towards the day ahead. The funeral. One large event for thirteen people she had known her entire life. It would be a full day of mourning for their losses. A day she would be on display for all of Eskham, in mourning instead of the joyous day it should have been. She let the sorrow wash over her, tears streaming down her face. It would be her only chance to feel it now, because alongside Lucian's family, with all eyes on her, she would show strength.

A sob escaped, and she let them go. Shoulders heaving, eyes burning, she let emotions flow, knowing she would lock them away after today. *Never again. Never again will loss weigh this heavily on me.* To experience such grief that stole her breath and made her feel like she was drowning was not something she ever thought she'd face.

She cried herself out, and rose from the bath, feeling older than when she'd stepped in. Dressing into the black dress she'd laid out for herself, she returned to her mother's side. "It's your turn," she told her, and she returned to her own bedroom.

A blue and yellow dress caught her attention, and she stared at it. Her wedding dress. Next to it, a yellow ribbon. She brushed her hair out and braided it, tying the ribbon at the end. *At least I get to wear something I was supposed to wear today.* A black cloak that Lucian had gifted her last winter hung over the back of her chair. *I don't remember that being there.* She ran a hand over it, soft and warm, but not her colour. Perhaps her mother had laid it out for her. The day was not that cold, though, so she reached instead for a cloak more suited for autumn, a dark blue riding cloak.

"Mother, Elaine will be expecting us," she called out. "Are you almost finished in the bath?"

"I am." The response did not come from the direction she expected, so she followed her mother's voice."

"Where are you?" she asked.

"I'm here." Her mother was at the front door. "One more house over, and it would have been ours." She pointed to the neighbour's house, and turned to hug Raven. "We are very fortunate."

Raven silently agreed. "Are you ready? We should go."

CHAPTER 20

The walk to church was quiet. Smoke lingered in the air, burning the back of her throat. Many villagers on their way to the funeral fell into step around them. No one had any words to offer, mute with sorrow, caught in the horrors of the attack. Elaine greeted them at the door. In the graveyard, Charles had his back to them as he stood over three bodies with a bowed head. She had never seen so many bodies together like this before. Tears threatened to rise again as Raven gave hollow words of comfort that would not bring back any of the dead.

The entire village had shown up, many speaking inside the church before making their way towards the graveyard. With so many dead, it was an unusual funeral, starting at the graveyard instead of ending there. The first to be buried was Hector. Her mother comforted Maria as they knelt before his grave, the two women crying together. All those Hector had trained knelt together, swords held over their hearts, heads bowed, a space where Zachary should have been, left empty.

Raven stood next to Elaine, her eyes stinging, already wishing it were over. Villagers knelt before Hector's body, speaking their last words to a man who had trained many. Hector's death was felt by all.

As men lowered Hector into his grave, her mother took her place by Raven again, looking around.

"Raven, where's Zachary?" her mother whispered.

The constant slips of mind were starting to bother Raven. "He's gone," she whispered back. "Remember?"

"Gone where?" her mother asked.

"With Death."

"Then should we not be burying him, too?" Her mother frowned.

"No!" Guilt washed over her as she caught her mother's look of hurt. "Please, just pay attention; we'll talk afterwards."

Raven let her mind wander as Hector's grave was filled. Zachary's absence earned a few confused glances in their directions. Out of everyone, he should have been the first one in line to bid farewell to Hector, the teacher he had looked up to, and who had inspired him to take on students of his own. Raven had a connection to each of those who died. Many had congratulated her and Lucian on their engagement, they had bought bread from her mother, and they had pulled together as a community more than once. Two were young parents of a four-year-old, who cried over their bodies, trying to wake them up. One had taught her to ride a horse, another to read and write.

When it was time for Rosamund, Raven knelt over the coffin. She'd seen the wounds on Rosamund's body when Elaine had cleaned her.

"You were almost my sister," she murmured. Words escaped her, so with a bowed head, she let tears fall. "I lost sight of you, and I don't know what happened. I'm sorry you were alone when you died. I hope you're at peace now."

Next, she knelt over Noah. "You were so young; I don't understand why you were taken."

As she reached Lucian's coffin, it was late afternoon, and Raven was all too aware that at that same time yesterday she had been talking to Zac about how Lucian had kissed her. The memory of Lucian's arms around her returned. His deep brown eyes gazing into hers right before he kissed her. His hand on her knee as they ate breakfast, his deep, joyful laughter rumbling from him. Raven let out a choked sob, Elaine and her mother tightening their arms on her. Pain overwhelmed her. Legs giving out, she fell to the ground at his grave, unable to hold back the stream of tears. She didn't care that the whole village was watching.

"This was supposed to be a day of joy," she whispered. "It's our wedding day, and already I miss your embrace, your voice, and your smile."

Suffocating pain blanketed her, spreading from her chest as her mother helped her to stand.

She moved away, watching Elaine and Charles. They had lost their home, and all three of their children. Sympathy for them gave her pause as their grief overtook them, and they embraced each other.

This day had been the longest in her life and had finally come to an end as dirt covered Lucian, Rosamund, and Noah's bodies. Grateful that her mother was not among the dead, Raven turned, embracing her tight. "I love you," she murmured as arms wrapped around her, just as tight.

Chapter 21

For long moments, Zachary lost himself in the endless dark. Voices drew him in, Darkness engulfed him. Only when he returned to himself did he remember who he was. *Where* he was. *I have to get out of here.* He longed for daylight, warm sun on his face, snow crunching underfoot. Anything else but the never-ending shadows.

How long have I been here? Red lightning flickered across the black sky, dark fog reflecting the blue moon in an unnatural haze. Screams of the dying echoed, and something moved in the dark, watching him.

"Isaac," his father had returned.

"You insist on calling me by a name I haven't used in twenty years," he growled. "I am Zachary Dale."

"No, you are *Isaac Blake*. Amelia should not have taken that name from you. Yours or Raven's. She is a Blake and should wear the name proudly. You will both reclaim your names."

"You would have us be proud to be the son and daughter of the country's most well- known murderers? It was your name we were hiding from!" Zachary glared.

His words were met by a cold smile. Nothing of the warmth he remembered remained. "Then stop hiding. Let people *fear* who you are, and the Darkness within."

"There is no Darkness in me." He wouldn't let his fear of the statement show.

His father watched him. "You cannot deny that it whispers to you." He pointed to Zachary's chest. "From within."

No! He didn't want to listen to this. "What do you want?" he demanded, shaking with anger. "You've trapped me here, have you come to gloat?"

"I've felt your presence disappearing. You're losing yourself. There will be moments where you cease to exist. That is the presence of Darkness claiming you." His father sounded pleased with himself.

"Please, Father, I don't want this," Zachary pleaded.

A cold smile crossed over his father's face. "You will. Soon, you'll have no thoughts but of the Darkness."

Zachary folded his arms. "Are you speaking from your own experience? Leave me alone."

His father's cold smile had returned. "Gone is the desperate little boy crying out for his father."

"My eyes are open to what you are. They said you were a monster, but I refused to believe it." Zachary couldn't believe his own foolishness. He had seen what his father had become and still insisted the man existed.

His father's shape became that of shadow. "**Yes, I suppose I am a monster, in the eyes of men. Those who gaze upon me see their own end, as I cast terror into their hearts.**"

"You enjoy it!" Zachary accused.

"**I do. As will you.**" The shadowed figure towered over Zachary.

"How did my father become...this?" He shook his head in disbelief.

The presence of Darkness nudged at him, trying to find a way in. His father was gone; everything was black. Zachary tried to move, yet it was as if he had no body. Only his mind remained, and whispers spoke to a deep part of him. *Don't listen.* But despite his efforts, he could not escape the voice that reached inside his very soul.

Isaac.

No. I'm Zachary.

Descendant of Death.

The presence reached into him; cold and emptiness spread around where he imagined his heart to be. Every nightmare he'd ever had was as fresh as the moments he awoke from each of them. Paralysed by fear, something watching him.

Surrounded by fire as his house burned, then his village. A man on a horse, coming towards him from fog. Fear gripped him as it had when he was a child, a heavy weight on his chest. His father, with dead eyes, staring at him as he'd done in the courtyard, and walking away. *Stop. Don't leave me.*

He tried to hold back the images, but they came at him faster.

Dark fury filled him. He tried to scream but no sound came out.

"Zac!" Raven's voice came out of the dark, filled with fear. "Please, don't hurt me."

I would never hurt her. This isn't real. He let out a silent scream, hoping for it to be over soon.

There was nothing, only a void before him, and he lost awareness.

The Shadow Realm pressed around him once more, and a dark figure towered over him.

"Why are you doing this?" he asked.

"I'm not doing anything," his father claimed.

Zachary collapsed, exhausted. Splinters of Darkness pierced his heart. "I can't take this any more," he murmured, closing his eyes. "Please, make it stop. Just let me go." The only response was silence, so he opened his eyes to find himself alone. "Please," he whispered. "Raven, help me."

The darker reflection of himself returned, kneeling before Zachary. "**Raven cannot help you.**"

He pulled himself up as his darker self drew a black sword. Pain pierced his entire being as the blade plunged into his chest. A scream rose from him and once again, he fell into nothing.

There was no self, only Darkness. His own name escaped him, memories gone as he awoke, surrounded by fog. He had been...where? Attempts to recall anything faded the moment he chased the memory. Pain stabbed through his chest.

"Where am I?" he murmured.

"You're back." A man stood in front of him, one eye white, one black, dark lines covered half of his face. "You were gone longer that time."

Gone? "Do I know you?" he asked.

"You haven't quite returned, have you? Are you still lost?" The man helped him to his feed

The man's words made no sense. "Lost? Am I not here?" Again he struggled to remember himself. "Why can I not remember who I am? Or anything?"

"You're Isaac," came the reply followed by a slow smile. "Isaac Blake."

Isaac. "You know me? Where are we?"

"I do," the man confirmed. "You're my son. We're in The Shadow Realm."

Isaac pointed around them. "I feel as if there is something familiar about this...Shadow Realm." It was the only thing familiar to him.

"I brought you here to connect you to your darker self," the man informed him

My darker self. A spark of a memory rose, gone before he could grasp it. "Your eyes and face. What are you?"

"I am Death," the figure said.

"Death? Then what am I?" Zachary asked.

"You are a descendant of Death, as is Raven."

Raven. "Is she here, too?"

"Not yet. *You* are to bring her here," Death replied.

He didn't know who Raven was, but he would do what was asked of him.

"How do I do that?"

"**Kill her.**" It was not the voice of Death, but something dark that spoke from the Realm itself.

Kill her. Raven. He recalled the face of a woman, long black hair, piercing blue eyes.

Something inside him fought against the fog, struggling to rise to the surface, screaming.

"No." The word came from him, a groan.

"Isaac—"

His memories flooded in. "It's Zachary." he glared. "You would have me kill my sister? Your own daughter?!"

"It seems she is the reason you're holding on. The very same reason you're here. You are protective of her, aren't you?" his father met his eyes.

"I would never hurt her. What did you do to me?" he demanded.

"You're losing yourself. It won't be long now," his father gloated.

"Until what?" he asked

Once again, he was alone, and he braced himself for more.

Chapter 22

Raven stood in the middle of Zac's shop, and the familiar smell of hot metal only saddened her that he was not there. Her mother stood beside her, hair loose instead of the braid she usually wore.

Her cousin had never been tidy, and his usual clutter showed in pages of orders, drawings, and notes. They would probably need to sort through it. Her mother's dislike of mess had been a cause of annoyance for Zac. She hoped there was nothing here that Zac wouldn't want to be found, as it was likely her mother would find it.

"Still as messy as ever, I see," her mother noted.

Raven grinned. "'Organised chaos,'" she quoted Zac's words. "He knows how to find everything."

She rested her hand on the hilt of the sword Zac had made for her.

Her mother's eyes shifted down, and she frowned at the sword. "Are you going to wear that in public?"

"I have to. A female blacksmith? I'll be here by myself all day. I think it's best to show the townsfolk right away that I mean business. That's why I brought the armour with me." The armour was beautiful, and she couldn't wait to wear it.

Her mother narrowed her eyes. "Perhaps we should talk to Lord Gerard, get you a bodyguard. He's a reasonable man, and on Zachary's wages, I think you can afford it." They had found a lot of money stored away in his locked chest; the secret wealth surprising the both of them. "These town folk are different from villagers."

A guard? She was capable of defending herself, and her mother's suggestion that she pay someone else to do it was bothersome. It would mean an Enforcer would have to be with her at all times. The very idea of it was irrational, not like her mother at all. At least it shouldn't be, but recently she wasn't sure what was happening.

"I don't need a guard; I know how to fight. You *saw* me fight." Her mother's expression didn't change with Raven's words. "Fine, I'll hire a guard." She gave in. *This isn't about the town folk; this is about him. She's scared he's going to come after me. What can a guard do against him, though?*

Her mother glanced around the smithy. "We need to clean up if you're going to open his shop."

Raven didn't like this. "No, this is his space. It doesn't feel right."

"Raven, we've talked about this. He's not here. He asked this of you. You can't run a shop with this kind of mess. You organise his orders, I'll clean the shelves. Good grief, it's a miracle he gets any business at all with this kind of mess." Her mother let out a loud sigh.

Raven started to pull the papers together, pausing as she saw the sword and journal drawings. She glanced over at her mother, who had her back turned, facing the shelves. Hiding them at the bottom of the pile, she looked over each order, working out the system. He wrote P on the orders that had been paid for. *D must be for delivery? C...for complete?* She figured the dates were when they were due. Separating the orders into piles, she understood the logic. She saw the same thing with papers next to swords.

"You call him messy, but he is quite organised," she commented, impressed. "Zac really knew what he was doing."

When no answer came, she glanced over. "Mother?"

Her mother pulled items off shelves, throwing them on the floor.

Raven rushed over. "What are you doing? Stop!" Tears of frustration stung her eyes as she pulled a dagger from her mother, grasp. "What's wrong with you?" she asked, helpless to hold back her irritation.

As if in response, her mother reached for another item on the shelf. An old leather journal. She opened the book and held it out to Raven.

"What?" she asked with impatience.

"You're angry," her mother announced with surprise.

"Of course I am. You just threw everything on the floor. Now we have to clean this up." Raven tried to hold the annoyance from her voice.

The journal was nudged into her hands with persistence. "This was your father's. It's yours now."

Icy fingers crawled down her spine. *That's his journal.* The very one she had just hidden a drawing of. "I don't want that."

"Raven, take it," her mother ordered.

With a sigh, she took it from her mother's grasp, and she flipped through it, paper rustling. There were drawings in the pages. A man burning. A hooded figure with black eyes. A bearded man that looked like...

"It looks like him," she said. "I didn't know he was an artist."

'Your father was very talented; he once drew a portrait of me. Unfortunately, that burned with the house."

"You never spoke of him like this. It was always the dark stuff," Raven commented.

Her mother flipped a page, stopping at a list of names. Staring at the names gave Raven a cold feeling.

Her mother ran her hand over the pages. "This was everyone Thomas killed."

A chill passed through Raven. "It is bad luck having this book. We should destroy it!"

Her mother shook her head. "No, read."

"You're not in the book…are you?" Raven asked, nervous.

"No. Not me," her mother said.

The name Blake jumped out at her. Not a name she'd ever been connected to, but one she recognised. "Who's Ethan Blake? Is he a relative?"

"Your grandfather. He was a very unpleasant man. But I wouldn't have met your father if it weren't for him," her mother told her.

"They…he…killed his own father?" Horrified, Raven flipped a page, scanning through the names. "I don't know anyone here, please tell me—" On the final page was her cousin's real name. "Isaac?"

"He died. *But he came back,*" her mother reminded her.

"I don't know if he can this time," Raven whispered with fear.

"But he's here," her mother said. "Can't you hear him?"

The silence was deafening, but it was only them in the smithy. "No, he's not. Mother, why are you doing this? Zac's not here! He's gone. Death took him, because of me!" *Always trying to protect me.* She pointed at her cousin's name. "Maybe this was his plan the whole time, to claim what was stolen from him. Zac's life. And I helped him get what he wanted."

"He's hidden in shadows and fog, but he's here," her mother insisted with a chilling calm.

Shadow and fog? She had said it earlier, when they first arrived. "The Shadow Realm? You can see him?"

Her mother nodded. "He's scared. Raven, help him. Before he loses himself."

"How?" She focused on where mother was looking. "Zac? Are you in The Shadow Realm?"

There was no answer, but for a brief moment she imagined he was talking to her, laughing with relief. His words, 'It's about time,' would be the first thing he'd say to her, before he became serious.

"Help him," her mother repeated.

Raven bit back frustration. "I don't know how. Zac, how am I supposed to help you? Mother can see The Shadow Realm, but I can't."

"You've seen it before, though," her mother murmured.

There was a knock at the door, interrupting them. "Zachary?" a woman's voice called out. "It's me, Julianna."

Raven opened the door, determined to get rid of whoever Julianna was, only to find herself meeting the gaze of the woman she had seen kissing Zachary only days before. Her own appearance seemed just as surprising to the other woman.

"Now isn't a good time. I'm sorry." She couldn't manage her usual polite smile.

"Where is he? He went back for your wedding, and no one has seen him since," Julianna said.

He must have told her who I was. The idea of being discussed with Zac's latest flavour annoyed her more than it should have.

"You haven't heard?" Raven's mother joined her at the door.

"Heard what?" Julianna asked. "He said he would be back this morning."

"Our village was attacked," Raven said, trying to be patient. "French soldiers arrived in the early evening."

Julianna gasped. "Is he…"

"No," Raven replied, glancing over her shoulder to where her mother had seen Zac. "Taken. But we're going to get him back."

Julianna's eyes widened. "Taken? By the French?"

Raven hummed in agreement.

"Then he's already as good as dead. They won't have mercy on him." Julianna took a couple of steps back.

"Have hope," her mother said. "He'll return to us. Raven's going to get him back."

"Mother, stop." Raven glanced at Julianna. "Is there something I can help you with?"

Julianna left without another word.

"Be polite," her mother warned.

"Sorry, her arrival was poorly timed." Raven almost laughed. Zachary had used the same words on her when she interrupted their kiss. "Do you still see him?"

"Yes. He says, 'The Darkness is here,' and that he keeps losing himself. He isn't sure how much longer he can hold on."

"Zac, I don't know how to bring you back, but I swear to you, I'll find a way," Raven promised. "Don't give up."

Chapter 23

Raven and Aunt Amelia stood right in front of Zachary in his smithy. Pride surged through him with the sight of a sword at Raven's hip. The one he had made for her. She wore a yellow ribbon in her braid, while his Aunt's hair was down, a silver appearance to it. *When did her hair change colour? Have I been so busy lately that such details escaped me?* He had never noticed how similar mother and daughter were in height before, with Raven the taller of the two. At that moment, both wore serious expressions, Raven's almost identical to Uncle Graeme's.

"Am I dreaming? Is this real?" he muttered. *I'm home!* "I've never been so glad to see you both!"

Raven didn't respond, but Aunt Amelia's gaze flickered towards him.

"Raven?" He moved within her eye line, waving at her. "Will you not welcome me back?" Again, nothing. He cursed under his breath.

"Shadow and fog."Aunt Amelia said, her eyes on his.

Shadow and fog? Zachary finally took in all his surroundings. "I'm still in The Shadow Realm," he muttered, his shoulders slumping. *Another trick of Darkness, to have me believe I was home.*

"What are you talking about?" Raven asked. "Mother, I fear you are losing sense." Her voice was tinged with worry as she cast a watchful eye to Aunt Amelia.

Aunt Amelia lowered her eyes, hurt in them. "Zachary."

She can see me!

"Aunt, can you see me? I'm here, but I'm not alone, Darkness is in here with me. I don't want to lose myself again." He took a deep breath. "I'm scared," he murmured, once again the little boy clinging to his Aunt after nightmares. "Help me."

The Darkness pulled at him, and his shop was gone.

I'm suffocating. Zachary couldn't breathe, and panic gripped him.

"**Isaac.**" A voice in the dark echoed, and a figure stood before him. His mirror reflection, white eyes, black lines over his face.

"That is not my name any more," he grumbled.

"**It is the name I gave you,**" a woman's voice echoed from behind him. "**Isaac Thomas Blake. Your father's son, no matter what name you go by.**"

Mother! The dark presence remained behind him, and he refused to turn around. He did not want to see Darkness wear her face.

"You're not her." Zachary's shoulders slumped.

"**Does it matter? Your father sent you to me. You will surrender, just as he did.**" In front of him, two figures fought, only for one to fall to the other's blade. "**When he killed his brother, there was nothing left for him to hold on to. He let go of all resistance. Not even your name would give him strength.**"

Tears streamed down his face as the apparition of his father cradled Uncle Graeme in his arms as he died. "Stop," he pleaded. "I don't want to see this."

"**This is where you really lost him,**" the voice told him.

The form of his father cried over his brother's body. Of Uncle Graeme's body.

"Why are you showing me this?" he demanded.

"**Because Raven will fall to your hand, as her father fell to yours.**"

He was back in his shop. Raven and Aunt Amelia were arguing about Uncle Graeme's journal. Aunt Amelia seemed strangely calm about it, not reacting with fear or worry as he would have expected. Raven, on the other hand, did not look happy.

The arrival of Julianna was not such a surprise; that woman had an appetite that almost equaled his own. But it was another that his thoughts strayed to. Dark brown eyes, and a smile that brightened his whole world. Delia's presence had always made him believe he could be a man worthy of her. *When I get out of here, I am going to visit her, as I should have done five years ago.*

"Zac, I don't know how to bring you back, but I swear to you, I'll find a way," Raven promised. "Don't give up."

The words repeated themselves over and over as he held onto them. Raven wouldn't give up; it wasn't in her to do so. *I'm going home.* The fear receded, allowing hope to swell in his chest.

"Mother, how is it that you can see The Shadow Realm, but I can't?" Raven asked.

"Probably because you don't want to," he joked.

Despite the Darkness pressing in around his mind, he let himself smile, telling himself he was going to be free of The Shadow Realm.

Aunt Amelia repeated his words.

"That doesn't explain how *she* can, though," Raven said. "Ever since that night, something's been wrong with her, Zac."

"I am right here." Aunt Amelia glared. "Do not speak that way of me."

"I'm sorry, Mother," Raven apologised. "But I'm worried. You do not seem yourself, and at times, you appear completely lost."

Raven was right. Something seemed amiss. "Aunt Amelia, she's right. Something is very wrong if you can see into The Shadow Realm."

"He's coming back for me." Aunt Amelia said.

Raven let out a sigh. "You keep saying that."

Zachary frowned. "Do you mean my father?"

Aunt Amelia opened her mouth and closed it again. "No. Why do you think I mean Thomas?"

"Do you mean Death is coming back?" Raven asked.

"Well, we cannot hide from him." Aunt Amelia flashed a bright smile. "He talks to me."

"Death talks to you?" Raven's voice rose.

Another knock of someone's fist on the door, and Raven scowled. "Please tell me it's not someone else seeking your bed," she grumbled. "Today is not the day for that."

She left him and Aunt Amelia to answer the door again.

"I may have a reputation for the number of women I share my bed with, but I never take more than one at a time," he replied, even though she couldn't hear him.

Aunt Amelia shook her head. "You are just as Thomas was, before he met your mother."

"Aunt Amelia. I ask you the same question Raven did. Does my father... Death talk to you?"

"I hear his voice, as if he's right next to me, just as you are," Aunt Amelia confirmed.

"Now?" he asked.

She shook her head. "No."

"What does he tell you?" he asked.

She met his eyes. "That your sacrifice is only the beginning. More is coming."

"You!" Raven's voice was filled with irritation. "What do you want? Why do you always come here when Zac's not here?"

Zachary glanced over to find the Enforcer at the door, just as Raven tried to shut it on him. He held it open with one hand.

"I heard about the attack on Eskham," he said. "My sympathies."

"Thank you," Raven's voice filled with pain."Can you let go of the door?

Now isn't a good time."

"Lord Gerard is waiting for the blacksmith," Markus frowned at her. "If he's not here, where is he?"

Her hand moved to the hilt of her sword.

"Raven, what are you doing? He's an Enforcer! You cannot threaten him!" He turned "Aunt, she's about to get herself arrested." His aunt mumbled back in response, but she seemed to not have heard him. "Raven, stop." *Oh, this is hopeless.*

Markus pushed the door open, his large frame in the doorway. "I allowed you to threaten me last time, but not today, Sunshine. Draw that and I will have no choice but to draw my own." He stepped into the shop, his eyes blazing. "Lord Gerard has requested his presence, and I'm to take him to the manor. The Lord doesn't like to be kept waiting."

Protective fury shot through Zachary. "Do not barge into my smithy and threaten my cousin," he roared. "I will kill you myself!" Dark rage took a life of its own as he glared at The Enforcer.

"I'd be careful, if I were you," Raven warned.

"Why are you always so hostile?" Markus demanded.

"You've barged in, uninvited, and after our last meeting, you're not a welcome sight," she told him. "Now leave."

"No. Where is the blacksmith?" Markus demanded.

Raven's anger got the best of her, and she started to draw her sword, but the Enforcer closed the distance between them in two strides, his hand wrapping around hers, pushing the sword back into its sheath.

"You look like a smart woman," he spoke down to her. "Let go of your sword."

"When I get out of here, I am going to make you suffer," Zachary promised. "You dare come in here like that?"

"Get your hand off me." She moved her hand as if to pull out of his grip. "Get out."

"Not until I know you won't try to use that on me. You're a fiery one, aren't you?" He glared down at her.

Zachary turned again. "Aunt Amelia, please."

"Please let me go," Raven pleaded.

"Let go of your sword and I will," the Enforcer instructed.

She must have done as he instructed, as he released her and stepped back.

"Touch me again and you will see fiery," she retorted.

"Just tell me where your cousin is. He was supposed to report to the manor today. Lord Gerard is patient, but he does have his limits."

"How is it that you've heard of the attack on my village, but don't know why Zac isn't here?" she demanded.

He knew her well enough to know she wanted to cry. "Raven," he murmured. "I'm right here. We'll figure this out. You'll figure this out." Of course, she couldn't hear him.

"His name wasn't in the list of the dead," Markus said.

"Tell Lord Gerard my cousin is away. Whatever business he has with Zac, will have to wait unless he wants to deal with me."

The Enforcer smirked. "You? You're going to step into the blacksmith's shoes?"

She folded her arms. "I am." His tone and smirk sent irritation through Zachary, but he could do nothing.

The disbelief in his face changed to one of confusion. "A woman blacksmith?"

"Yes, a woman blacksmith," Zachary said to no one.

"I learned from Zac; I'm just as good as him," she declared.

"He doesn't like you," Aunt Amelia had finally stepped in. "You should leave."

Markus finally left after glaring at both women.

"You can't talk to Enforcers that way. He can make things very difficult for you," Aunt Amelia said. "You also shouldn't threaten to kill one." Her eyes met Zachary's. "I taught you both to control yourselves better than that. You're behaving like your fathers."

There was another knock on the door.

"Now what?" Raven asked, pulling it open again, and her expression changed. "I'm sorry, I thought you were someone else."

From where he stood, he couldn't see who was at the door. "Raven, isn't it? Is Zachary here?" a woman's voice. *Delia!* He moved around to catch a glimpse, surprised to see a young boy by her side, hand in hers. The boy's hair was short, eyes light brown. Eyes he knew. The boy looked to be around five years of age.

No, it has to be a coincidence.

"Have we met?" Raven asked in confusion.

"Delia," Zachary said in wonder. "It's Delia."

"Delia," called Aunt Amelia.

Raven's eyes darted down to the boy. Zachary was already watching him, seeing a resemblance, fearful that there was none. He is *the right age.*

"Aunt Amelia," he urged. "The boy."

Can it be? He had hoped for a long time for children of his own, and now, presented with a very real possibility that he had one, he was afraid to hope.

"And who is this?" Aunt Amelia asked in her usual tone.

"This is Arthur." Delia smiled.

He'd once told Delia of his favourite stories as a boy, that if he ever had a son, he would name him for the noble King. *Do I have a son*? His heart pounded.

"He's Zachary's," Delia's words set the world spinning.

I have a son?! From spinning one moment, to standing still the next, Zachary lowered himself to one knee, crouching in front of the boy. "I have a son," he said aloud, even though only Aunt Amelia could hear. Elation soared and he reached for the boy. Eyes so like his own.

"Does he know?" Raven asked. "Please, come in."

"Raven, if I knew, do you not think I would have told you?" He shook his head, giddy with disbelief and joy.

Delia gave her son a sad smile as the two of them entered his smithy. "No."

"You didn't tell him he had a son? He would be delighted," Raven said.

They sat at the table.

"Delighted? I'm…" He couldn't find words as his heart swelled with joy.

Aunt Amelia laughed. "He would be overjoyed."

"My family prevented me from seeing him when they found out I was with child. But then they disowned me when he was born, and then disowned Arthur too."

"Your family disowned you?" Raven asked.

"I brought shame to them." Delia said.

Raven gave her a sympathetic look. "I'm sorry, who takes care of you?"

"I take care of us. I..." Delia bowed her head and a tear fell down her cheek. "It isn't easy."

"Oh. Is that why you're here?" Raven asked with sympathy. "Do you need help?" Raven turned to meet her mother's eyes.

"Help her!" Zachary shouted. "Aunt Amelia, You've seen that I have the money, more than enough. Give her whatever she needs!"

"Zachary would want you well taken care of." Aunt Amelia retrieved a leather pouch from his wooden chest. The one Tobias had given him only days ago.

"You would give this to me?" Delia's shock surprised him.

"Zac would never want to see his son in need," Raven replied.

"Where is he?" Delia asked, her eyes moving around the shop. "I heard Eskham was attacked. Is he alright?"

"No," Raven gave her a tight smile. "Murderers took him. But we're going to get him back. He has a son, and he'll want to be here for him."

Chapter 24

Raven waited alone in the empty room. Marble floors, with tapestries over the walls. She fidgeted with her braid, complete with yellow ribbon. *What if he denies me and takes Zac's smithy?* Zac had asked her to continue in his shop, but the decision was still down to Lord Gerard. She could only hope he was in a generous mood. It was uncommon for a woman to take such a trade, and she might not be welcomed.

"Raven." Lord Gerard entered the room. "Thank you for waiting. I've spoken with Charles Carter, Eskham has suffered greatly, and it saddens me to learn of the passing of your husband. Will you remarry?"

Remarry? The idea had never occurred to her. "Lucian is not my husband.

We were not married when he died." She averted her eyes. "I have not considered marriage to another. But if it is required of me..."

Lord Gerard smiled in sympathy. "Bachelors will pursue you when you have finished grieving. You have youth, and beauty that many will desire."

Heat rose to her cheeks.

"Lucian was a good man," Lord Gerard said. "So was your cousin. A talented blacksmith, his absence to his craft indeed a loss. I shall announce his passing within the week."

"He's not dead," she told him.

The look of sympathy changed to pity, and his hand touched her arm. "Raven, I know you want to have hope that he still lives, and that you'll bring him back. But very seldom do they come back when taken prisoner in acts of war. I'm sorry."

She let him believe what he wanted. It wasn't as if she could tell him about The Shadow Realm. "I will continue to have hope for his return."

He nodded. "Do what you must. He may surprise us. My Enforcers advised me you requested to speak with me."

"While my cousin is away, I want to continue his work." Raven put hope in her voice.

"Zachary spoke of your experience as a blacksmith, you learned from him." Lord Gerard said.

"I did," she confirmed.

His eyes remained on hers. "You're seeking my permission?"

"He rents the shop from you, so I thought—"

He cut her off. "It was Zachary's business. If his family members wish to continue running it, I see no problem with that. The rent remains the same." He turned to leave.

She hesitated. "Lord Gerard?"

"You have something else?" he asked, eyeing her.

"My mother worries; it's only to ease her concerns. While I stay in Oakborough, as a woman blacksmith, she'd like me to have the services of a guard." She gave him a small smile. "As you have said yourself, I may find myself pursued by interested bachelors. Some may not take kindly to refusal of such pursuits, and others may see opportunities where those of noble heart would not. It would be a comfort for me and my mother, to know that I am safe within the walls of Oakborough."

He studied her face, his arms folded. "That is a grave concern, and a large request."

She held out a purse of coins. "One I can pay for."

Lord Gerard laughed. "You already have to pay me for rent, and you offer to pay me more."

Raven lowered her arm. "I meant no offence."

"I took none, young Raven. With French soldiers this far inland, I cannot spare my Enforcers for such requests. There is panic in the streets, especially after the attack on Eskham. They are needed to make my people feel safe."

Her heart sank. "I understand." Fear spiked as she thought about the sort of people who lived in town. Her entire life had been spent in a village. She had heard stories of crime in towns, often unpunished, despite the presence of Enforcers. She turned to leave. "Thank you for your time."

His silence followed her from the room, and she raised her shoulders. *Zac trained me, I don't have need for someone else to do what I can do myself.*

As she walked through the manor, she passed Enforcers' dining quarters, laughter bursting from the room. Movement caught her attention, and she glanced up. Death, in the shape of her father.

"What are you doing here?" she demanded. "You probably shouldn't be here, looking like that. Everyone believes Zac to be held by the French." Disturbed by his resemblance to Zac, she forced herself to quicken pace.

He kept up easily. "Would you prefer this?" he asked, and his form changed, taking on the face of one she never thought to see again.

Tears sprang forth, a fist closing around her heart. "You come here to torment me?"

"Your request of the Lord was never going to be fulfilled," he told her. "If you want protection, call upon me."

She stopped, turning to face him. "Why? Are you short of men to kill, you would seek out more?"

"My daughter must be kept safe," he declared.

The word *daughter* filled her with disgust. "Don't call me that." She moved towards her horse. "I don't want your protection."

"You have it anyway. The Lord is an idiot." His laughter sent chills through her.

She glared. "Are you going to kill him, too?"

He chuckled, a chilling sound. "That thought may have occurred to me."

"You left the dead in your wake in Kempschester and Riverwick; Oakborough doesn't need that. It is a small town, and the people have done nothing to deserve the curse that your presence would bring upon them," she told him.

She climbed onto the back of Lance, having left Nutmeg with her mother.

Before she could ride away, he stepped forward and gripped the reins, Lucian's eyes boring into hers. "You mistake my offer of protection for kindness. I care little about these people. They will all die; it's just a question of when. I have stayed away from this town, and your village, to allow you to grow. If any of them make an attempt to harm you, their end shall be gruesome."

She stared down at him from atop her horse.

"Why?" she asked.

His answer was a cruel smile before he vanished from sight. She clenched her jaw in frustration. That he would return to The Shadow Realm in front of people showed how little he cared. With a quick glance around, no one seemed to have seen. She had come here with two requests, and had been denied one.

"Perhaps I should just return to Eskham, to the familiar," she muttered under her breath.

But as she rode from the courtyard, she knew she would remain in Oakborough. Zac had trusted her to keep his smithy open, and neither of them knew how long it would take to free him from The Shadow Realm. An idea occurred to her, and she could have groaned at her own stupidity. Death held the power to bring him back, and she had not thought to speak of such a request.

Chapter 25

The times between utter Darkness and being himself were growing longer. Each time the Darkness followed him, its grip grew tighter. He returned screaming, relieved at having a voice once more.

I'm Zachary. Every time the Darkness released him, he had to remind himself who he was, as his sense of self had diminished.

"Please," he groaned, without any idea of who he was talking to. "Stop." Unsure how much he could take, he feared what it would do to him. Darkness continued to show him Raven, bleeding, and pleading with him to stop. Fear in her eyes tore at him. "I will never hurt her."

But he was starting to doubt his own words. Something inside felt *different*, as if the grip on his heart was taking hold. His desire to leave The

Shadow Realm only grew, dreading the next time he fell into the void.

Instead, he didn't move. Either his father would appear, or the Realm would show him things, or Darkness would speak to him, wearing the face of a person. With his eyes closed tight, he shook with exhaustion. *I miss my family.*

A woman's singing voice pierced his trance. *Aunt Amelia?* Unsure if it was another trick, he refused to open his eyes. As the singing continued, he realised it was Raven.

"Mother, won't you sing?" Raven's voice was tinged with sadness. "You always sing."

Despite himself, he opened his eyes, finding himself in what used to be his home.

"I don't want to sing; he'll hear me," Aunt Amelia said.

"Who?" There was fear in Raven's voice.

"Your father," Aunt Amelia replied.

"He cannot hurt you," Raven promised as she dished up food for the two of them.

Aunt Amelia sighed. "No, but he watches me, and I don't want to hear his voice. Full of Darkness, it speaks to my soul, and calls me forth."

"What is he doing to you?" Zachary muttered.

"Zachary." Aunt Amelia's eyes lit up. Her hair had changed yet again, more silver than blonde.

"What happened to your hair?" he asked.

"He's here?" Raven looked around, her eyes not quite focusing on him. "Zac, I think I'm starting to feel your presence, and that of The Shadow Realm. I've been trying every day."

Excitement surged through him.

"Is he saying anything?" Raven asked her mother.

"Something is troubling you," his aunt said to him. "What happened?"

He wanted to blurt out everything, to confide in Aunt Amelia. But he was equally worried about her. "What's happened to *you*?" he asked instead.

He caught the tear as she turned away from him, and fury rose. "Father! What are you doing to her?"

"Shhh, Zachary, *please* don't bring him here." His aunt's voice shook.

She looked as she did the day they ran from Riverwick. Terrified. Suffering years of nightmares. "He continues to haunt you still." He searched The Shadow Realm "Let her go, she does not deserve your torment! She has suffered enough!"

Aunt Amelia whimpered, and Raven comforted her. "What is it? What's wrong?"

"He's here," Aunt Amelia said.

Zachary found himself face to face with his father. "You're always making demands. Come home. Help me. Take me, spare them. I grow tired of it. Your existence is because I allow it, but more burden than it should be." There was fury in his face.

"What are you doing to Aunt Amelia?" The words hurt, but reflected his father's anger, not backing down. "You continue to torment her."

"I do nothing of the kind," his father said.

Zachary glared. "Lies!"

Father moved towards Zachary. "I have no reason to lie. If she is being tormented, it is not my doing. Perhaps the ghosts she sees are her own."

"Please Graeme, Thomas, I can't keep hearing your voice." She had turned away from Raven. "Release me. Take me where I belong."

"Aunt Amelia! No!" Zachary wished he could step through the veil to shield her from his father.

"You plead with someone who no longer exists. Your children wanted you to live, I gave them that. I cannot give you what you want; it is beyond my ability now. I do not feel the calling for you any more." He turned to Zachary. "You, however. I did not bring you here so that you can speak with them."

Aunt Amelia's kitchen vanished, and shackles bound his wrists. "What are you doing?" he asked.

"You're more trouble than I expected. Now all you have is your own nightmares. You will face them," Death said.

"Please. don't leave me here." Pulling against the shackles, his struggles became frantic when his father walked away.

Shadows closed around him, and he had no way to escape the waves of despair and Darkness that crashed over him.

When he came to, Zachary was on his back. Once again, Raven's screams echoed in his mind. Everything The Realm was showing him filled him with dread. *What if I'm a danger to her? If she finds a way to free me, will it come to pass that she falls at my hand? I cannot let that happen. I cannot let her free me.* As much as he wanted to return to his family, to escape his prison, the desire to protect his family was greater. *I'm sorry, Raven, I know you will do everything you can to help me, and you won't give up until you succeed. I cannot allow you to do that. I cannot be the one you need protection from.*

Chapter 26

A week later, Raven lit the forge, a mixture of excitement and fear, in anticipation of what lay ahead. Her first day in which she would present herself as a blacksmith. Death's threats, Zachary's captivity in The Shadow Realm, and her mother's worsening all hung over her.

Elaine stood at the door. "Your house has never been so still or silent. The aroma of fresh bread and song have long been associated with your mother." Elaine moved over to her, touching her arm in comfort. "Charles suggested that she had been affected by the loss of Zachary, and the attack from France was quick and brutal. But she will recover. We will hear her voice, and have the warmth of her bread again very soon."

"Perhaps I should not have left her while she's like this," Raven pondered..

Elaine took in the sight of Raven's belongings that she had not yet moved into the bedroom. "You have already taken steps to do what Zachary would want you to do. Amelia is in good care; she has the support of many." She wrapped Raven in a hug. "Lucian and Zachary would be proud of you." Her hand reached for the yellow ribbon in Raven's braid. "You were to wear this on your wedding day. You bless my son to wear it still."

Raven pushed at the surge of grief. "I mourn him, and the day harshly ripped from us both," she murmured. "I wear this to honour his memory."

Once again Elaine cast a look around the smithy. "I worry about you here, alone," she said. "Should you not have security of some kind?"

"A request that Lord Gerard saw fit to reject," Raven told her.

Elaine shook her head. "Then I shall speak with him," she commented, and left.

With little more to do, Raven turned, picking up an order she had placed at the top of the pile. "I hope I'm doing the right thing," she muttered. "Zac, why did you ask this of me?"

She could almost hear his response. He would tell her that he trusted no one else to continue his business, no one else would care for it as she would.

"Raven?" A voice spoke from behind her.

She spun around. "Delia."

"I heard that you were opening today, I wanted to wish you good luck." The woman's smile was warm.

Usually she held no desire to know Zachary's women, and this one had hurt him. But with the knowledge that he had truly cared about Delia, and that she had birthed his son, Raven welcomed the presence. She couldn't turn her away.

"Thank you," she smiled back. "I hope I haven't made a mistake in doing this."

Delia remained where she stood. "I don't think you have. You look the part." She motioned to Raven's clothes.

Raven had donned a tunic and trousers in place of a dress. "This will either help them take me seriously, or I will be branded a fool in man's clothing."

"You are no fool," Delia replied. "I can come by in the mornings if you like. I know you must be overwhelmed in being here, and you look like you need a friend."

She had friends in Eskham, and while it was not all that far, they would be unlikely to travel. "I could do to have a friend here," she admitted.

Delia gave her a quick smile. "I must go, Arthur is waiting for me, but I will see you tomorrow."

Alone again, Raven sat on a chair, her hands on the table. She had made a promise to Zac, and she had no idea how to carry it out.

"Zac, I don't know if you're here, or if you can hear me," she whispered. "I'm going to keep my word. I just need to somehow see The Shadow Realm first." She had known about Darkness and The Shadow Realm from her mother's stories. Information given by Graeme. *How did he find it so easily?* The answer was right there, and she didn't want to consider it. But the more she resisted the idea, the more she realised there was no other way. Only Darkness would allow her to see what lay beyond human sight. Despite her realisation, she still tried to see the veil, pushing aside all thoughts of Darkness.

A footstep at the doorway announced someone's arrival. Opening her eyes she frowned. The Enforcer insisted on afflicting her with his presence.

"What are you doing here?" she asked, annoyed at the intrusion.

"I was sent here," Markus replied, meeting her glare with his own. "You requested to hire the services of protection."

Elaine's words in Lord Gerard's ear must have changed his mind. "I did not request you," she declared.

He flashed her a cold smile. "Well, Sunshine, you got me."

"No, he can send someone else. You are not welcome here." *He's a better choice than Death's offer, though.* At least he wouldn't kill people for the sake of it. The idea didn't move her displeasure at The Enforcer's presence.

"If you send me back, he will take that to mean you do not require the protection." Markus sat opposite her, not concerned that he was unwelcome. “I’m told you offered coin.”

She let out a laugh. “I’m not paying you.”

His eyes narrowed. “You cannot expect a man to spend his day providing you with a service without payment.”

She stood, moving away from the table to put distance between them. “I expect you to leave. You would have known I would not want you here. Why would you have accepted this job in the first place?”

He stood, and started to move towards the door. “Very well. But once I leave, you’re on your own. Lord Gerard will *not* send anyone in my place, nor will he be happy you wasted his time only to reject his offer,” he commented, reaching the door.

She forced down her frustration. “Wait.”

He turned. His smirk only added to her annoyance. “I knew you’d see sense.” His expression changed to one of sympathy. “I’m sorry to hear about your cousin’s passing.”

“He’s not dead!” Tired of people saying that, she stood, and returned to the forge; she had work to do.

Her idea to find The Shadow Realm would have to wait, for now. Raven busied herself so she wouldn’t have to talk to him. Even with her back to him, the heat of his gaze bothered her.

“You don’t have to watch me,” she told Markus without looking at him.

“You’re going to continue to take this manner with me, aren’t you?” he grumbled, and she tensed at his movement behind her. “I’m merely curious to see a woman blacksmith at work.”

He walked into her eye line. She frowned, and kept her focus down.

“Please, just keep your distance,” she told him. “I need to work.”

“Don’t let me stop you.” He chuckled.

Raven sighed. This was going to be a long day, and she was already tired.

Chapter 27

W*hy am I doing this? There are more important issues at hand.*

But she couldn't deny Zachary's request of her.

"Death." Her calls always went unanswered, yet his presence was often nearby. The dark presence and feeling of being watched sent fingers of ice down her spine, her skin crawling. "I know you can hear me. I can feel you watching me. Show yourself."

This time he appeared, wrapped in shadows. "I know what you want."

"Then free him. Let him come home," she pleaded.

"What will you give up?" he asked.

She had no words for that. All she had was her mother. *Can I give myself up for him?*

"I've seen you trying to access The Shadow Realm." He reached for her arm, bony fingers closing around it. Before she could pull away, her shop was gone. "Is this what you want?"

He had brought her to The Shadow Realm. "Where's Zac?"

"Raven?" Zac's voice was quiet.

She turned at his voice to find him on his knees, head bowed, black shackles around him, the chains seeming to come from the ground. He didn't raise his head to look at her.

"Zac!" Running to him, she wrapped her arms around him. "Oh Zac, I'm so glad to see you."

He didn't move, made no attempt to return the hug. "You're not real."

She pulled back, surprised at his reaction. "I *am* real. Zac, look at me. Are you alright?"

He still wouldn't look at her. Instead, he turned his eyes to Death "Why did you bring her here? Is this a new way to torment me? Have I not endured enough?"

He spoke in a flat tone, his eyes without their usual spark. Lifeless.

"She's determined to set you free, and she calls upon me every day for it," Death added.

"Raven, you have to stop." Finally he raised his eyes to hers. "Please."

She stepped back. "No, you know I won't do that."

"I gave myself up so that you may live. That's all I want. I want you to be safe." He muttered words that she couldn't hear.

She pulled at the shackles, but he tore his arm free of her grip. "I said stop, Raven."

"Let him go," she told Death.

Death's eyes shifted between the two. She didn't like the amusement on his face. *What game is he playing with us this time?*

"Take her back," Zac said in a low voice. "Raven, do not come back to The Shadow Realm. Stop calling for him. You can't help me."

"Why are you asking me this? What's wrong with you?" she asked, still pulling at the shackles

He shuddered, a whimper escaping from him. "Please, get her away from me."

Death's fingers pulled her away and Zac vanished.

"What happened? Where is he?" She demanded.

Amusement glinted in Death's eyes. "He'll be back in a moment. He won't want you to see this, but perhaps you should."

"What are you doing to him?" she demanded..

Before he could answer, Zac returned, and a scream tore from him.

"Zac!? Let me go!" She pulled her arm from Death's grip and moved towards him. He stopped screaming and raised his head, eyes white. She froze. "Zac?"

He said nothing, only stared at her blankly.

"Zac? Talk to me." Chilled to the bone, she couldn't look away from his eyes. *Why are they like that?*

"Who are you? Who's Zac?" His voice had changed, resembling that of Death's slightly, reflecting Darkness.

"Zac, we have to leave," she pleaded.

"Do you want to be released from The Shadow Realm?" Death asked.

"What is The Shadow Realm?" Zac asked.

"It is where you are." Death said.

Zac turned his head, looking around. "But this is all I have known."

"What? No." Raven held back tears.

"Do you know who Raven is?" Death asked. "Or Zac?"

"I know no such name, Raven or Zac," he admitted.

"Do you know who you are?" Death gripped her arm again, painfully, pulling her back.

Zac frowned. "I do not."

Raven gasped. "What?"

"It takes him a while to come back." Death told her. "I think he's willingly losing himself now, however. His fight has diminished." There was satisfaction in his tone.

"Then why do you hold him here? You have to let him go. Why have you restrained him? Why are his eyes like that?" Questions came spilling out.

"That is the Darkness within him, when he does not fight."

She stepped forward, unable to go far, held by Death's vice grip. "Zac, you have to keep fighting."

His blank eyes met hers, and he reached towards her. "I know you."

Relief washed over her. "You do. We're cousins. It's me, Raven."

"Raven." He stared.

Death let her go.

She grabbed his hand. "Please Zac, we have to leave." She hated to see him this way and glanced back at Death. "Please, just let him go."

"I will if you take his place," Death said.

Horrified, she shook her head. "No!"

Death smiled. "Very well."

"I've seen your face in the dark. You will fall by my hand," Zac said, and a deep shiver passed through her.

"Not yet," Death said.

She found herself back in the smithy. A tear escaped as she faced Death.

"Do you still want to free him?" Death let her go and stepped back. "Knowing what you know?"

"What did he mean?" she demanded. "He would never hurt me."

"Darkness has shown him that his greatest fear will come to pass," Death told her.

"Killing me is what he fears? Why would that be a fear? What's happened to him?" she demanded.

He grabbed her chin, fingers digging in painfully. "Because you and he will fight. I have seen it, as has he."

She shook her head. "No. He will never hurt me."

"Things are changing, Raven. Your sacrifice for your mother, his for you, that's what started this. It should have been you in The Shadow Realm, though, not him. The Darkness in him was but a spark compared to what lies within you. You are my daughter, and there will be a day that you will call me 'Father'."

"I will never call you 'Father.'" Disgusted, she pushed his hand away. "And I won't stop trying to free Zac."

"He doesn't *want* you to free him." Death told her. "Maybe he prefers The

Shadow Realm. You look up to him as a brother, but he had a sister, and she died with his mother. You are a constant reminder to him of what he lost."

His words winded her. Zac had told her about the sister who died at birth, but he'd never spoken of her reminding him of losing her.

"Your cruelty knows no bounds," she murmured. "He would *never* say that."

There was a knock at the door.

"Your protector is here." Death smiled at her. "I will see you again soon, daughter. You and The Enforcer."

"What do you mean by—" She was speaking to an empty room.

The knock came again, louder. "Stop, I heard you the first time," She called out, and opened the door.

He barged in. "Perhaps you should give me a key, so I don't have to knock."

Raven's shoulders shook. "I think not! You come in when I let you in, not a moment sooner." She propped open the door, to show the smithy was open.

Chapter 28

Raven focused on her work, humming quietly, the heat of the forge at her back. She had come to enjoy working on swords and understood why Zac often got lost in his work. It helped clear her mind, ease her sorrow. *Zac*. She went from missing her cousin, to grieving for Lucian. The yellow ribbon remained in her hair, pain always a splinter within her heart.

"You get the same look he does," Delia said.

Raven raised her head. "I do?"

Delia and Arthur had become a welcome sight. Their company helped distract her from the moody Enforcer. At only five, Arthur was a bright child.

"As if the whole world has faded away, and it's just you and the metal before you."

Raven smiled. "I never realised just how easy it was to forget everything when it's just me, my tools, and metal."

"It's been weeks; do you still have hope to get him back?" There was hope in Delia's voice.

That morning's events had lowered her hopes. *Is he still as I saw, or has he regained awareness?* She wanted him to meet his son. To know that Delia had not really abandoned him. *I'll get him back, even if it's just for the sake of Arthur.* "I don't know."

Delia's eyes were on Arthur. "It's no secret he favours the women, and they favour him. I knew what I was in for when I met him. What if he's got other children? Did he ever talk about wanting to be a father?"

Raven put down her tools. "He spoke of you a great deal. He cared about you, and he was hurt when you stopped coming around, but he didn't pursue you out of respect. Zac is not a man to turn his back on family. Had he known, he would have supported you."

Delia smiled. "I only ever hoped that Arthur would have a father, I just didn't know if that's what Zachary wanted. I shouldn't have taken that choice from him."

"He has a son?" Markus asked from the other side of the workshop.

Raven ignored him.

"What's he doing here again?" Delia asked in a low voice.

"My mother wanted me to have a guard while I'm in Oakborough. I spoke to Lord Gerard about it only to ease her worries."

"So he sent you an Enforcer you don't like?" Delia asked.

"He sent me one who, on our first meeting, I disarmed him and had him on his knees. Somehow, I'm supposed to trust that he can protect me." She scoffed, shooting a look in his direction.

Delia followed her gaze. "That explains the look of daggers. Are you certain you're safe with him? He looks like he doesn't like you very much."

Raven considered Delia's words. *Can I trust him?*

"As safe as with any Enforcer, I suppose." Raven said in a low voice.

"They're very serious about their duty. He won't turn down the coin."

Delia called over Arthur. "I'm going to get some food for Arthur. I'll be back tomorrow."

"I look forward to seeing you both." Raven said.

Delia called out to her son. "Arthur, say goodbye to Aunt Raven."

Aunt Raven. She couldn't deny the warmth the words gave her.

Raven farewelled Delia and returned to her work, only to feel like she was being watched again. An energy she was all too familiar with, beyond her sight.

"Stop watching me," she muttered. "I can feel your eyes on me."

"It's my job to watch you!" Markus growled.

"I wasn't…" Damn, she was about to blurt out who she was talking to. "Never mind. I can't work with you yammering on, and I have a customer delivery when I'm finished with this sword. Tobias Baxter. If you're going to escort me there, don't speak to me, nor to my customer."

He stared at her in disbelief. "I'm to believe Tobias Baxter is a customer? He's nobility; they have their own blacksmiths. Why would he hire you?"

Raven forced down her annoyance. "I don't care if you believe me or not. Just stop talking. I'm paying you for security, not conversation."

Raven knew she shouldn't talk to The Enforcer with such disrespect, and he was only doing what he was paid to do. She turned, positioning herself to study Markus. He had dark blond stubble lining his jaw, with blue eyes, and it looked like he spent a lot of time in the sun, his blond hair wavy and chin length. He was tall and had broad shoulders and a wide chest. If he weren't so surly…She lowered her eyes, guilt piercing her. Still grieving for Lucian, but looking at another man, even one as irritating as Markus. Hard as she tried, she couldn't deny that he was good-looking. She glanced up again.

"Like what you see?" he asked, his eyes on her. The same words she'd said to him when she caught him looking.

Heart pounding, Raven looked away, her cheeks burning.

"It's only fair, I was examining your curves, look all you like," he said.

"Fair?" she muttered. "It was unwanted."

"But here you are, unable to keep your eyes on your work." Markus gave her a smile. "It's alright Sunshine, you got a good glimpse, I don't mind."

"Sunshine?" He'd called her that before.

"You're just a ray of—"

"Please stop talking!" she demanded. "How many times do I have to ask you that?"

Embarrassment flushed through her, and he chuckled again, a sound that rumbled from him.

She loaded the swords into a wooden cart with a wheel at the front. On her way to deliver the order to Tobias, Raven glanced around at the streets. The air was cooler, lacking the sun's warmth as autumn pushed away the summer. Busy with whatever they were doing in their day, the townsfolk didn't pay heed to anyone they passed. In her village, she couldn't go anywhere without someone stopping to talk. Markus walked behind her, finally silent. It was late in the day, and she hurried so she would get home before dark. Arriving at a house made of stone, Raven hesitated. Tobias was a noble, and his business could get her more coin. *What if it's not up to the standard he wants?*

Before she could move, Markus moved forward and thumped his fist on the door, making her flinch.

"Do you have to do it so violently?" she muttered.

"Well, it looked like you weren't going to," he said.

"I told you to—" The door opened, interrupting her words.

A servant stood at the doorway. "Yes?"

"I'm here for Tobias." she said, pointing to the swords. "I have his order. From Zachary Dale."

The servant disappeared. Before long, he appeared, looking down at her.

"Tobias?" she asked.

"Yes. Can I help you?" He frowned and glanced at Markus with curiosity.

"I'm delivering your swords on behalf of Zachary," she advised him. "I'm his cousin, Raven."

"Who's he?" Tobias pointed at the Enforcer.

"I'm her security." Markus replied.

Tobias smiled at Raven. "I heard there was a woman blacksmith in town. I didn't know you were Zachary's cousin. Or that you'd be such a beauty, gracing my doorstep too."

Markus scoffed but said nothing.

Heat rose to her cheeks. "Here are the five swords you ordered." She pointed to the swords in her cart.

Tobias picked up one of the swords, examining the blade. "This isn't the work of Zachary. It is close, though. Did you make this?"

Raven opened her mouth. *How does he know that?* "Uh."

"It's alright," he smiled, his face softening. "I've been in business with Zachary long enough to know how he stamps his blades. You don't have a touchmark yet. If you're going to make a name of yourself, people like brands. People will want a Raven blade once they hear about the quality of your work."

Dumbfounded, she had no words.

Tobias smiled, glancing over the sword again. "A woman blacksmith is uncommon. But I can see you learned from your cousin. I'll make sure that word reaches the right people. I am happy to continue the business I had with your cousin, and I'll see that others do the same."

"Thank you," she said.

The servant who answered the door returned to retrieve the swords.

Tobias nodded to her sword. "Let me see?"

She drew her sword, handing it over. He turned the blade over. "See. His initials stamp his work." He pointed to the letters ZD inside a circle on her blade before returning the sword to her. "You carry a sword, do you know how to fight?"

"Zac trained me," she said proudly.

A glint in his eye confused her.

"Perhaps when you have a day off, you can show me," he said. His gaze shifted to Markus briefly "If your escort will allow it?"

"My escort doesn't get a say in what I do," she said. "I can come by at the end of the month."

"Not alone," Markus grumbled.

Raven clenched her jaw. Tobias glanced from her to Markus, amusement in his eyes.

"Thank you, you are most kind," she said and turned around. The door closed behind her.

"It seems you have someone intending to court you," Markus said as they started to walk back to her shop. "An unwed woman, your fiancé buried, you're going to find you attract a lot of attention from possible suitors. From a noble, though, is unexpected. Perhaps it is a mistress he seeks."

She reached for the yellow ribbon at the end of her braid. "What business is that of yours?" The idea was ridiculous, she was below Tobias's class, but his interest in her was strange. "You don't speak to me about my fiancé."

"Very well." He shrugged.

There was a twinge of something that made Raven look at him. He averted his eyes. She stopped in mid-step.

"This will never happen," she said, pointing between the two of them. "For starters, you're arrogant and annoying. You were too easily disarmed. That's not what I—"

Her words were cut off as Markus pushed her against the wall, arm against her throat. He leaned in, inches from her face.

"What are you doing?" she demanded. His arm pressed in harder, cutting off air.

"Now, I've disarmed you," he said with a smirk.

He stepped back, the tip of a sword under her chin. Her sword. He forced her chin up with the blade, forcing her eyes to his. His mouth curved into a smile. Shaking with anger, Raven glared.

A shadow appeared behind him. *It's him!* He had stepped in to help when the French soldier attacked her. *He's protecting me like he said he would.* She didn't move, and his eyes met hers. "How long have you been waiting to do that?" she asked Markus. *Please don't hurt him, he wasn't trying to kill me.*

"Since the moment you said, 'On your knees,'" he informed her and flipped the sword around, holding the hilt out to her. "You humiliated me; you didn't think I'd repay you for that?" The dark look on his face revealed his lingering anger over her actions.

The shadow figure remained for a moment longer, then disappeared again, and she let her shoulders relax.

Raven grabbed her sword. "I suppose we're even now, then," she said, resheathing the blade, and rubbing at her throat. "You didn't have to be so rough."

"That, my lady blacksmith, is why you need security," he commented.

The walk back to the smithy was silent. She kept an eye out for Death, fearful, yet hopeful that he would return. She wanted to try again to free Zac, and only he could get her into The Shadow Realm. Although she had no idea how she would get herself or her brother out. She needed to find another way in.

Chapter 29

His father had brought Raven into The Shadow Realm, and she had seen him when he wasn't himself, when he was lost in the confusion Darkness cast over him. Zachary remained where he was, shackles around his wrists, unsure how much longer before he lost himself completely. He wasn't sure he had any fight left.

No! I have to fight to keep Raven and Aunt Amelia safe. From him.

Him. His father. His deliberate torment left deep hurt within Zachary. He still struggled to accept that his father could become something so cruel.

"Zac." Hector had returned.

"Hector, I already told you, I don't know how to get out of here. I'm trapped here, the same as you." He raised his hands to show he was restrained.

Hector stared down at him. "I heard Maria crying. She needs me."

"You're dead; you can't go back," he sighed. "I'm sorry you're stuck here, Hector. I didn't intend for this."

"Then free me, as your father said," Hector demanded.

"I don't know how," he said again. "I cannot free myself; how do you think I can free you?"

This was his punishment: He was trapped here with a man he meant to comfort in his last moments. Hector left him but would be back to resume pleading to be freed.

Relieved at the quiet, he lay on the ground, looking up at the blue moon. "I'm not supposed to be here," he muttered. "I don't belong here."

"If you truly wanted to leave, you would have found your way out by now," his father's voice came from the dark. "I'm beginning to think you like it here. And why haven't you freed Hector yet? His presence bothers you, so release him."

Zachary remained on the ground, not moving. "I can't get out," he said. "You saw to that."

"Raven's still trying to help you," his father said.

"Go away. Why are you tormenting me?" Zachary grumbled.

"Isaac." His father stepped into his field of vision, looking down at him. Only it wasn't the father he knew now. It was the man he had known twenty years ago. Thomas Blake. No black lines, no Darkness rising from him, only his warm blue eyes and familiar smile.

Zachary sat up, slowly rising to his feet. "Father? Is it really you?"

"You've grown," his father said. "Look at you! My son, a man."

Overjoyed, Zachary relaxed. "Father. You're really here."

"Where else would I be? I promised you I would protect you," his father reminded him.

Zachary wrapped his father in a hug. "Father, I…" He pulled back. The moment contact was made, he could feel the Darkness within the figure before him. "You're him."

His father returned to his normal shape; black lines over his face, one eye black, the other white.

"You did that on the night you tried to take Aunt Amelia." Zachary recalled.

"I can take on the shape of either brother. I can also take on the shape of a loved one of those already passed. As Raven discovered when I showed her Lucian."

Zachary shook his head in disbelief. "You did that to Raven? But she's your daughter."

Why does this still surprise me? There is nothing but Darkness in him. Zachary worried about Raven, seeing the face of her dead fiancé.

"How quickly you forget when you see the face of your father. I am a killer, Isaac. Death, and Darkness," his father reminded him.

Grief surged through Zachary, pressing against his chest. He had never mourned his father, believing the man still existed. Now he missed the man he remembered.

"Stop calling me Isaac," Zachary demanded. His father's continued use of a name he no longer used set off irritation.

"Why? That's your name," his father said.

Zachary remained silent, keeping watchful. His father gave him a cold stare.

"While you've hidden away with your cousin and Aunt, I've spent the last twenty years killing those of Kempshire and taking them to the Crossover," his father said. "I let you live your lives in peace, but I always watched you, and Raven."

"Is that why you torment me? So I go as mad as you? I kill, like father, like son?" Zachary asked.

The chuckle that came from the figure before him was chilling. "You've already killed; so has Raven."

Zachary's chest tightened."She was defending herself, and our village."

"She was drawn to the death of her fiancé, moments before he died. Just as your touch led to Hector getting trapped here." Death looked around. A figure rose from the dark. "Darkness wants you here."

"What are you talking about?" Zachary demanded.

"The voices you've heard, the faces you've seen, that's Darkness trying to pull you in," his father told him.

"Why?" he asked.

His father smiled. "Maybe it recognises who you are."

"What happens if it pulls me in?" he asked, already knowing the answer.

"Zachary Dale will cease to be," his father confirmed.

No! "Like you ceased to be Thomas and Graeme Blake?"

His father smiled again. "Exactly. I gave in to Darkness, and you will, too."

Zachary glared. "Why do you want that for me?" Again, he didn't know why he was asking questions of the man before him.

"You have the Touch of Death; it's not about what I want. This is already your fate. You will embrace it. Your fight will be pointless." his father stepped away from him. "It's only a matter of time."

Horrified, Zachary turned his back on his father. "I won't do that."

"But you will. Just as your descendants will." Father stated.

He spun around. "No. Leave my son alone!"

"You have fathered more than one son," his father informed him.

He froze. "What?"

"With all the women who have been in your bed, you didn't think there would be more out there? You have a reputation. Look."

His father gripped his shoulder, and they left The Shadow Realm. The transition was unsettling; after spending so much time there, the daylight hurt his eyes. Horse hooves and metal on cobble hurt his ears as a cart passed by. A breeze ruffled his hair, cool on his skin, shackles gone.

"Look at where you are," his father commanded him.

They stood outside of a house he recognised. A young boy was playing out front. A girl came running out. They were of similar age to Arthur. Possibly a little younger.

"Twins," his father remarked. "I wonder if they have the same connection we had."

Zachary stared at the children. "They're mine?" he glared at his father. "Why are you showing me this?"

Father watched the twins. "They will all end up exactly where you are. You can prepare them. Get them ready. All of them."

Zachary couldn't look away from the children. He'd been overjoyed to learn of Arthur's existence. Now all he felt was dread. "For what?" he asked.

His father turned to him. "My fate is the same for my descendants."

Zachary narrowed his eyes. "They are children. I am not doing that. They are not doing that."

He searched the streets, people hurrying by. His father had given him a chance to claim his freedom. A few weeks ago, he would have run the moment he set foot in the street. Instead he waited for their return to The Shadow Realm.

His father watched him. "You've given up. All that yearning for freedom, and you don't take it when given the first opportunity. Run back to your cousin. Don't you want to meet your children?"

"Just take me back." He couldn't deny there was nothing left in him. Weeks of a waking nightmare, and his presence here would lead to Raven's fall. He didn't want his children to be in his life if he was losing his fight. "Before someone recognises me."

It was almost a relief that they had returned to The Shadow Realm. His father turned to leave.

"How did you know?" he asked.

"I *feel* them, the same as I feel you and Raven. There is a link in our family that connects us all. Maybe it's the Darkness in the bloodline." His father vanished, and Zachary was left alone again.

He watched the twins through the veil. A woman stood at the door. Grace. She had been his solution to feeling better about Delia's rejection.

"Giselle, Joseph, stay close to the house," she warned.

"I wish I could be the father you deserve." He knelt to peer into the twins' faces. The girl looked like her mother, but Joseph had the same dark hair and brown eyes as Zachary. He'd wanted fatherhood, and suddenly, he had three children, and he wanted to be in their lives, to get to know them. "I'm sorry," he whispered. The girl looked up, her eyes meeting his.

"Hello," Giselle smiled.

Zachary froze.

"Hello," he replied. "You can see me?"

"You're right there, of course I can." She laughed.

"What are you doing there?" Joseph asked.

"**Isaac**."

The street faded, and Raven stood before him with black eyes, dark lines across her face.

"I'm not Isaac." *I'm Zachary.* "I know you're not her," he called out to Darkness.

The apparition of Raven smiled. "**Does it matter? This is all of our fate, cousin. None of us can escape it. Our children, and *their* children will all give in to Darkness. We are Death's descendants.**"

Isaac. Zachary. Isaac.

Darkness surrounded Isaac, and once more he fell into the void.

Chapter 30

Raven opened her eyes, the dark room bringing her back. Dreams of Zac and The Shadow Realm disturbed her. She sat up. Her mother was coming to visit in a few days, she needed to make sure the shop was tidy. It made her smile to see her mother's happiness with Arthur. She climbed out of bed and dressed into a light blue tunic and brown trousers, pulling her hair into a braid. It always got her stares but was easier to work than in a dress.

Before Markus arrived, she reached out to Death.

"Are you there?" she spoke to the empty room. "I know you watch me; please hear me now."

Just like that, he was there in front of her. She suppressed a shiver and stepped back involuntarily. His empty stare was as unsettling as the first time.

"You're afraid of me." Amusement lit up his eyes.

"I'd be stupid not to be." She frowned at his smile. "That pleases you."

"Of course. I live for fear. My daughter has no need to fear me, though. I look forward to our morning conversations," he said.

Even his smile made her uneasy.

"Don't call me that." She couldn't deny she was his daughter, but she didn't like the way he used the word. "My father died twenty years ago. Killed by his brother."

He took on the form of Graeme. "But my death didn't last, did it."

His amusement disturbed her, but she pushed it down.

She studied his face. "How does that work? Are you one being, or two souls trapped as one?" Curiosity was getting the best of her.

"I am one being, formed from both brothers, so I can appear as either Thomas or Graeme. Is this why you called me here, or was it to talk about your cousin?" he pressed her, reminding her why she had called him.

She had been drawn into a conversation and forgotten her reason for calling on him. "Please free him."

"He can walk through the veil any time he wants. But he doesn't want to. I granted him time in this realm today, and he demanded I take him back." Death chuckled. "He has no fight left in him."

"But he has a son, and a family," she said. "He would never abandon us."

"He knows." His smile flashed again. "Once you're in The Shadow Realm, what's important in this one tends to fade away. Maybe he's happier there. He falls into the shadows for long stretches of time; I think he prefers it. He's going to surrender to Darkness very soon." Death reached towards her. "But it's already inside you, waiting to be released."

He would never give in to Darkness. "Just let him go," she requested.

"He made his choice. For the sake of your mother. For you. She was more than willing to take my hand, though; she knew her time was up." His eyes met hers, a piercing stare. "If you want, I can take you to him."

There was a knock. She recognised the heavy thud of Markus's fist on the door.

Death smiled. "Perhaps later."

"I'm closed," she called out. "Please." Raven didn't care about the Enforcer reporting for his work.

Death returned to The Shadow Realm without a word.

"Miss Dale, open the door." Markus banged on the door again.

He's persistent today. "No. You can have the day off today."

"If Zachary's back, will you still be needing me?" he asked through the door.

She opened the door. "What?"

He blinked at her in surprise. "Your cousin."

"No, I heard what you said, but you're not making sense," she said.

"He's not back?" He glanced around the shop. "He was seen outside a house on West Street."

Her heart skipped a beat. "Are you sure it was him?"

"There were two; one looked just like him. They didn't come back here?" he asked, looking around again.

One of them did. Raven frowned. *Did he release him after all? Why wouldn't Zachary come home?* "No," she said. "Where were they seen?"

"I can take you there," he told her.

She grabbed her sword and stepped outside. "Let's go."

They walked at a brisk pace, Markus at her side. A stranger's eyes followed her with a hint of a smile as he veered towards her. Fear spiked as she stopped walking, the look in his eye compelling her to reach for her weapon. He eyed her hand and raised his dagger.

"Keep walking." Markus said, drawing his sword. "She is under Enforcer protection."

The stranger barely acknowledged Markus, but he did continue walking, passing by Raven, his footsteps loud.

Taking a moment, she raised her eyes to Markus, to find his filled with concern.

"Are you alright?" he asked, returning his sword to its sheath.

She loosened her hand from the sword hilt. "I froze."

"I know. That's why I'm here." His usual gruff voice had changed, a calming tone to it.

"I don't understand why I froze. Zac trained me; I should have drawn my blade," she said, disappointed in herself.

"It's different when you're face to face with a soldier, than it is with a would-be mugger." He glanced over his shoulder and placed his hand on her lower back to guide her away. "Trained or not, you're still going to feel fear. No one's immune to that."

"He was going to mug me? But I don't have anything on me, other than my sword." *I'm talking nonsense.* "Thank you."

"It is why you pay me," he noted.

"Yes, I suppose it is," she agreed.

She glanced behind where the stranger was walking away. A familiar shape, a dark shadow trailed him. She quickened her pace and turned away. The man had been about to hurt her; he deserved the worst of what that shadow would give him. Hopeful that Markus wouldn't see, she attempted to keep his focus on her.

"What if he had challenged you? You're not wearing armour," she pointed out.

"I prefer not to," he admitted.

His hand remained on his sword, ready, as they walked.

"Why not? You're an Enforcer, you're supposed to wear armour."

"Zachary was going to make new armour for the Enforcers. When he disappeared, Lord Gerard sought out another blacksmith. The armour is..a little small. It's uncomfortable."

It hurt that Lord Gerard had not hired her for that. "Did you not think to get it fitted?" She asked with a frown.

He stopped, giving her a curious look. "You're upset about my armour?"

"No, I'm upset that the man I'm paying to protect me is not wearing armour. He could have stabbed you," she said.

Markus seemed taken aback. "I'm touched by your concern, Sunshine, but I can protect you with or without armour. Have more trust in me than that." He resumed his path, and she kept pace. "There is a woman blacksmith I know of who makes good armour that I've considered hiring, but she's a real pain." He glanced down at her with a small smile.

"Is that right?" She raised an eyebrow at him

"I think my presence displeases her," he admitted.

Despite herself, she couldn't hold back the smile. "Perhaps if you grovel, she may consider making you a cuirass that fits."

He chuckled. "Are you trying to get me on my knees again?"

The laughter that burst out of her surprised her. After her near miss, it seemed out of place that she would laugh at such a time.

"We're here," he said and stopped. "This is where he was seen."

Raven looked around. "What would he have been doing here? Why didn't he come to see me?" The idea of Zac returning without seeing her stung. *What was he doing here? Why would he not come home?* Death's words echoed in her mind. He had granted Zac a chance at freedom. *Was this what he spoke of?*

Markus put a heavy hand on her shoulder. "I don't know his reason. He's rather protective of you, though, so I'm sure he'll come home." His words were soft.

His hand was a comfort, so she didn't ask him to remove it.

Raven noticed two children playing in the street. "Aww, they're sweet."

"The twins? Those are Joseph and Giselle Slater," he said.

Twins?

"Who is their mother?" she asked, glancing around the street.

"Grace Slater," he replied. "Her husband died at war."

She faced Markus. "Do you think he was here watching the twins?"

"Why would he be...*oooh*." Markus eyed the children. "Do you think they're his, too?"

"It's likely," she affirmed, watching the children. The boy did show resemblance to Zac.

"But how would he know of them?" he asked. "Are there more?"

Zachary's habit of bedding women was known by many. She had always figured it was a way to cope with the loss he had endured, and she was just grateful it wasn't gambling or drinking. Although for a while, it had been fighting. Secret fight clubs that Lord Gerard had put a stop to, locking up anyone caught there. Zachary had been lucky.

"How does a man like that have so many women?" Markus wondered out loud.

She walked away, leaving Markus behind.

His footsteps pounded the road as he ran to catch up. "Please stay close; that mugger could come back."

He's probably dead by now. She pushed down a flicker of guilt. *I should not feel guilty; he pulled a dagger on me.* Remorse turned to anger at the idea. "Sorry. I didn't want to hear you speak of my cousin that way."

"How did he..." He let his words trail off. "What happened to his eye?"

Zac had endured a lifetime of questions about his eye. He'd told her it had been like that since he was struck by the dark lightning that burst from his father.

"It happened before I was born. He was close to where lightning struck." Another lie. She noticed how much easier it was to lie these days.

Markus took a while to respond. "He's lucky he didn't die then."

"Lucky," she agreed.

Up ahead, a crowd drew their attention. Markus walked a little ahead of her. Pulled forward by the familiar flutters within, she already knew what they would find. She hung back, feeling no need to see Death's handiwork. Realisation spread across Markus's face, and he shot her a look that set off worry.

He made his way back to her, gripping her arm. "He's dead. The man that was going to attack you."

Raven remained silent.

"Can you at least try to look surprised, or show regret?" he demanded.

"Regret? Why? Had you not been here, that could be me on the ground." His fingers tightened around her arm, and he pulled her away from the crowd. She tried to pull her arm out of his grip. "Stop, you're hurting me," she requested.

They got distance from the crowd before he stopped and turned to face her. "Do you know who did this?"

She avoided his eyes. "Why would I? I was with you."

"Look at me, Raven." His words were spoken with authority, and she had no choice but to meet his hard glare, surprised at his use of her name instead of 'Miss Dale.' "Your cousin was seen in town on this very day. Was this his attempt to protect you?"

"You're accusing Zac of doing this?" Fury hit her in waves. "He's protective, but he'd never kill someone over it. Injure, yes, but not kill." Again, she knew she was lying. Zac would likely kill to protect her. But it wasn't her cousin who'd done this.

His eyes narrowed as he studied her face. "Are you sure?"

Tingling started at the back of her neck. *He knows something.* "I am." She confirmed.

His chin lifted.

"You look like you want to say something," she noticed.

Instead he turned, pulling her with him.

"What are you doing?" she asked.

"I'm taking you home." His voice was terse.

She stumbled behind him. "Please slow down. You don't have to hold my arm so tight."

He let go. "Walk."

She pulled away, walking ahead of him.

"It's happening again." Markus spoke under his breath, but she was close enough to catch the words.

"What?" she prompted.

That he seemed to know something worried her. The names of her father and uncle were well known across the entire country, but he knew something. She was sure of it. She never thought she would see him that afraid. Raw fear shone through his eyes. Before she could say something, they reached her shop. Without a word, she unlocked the door.

"Raven."

She turned to face him.

"I'm sorry for how our first meeting went. I shouldn't have mistaken you for one of Zachary's women. I regret that I offended you. That was wrong of me."

Raven lifted her eyes to his face. He looked to be speaking in truth.

"Thank you," she replied.

He turned and walked away.

The dark presence remained, cold emptiness emanating to her right.

"Don't hurt him," she requested. "He is not a threat to me. He's my protector, too."

Something shifted in the presence, as if he were acknowledging her request.

Chapter 31

Overhead, a dark sky threatened rain. Clouds had moved in quickly, covering the sunshine from that morning. Raven led her mother to the place where she had seen the twins. Where Zac had been seen. *Is he still here?* A cold wind tugged at her clothes, and she regretted not having a cloak. Autumn would be over before long.

"They went in that house," she said. "This is not a poor neighbourhood, so I wouldn't say she's struggling."

Her mother stared. "I really need to have a word with Zachary about his vices." She shook her head. "What do you have in mind, Raven?"

"They are family. If she wants no part, then we let her be. Zac wouldn't want to abandon children," she said.

Her mother nodded. "Very well, lead the way."

Markus followed behind as Raven and her mother walked towards the house. It had been a couple of days since the body, and he had barely looked her in the eye. Once again, the idea that he knew something nudged at her.

"You don't have to be here," she told him.

"Yes, I do," he replied, avoiding eye contact. "You are my duty."

Perhaps I should stop paying him. We'll see how quickly that changes.

Her mother turned a bright smile on Markus. "You're different from the Enforcers I've known."

His expression softened as he smiled at her mother. "I've heard they're quite brutal in the bigger towns."

Raven frowned. "She didn't say she was from a bigger town."

Markus blinked. "Zachary mentioned once he was from a bigger town further West."

"He wouldn't say that." She cast a glance at her mother.

"Raven, calm yourself." Her mother nodded to Markus. "We did hear of some violent ways of Enforcers. It was normal for them. Many were returned soldiers, but a large number were nobility. They liked to abuse their power, lord it over the poorer folks."

Her mother made no attempt to hide that she liked Markus's presence. His mannerisms around her were different, more respectful than he had been.

Markus raised his fist to the door. "Markus, no, this requires a gentler knock," she said. "She's never met us, so we don't want to scare her."

Markus knocked on the door softly and stepped back.

The door opened, and the woman she had seen before stood before her. Grace took in her appearance before her eyes shifted to Amelia. "You're Zachary's family," she said. "Please, come in."

"You know us," her mother said as they stepped through the door.

Grace glanced at them. "Of course. I made sure to know who you were."

"Your children…" Raven started.

"Yes, they're his." Grace answered the question before Raven could ask it.

"You never sought to tell him?" *How many more women have his children that he doesn't know about?*

"Zachary is a complicated man." Grace said. "I was not in need of support and didn't want to force him into marriage. He has trauma over his own father, so I wasn't sure he was ready for fatherhood…or for a family."

"He told you about his father?" Her mother frowned.

"Not much. Just that both his parents died when he was very young. His father was a soldier or something?" Grace glanced between them. "Have you received any news on Zachary?" Her eyes lifted to Markus. "Aren't you an Enforcer?"

"He's my guard." Raven said. "I'm running the smithy in Zac's absence."

"His absence? I thought he was back?" Grace said.

Markus's eyes met hers.

"Back?" Raven asked.

Grace glanced around at each of them. "I'm sorry, he's not back? I heard he was seen out on the street. I assumed he'd sent you here about the twins."

"Zac didn't send me," Raven said. "I saw your twins."

Grace gave her a long stare. "Well, I suppose I should introduce you. Giselle! Joseph! Some people are here to meet you!" The four-year-old children came running and stopped when they caught sight of Raven and Amelia, their eyes big as they stared.

"Children, this is your father's cousin and aunt," Grace said.

"Hello," Giselle said first, giving Raven a smile.

Joseph just stared before turning his gaze on his mother.

"Go on, say hello," Grace instructed.

"There's a man in the shadows," Giselle said. "He's sad."

Chills crept up Raven's spine. "What?"

"They've been talking about that all morning, I don't know what she's talking about." Grace said.

Raven lowered herself to her knees. "What man in the shadows?" she asked.

"He was watching us," Giselle said. "But then he went away."

"Did you see him, too?" Raven asked Joseph.

His hand was in his mouth as he blinked at her. Slowly he nodded, eyes wide.

"He's a bit quiet around people he doesn't know," Grace said.

"I'm Raven. This is my mother, Amelia," Raven said to the twins. "I hope we can get to know each other."

"Raven, is my father dead?" Giselle asked.

Horrified, Raven glanced up at Grace.

"No!" she whispered. "He would like to meet you when he comes home." She smiled at the twins. "Both of you."

"Where is he?" Giselle asked.

"He's…not here right now. But he'll be back soon," Raven's mother spoke up.

Relief flooded Raven. Mother was having a good day; no unusual statements. Like herself, almost.

Raven smiled at Grace. "Are you alright with us being here?"

"It was an unexpected visit, but I'm happy you're here," Grace said. "They've wondered about their father, so I'm happy they can meet his family."

"They have a half-brother, Arthur," Raven said. "Delia's his mother."

"I thought that might be so. I knew when I was with Zac that he hadn't let go of her. I've seen her with the boy," Grace's eyes crinkled.

While Grace and Raven's mother talked, ice ran down Raven's spine and she straightened, carefully glancing around the room. That feeling of being watched had returned. She caught Giselle's eyes on her.

"Do you see him, too?" the girl asked.

Raven's mother looked over, eyes wide.

"See who?" The hairs on Raven's arms stood up.

"Giselle, don't tell her." Joseph whispered. "He might see."

Raven lowered herself to Giselle and Joseph's level. "You can tell me." she whispered. "What do you see?"

"He's mostly in shadow, but he watches us. Like now. He's not the sad man we saw earlier, but someone else." She lowered her voice. "He's scary."

"You can see him?" Raven asked.

Giselle pointed to the corner of the room. "He's there."

Raven raised her eyes to the corner, seeing nothing. He was there, though; she could sense the dark presence. The same she had felt watching her many times. He had killed twice now to protect her. Death.

"Leave them alone," she whispered. "Watch me if you must, but not them."

The room fell silent. Markus, Grace, and her mother's eyes were all on her. She forced a smile, while Grace's expression was one of horror. The look on Markus's face was unexpected, though, as if this was of no surprise to him.

"You did it!" Giselle said. "He's gone!"

Chapter 32

Weeks had passed and Raven had begun to enjoy working as a blacksmith.

She was so focused on lighting the forge that she didn't realise that Markus had walked in until he entered her periphery.

"Raven." His mouth pressed into a hard line, eyebrows drawn together. "I need you to come with me. Now."

She didn't stop. "You can see I'm busy. What is it?"

"Lord Gerard has sent me for you. Your presence has been requested at his manor. Your cousin's horse is saddled and waiting outside."

"Why doesn't he come here?" Raven frowned. "What does he want?"

"I'm sorry, but I've been given clear orders to escort you there immediately," he said apologetically.

She met his eyes. She noted that at least he was looking at her this time. "You can't tell me why?" she asked.

"No." He shook his head.

She found his lack of answers irritating.

"But you know what he wants," she clarified, forcing herself to stay calm.

Unsure why she was resisting his orders, she frowned at him.

"I do." He crossed his arms over his chest. "I will carry you if I have to."

There was no amusement in his eyes, only the hard glint of determination.

"No you won't. Just tell me," she pleaded so she could get on with her day.

"I cannot." Markus took a step towards her.

She stepped back. "Markus, I know you love your duty and orders and all that, but I have a lot to do today." She pointed to the orders on her workbench. "If you know what he wants, then stop wasting my time!" Raven knew she was being difficult but didn't care.

Markus closed the gap between them, and with quick movements, he lifted her over his shoulder.

"What do you think you're doing?" Furious, she squirmed. "Put me down! Immediately."

"I cannot do that," he said, wrapping one hand around her legs and the other across her back. "Stop squirming, or I'll drop you." He moved towards the door.

Humiliated, she stopped struggling, realising that there was no point. Outside, sunlight held little warmth.

"Please put me down," she pleaded again.

"Not until you're on the horse," came his reply.

"Please don't do this. You're taking me away from my work." She hadn't spoken with Death yet. But Lord Gerard's summons scared her. Markus didn't have to tell her what it was about, for her to be concerned. Somehow, she felt Death's involvement.

"Your work will have to wait. This cannot," he told her.

He forced her onto the horse, and instead of taking his, he climbed on the back of Lance, cutting off any chance she had of escaping, with his arms on either side of her, as he grasped the reins.

"Don't you trust me?" she asked.

"No. We're going to the manor, so you'd best accept that now," he advised her.

Desperate, she sought a reason for him to release her. "I don't have my sword," she said.

"You don't need it. I *am* your sword," he declared.

It was hopeless; she wasn't getting out of this. Raven gave up. As they rode towards the Manor, Markus's body pressed against hers with every movement of the horse. He wasn't wearing armour, and his torso was warm through the tunic. With nothing to hold on to, she leaned against him for support, his body firm as it pressed into hers. Hooves on stone filled the silence.

The early morning foot traffic had picked up, townsfolk talking amongst themselves, and as they rode past the market, voices and laughter rang out.

They arrived at the manor, and the Lord was there to greet them. "Bring her," was all he said and strode inside.

"Do I need to carry you over my shoulder again?" Markus asked, next to her ear.

"I can walk just fine," she replied through clenched teeth. "I'd rather you not touch me like that again."

He climbed off the horse and helped her to the ground. She pulled out of his grasp, eager to get away from him. Markus led her towards the manor. She walked through large wooden doors, down a large hallway with many rooms. In the kitchen, cooks moved around shouting orders at each other, her mouth watering as the aroma of cooked meat and various scents towards her.

They arrived in the parlour, and she found the Lord flanked by four Enforcers.

"My Lord." She nodded her head in respect. "Can you please tell me why I am here? Your Enforcer saw fit to drag me here, so I assume it's of importance."

Lord Gerard glanced at Markus, who smirked. "She wouldn't leave," he said. "So I carried her over my shoulder. You said to get her here by any means necessary."

Lord Gerard attempted to hide a smile. "Thank you, Markus," his smile faded. "It's about your cousin," he said to Raven in a sombre tone.

Zac!

"You've seen him?" The hope in her voice made Enforcers look at each other.

"I have received news that a body was found outside the town walls," he said.

Everything stopped, ice spreading through her body. "What?" *No, not Zac.* Tears welled in her eyes and the ground fell away. It wasn't until Markus's hands caught her that she realised her knees had buckled. "Zac?" she asked, stepping away from him, towards Lord Gerard. "Is he…?" *What did he do to Zac?* Despair turned to rage directed at Death.

"It's not Zachary's body, but someone witnessed the event," Lord Gerard faced her, his eyes grim, mouth pressed into a hard line.

"I don't understand. What does this have to do with my cousin?" she asked.

Fear enveloped her in a vice grip. Something had happened, and what he said next would change her life. She didn't know how she knew.

"They recognised Zachary *over* the body," Lord Gerard told her. "*With a bloodied blade.*"

Raven stared, confused. "Zac? He wouldn't kill anyone."

"He was *seen* killing someone, Raven." His tone hardened. "He's killed *my Captain.*"

"No, he would never do that." She shook her head, fighting against tears.

"I have heard of prisoners being converted to the enemy's cause," an Enforcer spoke up. "Perhaps the French sent him to break our defence."

"No, not Zac." Dread crashed through Raven, and she caught Markus staring at her. His earlier accusations rang in her ears. *Is he going to say something?* "Your witness is mistaken, it was not him! I refuse to believe this."

Lord Gerard watched her, a coldness in his eyes she hadn't seen before. He turned to one of his Enforcers. "Dispatch a call for soldiers." His eyes were hard as he studied Raven. "What you believe about your cousin is insignificant. If he is seen, he will be arrested on sight. If you see him, you are not to offer him shelter, or you will be arrested, too. Do you understand?"

"Yes, my Lord." Struggling to hold her anguish, she needed to show that she would not be a problem. Raven silently cursed Death again.

"Enforcer Markus has been permanently assigned to you. Night and day. He will be reporting anything unusual to me." The Lord faced Markus. "Any sign of him, and I know about it the moment you do."

"Yes, Lord Gerard," Markus agreed. He opened his mouth as if to say something else, but his eyes darted towards Raven, and he closed it.

"What of the smithy, Lord Gerard?" Raven asked.

"Under normal circumstances, the shop of a murderer would be seized. However, you have quickly earned favour among my Enforcers. For some reason, they seem to like you. I've also had Tobias highly recommend your services. You will continue to run the shop as you have been." he turned. "You may leave."

Raven's vision blurred as Markus led her back to the horse outside. She needed to be free of Markus to speak with Death. She would be demanding answers.

Chapter 33

Back at her shop, she hesitated before going inside. She needed Markus to leave so she could demand answers of Death. She wanted to know why he had killed this time.

"You don't have to follow me in," she said.

"I do," he replied. "I know you don't want me here, but I have my orders." His voice was low, and she hated the sympathy in it.

His orders. Raven pushed down the frustration as Markus followed her into the shop. Once inside, Raven swayed. In such a short time, everything had fallen around her. With Zac being suspected of murder, many would be watching her. Death had done this; destroyed her cousin's life.

Markus's hand lightly touched her elbow. When her legs threatened to buckle, his grip tightened, sliding up her arm, his other hand on her waist.

"Perhaps you should sit down?" His voice was gentle.

Warmth of his hand seeped through her tunic. "Markus."

"Yes?"

"Your hand is on my waist," she pointed out.

He removed his hand immediately. "Sorry."

Raven moved towards the work bench, wanting to be sick.

"I'm sorry about your cousin," Markus said.

Again, she hated the sympathy he was showing. It was as if he were trying to get her to drop her guard.

"I need to be alone," she said.

"I have my orders," he reminded her.

"Damn you with your orders. Just leave! I don't want you here, I just want to be left alone. Please, Markus." She pointed to the door. "Just leave."

Markus frowned. "If I leave, are you going to sneak your cousin in here?"

Fury burned through her. "You dare accuse me of that? Can I not just have a moment by myself after I've learned that the entire town is going to be seeking him out? Hunting him?"

His expression softened. "You know I can't leave. But I will give you time. I can understand it was a lot. I'll be outside."

As soon as he left, Raven let tears fall.

"Zac, where are you?" Raven's throat tightened and she shook her head. "I know it's not you. It could only be him." The shop was empty, but Death's presence was close. "Death, what have you done? Why would you do this to him?"

Her question was pointless. Death's humanity was absent, and only he would know why he did such things. She couldn't tell anyone the truth. An arrest-on-sight order would never be successful for him, though; not if he could melt away like a shadow, into another realm.

"Show yourself," she said, anger in her voice. "I know you're there. I can feel your presence."

The door behind her banged closed.

"Damnit, Markus, I told you to go. Why is it so hard for you to do as I ask?" she demanded.

The silence made her turn around. It wasn't Markus but a man she didn't know. "Who are you? What do you want?"

"Where's Zachary?" he asked, a dangerous glint in his eyes.

"You *know* he's not here," she said. He moved towards her, and she glared. "That's close enough," she warned. He kept moving, and she reached for her sword, only to find it not at her hip. "I said stop."

"When we find him, we'll hang him for his crime and burn his shop. It's best you go home, village girl. You'd be safer there," he instructed her.

"Lord Gerard has declared that this shop is mine. I'm not going anywhere." She moved back, searching for her sword on the bench while keeping her eyes on him.

Light reflected off his dagger. "Tell me where Zachary is."

Death emerged from The Shadow Realm as he stood behind the man in shadow form.

"Please don't." She wasn't quite sure who her pleas were for.

The man rushed at her. Unwilling to have Death kill for her again, she slashed with her sword, slicing across the intruder's throat.

He gurgled and fell. Standing over him. Raven's hand shook. *I just killed someone. Again.* The sharp smell of urine filled the air.

She glanced towards the door to make sure no one saw. Dropping her sword, she stared at the body.

"You were going to kill him," she said.

"**I was. It seems I'm not needed. You really are my daughter.**" The pride in his voice was unmistakable.

She suppressed the shiver. "Stop calling me that."

He took on the shape of her father. "You cannot deny you are my daughter, Raven."

She couldn't, but it didn't mean she was going to be proud of the fact. "Why do you keep killing people?" she asked.

"I'm protecting you." His response was so matter-of-fact.

"Why? I didn't ask for it." She glared, but couldn't hide behind her anger from the fact that she had killed.

His smile set off dread again. "You'd be surprised how many times I've stepped in," he admitted.

"I don't want to know that! It's your fault he was in here to start with. You framed Zac for murder. I know it was you. You made sure someone saw. You wanted him to pay for a crime he didn't commit. Why?" Her words spilled out of her.

"I'm removing his attachment to this life. If he's hunted, it might push him to Darkness quicker. He's resisting," he remarked.

"Please, just let him go, and leave us to live our lives," she pleaded.

He turned his head towards the door. "How will you explain this to the Enforcer?" he returned to shadow form and was gone.

Raven fought against the rising panic. If she was caught with a body in her shop after the warning she had received, no one would believe her. *He wants me to be arrested. No doubt so he can offer me a way out, involving The Shadow Realm. I have to get rid of the body before Markus sees this.*

Heart pounding, she leaned over and grabbed his feet and started to drag the body scraping across the ground, leaving a trail of blood. As she glanced towards the door again, a figure stood in the doorway. Raven straightened up, heart racing. *How am I supposed to explain this?*

Raven's gaze drifted from the body to Markus, trying to evaluate what he would do. He had been ordered to report anything to the Lord.

"Are you going to..." She couldn't finish.

Markus bent down, retrieving the dagger. "No. He would have killed you. This isn't something I'm going to tell the Lord about."

"Then what will you do?" Her heart thundered in her ears.

"Get rid of him," he said with a shrug.

"What?" Those were the last words she expected from him. Surely he was planning on arresting her. Taking her and the body straight to Lord Gerard. "Why?

His eyes shifted over her face. "Were you not attempting to hide him anyway?"

She had no answer for that.

"Let me remove him for you," he offered.

She narrowed her eyes at Markus. "You would do that? Why?"

"Can you trust me?" he asked.

She scoffed. "No."

He laughed. "It's good that you're suspicious of people, but you have no need to be so of me."

Raven glared at him. "This is funny to you?"

He moved towards her and grabbed her arm, pulling her towards the seat. "No, it's not funny. Let me take care of this for you. It's the least I can do."

She stared at him with suspicion. "Why would you? You could be free of me."

The intensity in his eyes made her stomach tighten. "Wipe down your sword. I'm taking him out the back door. Clean the blood off the floor while I'm gone," he commanded.

The back door of the shop led to an alley that no one used. Markus grabbed a blanket from her bed and wrapped it around the body. She held the door open as he heaved the corpse over his shoulder. "Don't talk to anyone," he ordered her and left through the door.

Raven did as he instructed, first cleaning her sword, then the floor. Spotting blood on her tunic, she pulled it over her head and threw it into the corner. Grabbing another, she finally sat down, her back to the wall, staring at the spot where the body had been.

Why don't I feel guilty?

A shadow fell over her. Markus had returned. He said something but she couldn't hear over the roaring in her ears. Suddenly he was kneeling in front of her. "You have blood on you," he said.

"No, I changed my tunic." She pointed at the one she'd discarded. "I have to hide that." He reached a hand towards her face. His hand cupped her cheek and his thumb stroked under her eye. Startled that he would dare touch her, she met his eyes. "What are you doing?"

"Wiping away the blood," he replied. "Are you alright?"

She shivered. He rose to his feet and removed his cloak, wrapping it around her. The weight on her shoulders did little to comfort her. He then lifted her to her feet, guiding her to her bed. "The floor is no place for a lady to sit."

She sat on the bed, staring at his feet. "I don't feel guilty," she repeated. "Why don't I feel guilty?"

He lowered into a crouch, down to her eye level. His eyes were dark as he lifted her chin to meet his. His breath was warm on her cheek. "Because you know that if you hadn't, it would be your blood on the floor."

A sob escaped her. "I'm a killer," she gasped. "Just like my father. His shadow hangs over me."

"Your father?" he asked.

Raven shook her head. She had said too much.

"Maybe get some sleep," he said. "It's been a stressful day for you today."

"Why are you being like this?" she asked. "Why are you helping me?"

"Because I thought I'd give you a break." He cracked a smile. "We can go back to glaring at each other tomorrow."

She couldn't resist her own smile.

"Get into bed," he instructed.

She shook off the cloak and did as he ordered. He pulled a blanket over her.

"Where did you take him?" she asked.

"No." he said. "You don't need to know that. Just trust that he's gone."

"alright." She closed her eyes, and the dark shadow of Death loomed over her. She opened them again. "Please don't leave. I don't want to be alone."

A chair scraped over the ground as he pulled it towards her bed. "I'm not going anywhere. You're safe. Sleep."

She closed her eyes, exhausted, yet unsure she would sleep.

Chapter 34

Fog and shadows surrounded Raven. Zac's face appeared before her, only to fade into the Darkness.

"Raven, help me." The desperation in his voice tore at her.

"I'm trying," she called to him. "I don't know how to get you out."

He stood before her. "The Darkness is trying to claim me. I don't want to go."

"Hold on. I'll find a way," she promised.

Death's hand grasped her shoulder. "You're too late. It's only a matter of time before Isaac is no more. Let him go, daughter."

Tears slid down her cheeks.

"No!"

CHAPTER 34

"Raven." A voice spoke to her, pulling her out of her dream.

"Zac?" she asked, sitting up.

"No, Markus." He knelt by her bed. "You were having a nightmare and calling out in your sleep." He frowned. "Who's Isaac?"

He was rubbing her back to calm her down, his presence more welcome than she would have liked. His face was in shadow. Unsure if her heart was pounding at his closeness or her nightmare, she held her breath. He was so close, yet she didn't pull away. Instead, she gripped his arm, fearful of being pulled back into the dream. His hand stilled on her back, his breath ragged.

Say something. "It looks like I got you on your knees aga-."

Her words were cut off as he pressed his lips to hers, his hand on her back sliding up to the side of her neck. Lucian's face flashed before her, and she put her hands on his chest and pushed.

"I'm sorry. I shouldn't have done that," he said, without regret.

She couldn't deny that the kiss had done something to her. Or that despite his words, he wasn't moving away. Unsure she wanted him to, she realised her hand was still on his chest. "You kissed me," she said, stunned.

"I did. I'm sorry." Again, he didn't look sorry.

"Are you?" she challenged.

His smile sent shivers down her back. "No. Not really."

"How long have you been wanting to do that?" she asked.

"Since you told me to get on my knees. You're not threatening to kill me, I take this to be a good—"

Raven grabbed the front of his tunic in a fist and pulled him towards her. "Stop talking," she said and met his mouth with hers.

He let her pull him on top of her on the bed. With his hands on either side of her, his body pressed against hers, and their kiss became hungry. They moved further onto the bed, his hand sliding up her body before he pinned her arms above her head. He pulled away from the kiss, inches from her face. His eyes burned with desire, weakening her. She lifted her head, trying to kiss him again, letting out a groan of frustration, her arms still pinned. She fought against his grip, which only tightened. His woodsy smell filled her senses.

He lowered his mouth to whisper, breath tickling her ear. "Do you want me to stop?"

Nipping at his jaw, she stopped fighting against him. She was betraying Lucian's memory, but couldn't deny her body was responding to his, that she yearned to have more.

"No," she said finally. "Don't stop."

With one hand, he caressed her cheek. His other hand moved to her body.

She struggled to take his tunic off. Markus lifted himself enough to pull it over his head. She slid her hands across his torso and up to his bare chest as his slid under her tunic, over her stomach, cupping her breast. He lowered his head once more, kissing her jaw.

Desire heated her. "Markus. I want—"

His kiss cut off her words, hands creeping again. As his thumb brushed the underside of her breast, she started to peel her tunic off. Markus pulled back, to let her remove it, where he threw it across the room. His eyes strayed down to her body, a shocked smile on his face. As he lowered his head again, his lips blazed trails across her breasts before he buried his face in them. He took a nipple in his mouth, and she sucked in a breath, fingers tangling in his hair. His tongue flickered against her skin, sending more heat through her body. He moved down to her navel and undid her trousers. She squirmed out of them, laying before him naked and vulnerable. He rose from the bed, looking down at her.

"There she is." His cheeks were pink, breathing ragged as he ran his eyes over her exposed body, a smile crept across his face.

"Who?"

"The woman who commanded an Enforcer to get on his knees. The fiery belle. My Sunshine. What commands do you ask of me?"

Usually, she hated the name he gave her, but it was growing on her.

Raven bit her lip. "No," she murmured. "This time, I'm yours to command."

She caught surprise in his face for just a moment, replaced by a wicked glint in his eyes.

"Will you be obedient, no matter what I say?" He breathed.

"I will," she said.

"That's my good girl," he growled. "Get on your knees."

Excitement coursed through her as she moved to kneel. Markus moved her to the edge of the bed, pressing himself against her.

"I'm going to kiss you," he said.

"I won't stop you," she whispered.

"Not here." His fingers pressed against her mouth, and she nipped at them. They moved from her mouth. "Here." He touched her between her legs softly.

Heat swelled within, moving towards her core. He knelt before her, locking his arms around her thighs. "Hold my shoulders." His voice was husky, and then he pressed his lips against her thigh, sending a shiver through her. Slow kisses, from one thigh to the other and back again. Raven's heart was skipping, her face hot.

His breath whispered against her as he paused, smile widening, eyes gazing into hers, reflecting lust.

Don't stop," she whispered.

He barely touched her, but it was enough. Sensitive, she gasped as his lips brushed her inner thigh, trailing up. The stubble on his chin only heightened the feeling, and he then pressed his mouth to her sex. She gasped. Raven had never imagined someone would be kissing that part of her body, and would never have known to expect this. The feeling of Markus's lips on her sent fire burning through her entire being. Then his tongue stroked through her, eliciting a soft moan from her.

Gripping his shoulders, she couldn't look away as they locked eyes. He maintained his licking, swirling his tongue, and sucking on her. Sparks inside her core heated and spread as she threw her head back, unable to hold back another moan.

"Eyes on me, Sunshine," he ordered her.

She lowered her eyes again, gazing into his. Her breaths came in short gasps, and she whispered his name. His mouth stretched into a smile. She pushed into his face, arching her back. Her body tense with shivers rippling all over. His arms around her tightened.

"Markus, I—" pleasure exploded, deep within and with it, another moan. Quivering, she couldn't hold herself up any more. Markus's arms moved, gliding around her lower back as he lowered her onto the bed. Shudders continued to tear through her, and Markus crawled his way up her body. He found her lips again, his kiss forceful. She ground herself against him, already feeling his erection.

"Look at me," he commanded.

She was looking. His jaw, chest, arms and torso.

"Do you want me?" he asked.

She nodded.

"I can't hear you."

"I want you." Her hands roamed over his body.

He reacted to her touch.

"Do what you will. My body is yours." *It should have been Lucian's*. Tears sprung to her eyes at Lucian's name.

As he lowered himself, she tensed.

"Will it hurt?" she asked.

He paused, staring. "What?"

"I don't...I haven't...."

"Oh." He kissed her again. "I'll be gentle. Tell me if it hurts."

He entered her slowly to ease in. It hurt, but there was a pleasure in the pain.

His lips were on her throat, their bodies pressed together. "Are you alright?" he asked in her ear. She nodded.

He lifted himself until he was almost out of her and thrust again.

"Markus." Unable to hold back her gasping moans she clung to him.

His movements became faster, as she drove up to meet his thrusts.

"Tell me again," he grunted.

"I'm yours to command," she rasped, hoping it was the right words. "My body is yours." She gasped as he filled her again. "I'm yours."

Her last words had an effect on him. "You're mine." He repeated, his words coming out in a low grumble.

She neared climax again, her back arching. "Markus." His name came out in one long moan.

His thrusts were hard and fast. Her release approached quickly. His followed soon after, and he collapsed onto her.

Breathing hard, she twisted her fingers through his hair. Their bodies slick with sweat, pressed together, heaving in unison. Fine tremors ran through him, his head on her chest.

Chapter 35

Thoughts of Lucian pierced her heart. Last night washed over her, along with grief and guilt. Raven opened her eyes, hot tears spilling over. *I should be married by now.* Markus lay on his stomach, still asleep, his usual hostility gone, replaced by a peaceful expression. She reached towards his face but stopped. She liked this side of Markus. Almost vulnerable instead of the Enforcer.

She grasped the end of her braid, hair messy from the night before, and untied the yellow ribbon. She looped it around her fingers, no longer holding the sorrow back. *Lucian, I can't deny myself for a ghost. I'm sorry. He's here, you're not.* She rolled away from Markus, placing the ribbon on her side table.

CHAPTER 35

Daylight streamed in around the shutters as she sat up. Raven caught sight of Markus's back and gasped. Scars that she hadn't seen last night, criss-crossed across his back and without thinking, she traced her fingers over them. He moved under her touch, a smile on his lips. Her fingers stilled.

"That feels nice," he said. "Keep doing it."

"What happened?" she traced her fingers across the most noticeable line.

"Have you never seen the scars of a whip?" he murmured sleepily.

"You were whipped?" she asked horrified.

"Five lashes from an Enforcer when I was fifteen. I was caught stealing." He held up his hand, and her eyes were drawn to his pinkie. At least, what was left of it. Half of the digit was missing. She hadn't noticed that before. "He wanted to remove my whole hand. I'm grateful it's not my sword hand."

"Yet you became an Enforcer?" she challenged.

He opened his eyes, meeting hers.

"Sometimes our paths take us in directions that surprise even us," he spoke slowly. "My father was a peasant; my becoming an Enforcer was unexpected, even to him."

"Would you whip someone?" She couldn't hold back her curiosity.

"Never." He lifted his head. "Come here."

He pulled her to him, turning her around and wrapping his arms around her. She sighed in contentment.

"You sound pleased with yourself." His breath tickled her ear.

"Last night was unexpected," she admitted.

He nuzzled her, nipping her ear. "I can make you happy again this morning."

Desire for Markus filled her, and she wanted more. The memory of his words last night sent shivers through her. "Can we just stay like this for a moment?"

"Anything you want." His lips on the back of her neck brought back heat, his arms wrapped around her tight.

"All this time?" she asked. "You wanted me even though we loathed each other."

"Are you going to pretend you didn't want me too?" He kissed her shoulder.

"I didn't," she said.

He chuckled.

She rolled over to face him. "You have a lot of confidence in yourself."

"Maybe I just recognise hidden lust when a woman claims to despise me," he boasted.

"You're ruining the moment." Raven started to sit up.

"I'm sorry," he said. "Stay." He pulled her back towards him.

She didn't fight him, as they lay face to face, their eyes locked. Caught in his embrace, her heart pounded as she wrapped her arms around him. The warmth made her drowsy.

"Don't let me fall asleep," she murmured. She was forgetting something.

"Don't fall asleep," he said.

An annoying thumping cast Raven into confusion. She groaned, but it continued.

"Go away!" She tried to crawl back into sleep.

Markus shook her. "Raven, someone is at your door."

She sat up. "I told you not to let me fall asleep."

He smiled. "Sorry, I was busy falling asleep myself."

"Stay here." Raven pulled on yesterday's tunic and trousers, moving towards the door. "What?" she demanded, opening the door.

Tobias opened his eyes wide. "Did you not receive my invitation?"

Damn. She had forgotten she was supposed to be up early to go to his house. "I'm sorry Tobias, it slipped my mind. A lot happened yesterday and..."

His eyes darted behind her. She followed his gaze to find Markus wearing only trousers walking towards her.

"I can see that. So, you favour your guard then. That explains a lot," he said, with disappointment in his tone.

"Not for much longer." She grumbled. "It seems he doesn't know how to follow simple instructions." She glared at Markus. "Give me a moment." She said to Tobias. "I will accompany you, if your invitation is still open."

"Perhaps another day," he said with a forced smile. "I'll leave you to your protector."

He turned to leave.

"Tobias?" She called him back.

"Yes?" He glanced over his shoulder at her.

"This doesn't change our current business?" she asked.

He smiled. "A true businesswoman. I am a man of my word; I do not back out of deals."

She closed the door. "Why did you do that? I told you to stay," she grumbled at Markus

"Your hostility has returned," he noted.

"Because you could have cost me a high-paying customer. Why couldn't you have listened to me?" she demanded

"In case you haven't forgotten, someone tried to kill you in here last night," he reminded her.

"You don't need to remind me of that." She walked towards her bed.

"Then let me do my job. Let me keep you safe," he offered.

Raven picked his tunic from the floor and threw it at him. "Then do it fully dressed. You're out of uniform, Enforcer Markus."

"I want a new uniform," he said. "One which doesn't involve clothes at all."

She stared at him. "You're impossible!"

"With the Lord after your cousin, I should stay with you. I do have my orders. I'm not sure he quite meant *this,* though." His face lit up.

She'd forgotten about Zac.

He watched her. "I saw that look yesterday. You don't believe it was him. Even though he was recognised."

"I *know* it wasn't," she affirmed.

"Who else would it be then?" he asked. "Unless he has a twin no one knows about."

His words were meant in jest, but he couldn't know how close he was.

She glanced at Markus, taking in his open concern. As much as she wanted to confide in someone, she couldn't. She had lived with her mother's fear of what would happen if anyone were to discover their connection to the killers of Kempschester. No one knew what really happened, but rumours had still spread across the country. The way he met her gaze set off a concern within her.

"I just know he wouldn't hurt anyone," she said finally. "Not without reason. Whoever saw him was mistaken."

"Is that what you're sticking to?" he asked.

"What do you mean? It's the truth." Her voice trembled.

Uncomfortable under his stare, she turned away.

"Which twin was his father?"

Raven's heart leapt to her throat, and she spun around. "Excuse me?"

"I know of the killers of Kempschester. The Shadow of Death, and Grim the Reaper. You and Zachary are their children."

Raven tried to feign innocence. "The killers of Kemp…What are you talking about?"

His tight smile suggested he wasn't falling for it.

"I'm going to tell you what I think," he said. "Someone mistook Zachary for his father, or yours."

Raven clenched her jaw together to remain silent.

He reached for her hands. "Raven, my father was there. He told me stories of the Blake twins my whole life. One of the brothers killed the other, then was hit by lightning. My father is not sure how anyone would survive that. Or how he disappeared into thin air afterwards, before he burned down all of Kempschester."

Raven pulled her hands from his. She couldn't talk to him of Shadow Realms or Darkness. "Do you hear yourself?" she asked. "You sound mad." To her own ears, her denial was weak.

"You can trust me," he said. "I already know everything. I won't tell anyone. You don't have to carry such a dark burden any more. What is it you're afraid of?"

"That there is the same Darkness in me," she blurted before she could stop herself.

Markus caressed her cheek, tucking loose strands behind her ear. "That is what you fear? That you are like your father?"

She'd said too much, but it was too late to take the words back. "I killed a man and felt nothing. No remorse."

Understanding filled his eyes. "You killed a man that would have killed you. That's not Darkness, that's survival. You shouldn't feel guilty about surviving. You didn't seek to kill him, he attacked you."

The desire to tell him everything almost had words spilling over, but she held back. "I'm scared," she whispered.

His arms wrapped around her, the closeness a comfort, as was his warmth against her. She leaned against him, tears spilling over.

"You're not like your father." He tightened his embrace. "I see a beautiful, passionate woman who worries about Darkness. If it were in you, there would be no fear of such things."

His words made sense. She didn't imagine Death worrying about such things. She leaned into his embrace, trying to shrug off her fears. Just having his arms around her helped. Strong arms, warm body, she smiled.

Finally, she lifted her chin, meeting his eyes. "Your father?" she asked.

"He was a servant and worked in the house of Lord Samson. He often saw Thomas and tended to his brother in the Enforcer quarters once. The day Thomas was to be executed, the servants weren't allowed in the courtyard, so watched everything from the window. They fled as Kempschester burned."

"How did you find us? You ended up in the same town we did?" she asked with suspicion.

"No. We ended up a few towns over. But your cousin passed through one day, five years ago, meeting with blacksmiths. My father recognised him immediately. He thought The Shadow of Death had come for him, something he had feared for twenty years."

"Then you end up as an Enforcer here? Were you watching him? Or me?" Betrayal burned through her.

"I followed Zachary to make sure he wasn't who my father thought he was."

"You followed him?" Her pitch rose. "Were you following me, too? Is that why you somehow became my guard?" *I was an idiot.* She pulled away and pointed to her bed. "And that? What was that?"

He met her eyes. "That was me giving in to something I wanted since the day we met. I could not deny what I felt for you. That was real, Raven. You can trust me."

"Can I?" She shook her head. "I was starting to. Why would you go through all of this?"

"My father was scared." Markus sighed. "He's been haunted by nightmares since that night. Word spread that Thomas wasn't finished with the people of Kempshire, and that any survivors were cursed. He's been waiting for Thomas's shadow to darken his doorstep for twenty years."

"What is your plan, then?" she asked. "You took on a job, to protect the daughter of a murderer. What were you going to do if he showed up?"

"I hadn't thought that far," he admitted.

"I don't think you knew what you were in for. Thomas isn't just Thomas. He's both of them," she revealed.

Confusion clouded his eyes. "Both of ...?"

She sighed internally. She had said too much, but it was too late now. "The twins. My father and my uncle. Something happened when the lightning struck, and Thomas and his brother became one being."

"I thought Thomas killed Graeme?" he asked.

She nodded. "He did. My mother heard my father tell her to run, right before the lightning hit. Zac heard the same, then he heard my father telling Thomas to kill them all."

"Is that where he got his ...?" He pointed to his eye.

Raven nodded.

"So, how do we stop him?" he asked.

Raven laughed. "Stop him? He calls himself Death, there is no stopping him. You wouldn't even be able to contain him, he'd just vanish right into The Shadow Realm."

The helplessness settled over her. There was no way to escape her father if he came for her. Whatever he had done with Zac was probably in store for her.

"Do you believe he would hurt you? Or Zachary?" Markus asked.

Zac. What if he's dead? "I do. He's already done something to Zac he's not himself. I don't know how to help him, or if he wants my help." A spark of defeat lit within her. Determined not to give up, she pushed it down.

"Where is he?" Markus asked.

"He's in The Shadow Realm," she said.

"Then we find a way to get him out," he stated.

"You think I haven't already tried? I have no way in without Death, and it's not as if he will let me walk out with Zac."

"Then let me come in with you," he offered.

She laughed. "And do what? He'd gut you and leave you there without a second thought, and probably go after your father."

She moved away from Markus. It was a relief to share her secret with someone, but she should have kept silent. Death had told her there would be a fight between her and Zac, one that she would lose. If Markus tried to intervene, it would not end well for him.

"This isn't your fight," she told him.

"I think it became my fight the moment he killed someone in a town I have sworn to protect. From what I know about him, where there's one body, more will follow." He reached for her. "Let me help you, Raven."

"You can't. The best thing we can do is run, as mother did with Zac twenty years ago."

"You would run?" He asked in disbelief.

She sighed."Run, hide, disappear, it doesn't matter, he'd still find me."

"This is a small town compared to Kempschester. The people here have no idea what's about to happen. Do they not deserve a fighting chance? To know of the Darkness blanketing their home?"

"You want to tell the townsfolk that the Killer of Kempschester, the Shadow of Death is here? Do you not realise the panic that would cause? There's nothing I can do," she said.

"If you do nothing, then you're right, there is Darkness in you," he pointed out.

The words were like a slap. His eyes darkened as he watched her.

"I understand your father's fear. But he and you aren't like us. like me. I am the daughter of half of Death. Zac is the son of the other half. That's different to surviving like your father did. My mother was married to one of them. She loved him. But I've grown up on her fear. Stories of black eyes and The Shadow Realm and of Darkness."

"You don't strike me as someone who would run. You would defend these people. Isn't that why you had your cousin train you? To defend yourself, and people who can't protect themselves?" he asked.

He had a point. It wasn't in her to turn her back on people over her own fear. But at that moment, her fear was for him.

Chapter 36

Raven walked through what should be a town. Burned buildings, ash, and blackened bones surrounded her. Their deaths echoed, screams that she felt within her soul. Kempschester. A town she had never seen, but there was no other that could show such destruction and death. Why am I here? Is this a dream?

This is where Death's Descendants will fight. This is where you will fall, by his hand.

Pure Darkness, the voice came from everywhere and nowhere all at once. Swords clashed and she followed the sound into a courtyard. Two people fought. Zac, his eyes white, black lines across his face, wisps of Darkness rising off him. The other was her, as Death watched, a smile on his face. Her brother had taught her everything she knew; he would know every move before she did.

Death's eyes met hers. "Prepare yourself," he said. "It is your time."

Ice gripped her heart.

"Tell me where Zac is," she said. "This doesn't have to come to pass. Let me bring him home."

The town around her shifted to that of a village. Burned ruins and just as in the streets of Kempschester, the dead lay as bones. Everything was destroyed, yet a stable remained. Drawn towards it, she walked in, to find two men facing her. She froze, but their conversation continued; they didn't react to her presence. Death smiled at her cousin.

"I'm proud of you, my son," he said to Zac. "You have made the right decision."

Zac was different, as he had been in the courtyard, his arms covered in the same black lines. There was no warmth in the smile he returned to his father, but a dark surrender had taken place.

"Zac?" Unseen, she got closer. "Oh, Zac, what has he done to you? I'm sorry I couldn't help you."

"I'm not." His voice wasn't spoken but whispered within her. "You'll resist, but it won't be long before you yield."

"Yield?" She took a step back. "Yield to what?"

Death turned his gaze onto her. "To me, daughter. To the Darkness already wrapped around your heart, embedded in your very soul. You know where we are; what will you do?"

"No!" Raven sat up in a panic, pushing Markus away to climb out of bed. Heart breaking, tears fell down her cheeks. "No, Zac."

"Raven, what is it?" Markus stood in front of her, gripping her arms. "What happened?"

Unable to form the words, tears streamed down her cheeks. Six months had passed and she was no closer to freeing Zac.

"Raven, you're alright. You're safe." He pulled her into an embrace, his arms a comfort. "I'm here." He murmured. "Tell me what happened."

"It was a dream." She whispered. "A village that burned, Riverwick. Zac was there…with him."

"Him? Your father," he commented.

She shuddered. "Don't call him that."

She pressed her head into his chest, relieved as his arms tightened around her.

"Zachary, you think he's at Riverwick?" he asked.

"I know he is. I've lost him." The loss of her brother resounded within her chest, her heart breaking. "Oh, Zac, why?"

Markus frowned. "Lost him? He's dead?"

"No, worse: He's given in to Darkness."

"Then we go and get him." Markus lifted her chin. "We bring him back and free him from the Darkness."

A spark of hope quickly died. "I don't know if there is a way to free him. Once Darkness has him, it won't let him go."

"So, you'd give up on him?" he challenged.

His words reminded her of everything Zac had done for her. His protectiveness, and how he would never give up on her.

"I don't know how to get to Riverwick." she admitted. "I cannot ask my mother. I believe it would break her entirely."

He considered her words, his eyebrows drawn together.

"Then we'll ask my father. He'll know the way to Kempschester. We can find Riverwick from there," he said, his words giving her a flicker of hope.

"You'll do that? You'd help me bring Zac back, with no guarantee that it will work?" she asked.

He nodded, smiling down at her. "I know how important he is to you. We won't know unless we try."

The dream hadn't let go of her yet. Fighting Zac. She wanted to deny that it would happen, but unable to, fear crawled across her skin. The familiar shiver on the back of her neck was enough to convince her: One of them would die. Death had told her to prepare. To think about raising a sword to her cousin, the one who would do anything to protect her, went against her instinct.

"I need you to teach me how to fight," she said.

Markus's eyes widened. "I thought you already knew how to fight."

"I know the way Zac taught me. But if I'm to fight him, I will need something new. Teach me to disarm someone without killing them."

Chapter 37

Zachary had battled the apparitions that Darkness threw at him for an eternity, and it wore at him. Long moments of empty nothingness stole his existence, and it took longer each time he returned to remember his life outside of The Shadow Realm. The hope he clutched at with desperation that he could escape, had long since withered. Darkness clawed at his heart, trying to find a way in and his strength to fight it waned. Unsure if he had ever existed beyond Darkness, he fell to his knees.

The constant night, dark fog, and strange blue light of the moon were always there every time he opened his eyes. He couldn't sleep without dreams being invaded by the same visions. Tears streamed down his cheeks as he shook with exhaustion.

"**Isaac.**" The voice came from the dark again.

"Please, stop," he begged. *I can't take this any more.* He kept his eyes down, not wanting to see who it was trying to pass as this time. The worst it showed him was a dark version of Raven, over and over again. Her black eyes revealed an absence of humanity, a cold smile. He didn't know what was real any more or if he was Zachary or Isaac. This had been a slow torment. "I'm *Zachary,*" he told himself, again collapsing completely. "Zachary Blake. No. Zachary *Dale.*" He repeated the name, fighting to hold on to who he was.

He rolled onto his back, arm covering his eyes.

"Father, please," he called out again, knowing it was pointless. Helplessness stung. "Please, just kill me."

"Little Zac." This voice was human, without the echo of Darkness. He lifted his arm. Hector stood over him.

"What do you want?" he demanded. Hector's presence was a constant reminder of what he had done.

"I need to leave; the other place is waiting for me," Hector said.

He sat up. "What other place?"

"I don't know. I belong *there,* not here." He studied Zachary. "You were once like a son to me. If I had known you'd be my captor, my killer… I would never have welcomed any of you into my life."

The years in which Hector had been a father figure flashed before him. He had lost both his parents, but Aunt Amelia had taken him in. She hadn't known how to handle his rage, nor the fights he started with other children of the village. Hector had been so patient and kind. Every time Zachary got in trouble, Hector had accepted responsibility for him. Everything changed for him when he began training.

"I'm sorry, Master Hector." He bowed his head. "You don't deserve this."

Hector stood over him, anger darkening his face. "Something is clearly tormenting you, and it won't be long before you fall into whatever Darkness has a claim on you. You're on the verge of madness, I can see it in your eyes."

The Darkness had said the same. Unsure if Hector was real, Zachary struggled to his feet, stumbling away.

"Don't turn your back on me, you little monster. You put me here, you're the one holding me here."

Darkness pressed in around him again, gripping his heart. Hector no longer stood before him. Zachary had returned to the darkest centre of The Shadow Realm. There was a calm closing in. After months of fear and struggle, he yearned for that calm. "**Stop fighting. All this will cease when you surrender.**"

"Leave me be," he pleaded. Fog twisted around him, tightening its grip. "Raven, Aunt Amelia, I'm sorry."

He sought his sister out, finding her in his shop, locked in training with Markus. A bright light shone from the Enforcer, with a blue glow. Raven, pale yellow, but a dark fire burned from deep within. She lifted her eyes to the Enforcer, her face lighting up.

"Do you see it?" This time it was Uncle Graeme that stood before him.

"That's the Darkness she fears that she would inherit from you," Zachary said.

Uncle Graeme's smile was that of satisfaction. "To see that, it means you've let it in."

"I just want it to stop," he pleaded. "It torments me, and it never stops."

"You know how to make it stop. How much more will you take before you go mad?" Uncle Graeme asked.

It surprised him to see Raven smiling at Markus. *How did she warm to him so quickly? Did Raven give up, or is she still trying to find a way to free me?* If she had, perhaps it was a good thing. He wasn't sure he could trust himself.

"I see the effect Darkness has taken on you. I do not think you will know how much until it's too late," Uncle Graeme noted.

Zachary wanted to deny his uncle's cruel words, but there was truth in them. Death's words. After all this time being surrounded by Darkness, it had found its way in. A deep cold seeped into him, and he wasn't the same as he had been. The Touch of Death would make him a risk to those he loved. "I don't want to lose myself," he said. "I won't let it in as you did." He held his hand up, the one that had taken Hector's life. "I won't use it."

Death took on his father's face and grasped his shoulder, almost tenderly.

"I know it hurts, and you're tired of fighting. You know how to make it stop. Give in to it. Turn away from Raven, and welcome what you are now. You cannot go back, anyway, not while you are hunted."

Defeat was the only thing Zachary had felt in a long time. And hopelessness. If he could get home, he wasn't sure he would remember how to be Zachary any more. All he saw was never-ending torment, without peace. There was only one way to stop the never-ending struggle.

The last of his defence slipped. Darkness crashed over him like a wave, washing away his fight and everything he still held on to. He no longer possessed the strength to push it back. The calm was welcoming, and he gave in to the dark, cold energy that flooded him. Black lines crept around his arms, like those on his father's.

"Show me what I'm supposed to do," he whispered.

He turned his back on Raven, letting the shadows close around him.

Triumph crossed his father's features. "Who are you?"

Zachary Dale. The name seemed unfamiliar, like it didn't belong to him. There was another name, rising up to the surface. One he hadn't used since he and Aunt Amelia had run from Riverwick. "I am Isaac Blake," he said, his voice low, with a slight echo. "I am the son of Death."

"Are you ready to release Hector? Let him have the peace he seeks."

"I am." He hesitated. "Will you show me how?"

"You *know* how. But just this once I will guide you. First, call Hector. Summon him to you."

"Hector." The name came out of him a whisper that echoed in The Shadow Realm.

The man who he had once looked up to, his mentor, appeared before him.

"Zac? What happened to you?" Hector asked. His eyes landed Isaac's father. "You!"

"I will take you where you want to be," Isaac said.

Hector smiled. "Maria."

"You are not mortal; you no longer belong in the mortal realm," Isaac's father said to Hector, then turned to Isaac. "Put your hand on his shoulder, and I will guide you both to The Crossover," his father instructed him. "But next time, you're on your own."

Isaac was distracted. Something connected him to Hector, and the need to release him grew. It had been there the whole time. "I think I can feel the way," he said.

"Then go. I'll follow you."

The fog and darkness around them disappeared, replaced by a feeling of peace. Opposite to the never-ending gloom of The Shadow Realm it was filled with a soft warm glow. A world that didn't want him. Pressure pressed against him, like a current, pushing him towards The Shadow Realm."What you feel is because you are still amongst the living. Release Hector," his father instructed him.

"Where are we?" Hector asked.

"This is The Crossover," his father said.

"Here you will find peace," Isaac said. "Maria will join you here when it is her time. You're home. I release you."

"Thank you." Hector's smile was wide.

"We must go," his father said. "Can you feel The Shadow Realm?"

The Shadow Realm pulled at him. "I can; it feels like it's calling to me."

"It is. Allowing the Darkness in, you'll always be able to find The Shadow Realm, and find your way back."

Isaac let the shadows pull him back, engulfing him.

"Do you still wish to go home?" his father asked.

Home. Images of his family filled his head. Children he had never known. A woman, Aunt Amelia… his aunt. His cousin, no, sister…Raven. For so long, all he had wanted was to return to them, to escape the pressing dark of The Shadow Realm. But he had been in the dark so long that that life seemed like it was someone else's, or a dream. There was no going back. Releasing Hector had changed something within him, and he understood his purpose. "I *am* home," he said.

A low chuckle came from his father. Triumph flickered across his face.

"You will have to go to the mortal realm when you hear the call."

"The call?" He had no clue what that was.

"Souls of those to die will call to you. You will answer that call, you won't be able to resist." Father looked at his face. "Your face shows the Darkness within you. Your good eye is white. That will alarm many people. You'll need to learn to control that."

The idea of causing fear to people filled him with glee.

"Let them be alarmed," Isaac said.

"No," his father said sternly. "To walk among them, you must look like them. You must look human."

"I do not want to walk among them," Isaac muttered.

His father's eyes were on him. "It is necessary."

He met his father's gaze without flinching. "You could change your shape, yet you chose to show your Darkness. Your shadow self."

"My desire to live among them is no more, but you must learn to contain yours. That is how you will control your Touch of Death," his father told him.

"Then how do I?" He still didn't care about what his father was telling him.

"Can you feel the Darkness inside you?" His father put his hand over Isaac's chest. "In there. Call it all inside you. Summon it to respond to you."

Isaac tried as instructed. and nothing happened. His father laughed, a sound similar to the laugh he knew.

"It's alright. It took me a few years to gain control of that," his father said.

After years of seeking out his father, he had finally found a connection with him. His father was different, but the man he knew was still there, just a darker version of him.

"Is this why you trapped me here? So I'd become like you?" he asked.

"No. I trapped you here because your desire to connect with a father that ceased to exist was a constant reminder of who I used to be. But when I saw Darkness trying to win you over, I saw a way we could connect without you attempting to remind me of Thomas Blake."

"But you said, yourself, you're still him." Isaac pointed out. "You still refer to me as your son."

"I was Thomas and Graeme. But now I am Death. I have my purpose, and it is not to live as a mortal man, as the father you refused to mourn. Now, you have your own purpose. You must let go of your own connections within the mortal realm."

*Am I ready to let go of...*he tried to recall names. *Aunt Amelia and Raven. Delia.* The boy with the brown eyes, his son. He cared little for what his father called the mortal realm, but his attachment to his family wasn't quite gone. The Darkness had created some kind of connection between the two, her presence at the edge of his mind.

"I can sense Raven," he admitted.

Father smiled. "That does not surprise me. We had a connection; I believe the Darkness has opened something similar between the two of you."

"We are to fight," Isaac recalled.

"Not yet, but soon. Come with me." His father's arm gripped his shoulder, and The Shadow Realm vanished.

His heartbeat started, and he held a hand up to his chest. "Why does it do that?"

"The Shadow Realm is a realm of the dead, not living." Father pressed his hand to his own chest. "Mine has not beaten for many years. Yours will soon cease as you spend more time in The Shadow Realm."

Before Isaac could answer, he realised where he was. "You brought me back to Riverwick?"

Chapter 38

As they prepared to leave, worry churned in her stomach. She didn't want to be responsible for leading him to his death. *What if he wasn't in my dream because he was already dead? I've already seen one man I care about die. I cannot watch another.*

The idea of enduring that loss again overwhelmed Raven. Pain over the loss of Lucian still pierced her heart, despite her growing feelings for Markus. *I cannot put myself through that again.*

"I don't think you should go," she pleaded with him.

"Are we having this conversation again?" Markus shook his head. "I am not about to let you go alone. It is too far for you to ride unaccompanied."

"I don't want you to come with me," she said. "I release you from being my guard. You should return to your Enforcer duties."

He lifted the saddle onto Lance, ignoring her words.

"Did you hear me?" she demanded.

"I heard you." He still didn't look at her.

"You're not coming with me," she repeated.

"You don't have a say in this, Sunshine." His stern glare had returned. "Lord Gerard has already granted me leave. You are my duty, and I will be going with you, whether you want me to or not." He finished with the saddle and turned to face Raven, lifting her chin. "I know you're scared; I just want to protect you."

"Your duty?" Raven shook as she pushed his hand away. "I'm not your duty. You think because we share a bed, I'm yours to protect. You're wrong. I don't need you."

She eyed his horse, yet to be saddled.

"I see we're back to this," he grumbled. "This is going to be a long journey."

Raven mounted her horse.

"What are you doing?" he demanded. "I'm not ready yet."

"You're not coming," she said.

He forced a laugh. "Get off the horse, Raven."

"Go back to Lord Gerard. I will not pay you for your services any more."

She pushed Lance into a gallop, leaving Markus behind, holding back tears. It would have been a comfort to have him with her, but Death had shown her he had no hesitance in killing.

"Raven!" Angry curses followed her.

She didn't look back, determination set in. It would take him time to ready his horse, giving her enough of a head start to face Zac and Death alone before he could interfere or get himself killed.

I won't let him die because of whatever curse plagues my family. The idea of another loss was too much to bear. *I made a mistake letting him into my bed. I should have just asked for another Enforcer, anyone but him when Lord Gerard told me of the murder.*

The cool wind whipped around her cloak and she pulled it tight, putting as much distance as she could between herself and Markus, hoping yet doubtful that he would not follow. His interest in money had brought him to her; she was unsure whether her threat to cease payment would be enough for him.

Reflecting on her haste, a spike of regret made her question her decision, but it was too late to turn back. Instead she urged Lance forward. She wouldn't be able to keep the horse at this pace for long, but time was everything.

She reached a stream, and she paused, allowing Lance to drink water, watching over her shoulder. She grabbed an apple from the saddlebag. As she bit into it, the crunch brought a smile to her face. A memory of Zac bringing her basket of apples overwhelmed her.

"Raven?" Zac's voice had a hint of amusement in it. His footsteps were loud as he walked into the house.

"I'm in the kitchen," she called out.

His footsteps led towards the kitchen. In one hand, a basket filled with apples, as he bit into an apple in his hand.

"Where did you get those from?" she asked. "Have you been stealing again?"

He rolled his eyes. "You always think the worst of me!"

"No, I know you." She grinned at him. "You can't help yourself."

Zac put on an offended face. "I haven't stolen since..." He stopped, as if trying to remember. "Well, last week." His smirk crept across his face. "But this time I cannot take credit for this. These are a gift."

He placed the basket on the table in front of her. At the top was a yellow rose, and a red one. Her heart pounded. She knew what this meant. He crunched on the apple again, and she couldn't help but laugh. "You stole something meant for me."

"If I'm going to be the messenger, then I get something for my troubles. They're a good harvest, sweeter than last year's, try one."

Raven lifted an apple from the basket and put it to her mouth. "Who's it from?" she asked, eyeing the roses.

Her brother said nothing, only giving a small smile as he watched her. She bit into the apple. Juice ran down her chin, the apple crisp and sweet.

"Lucian," he said finally.

"The one you fight with?" she asked.

"He's asked that you give him his answer this afternoon. He will come by to take you horse riding."

She lifted the red rose from the basket and breathed in its scent. This was a meaningful gift, its intention clear. Lucian Carter wanted to court her.

Lance's movement brought her out of her memory. He'd finished drinking.

"We're a long way from Eskham now," she murmured, petting the horse's head. "I miss how simple life was. I was to be married, I had my family and had very little to worry about. Now Lucian's dead, Zac's in The Shadow Realm, and Mother's talking nonsense." She had never felt so lonely in her life. *My father is Death, he either wants to protect me or kill me, and I'm supposed to fight my cousin. I ran away from the only person left in my life I can talk to about this to face my own end alone. I'm an idiot.*

She hadn't got far when the sound of a horse galloping drew her attention. Without a backward glance she nudged Lance to pick up speed. Markus advanced, hooves thundering behind her.

He caught up quickly, his horse larger and faster.

"Stop the horse." His eyes glinted. "Raven. Now."

The edge to his voice indicated his serious mood. She pulled on the reins, bringing Lance to a stop.

"Off," he ordered.

She dismounted, fearful of his anger on display. Markus dismounted, and reached for something in his saddlebag.

When he pulled out the shackles, she took a step back. "Why did you bring shackles?"

"For your cousin. But right now, they have another use." The chains rattled as he turned to face her.

Before she could move, he marched over her and locked one cuff around her wrist. The metal was cold and heavy. He closed the other around his own wrist before taking her sword from her.

"What are you doing?" she demanded, trying to pull her wrist free.

"Now where you go, I go." His anger didn't appear to be cooling. He pointed to his horse. "Get on the horse, and we ride together."

"Why did you bring those?" she asked again, climbing on to his horse with care.

"Lord Gerard gave them to me so I could bring Zachary back." He connected the horses' lead ropes, and climbed onto his horse behind her.

"You...what?" her own voice was like ice, but heat flushed through her. "All that talk about proving his innocence. You told him?"

"He demanded answers, so I told him that you knew where Zachary was," he admitted.

"You lied to me." She had never experienced such hurt. "You've been playing me."

He sighed. "No, but I was charged with the duty to find Zachary. You were there when he declared it."

She wanted to yell, to cry, but it would do her no good. His actions were like a blow to the stomach. Instead, she remained silent.

"We're going to ride in silence?" he asked.

"I have nothing to say to you," she muttered.

His voice softened. "Raven, I'm sorry. I cannot go against orders."

She didn't respond, annoyed at his body pressed in against hers.

The breath he let out was noisy. "I see you're back to being difficult."

"Difficult?" she fumed. "I told you Zac was innocent, and you still seek to arrest him! Following orders?! Did anything have any meaning to you?"

His hands closed over her arms. "Yes. You did. You *do*."

She held up her hand encased in metal. "Then release me."

"I cannot do that," he argued.

"Stay away from me. Hedge-born yaldson." She hurled the worst insults she could think of at him.

"Raven..."

"Stop talking." The hurt buried deep in her heart.

"I understand your anger, but throw insults at me, not my mother. She was no prostitute, nor did she bear an illegitimate child. I'll give you your space."

"Give me my sword back," she grumbled.

"You don't need it; you have me," he said, with tenderness.

Chapter 39

It was strange being back in Riverwick. Isaac glanced at the orchards and empty fields he had run through as a young boy. This was once his home. His father led him to the stable that still stood.

"Why are we here?" he asked.

"Because I needed somewhere that no one would come looking," his father said, back in his natural shape, with the two different-coloured eyes. One black, and one white. "Locals think this village is cursed," he added. "They think the river is cursed, too, but that's just your cousin."

My cousin? Unsure what it had to do with Raven, he remained silent.

"No one will come here." His father glanced over his shoulder. "Unless he's stupid enough to because he thinks he'll find answers."

"You saw me?" Isaac recalled the feeling when he'd been here.

"I did. I tried to warn you away, but you wouldn't listen. I watched you from the door of the stable."

Isaac frowned. He hadn't thought much of the stable the day he had come here. He walked in. A large grey dog lifted its head, looking at him. It stood up, moving quickly towards Isaac. He stepped back as the dog pushed its nose into his face. He'd never seen a large dog this close before.

"**Hunter.**" His father's voice boomed, and the dog backed off.

The name sparked a memory. "Hunter?" he asked.

"Ever the loyal companion." His father's hand moved over the dog's head.

Isaac glanced down at the dog. "Does he remember me?"

"It seems he does. Follow me," his father instructed.

Isaac followed him to the back of the stable. There he found a familiar black horse with a white mane, and a white horse. Guinevere and Willow. The horses' eyes were black.

"I don't understand. How are they still alive after twenty years?" he asked.

"The Shadow Realm has extended their lives somewhat. And mine. It will likely extend yours, too," his father revealed. "You'll need a weapon."

"A weapon?" he repeated "Why?"

A black scythe appeared in his father's hand. "They're as afraid of this as they're afraid of me. It's made from the essence of pure Darkness. You'll need one of your own."

Isaac looked at the scythe. "For someone wanting to cut ties with your mortal life, you certainly keep connections to that life close. A scythe? The horse and dog?"

His father's head turned as if he heard something. "I have to go."

"Where?" he asked.

His father tilted his head, watching Isaac. "The dead call to me. Learn to access The Shadow Realm while I'm gone. Find your weapon." He climbed onto the back of his horse.

The horse and dog vanished when his father did; into The Shadow Realm.

With nothing left to do, Isaac wandered what remained of the village. He found himself at the graveyard, staring at the space where his mother was buried. There had been pain the last time he visited, but now there was nothing. A woman who died a long time ago, he couldn't recall her face.

"Raven is coming for you," his father said as he returned. "Her Enforcer is with her." A look of disgust was apparent on his face as he mentioned Markus. "Although I wouldn't say they're on friendly terms right now. She's not all that happy with him. If she brings him here, it will give me the perfect chance to kill him."

Isaac turned from the graveyard. "How does she know I'm here?" She hadn't given up trying to find him, after all.

"I showed her," his father admitted.

"You showed her? How?" he queried.

A cold smile crept across his father's face. "In a dream. While you struggled with Darkness, I let her see what you would become."

His father led him away from the graveyard, the horse and dog following behind.

"You can do that?" Isaac asked.

His father chuckled, a chilling sound. "I reach out from within The Shadow Realm. People can see me in their dreams, or what I want them to see. Many who were here that night dream of me." His smile was dark, with a hint of joy. "Remember the nightmares you had as a child?"

Realisation sunk into Isaac. He stopped, turning to face his father. "You forced nightmares on me?"

His father watched him closely. "That angers you."

It wasn't anger, but confusion that he felt. "You deliberately tormented a child, already traumatised by the loss of his parents and the sight of his father becoming something—"

"Of nightmares?" His father's laughter was not that different from what it used to be. "I wanted you to stop crying out for me. Every time you did, I heard it. You speak of me tormenting you, yet I was haunted by you. I considered killing you." He paused. "Do you think your dreams of my sword and journal were your own?"

"That was you?" he asked in disbelief.

"I was going to kill you. Then decided it would be more satisfying to bring you to The Shadow Realm instead."

"Is that why you brought Raven here?" He didn't want Raven to come to Riverwick. She would try to free him, when he didn't need her to.

"Not yet. Her turn will come." His father rubbed the muzzle of his horse. "The children of Death, reunited in Darkness."

They continued walking towards the stable.

"She will try to get me to go home," Isaac pointed out. "She doesn't give up easily. She's very stubborn." He shot a look at his father. "Like Uncle Graeme."

"Calm yourself," his father told him. "She cannot do anything. She needs to see you as you are."

They reached the stable. Guinevere returned to her stall. Isaac stood at the doorway of the stable.

"Is that where you went before, to make her dream?" Isaac wondered if her dreams she'd been so afraid of were caused by her father.

His father's smile was cold. "Duty called."

"You killed someone," he stated simply.

"Does that bother you?" his father asked.

"No," Isaac said, surprised. *It should bother me, shouldn't it?*

"Good." His father's approval shone through."Your time will come; you will feel drawn to your first kill."

"How will I know where to go?" Isaac asked.

"You'll know. It's hard to resist." His father put his hand on Isaac's shoulder. "I'm proud of you; you've made the right choice."

"The right choice?" He couldn't deny that his father's pride affected him.

"The same choice I did. To not fight what you are, what is in you. Raven will. My children were always going to. As will your children."

Arthur. Joseph. Giselle. Their faces flashed before him. "When?" he asked.

"Not yet. The Shadow Realm. Try again."

Isaac had found his connection to The Shadow Realm but had yet to gain control enough to enter without his father's help. He let the Darkness into his heart, reaching out for the energy.

"Do you see the veil?" his father asked.

"No," he admitted, deflated.

His father vanished, but he remained close by. The spark of Darkness connected them both. His father's presence was like a cold emptiness that nudged at him.

Find me. The voice was not spoken, a rush of whispers that he heard within his mind. For Isaac to hear that, meant that his father had taken on his other form. One that had once filled him with terror, given him nightmares.

He sought out the presence, tried to see through the veil. "I can feel you," he said. "I can feel The Shadow Realm. Why can't I—?"

His father returned, only for his fist to connect with Isaac's face. "**What good are you if you cannot find your own way in?**"

His father hit him a second time, the pain pulsing through his face. Anger flared in Isaac, fed by the Darkness inside him.

"Stop!" He fumed and took a swing.

Again, his father vanished before he could make contact.

"**Try again**."his father said, using his scythe to pull Isaac's legs out from under him. Laying on his back, breathing hard, Isaac gazed up at the cloudy sky. Finding the blade at his throat, he lay perfectly still, eyes on his father.

"You don't scare me," he grumbled.

"**Then you're an idiot.**" The blade pressed in. "**You are useless to me. I'll leave you here so Raven can take you home and bury you. You haven't given into the Darkness at all.**"

"No, please," Isaac pleaded. "I can do what you ask of me. Let me try again."

The blade pulled back, his father watching him. "**Get on your feet.**"

Climbing to his feet, Isaac glared.

"**Your eyes are white, Darkness shows across your face, but you haven't embraced it entirely. You hold on to something. Is it Raven? Or your children? Or that woman, Delia?**" his father taunted him, then swung his scythe again.

Isaac stepped back, throwing his arms up in defence. The scythe met his own with a thud. In his moment of desperation, he had called on a weapon identical to that of his father's.

He swung, and his father passed into The Shadow Realm again.

You've found your inner Shadow. His father's voice came from The Shadow Realm. **But is that all you can do?**

"Are you done hiding like a child?" Isaac taunted, stepping through the veil. His scythe vanished; a sword took form in his hand. He moved quickly, stepping forward with a thrust of the sword.

His blade pierced his father's shoulder. His father's shape changed, looking like Thomas again, staring down at the blade. "You *do* have it in you. Good." he looked up at Isaac. "You can remove the sword from me now."

Isaac removed the sword. "I'm sorry, I—"

"Don't panic. Blade or fire, I seem to be immune to the same mortality everyone else is plagued by. Of course, I had to die first, for that to take effect." he smiled at Isaac. "Now you've truly embraced Darkness. You followed me into The Shadow Realm like it was nothing, and it's wrapped around you."

Isaacs arms had deep black lines twisting around them, Darkness rising off him like it did his father. "Will I change shape like you?" Isaac asked.

"I don't know. Perhaps." His father turned as if listening. "Stay here."

"No!" Isaac said. "Let me come with you. If I'm going to take this on, you can show me how it's done."

His father smiled. "Very well."

In The Shadow Realm, the fog enveloped them completely. When it pulled back, his father stepped through the veil. Isaac remained where he was, watching as his father knelt over a figure on the ground. Dark flames that burned inside his father surrounded the two of them as his father used his Touch of Death. "That's what it looks like," he pondered out loud. *Will I know how to do it again?* Wanting to practise emerging from The Shadow Realm, Isaac stepped through the veil. It was a strange feeling, but he was getting used to it.

His mind clouded over. Something spoke to a deep part of him, his chest felt like ice. He let out a grunt, turning his head. A whispering started, as if someone were speaking to him.

"That's your calling," his father said, suddenly beside him. "Follow it."

Isaac returned to The Shadow Realm. "How do I know where to go?"

"Let The Shadow Realm take you where you need to be."

"Will you be with me?" Isaac asked, nervous.

His father's hand gripped his shoulder. Closing his eyes, he focused on where the whispering led him.

Stepping through the veil again, he found himself in the middle of a battlefield. Beside him, his father laughed. Isaac glanced at him, swords clashing, men screaming. A heavy patter of rain fell, hitting the ground, saturating him within moments.

"It's been a long time since I've been here. Your first calling…" His father didn't finish the sentence, instead shaking his head. "A battlefield." His laughter struck a chord in Isaac, a sound he remembered from years before. He couldn't help but smile.

They walked past the soldiers fighting. Isaac knew the way. "Why is it the dying we get called to?" he asked.

"Because they will soon enter The Shadow Realm," was his answer. "I take them to The Crossover so I don't have to endure their presence."

Isaac stood over a man. "I know him."

The man opened his eyes. "Zachary?"

"Gideon," he growled.

"Why are you here?" Gideon spoke as if words pained him. An arrow stuck out of his chest. "Who's he?" The soldier's eyes widened. "What's wrong with your face?"

"He is Death." Isaac said, kneeling. "My father. I am here because your fight is over."

Chapter 40

Cold wind tugged at their cloaks. Grey clouds separated them from the sun's warmth. She pressed a hand to her chest. Something was telling her to turn around, to return to Oakborough. A chill set in that she couldn't shake, the feeling that Zac was already lost.

Walls of a town rose from the horizon. The word 'Kempschester' hung from above an archway. Markus climbed off his horse, forcing Raven to do the same. He grunted as he tried to push the gate open.

"Do you need some help?" Raven laughed harshly.

Markus examined the large gate. "It won't budge. I don't know if something is blocking it, or if it's stuck. We'll try the other gate."

Kempschester was a large town, over twice the size of Oakborough. The ride around it was not a quick route. Trees and overgrowth had spread across what used to be a road. This close to the town, dread clawed deep within her, but she forced herself to ignore it. On the other side, they reached a large trench, filled with bones.

"I heard about this," Markus said. "My father said that during the pestilence there were too many dying, so they threw the dead in a mass grave."

She clenched her jaw at his attempt to hold a conversation as if he hadn't betrayed her and shackled them together.

The overwhelming sense of suffocating returned, and her legs buckled, but she caught herself. She'd felt something similar the night the French attacked, but less than what pressed against her now.

"Raven?" He cast her a look of concern.

She said nothing.

"Please Raven, if you're going to faint, let me help you," Markus offered.

"I'm not going to faint." She pointed at the bones. "There are more of them." She moved her hand towards the town. "In there. I can feel them." The screams of the dead were deafening.

"You feel them?" He eyed her with disbelief.

"It comes hand in hand with being the daughter of Death," she said, her voice still cold. "I hear the dead, feel their last moments. A curse he calls a gift."

He didn't move, his eyes filled with confusion. "There is a lot you haven't told me."

She raised her hand, rattling the chain between them. "You want to talk about that now? I was right not to tell you everything. Would you have told Lord Gerard that, too?"

"You don't have to continue with the hostility, Raven. Please, can we move beyond this?" he pleaded.

"No!" she snapped.

"Very well, then I'll drag you with me."

As he moved towards the gates, she dug her heels in. "I'm not going in there." Her instincts were screaming at her to leave and get far away from this place. Death's presence lingered here, the air heavy with danger. *Is this where Zac fights me?*

"alright, you're testing my patience." Markus wrapped the chain around his hand, and he pulled her to him. "I don't want to drag you, but I will."

"I'll walk." Raven narrowed her eyes at him as they passed through the destroyed gate.

The entire town was empty and silent. Their footsteps and the horses' hooves echoed on the cobblestones. Streets that should be full of people going about their day instead were filled with the bones of the dead. Buildings half in burned ruins, many were blackened and destroyed, while some had walls that still stood.

"My father described it; I could never truly grasp it until now," Markus said in a low voice.

Tears streamed down Raven's face. "So many people died here," she whispered. "I can feel it. Their pain and fear, it's suffocating. I can hear their screams."

Markus dropped the chain and cupped her cheek. With both his thumbs, he wiped at her tears. "It's alright." His stern expression softened. "You're here, with me. Anything that happened was twenty years ago." He tried to comfort her.

Her heart melted at his touch, but she wasn't ready to forgive him.

"We'll look at the estate; then we can leave." Markus stood over skeletal remains. "To burn to death, what a horrible way to die."

"Not all of them burned," Raven clarified. "Some people were running for their lives." Their fear crashed against her in waves.

Markus looked at the bodies around them. "He gave chase." His eyes widened. "He killed them all."

"Then he went to Riverwick," she affirmed.

Markus was horrified. "How did my father escape from this?"

An archway above them had a K on it with a coat of arms of a horse and sword.

"That will be the Lord's sigil." Markus said. "My father said he served Lord Philip for years, but his son Samson was Lord when this happened."

Raven froze. Dark energy pounded against her. "They died quickly here," she whispered.

"Lightning struck a man, then burst from him, no one would have had time to run," he replied.

"I think this is where he became what he is now." She talked more to herself than Markus.

"I thought he was already a killer." He frowned and turned towards the house.

"No, I mean, Thomas and…my father. They became one. Here." She pointed at rubble.

He stopped, turning back towards her. "They became one?" His eyebrows drew together. "I'm not sure I understand."

"I mean, my father, and my uncle, Zac's father, the Blake twins, merged. They became something that isn't quite human. Zac and my mother saw what he became, and they ran. Rumour spread across England about the Killers of Kempschester. People used to call him The Shadow of Death. He calls himself Death, and this is where he became that. A being of pure Darkness, hunting anyone who survived that night, and killing people all across England."

Except for Oakborough and Eskham. For some reason he had not been seen there. *Proof that he'd been watching us. Watching me.* A chill made the hairs on the back of her neck lift. Her cousin and mother had run, thinking they had escaped him. But his lack of presence should have been a warning.

"I believe you," Markus said. "That your father and uncle are…something. That you can sense the dead, or hear them, it makes sense. I cannot imagine what it would have been like, to grow up, knowing you were the daughter of such a being. A monster. I understand now why you said you were afraid his darkness was inside you."

She met his eyes, seeing his sincerity shine through. "Thank you." She smiled, melting a little more. "Can we leave? I don't like being here."

He nodded."I want to get a closer look at the house first." Markus said. "This is where my father worked. I would have been a servant, as he was."

Inside, debris was scattered around, walls blackened. They found their way to a large bedroom, mostly untouched by the fire.

"This is bigger than my entire house," Markus grumbled. "The rich really do live in luxury."

Light caught the blade of crossed swords hanging on the wall. Markus stopped in mid-step, staring up at them. He reached up, pulling one down, examining the blade.

"What are you doing?" Raven asked. "I don't think you should touch anything."

"Well, I don't think he'll be needing it," Markus said. A loud sound echoed down the hallway, and his eyes widened. Pale, he put the sword back. "Let's go." He led her quickly towards the door.

"What's the hurry?" she asked. "You forced me in here, now you want to leave?"

Markus shot a look over his shoulder. "I've realised that poking around in the house of a dead man might not be the best thing to do. What if he haunts this place?"

"Then he's going to be angry about you moving his sword." Raven glanced around the room. "He's not here. He died outside."

"You can feel that?" Shock flickered through his eyes.

"I can," she confirmed.

"Did you know people in your village would die?" he asked.

She froze. The question was unexpected. "Yes," she admitted. "I had a vision. Two, I think. But I knew something was coming."

"The one you were to marry… Did you know…" he stopped as if unsure how to finish his sentence.

Her heart raced. "You're asking me if I knew Lucian was going to die?"

He nodded.

"Yes," she confirmed. "I rushed towards him but I knew it was too late. I couldn't do anything but watch him die." This was the first time she'd talked about it since Lucian's funeral.

"You still grieve for him." There was no hurt behind his voice, only acceptance. His hand cupped her cheek and she leaned into it. "It's alright to grieve the ones we lose, the ones we love. I've noticed the yellow ribbon in your hair. Is that for him?"

The last of her rage collapsed. *He noticed.* "It was a ribbon to match the dress I should have worn," she murmured, another tear sliding down her cheek.

His thumb wiped away her tears. "You still call out to him in your sleep. You're not ready to let him go yet, are you?"

She shook her head.

"I'll be waiting, when you are ready. No matter how long it takes," he promised.

She wanted to be angry at him. She wanted to hate him. He certainly deserved it, but when he spoke this way it was difficult to hold on to anger.

He cast another glance around the room. "We should leave. I don't like standing in the room of a man whose death you can hear."

Markus led Raven from the room.

"You can ask me," she said. "You must be curious."

A heavy silence fell as he considered what she'd said. "You would tell me, if it was my death..." He shook his head. "I'm not sure I want to know. Not if there's nothing I can do about it."

"Wouldn't you want to fight it?" His acceptance of death intrigued her.

"I will fight hard to live, but we will all die eventually. When our time is up, it's up," he murmured.

In the courtyard, they retrieved their horses and the feeling of being watched returned.

"He's watching us," she whispered.

"That means he knows we're coming." Markus said. "Will he still be in Riverwick?"

"I don't know, but we have to go," she told him.

Markus glanced at the sky. "It will have to wait until morning; we need to take shelter. It will be dark soon."

Raven stared at him. "Not here!"

"There's a town nearby, Hazelbury, we'll go there," he said.

Leaving Kempschester, they rode towards the river. The walls of a town just below the mountains were noticeable. "Is that Hazelbury?" she asked.

"I think so. I was very young when my mother and father and I left. But Father told me Hazelbury was close to Kempschester. I think that's the Lord's manor." He pointed to a manor with high walls built into the side of the mountain.

"Do you remember anything?" she asked.

Markus shook his head. "Sometimes I think I do. Like feelings, and brief glimpses of memories I can't quite reach."

"Feelings?"

"Of feeling safe, protected. Loved."

Raven smiled. "What are the memories?"

"A woman's voice whispering my name and humming. A man with blue eyes looking down at me, I think my father. Him picking me up, talking to me." Markus's face filled with joy as he recalled his memories, but his smile faded quickly. "I can hear screams, and voices nearby filled with panic."

"When he chased people," Raven said, her eyes on Markus. "You remember that night."

His face had darkened. "I think so. I never had the same feelings after that. Father lived in terror that The Shadow of Death would find him, and we never escaped your father's shadow."

Zac had awakened that fear. "I'm sorry," she said. "My mother lived in the same fear, and Zac had his own memories of the event, and of his father. I grew up on their stories but could never talk about it. I never thought there would be anyone else living with that too."

As they approached Hazelbury, Markus turned his head towards the mountains. "I remember these mountains," he said. "There was snow on them!"

Raven glanced at the mountains. "I was born in Eskham. I have no connection to Riverwick, or Kempschester at all. No memories."

"Maybe it's good that you don't," he remarked. "You know your father for who he is now. Zachary's memories of his father interfere with acceptance of what he became."

"I worry about Zac. In my dream, he looked so much like his father," she said.

He turned his attention to her. "What do you mean?"

"His eyes were both white, with dark lines on his face. If he's been in The Shadow Realm all this time, what could it have done to him?"

As they approached the gates of Hazelbury, people stared at them, murmuring amongst themselves. No one stopped to talk, and Markus found the inn.

"Let's stay here for the night," he murmured. "We'll ride to Riverwick in the morning."

Tying their horses to the bar at the front, they walked inside.

Chapter 41

Tired from the day's riding, Raven lay on the bed, her arm over the side. Markus sat on the floor, his back against the bed. He had rejected her pleas to remove the shackles. She closed her eyes, and sleep pulled her from the room.

Once again she stood in the courtyard of the Estate. This time it was empty; fog surrounded her.

"Raven."

She turned at her name, face to face with her cousin. "Zac?" There was nothing left of him in the man that stood before her. No warmth or mischievous glint in his eyes, only emptiness.

"Did you know Aunt Amelia let me choose that name?" he asked. "It was the

closest name to my own I could think of. A child, choosing his own name," he scoffed. "I've been Zachary longer than I was Isaac. But I should never have turned my back on the name my mother gave me. Named for her brother, and my father. We are Blakes, Raven, you cannot escape that. You cannot escape who your father is."

"I know," she admitted.

He raised a black sword. "This is where we fight."

"We don't have to. We can just go home. Mother misses you. Please, Zac."

A shadow of his smile. "I never could walk away from a fight. Are you ready?"

Screaming ripped Raven from the dream, bringing her back to Hazelbury. Her wrist was bare, the shackle removed. She sat up. "Markus?"

His silhouette stood at the window. "Shhhh. Something's out there."

"What's happening?" she asked. "What are you doing over there?"

She climbed out of bed, joining him at the window. The panic of townsfolk rose in screams as they ran. Under the full moon she could see that a figure on a horse chased them, and the howl of a dog raised the hairs on her arms. The figure grasped a scythe in his hand. As he passed by their window, he stopped and turned his head towards them.

"Get down." Raven pulled Markus with her to the floor. "It's him!"

"I think he saw us," Markus murmured in her ear. "Him? You mean your father. He really isn't human. What is he?"

"Death," she reminded him. "I think he's here because of us."

Markus raised himself to look out the window.

"No, he's here tormenting the people. I can see someone on the ground; he's crouching over them."

Raven peered at the street below. "Did he kill them?"

"I don't know. But if this were our town, someone would have stepped in. Look, the townsfolk won't go near him. They only watch."

"They're terrified. Has he been tormenting them for twenty years?" The idea of it filled her with horror. "They're afraid that if they intervene, they'll invoke his wrath."

Markus crossed his arms. "How did he know we were here? He looked straight at us."

"He told my mother he can sense me," Raven admitted.

Markus helped Raven to her feet. "I don't know how to protect you against something like that."

She bristled at his words. "I can protect myself; I don't need you—"

"Not against him," Markus argued. "He's not a French soldier invading your village, Raven, nor a man in your shop. He isn't human."

As they watched, Death rose to his feet, and he and his animal companions disappeared.

Markus stepped away from the window. "He's not bound to our world. To fight him is a battle already lost."

"I fought him," she replied.

"And where did that get you?" He paced the room.

"Are you afraid?" she challenged him. "Do you want to leave?"

He pulled her to him. "That's not what I'm saying. I won't leave you, not now. I just don't know how to protect you from him."

She leaned her head on his chest.

"If I fall…" He stopped.

Raven pulled away. "Don't talk like that."

Markus grabbed her wrist and pulled her back to him. He kissed her, hard, his hand sliding up, gripping her arm tight. "I'm not trying to scare you. We need to prepare ourselves for what we're about to face if he comes after us. Or if Zachary has joined him."

"I've been afraid of this my whole life," she whispered, leaning into him. "I always thought it was something I'd have to face by myself. Or with Zac."

Markus's arms slid around her, his embrace a comfort. "You're not alone," he whispered into her ear. "When we find Zachary, we'll bring him home."

She could tell he didn't believe it, but she didn't care. "My brave Enforcer," she cooed.

"We have a long day tomorrow. Let's get some sleep." But the way he looked at her, it was unlikely they would get much sleep.

"This doesn't change where we are," she whispered.

"I know, and I meant what I said." His fingers lifted her chin, his touch light. "You can still give in to desire while your heart heals. I know you protect yourself." His hand rested on her chest. "You protect your heart. I understand."

She hesitated. "Markus?"

His breathing changed. "Mmm?"

"On your knees," she ordered. "I want your tongue…" She trailed off.

Understanding glinted in his eyes. He sank to his knees before she finished talking, and pulled her trousers down. His arms wrapped around her legs. With a widening grin, his lips pressed into her, then his tongue. Warmth tingled up her spine, racing to her core. As his tongue found the spot that sent fire burning through her body, she caressed his hair, and let out a moan.

"Good morning, Sunshine, have some breakfast." Fingers stroked her face, pushing her hair back.

With a groan, Raven opened her eyes to light shining in the room. Markus lay over her, his eyes warm, corners crinkling as he smiled at her.

She squinted. "You went to get breakfast?"

"No, they brought it up. No charge." He kissed her forehead. She screwed up her nose. "You are not a morning person, are you?" He laughed. "Although I cannot blame your exhaustion, we didn't get much sleep last night."

"Can you throw me my clothes?" she asked.

He stood, grinning down at her. "And cover such beauty?"

She attempted a smile. "You're right. I'll stay undressed." His grin grew wider. "Although, I'm not sure the townsfolk will like me riding like this through their streets. But I'm willing to try it if you are. Although I might get horsehair in my—"

"Enough!" His smile faded. "You made your point." He threw her clothes at her from the floor. "At least let me have my fun for a moment."

Once dressed, Raven moved towards the breakfast. Cinnamon, nutmeg, and porridge teased her senses. "Smells delicious. For what reason did we get a free breakfast?"

Markus took a seat, spooning pottage into a wooden bowl and passing it to her before pouring his own. Made of wheat cooked in milk, combined with cinnamon and honey, the breakfast had a sweet flavour.

"It could have something to do with a disturbance outside our window?" he hinted.

His expression was serious, but she caught the glint in his eyes. "Markus?"

He paused with the spoon at his mouth.

"Did you complain to get us a free breakfast?" she demanded.

He winked at her. "I may have mentioned that it sounded like someone was dying outside our window last night, and my woman didn't get a lot of sleep."

My woman. The words made her tingle. "Your woman?" she asked.

Markus flashed her a smile, leaning across the table and grasping her chin. "You caught that, did you?" He lost his smile. "Should I not have said that?"

"Don't look so worried." She laughed. "If you want to call me your woman, I won't stop you."

The grin on his face returned. Raven couldn't help but watch him as she ate. Their first meeting had been quite unpleasant; she would never have guessed she'd lay with him, or travel to Riverwick with him. With all the time they had spent together, there was no other way for them.

"I like you watching me, but eat, so we can go," he told her.

Chapter 42

Neither of them knew where they were going, and she was hesitant to ask anyone about Riverwick. Instead, they just followed a road, hoping for the best. The sun shone down, warm on her back. Tilting her head back towards the sky, she started to relax as the warmth seeped into her.

"You're not going to fall asleep, are you?" Markus's voice pierced her trance.

She sighed but said nothing, returning her eyes to the road. "Why is this taking so long? Are we going the right way?"

He pointed to signs. "Yes, that way."

It wasn't long before they caught sight of a village. "Is it Riverwick?" he asked.

She said nothing as they approached, until she saw that the village was completely destroyed. Burned. "This is it," she said finally. The feeling of death surrounded her once more.

"He burned his own village," Markus observed. "That is dark."

"His home had already been burned by then. The villagers turned on him. His uncle turned on him."

"He killed people. Including his own brother." Markus glanced at her. "Are you defending him?"

"No! Of course not!" She frowned. *Am I?*

The bones of villagers lay scattered around the village, just as in Kempschester.

"He ran them down here, too," Markus lamented. "He slaughtered his own people, in cold blood."

"This should have been where I grew up," she explained. "With my mother, Zac, and our fathers." They came across what looked like the ruins of an orchard, and barren fields.

Zac waited in front of them. "What are you doing here, Raven?"

He looked as he had in her dream. His voice had a slight echo to it, his face with black lines, Darkness rising from him like black smoke. She climbed off her horse and gazed into his white eyes. "Oh, Zac, no."

"Zachary is no more," he told her. "I am Isaac Blake."

She gasped. "You're using that name now?"

"It is my name," he said simply.

"Wait, he's Isaac?" Markus asked.

"Are you truly lost?" She ignored Markus's question.

His face remained expressionless. "Go home, little Raven."

"You don't call me that," she protested, annoyed that he would use her mother's name for her. "I've come to take you home." Her heart was breaking.

"I *am* home," he said.

Her heart sank. "No, this isn't your home."

He pointed to the ruins of a house. "I grew up there, in that house."

"Where is he?" she asked.

He gave her a cold smile. "Don't worry about our father." Zac's eyes rose to Markus, still on the back of his horse. "He's somewhat disappointed that you took an Enforcer to your bed. I can't say I blame him. Especially *that* one. Weren't you the one angry over the way he looked at you?"

"Who I choose to bed is none of your business, nor his," she said. "Zac, this isn't you."

"Isaac," he corrected. His eyes returned to her. "But it is," he said, taking a step forward. "And it will be you, too."

Horrified, she stepped back. "I would never give in to that," she whispered.

"The Darkness is already in you, Raven. I've seen it. It burns in you, a black flame."

"It clearly has a grip on you," Markus said from his horse. "Raven isn't that weak."

Zac laughed. "Weak? You think me weak? I can kill you *with a touch*." He stepped forward, advancing on Markus. "Didn't I tell you I'd burn your eyes out of your head if you looked at her again?"

"My gaze is not unwelcome as it once was," Markus said, dismounting his horse. He pulled the shackles out, and Zac let out a chilling laugh.

"Are those for me?" The black sword from her dream appeared in Zac's hand. "You'll die before you get those on me."

Raven stepped in between them. "Zac, please, I don't want you to hurt him." She looked up at Markus, into his eyes before turning her gaze back to her cousin. "It would hurt me if you did. I know you'd never hurt me, no matter what you become."

"Very well." He stepped back, his dark presence wavering. "Just leave, Raven, you've come all this way for nothing." Shadows closed around him, and he disappeared.

Markus reached for her. "Raven?"

"I've lost him, Markus. He's not Zac any more." She shook her head, trying to hold back the tears, and failing.

"You said your father took him to The Shadow Realm. Perhaps that changed him. If he was in there the last few months…"

"I never thought he would give in to Darkness." His words from years before whispered, a reminder. "When we were children, we often spoke of our fear of Darkness. We agreed that if one gave in, we would fight to bring the other back." She let out a breath.

"I don't understand why he sought out his father. Did he not know the monster he had become?" Markus muttered..

Raven glanced where Zac had been. "I can't give up on him. Markus, please."

He gave in to her. "What do you want to do?"

Before she could answer, something drew her attention. One of the remains of the houses drew her forward.

"What is it?" Markus asked with a hand to her shoulder.

"Of all the people who died in this village, the worst of it is here. A cold energy remains, like something that clings to the house. Or what remains of it."

"It is my daughter's death that you feel," Death said, his sudden appearance startling Raven. "Her essence remains, unable to leave this world, attached to this place."

"How is her presence so cold?" Raven asked him.

"You are drawn to it, aren't you? Is there anything else here you sense?" He answered her question with one of his own.

A strange whispering started, drawing her elsewhere. She stared in the direction she was being pulled.

"Follow it," Death instructed her.

She climbed on her horse, riding from the village.

"Where are we going?" Markus asked when he caught up with her.

"I don't know," she said. "There's something there; I have to see what it is."

They rode towards the forest. Something was drawing her forward, and she didn't understand what it was.

As they entered the forest, Raven shivered. It was dark, silent as a grave. Deer scattered from them.

"I wish I'd brought my bow." Markus muttered. "I didn't think there would be good hunting here."

The idea of venison appealed to her. "There would be no one to stop you, either. No Lord is sending scouts to stop illegal hunting."

They went deeper into the forest. "Raven, where are we going?" Markus's tone was sharp.

Finally, she stopped at the river. "The same as the energy at the house," she noted. "Cold, and dark."

"Your sister," Death said. "The very river she drowned in."

"Can you please stop doing that?" Markus demanded.

"Why do you follow us?" Raven asked.

Death said nothing.

Raven dismounted, moving towards the river. "Mother told me she drowned when the river flooded."

"She was claimed by the river, carried away. As that of her cousin, she remains here, the river her realm."

"The whole river?" Markus asked.

Raven put her hand in the water. "*She's become the river.* Do the people feel this?"

Death smiled. "They believe it to be cursed, something else they attribute to me."

"Why do I just sense her here, though?" Raven moved her hand through the water, hearing a child's laughter, followed by screams and fear.

"Do you feel anything else here?" Death asked instead.

His answering her questions with his own was starting to irritate her. But she glanced around. This whole area held pain.

"Someone died here," she whispered.

He changed shape, his eyes matching hers. The face of Graeme. Her father. "Do you feel who died here?" he pressed.

She looked around. "No. I can feel that it was two people." She pointed. "One over there, leaning against a tree."

"Reynold," he said. "He was a good man. An Enforcer, too."

"But you killed him, didn't you?" Markus said. "You don't seem all that worried that you killed a good man."

Death shot him a look before turning a smile on for Raven. "You feel his death, don't you? His final moments. Just as I did."

"I do. It hurt him that a friend was the one to take his life. He grieved for his family." She gazed down at the spot, tears running down her cheeks. She held a hand to her ribs, pain in her chest. "The sword pierced him, here. His own sword."

"Isaac has the Touch of Death, inherited from his father. You are drawn to it, as I was." Death commented.

"I've never experienced this before," she revealed.

"Because you've never been here before. Coming to Riverwick has created your connection with the deaths at my hands."

"Who was the other one?" Markus asked. "You said two."

Raven turned, drawn to a place not far from where Reynold had fallen. "Here," she said.

"What do you feel?" Death asked.

"Betrayal, then forgiveness." She pressed her hand against her abdomen. "The sword pierced here. I feel this one more." She let out a groan and fell to her knees.

Markus ran to her. "Raven!"

"I'm alright," she groaned, sweat lining her forehead. The pain was as if a sword really had pierced her. She glanced down, blood forming on her tunic, warm and sticky.

"That is not alright." Markus glared up at Death. "What did you do to her?"

"*You* died here," she gasped. "Graeme, my father. Thomas killed you."

"Is she dying?" Markus pulled Raven to him, glaring at her father.

"No, she is feeling my death. It will not kill her," Death replied.

"How do you know?" Markus's voice rose. He lifted her tunic. Raven looked down, a wound in her abdomen. "This looks fatal. Whatever you're doing, let her go, please."

"Markus," she gasped out. "It's not him."

"I know she won't die because I'm not being called to take her to The Crossover. If Isaac were called, he would be here already."

Cold washed over Raven, and she shivered. "You loved your brother," she whispered. "Even though he killed you." She closed her eyes, almost hearing words.

"I want to go home. Please. . .take me. . .home. . .Amelia," she whispered. "She must know. . .I didn't leave her. . .Promise me. Bury me next to my daughter." She opened her eyes. "Mary, my sister. Is this why she is here? Drawn to the death of her father, as I was?"

Death's face was blank. "You heard my last words?"

His voice from the past, a normal voice, pained, human. "I can hear them as clearly as you speak now."

The pain started to subside. With Markus's arms still around her, she looked up at Graeme. "Why do you take on his face?"

"So you recognise me as your father. You want to ignore it, but you cannot change who your father is, any more than your Enforcer can."

"What do you mean by that?" Markus demanded.

"You're giving me stares as if you'd like to kill me. She is my daughter, and you can't change what she will become. She will live, long after you have died. She won't mourn you."

Markus started to rise, but Raven gripped his arm. "Markus, no. Please don't."

His face was a mask of fury as he gazed down at her. Reaching up, she pressed her hand to his cheek. "You cannot fight him," she whispered. An urgency rose inside her chest. She had to leave, now. *Mother*. "Please, take me home."

His eyes softened "Home?" He lifted her in his arms. "We came all this way. You'd leave without Zachary?"

The urgency turned to ice. "Mother." She turned her gaze to Death. "Please, don't."

"Your gift has shown you what will happen." Death smiled at Markus. "You heard her, take her home."

"You don't give me orders." Markus glared.

"Let Zac come home with us," she pleaded.

She could feel Zac close by. A chill ran up her spine. "Zac?" she called out. Only silence greeted her, but his presence remained. "Zac, please. Something is going to happen to Mother. Don't let him take her from me."

Again, only silence.

"He has made his choice. You must make yours. Isaac, or your mother."

For Zac to not step in, he truly was lost to her. A tear slid down her cheek, her heart heavy.

"Raven?" Markus's voice made her jump.

"Take me home," she whispered.

Chapter 43

Isaac watched Raven leave Riverwick, her voice and the Enforcer's fading.

"I thought we were to fight," he said as his father's presence burned beside him.

His father's eyes were on Raven. "Not yet. Soon."

"What did you do to her in the forest?" Isaac asked.

"You saw that?" his father turned away.

Isaac followed him. "Was she hurt?"

"Raven is already well connected to her gift. It's manifested in a way I could not have seen. Stronger than I experienced." There was a tone of disbelief in his father's voice.

"Her gift?" He urged his father to continue.

"She is drawn to death." His father pointed around Riverwick. "She could *feel* their final moments. She experienced *ours* in the forest."

Isaac glanced around at the bones of people he had once known. "I remember that night," he reflected. "We came here hoping James would help us, and the village was burning. I saw you."

"I remember." His father smiled.

"You could have killed us, but you didn't," Isaac recalled.

"I wanted to let Amelia go. I marked everyone in Kempschester and Riverwick for death. That's why I told her not to come here. She loved me; I didn't see any reason to punish her," his father said.

"I was on your list, though." Isaac said, following him.

"You cheated your own death. That took me by surprise," his father admitted. "But that night I was busy. I've spent twenty years chasing down anyone who escaped."

"Is that why you came for Aunt Amelia?"

"It is her time." His father's eyes returned to the retreating backs of Raven and Markus. "Raven will not reach her in time. That Enforcer's time nears, too. He has the stink of Kempschester. But he will learn something about his family first." He turned away, moving towards the stable.

"She will fight you." Isaac warned, walking beside him. "I think she loves him. I saw it in her eyes when I threatened him."

"She will lose," his father said. "But it's not me she will fight."

"She won't fight me," Isaac disagreed. "She still thinks she can convince me to go home."

"That will change," his father informed him.

They stopped at the door to the stable.

"How do you know?" Isaac glanced around, finding Hunter watching him.

His father's only answer was a smile.

"Why do I feel like you're pushing pieces together to make this happen?" Isaac wondered out loud.

His father offered him a triumphant smile. "I'm merely guiding you to what I have seen." His eyes unfocused.

"Duty calls?" Isaac asked with a smile.

Death moved into The Shadow Realm, and half-turned, his eyes on Isaac before shadows and fog closed in around him.

A nudge at his back made him turn around. "Hunter, you're a lot bigger than you used to be." He laughed, giving the dog a scratch behind the ears. "You're not a puppy any more, are you?"

The dog let out a low growl, then threw back his head and released a mournful howl. Returning howls echoed nearby, and Isaac caught sight of wolves closing in. Hunter lowered his head, growling at the nearest wolf, showing his teeth. The two stared each other down, snarling before the wolf moved off, taking the pack with her. Isaac scratched the dog behind the ears again.

"Good boy," he said. "Thank you."

Memories of running in the snow with Hunter running after him overwhelmed him. He knelt down to Hunter's level. "Are you still that puppy?"

His father returned. "On your feet. He's not a pet." He reached his hand out.

Isaac grasped the outstretched hand, letting himself be pulled to his feet. "Where did you go this time?"

"I don't care to know where it takes me," his father informed him. "You did well with your first kill. Gideon, was it? How did you know him?"

"I made him the sword that lay beside him." He frowned. "He tried to steal your sword from me. I didn't take that too well."

"Of course you didn't."

They stopped in front of where his house once stood. "We were not peasants, were we? Our house was bigger than most." Isaac recalled the house.

"You've spent twenty years living as one, but you were never a peasant. Yeomen were above them, but we took care of them. You had a comfortable life. You should rest; you'll need it with what's to come."

Father slipped into The Shadow Realm and was gone.

Weariness passed through Isaac. He returned to the stable and lay down, closing his eyes. Sleep finally claimed him.

Isaac woke to find his father had returned, feeding the horses. The calling pulled at him.

"How long have I been asleep?" he climbed to his feet.

"Half a day. You fought too long. I let you sleep. Your body has experienced a lot in a short time."

"Another one calls to me," he confirmed.

"You don't need me this time." His father's unblinking gaze focused on Isaac.

He let himself be pulled through The Shadow Realm. Stepping into a house, a woman started to hum. A familiar sound that pierced his memories. Singing to him as he awoke from nightmares. Singing as she baked bread.

He froze, the smell of warm bread wafted around him.

"I made you some bread," Aunt Amelia said, and parts of a song drifted to him.

She turned as he entered the kitchen. Her eyes glimmered with joy.

"I knew you'd come home." She held a slice of bread out to him. "Something for you to eat before we go."

He'd surrendered to Darkness, releasing all his fear and worry. Now, overwhelmed by the memories of Aunt Amelia doing everything she could to make him feel loved, it all came rushing back.

"Father," he muttered. "Not her."

His father was beside him in an instant. "You cannot deny the call," he said. "If this is where you were drawn to, you must take her."

"She was like a mother to me," Isaac shook his head. "I cannot do this."

"You're allowing your humanity in," his father said, narrowing his eyes at Isaac. "Don't let your mortal attachments get in the way of your duty. It is her time, and it is on you to take her."

Isaac stared into Aunt Amelia's trusting eyes. "No, please."

His father changed shape, scythe in hand. "**If I have to do it, I will take you, too. Perhaps I have misjudged you**." He grabbed Isaac by the throat.

"Don't hurt him." Amelia called out. "I'll go, just don't hurt my boy."

"**Stay out of this, Amelia,**" his father ordered, fury ringing in his voice.

Isaac couldn't breathe, his father's hand cutting off oxygen as he was lifted into the air. "Please, let me go," he choked. His father threw him and he hit the wall, grunting in pain.

"**If you don't do this now, you will not be released from your calling. It will only grow. You will end her life either way,**" his father declared.

"I won't do it," Isaac said, defiant.

"**You will. You won't be able to resist it**." his father said. "**The longer you deny what you are here for, the louder it will get. The calling will be too much for you to resist. She will die in a violent way. Is that what you want?**"

Isaac rubbed at his throat and met his aunt's gaze.

"It's alright," she whispered. "If it's what you have to do, then you must."

"No." He shook his head again. "I won't do it."

"**Very well. Stay here. Be the son one last time.**" His father returned to The Shadow Realm.

"He knew," he muttered.

Aunt Amelia approached him with caution. "If Raven saw you like this, she would be heartbroken."

"She saw me," he said. "In Riverwick."

Aunt Amelia moved past him. "Sit with me, Isaac," she said, taking a seat at the table. Once again she held the bread out to him.

He followed her, keeping his distance. *She called me Isaac.*

"How long were you with them?" she asked.

Surprised at her question, Isaac frowned. "You know why I came here; you would sit and converse with your would-be killer?"

"I would sit and converse with my nephew, whom I have not seen in months," she affirmed.

He took the bread. "You were expecting me?"

She gave him a small smile, unflinching. "I felt it the moment I awoke. I made this bread just for you."

Taking a bite, he chewed. He couldn't remember the last time he'd eaten, and he missed his aunt's baking. The night he'd come for dinner, he hadn't had a chance to sit down for food before the village had been attacked.

"We met your sons and daughter," Aunt Amelia said.

"I know." He smiled at her. "I'm a father."

"There's that smile of yours." She reached for his hand, but he pulled it away.

"Careful." He warned. "I don't want to hurt you. My touch, it..." He sighed. "I took a life."

"You gave in to the Darkness," she confirmed.

He nodded. "I couldn't fight it. That long in The Shadow Realm, I lost myself. Haunted by my father, Uncle Graeme, mother, you, and Raven."

"You saw your mother?" she asked.

He shook his head. "It wasn't her. Father took her shape to torment me."

"He can do that?" Her eyes widened.

"It was either him, or Darkness. I don't remember." It had become muddled.

She said something, but he didn't hear her words; the pull came again, stronger, darker. He groaned.

"What is it?" Concern filled her eyes.

"Father was right," he said. "I can't fight it, Aunt."

"Then don't," she said simply.

"I cannot do this to you, or Raven." Darkness flooded through him. "How are you so calm? You're going to die."

"I was supposed to die. You and Raven didn't stop that, you only delayed it." She reached across the table. "Your father's shadow has hung over us from the day we fled Kempschester. A widow and a frightened boy, perhaps it was always going to be this way. I'm glad it's you."

"I was a nightmare for you then, too," he muttered.

"You were just a child, and you had suffered great loss. It is not your fault you became angry." Her eyes bored into his. Everything about her had changed. Silver hair in a braid, the last few months had been leading to her death. "How will it happen?" she asked.

He lifted his hand to his chest. "I will place my hand over your heart, and I'll take your hand."

"Will it hurt?" Her eyes were on his, and for the first time she showed fear.

"I don't know. Both times before, they were wounded and in pain already." He didn't know how to prepare her for what was coming.

"Both times?" she pressed.

"I didn't know what I was doing with Hector," he admitted. "I was only comforting a dying man. But Gideon, I did."

Another wave of Darkness rose within him, with it the urge to kill. A lust he had never experienced before. "The longer I leave it, the less of me I'll be," he said. "I can feel myself slipping away."

"Then do what you came here for," she said, her eyes watery.

There was no point in fighting it any more. "Where?" he asked.

"I always hoped I'd die in my own bed," she whispered.

He followed her to her bedroom. Aunt Amelia lay on her bed and smiled up at him as he pulled up a chair beside her. He hesitated.

"Don't worry about me. I have lived a good life," she said. "I got to see my daughter become a beautiful young woman. I got to see her happy."

"You met her lover? The Enforcer."

She laughed. "I never imagined she'd take an Enforcer. But he's different to those we knew. He makes her happy. It's all a mother wants."

Isaac took her hand in his. "This will hurt her," he murmured.

"Not as much as it's going to hurt you," she whispered. "You grew into a fine young man. You're going to live with this for a long time." She braced herself. "I'm ready."

He laid his hand over her heart. "Your fight is over," he whispered. "You have nothing more to fear."

Isaac couldn't hold it back. Like a wave washing over him, Darkness took away his fear, his resistance to what he'd been called here to do. Energy passed between the two of them. Her eyes turned white. "You'll awaken in The Shadow Realm, and I'll be there to take you home."

"Home?" she asked.

"A place of peace," he smiled at her, hoping it was of comfort.

He let the fire burn through him. Aunt Amelia's eyes widened. "Does it hurt?" he asked.

"No. I'm tired," she said.

"Then rest," he told her.

Her eyes closed, and he felt her life slip away.

A gasp came from behind him. Raven had returned.

Chapter 44

Urgency had Raven's heart pounding as they left Riverwick.

"If he takes her, after all this, I'll kill him," she promised. *How will I kill Death?*

"I'm sorry we couldn't bring Zachary back." Markus rode beside her, regret glinting in his eyes.

"I can not blame you," she said. "Zac is…." she hesitated. To say the words would make it reality, and there was no taking them back. "He is lost. There is no bringing him back." Pain squeezed her heart. "I lost him the day I lost Lucian."

"What will you do?" he asked.

The only sound was that of their horses' hooves on the dirt track. Behind her, voices of the dead still whispered; ahead of her, more sorrow. "He would never give up on me, and would find a way to free me, no matter what." She didn't want to, but there was only one way left to free her cousin. "I wanted to free him from The Shadow Realm, but there is no way to bring him back; he has given in to Darkness." The ache deep in her soul made Raven weary. "There is only one way to free him now."

Markus's silence stretched out. "You mean to kill him."

In such a short time, Zac had ceased to exist, his darker, shadow self replacing her cousin.

"I mean to kill him," she confirmed.

There was no surprise from Markus, no attempt to talk her out of what she knew she must do. Only a look of understanding.

"I cannot say I like your cousin much," he confessed. "But it pains me to see you in such anguish. Such a decision comes with a heavy burden."

"It's what Zac and I agreed on," she explained. "We swore we'd always fight for each other until we had nothing left to fight for."

"You believe there is nothing left to fight for?" His voice softened.

His question hurt. Zac really was gone.

"I believe there is going to be a battle between us, and it won't end well for either of us," she told him. *Is it my end I can feel, or his?*

Their conversation turned to silence. The curse she had inherited from Death - a constant warning that her mother's fate would soon play out.

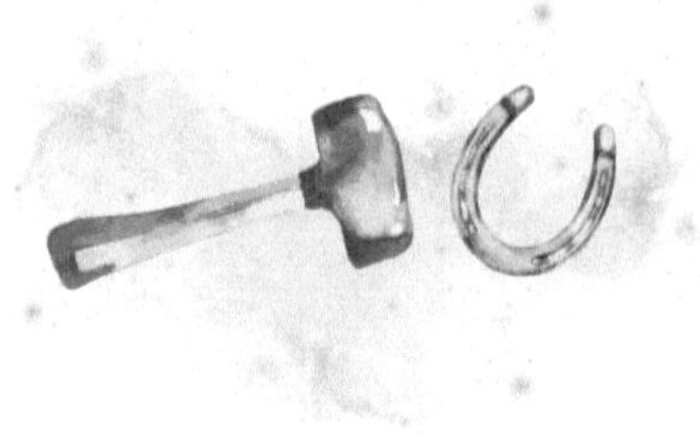

Raven stood face to face with Zac. Mother lay on her bed, eyes closed. The cold fear that had gripped her the entire way home now buried itself deep inside her. She was too late. Glaring, betrayal burned, turning sorrow to bitterness.

"Raven, I'm sorry," Zac murmured.

He was different, no longer the man she'd seen in Riverwick. Darkness had receded, but she wasn't in a forgiving mood.

"She's gone," Zac said. "I have to go. I need to take her to—"

"You're not going anywhere." She gave in to rage and drew her sword. "You wanted to fight, then we fight. Here and now."

Footsteps behind her announced Markus's arrival. "Raven, know what it is you do," he warned, a gentle tone to his voice.

"Back off, I know what I do." She didn't look at him; her attention zeroed on Zac. "I told you he has to die; this only confirms it."

Raven's eyes darted towards her mother, and grief clawed at her heart, becoming twisted. "Draw your weapon," she ordered.

"I'm not going to fight you," he argued. "If I don't take her, she—"

Raven didn't let him finish before she attacked. She swung upwards as Markus had shown her. Zachary's black sword blocked hers, and she pulled her dagger, stepping forward, ready to plunge it into his chest. Death appeared. His bony hand gripped her wrist.

"Stop," he said, piercing blue eyes meeting hers before he took on the dark shape. "**Not yet.**"

"You don't get a say in this. He killed my mother, he has to die," she didn't recognise her own voice, icy, tinged with a dark tone. Flames of something she didn't recognise consumed her until all she desired was to kill.

He shifted his grip to her arm. "**I said not yet, daughter.**"

"Let me go." she shifted her sword, turning in his grasp. "I don't care what you call yourself, get in my way, I'll kill you too."

"**I give you one chance to calm yourself so that you may say goodbye to your mother before Isaac takes her to The Crossover. Take my offer.**" His fingers tightened painfully on her arm, his meaning clear.

Pain shot up her arm as he showed her his willingness to carry out his threat.

"**Make your choice,**" he demanded.

She cast a look at Zac, then her mother's body, before bowing her head. "Please, take me to her," she said at last, her fury becoming an ocean of grief threatening to drown her.

They were in The Shadow Realm. "Raven?" her mother's voice broke her heart.

"Mother?" she sobbed

"Do not be angry at Isaac, little Raven." Her mother reached for her, wrapping her arms around Raven.

Raven softened, and returned the embrace, but the pain in her chest remained. She shook her head, her eyes stinging.

"It was my time, Raven. Even the daughter of Death cannot fight mortality." her mother's voice was soft, comforting.

"I'm not ready for you to be gone." Hot tears streamed down her face as she lost the fight to stop them.

Her mother pulled back, and she wiped tears from Raven's face. "We never are. That's part of life. My little miracle, I'm so proud of the woman you have become. Continue to be that woman. I know you'd be happy with the Enforcer."

Raven almost laughed. "I should have known you'd know."

"I'm your mother; I know everything." She smiled. "You think I wasn't young once, trying to sneak in glances, unable to contain myself?"

Her mother's eyes darted towards Death. "Your father was intimidating when I first met him, but he soon won me over. It was hard to resist him." She reached a hand to Death's face. "Let me see my husband one last time," she requested. "My Graeme."

Death's eyes lingered on her mother's. "**I am not your husband, Amelia. Not any more.**"

"I know he's still in there, and that he still remembers his wife, and all that we lost. Please. A dying wish."

He gave her a hard stare. "**Your husband died. I see no need to show you what no longer exists.**"

"Consider it a kindness," her mother pushed. "You showed me that night."

Death remained in his shadow form.

"Then let this be my goodbye." Her mother's voice was barely audible, and she stepped forward, pressing a hand to the back of his head and kissed Death.

Raven's heart broke for her mother. She had loved her husband and lost him without a chance to say goodbye. As they pulled apart, Death had taken on the human appearance, his face expressionless.

"Graeme." Her mother reached for his face.

He caught her hand. "I showed you kindness, as you asked.. It is time to go."

"You returned my kiss. There is a flicker of humanity in you." Her mother smiled.

"Merely an echo of who I once was. Are you done?" he demanded.

"I am." Her mother's disappointment shone through.

"It's time to go, Amelia. You had borrowed time. That time is up." He stepped back, away from her touch.

"I know." With teary eyes, she smiled at Raven. "Be happy, my daughter." She held her hand out. "I'm ready."

"Isaac," Death instructed. "It must be you."

Zac refused to look at Raven. "Aunt Amelia, it's time to go."

Her mother turned her gaze to Death. "Graeme, please be gentle on our daughter. She is as strong-willed as you were and can be unforgiving. She has a fiery temper, just as you did. Please let her live her life. If she wants you in it, welcome that."

"I don't." Raven blurted out. "He's Death. There is no room in my life for the Darkness he brings." She glared at her cousin. "Nor you."

Isaac grasped her mother's arm, and the two disappeared, leaving Raven with Death.

She eyed him sideways.

"You'll change your mind," he told her. "Once you let the Darkness in, you will not be afraid of me, nor will you hate me. You have no reason to, Raven."

"There will be nothing you can do to make me give in to that," she told him defiantly.

"We'll see," he mused.

She studied his face, wondering at the father he should have been. Had she grown up with her father, what would he have been like? She pushed it down. It would never be, and there was no point pondering on it. "I never wanted any part of what you are, who you are. Zac…Isaac may have sought you out, but I never did."

He half-smiled. "I know."

Disturbed, Raven faced him, attempting to ignore the fear that rose. "Is this really what Thomas wanted for his son? For him to be a killer? To kill the woman who was a mother to him?"

"He is the son of Death," he said, as if it were the only answer to her question.

Grief and anger had a hold of her now. For her mother, for her cousin, always like a brother.

"Why did you have to do that to him? You took my brother from me." Anger flared within her, and she struggled to contain it.

"He is not gone. This was always his fate." His eyes on her were an uncomfortable reminder of what he was.

She couldn't face Zac, not now. "Keep him away from me," she told Death. "If I see Zachary, Isaac, whoever he is, he dies. I will not hesitate to kill him next time."

His smile returned. "I know."

"Please, take me home," she pleaded.

The Shadow Realm receded, and she found herself standing in the bedroom. Markus stood in the middle of the room; his eyes widened when he saw her.

"Raven?" He stood straighter.

"Markus." Her voice was flat.

He studied her. "What happened?"

"Stop talking," she said. "I just need your arms around me."

He lifted her chin with the crook of his finger. She met his eyes, her hand trembling as she reached for his. Then his arms were around her, strong and warm. In his embrace she leaned against him, letting the tears flow.

Chapter 45

Isaac escorted Aunt Amelia to the same place to which he had taken Hector and Gideon. He didn't want to be in this place for long. He knew his mother was here and wanted to leave.

"Is this Heaven?" Aunt Amelia asked.

"I don't know if it's Heaven, or if Heaven truly exists, but you will find peace here." Isaac said. "This is The Crossover. It's another realm."

"Like The Shadow Realm?"

"Not quite. It's the opposite. You will find your family here. Loved ones. There's no fear or Darkness. Just peace."

"My parents?" She glanced around with hope.

He nodded. "I have to go. I'm sorry, Aunt, I truly am."

"Will you ever find peace?" she asked. "Now that you're..."

I'm a monster. With his heart heavy, exhaustion set in. "I don't know."

"You still have a choice." Aunt Amelia declared. "You can walk away from it. You have a family."

"I don't think I can. I let the Darkness in; I ended your life. There's no returning from that. I can't expose that to my children." They would still get caught up in this, and the knowledge weighed on him.

"Don't abandon Raven. You two need each other," Aunt Amelia said in a soft voice.

"I don't think she wants to see me any more. She tried to kill me when she saw you were dead." The look in her eyes had hurt. Her dagger had come close to piercing his chest. If his father hadn't stepped in, his cousin may have killed him.

Aunt Amelia touched Isaac's shoulder. "I see a lonely life for you. It's not something your mother would have wanted for you. Her little boy."

"I suppose she'll tell you soon enough." He turned away.

"She's here?" The hope in her voice was unmistakable.

"This is where my father told me he brought her." His father had told him he'd freed the lost souls so they would leave him alone.

"You haven't sought her out? You lost her so young. The two of you were so close," she reminded him.

"I can't." He shook his head. The idea of seeing her while he was like he was only filled him with dread.

Aunt Amelia put a hand on his arm. "Zac. Isaac, you have what many others do not have. A chance to say goodbye. Raven had her chance with me; you should get yours."

"I have to go," he said.

"Amelia?" A voice behind him froze him in his tracks, memories of a long time ago rising up. "Not you. I'm sorry."

"You have that chance now," Aunt Amelia reiterated. "Don't let this pass you by; you'll regret it."

He turned, her familiar brown eyes on his. It was as if he were a boy again. Everything in him wanted to run to her, to feel her arms around him.

"Thomas," his mother said warily. "You brought Amelia?"

Annoyed that his own mother could not tell him apart from his father, he sighed, reaching for The Shadow Realm.

"Isaac?" Her voice filled with delight and joy. "My little Isaac?"

"Mother." He ran forwards, wrapping his arms around her. She was so small in his arms. Not at all how he remembered. He stepped back, staring down at her in wonder.

"You have your father's curse." There was no horror in her eyes, only sadness.

"I gave in, I couldn't fight any more," he apologised. "But somehow I broke free when I was called to Aunt Amelia's."

His mother grasped his chin, as she had years before."You've chosen a path that is only filled with Darkness and death," she said. "To bring souls here, to a peace you will never have. I always hoped you'd live a happy life, not one fated to follow in your father's footsteps. Is this really what you want?"

The disappointment in her eyes tore at him. "It's too late to ask that now," he muttered. "It doesn't matter what I want."

"It's never too late. What were you doing with your life before this?" She smiled. "Are you a farmer, or did you choose another trade?"

He smiled back, his chest lighter. "I'm a blacksmith. A successful one, at that." Only now, he had lost his shop to Raven. She would never give it up now.

"A blacksmith?" Her pride shone through. "Riverwick needs a good blacksmith."

"I don't work in Riverwick," he said with a frown. *Does she not know?*

"Did you move to Kempschester? Or Hazelbury? They have good blacksmiths there." Excitement glinted in her eyes. "I'm from Hazelbury. Is it still thriving?"

He stared at Aunt Amelia for help.

"Riverwick burned down. As did Kempschester," Aunt Amelia said. "Thomas and Graeme burned everything."

His mother blinked. "Oh. He didn't tell me that."

"Father destroyed them. Uncle James, John, Susanna all died. Aunt Amelia took me and we ran," he explained.

His mother looked at Aunt Amelia. "You sheltered my boy?"

"I did," Aunt Amelia agreed. "He grew up too fast, but I kept him safe."

"I thank you, my sister." His mother hugged Aunt Amelia.

Isaac stepped back, looking at his two mothers. The woman who had given birth to him and loved him right up until she died. His aunt, who had done her best for him in the years that followed.

"I love you both," he said before he could help himself. "Mother, I missed you every day after you died, and I never forgot you. Aunt Amelia, you sheltered a broken boy, and it means the world to me that you were there. You were so forgiving and gentle, and the mother I needed in her absence. I'm sorry."

A man and a woman appeared. The man had light brown hair and blue eyes. The woman had blonde hair and brown eyes. Aunt Amelia caught sight of them. "Mother? Father?" she choked with emotion.

"Oh, Amelia," the woman said, pulling her into a hug.

He turned to leave, joyful at his aunt's reunion with her family. Darkness had lost its grip on him, and he knew what he was going to do now.

"He has children of his own now." Amelia's voice pulled him back.

"I'm a grandmother?" His mother's eyes lit up.

He needed to leave, but he was stalling, listening to their conversation.

"They're beautiful children. Isaac here really does love the ladies." Amelia laughed.

"He's just like his father." The amusement turned to sadness. "I never wanted this for you, Isaac."

The Shadow Realm pulled him back.

Darkness lost its grip completely, and he fell through the veil, hitting the ground hard. His heart pounded.

"You did well," his father said.

"No. Don't do that," he grunted, climbing to his feet. His father raised an eyebrow. "Don't act like a proud father. You don't have the right to do that.

Not any more."

"There was a time you would have loved my approval," his father noted.

"No! You have his memories, and his face, but the man he was, he would have been horrified." Isaac glared.

His father glared back. "I am still your father, Isaac. Watch your tone with me. I can put you back in The Shadow Realm."

"You're not him. I remember what he was like, and you're not him. He was a loving man, trying to do the best he could." The pain of losing his father again hurt more than he could have thought.

"You knew nothing of your father and the man he was. Nor your uncle." His father's smile sent chills down Isaac's spine. "I was a killer. As Thomas, and as Graeme. I protected you from it at the time, but I committed many atrocities at war. I am still me, just with a power that you seem to have inherited."

Isaac held his hands out in front of him. "The Touch of Death," he whispered, horrified. "I killed the woman that took me in when you..." Isaac stopped. "I killed her. Where's Raven?"

"Raven is with the Enforcer. He comforts her. I would stay away from her. She made it clear she will kill you if she sees you again," his father affirmed.

"Oh Raven, I'm sorry." Isaac turned his back on his father.

"Where are you going?" his father demanded.

"Well, I can't go home, you've framed me for a murder, and my cousin, my little sister doesn't want to see me. You've destroyed my life!" Isaac truly hated his father and wanted to be free of him.

But as he walked away, his father followed him. "That town is not your home, anyway. You are from Riverwick."

"You burned Riverwick!" Isaac yelled. "It no longer exists! The bones of the villagers still litter its ruins. People you knew," he sighed. "I can never see my children again."

"They will join us soon enough." His father's smile filled Isaac with dread.

"No! This will not be their fate," Isaac said. "I will not let that happen. Not to my children."

"You gave in, just as they will," his father declared.

"I cannot undo what I did, but I will not do it again. I'm leaving. Don't try to find me. Leave my children alone." He stepped into The Shadow Realm, ignoring the Darkness that pressed in around him. *Where do I go?* He had no where he could call home any more; it was time to make a new one.

Chapter 46

Raven leaned heavily on Markus, his arms around her. Villagers surrounded her, their sobs loud. Behind her, Grace and Delia with Giselle, Joseph, and Arthur. All she needed was to get through the funeral, and she could collapse into Markus's embrace, let herself fall asleep and not have to feel. The dark sky threatened rain, and she glanced up, hopeful the weather would hold out.

Raven gazed into her mother's face. To stand in front of an empty shell of a corpse, with her essence elsewhere, made it a little strange to be addressing the body.

"She looks so peaceful," she murmured.

"I'm glad you got to say goodbye." Markus nudged her forward.

She moved as if in a daze, kneeling beside the coffin with Markus beside her.

The tears flowed then, and Raven didn't try to hold them back. Many loved her mother and had lined up to say their goodbyes. Raven had let them go first, so she could be with mother before she was carried to the graveyard.

She held her mother's cold hand. "You weren't supposed to leave me so soon. We should have had many more years together." She sighed. "What's the point of this; she cannot hear me."

Markus rubbed her arm. "I think she can. Keep going."

Raven took a deep breath. "We never got to have a normal life, that didn't include fear of Darkness, my father, and shadow realms." She touched her mother's cheek. "But you did your best for all of us. You gave us a loving home. You let me learn to fight, even though it terrified you. You gave me your strength and your heart, and I will carry it with me. I will never forget who you were. You were the light in this world of Darkness."

Overtaken by sobs, Raven bowed over the coffin. Markus's arms wrapped around her.

"Why did he do it?" she choked out. "Why did he have to take my mother from me, Markus?" Unable to see her mother's face through tears, the sorrow was suffocating. Raven knelt there for what felt like an eternity, in Markus's embrace, holding on to him for dear life.

"They want to take her to the graveyard," he stated, his mouth close to her ear. She didn't answer. "Raven."

"I can't." She raised her eyes to his.

"You can." he insisted. "I've got you. We walk behind her. If you can't walk, I'll carry you."

She half laughed but let him guide her to her feet.

"Oh, my dear, you have lost so much." Elaine's voice was deep with sympathy. "Lucian, Zachary, and now your mother." Her hug did little to comfort Raven. "Your mother's song is already greatly missed in this village; we'll all feel her loss."

"Will you hold her?" Markus asked Elaine. "I have to help carry the coffin to the cart."

Raven was passed to Elaine. She lifted her head to watch as Markus joined others to lift the coffin.

"You've got yourself a good man there," Maria observed from beside Elaine.

Raven remained silent.

Maria continued talking. "He looks like he comes from a good family. Good upbringing. Does he make you happy?"

"He does," Raven agreed.

"It's alright to love another. Lucian would understand," Elaine whispered. "Will you marry him?"

Raven watched Markus. She had not considered the idea of marriage since Lord Gerard had spoken of it just after Lucian's death.

"I don't know," she admitted. "I should be married to Lucian by now. The idea of marrying someone else only makes me feel…" She paused. *What do I feel?*

"You feel guilty." Elaine's eyes bored into hers. "I don't want that for you, Raven. Lucian wouldn't either. It would make him happy to see you happy. If your life has taken you to that young man, perhaps it is Lucian giving you his blessings. I certainly give you mine."

Raven took in Elaine's words. Society would expect her to marry, and soon. It was already public knowledge she had lain with Markus; men would not exactly be lining up for her hand with him around.

"I thank you for your kind words, Elaine," she said as Markus returned, wrapping his arms around her again.

The cart moved towards the church and they followed behind, villagers singing, someone played a flute.

"You're a good man, Markus. Take care of her," Elaine requested.

"I think we both know Raven well enough to know she doesn't need anyone to take care of her," Markus said in a low voice to Elaine. "But I will certainly be strong for her when she does need it." He squeezed Raven.

With her eyes on the cart, Raven's heart ached. She'd had a chance to say her goodbyes, but it didn't help. All the time in the world to say goodbye wouldn't help.

"Markus," she began, "I can't do this. I cannot watch them bury her."

Elaine's arms went around her from the other side. "You saw me bury three of my children. I know this is not easy. You lean on us and cry all you need, Raven. This is the most difficult part of life, and you have the entire village holding you up."

Supported by both Markus and Elaine, Raven's heart swelled with gratitude. They stopped at the graveyard, and she let herself be led to her mother's grave. A drop of water landed on her cheek. Then another. The sky opened up, and a cold downpour descended.

Markus walked Raven into her shop. "Get your clothes off and into bed," he ordered her. "I'll look after you, Sunshine. I'll get you some food."

She wasn't hungry but saw no need to tell him. She started to unfasten her cloak, but his hands pushed hers out of the way. He unfastened it and hung it over the back of a chair. Too tired to fight, she let him remove her tunic and trousers. Pulling her nightdress over her head, he guided her to her bed, pulling the blankets over her. He moved away, and soon returned.

"Maria wouldn't let me leave without this," he revealed, laying a loaf of bread next to her bed. "She found it in your mother's kitchen, laid out as if for a guest. One slice was missing."

"She hasn't baked for months!" Raven broke an end from the loaf and took a bite. She forced it down and put the bread back. With her mother gone, it no longer tasted of warmth and joy, but of bitterness and grief.

"Oh, of course you're not hungry." He lay on top of the bed, facing her. "What can I do?"

"Just stay with me?" she requested. "I don't want to be alone tonight."

"I'm not going anywhere," he agreed.

Raven closed her eyes. She dreamed of her mother, her smile, the glint in her eyes.

When she awoke, Markus was still fully dressed, laying on top of her bed, his eyes closed. She watched him, his face relaxed. "I'm glad you're here," she whispered.

His eyes opened. "Where else would I be?"

"I couldn't have gotten through today without you. I'm glad you were with me," she admitted.

"It was an awful day for me," he confessed.

"How?"

"Your fa...Death threatened you. I had my hand on my sword when you and he disappeared. Zachary told me he would cut out my heart if I hurt you, and then he was gone, too. I didn't know if I would ever see you again," he said, his voice husky. "I was ready to ride back to Riverwick, and I would have burned it down all over again to get you back. I'd never felt such rage, or fear."

"Fear?" she pressed.

"Fear that I'd lost you." He caressed her face, tucking loose strands behind her ear. "No matter what world you were in, I would have found you to bring you back into mine."

"Yours?"

"In my world, where I am Lord, and you are my Lady Sunshine."

Raven gazed into his eyes. Her heart ached. "Enforcer Markus, are you trying to tell me—"

"I am," he said. "You are my world, Raven. You have disarmed me and brought me to my knees." His kiss was tender. "And I will tend to your broken heart."

Her cheeks were wet. "I can see no other in my future. Only you." She pressed her forehead to his. Markus's lips found hers, the kiss consuming as she gave in, wanting every part of him.

Raven pulled away, reaching for the yellow ribbon. "I wore this as I mourned Lucian. I still feel his loss, but I pass this token to you, to show that you now hold my heart."

Markus took the ribbon. "Then I shall never let go of it."

Chapter 47

Winter was setting in early, and with only the clothes on his back, Isaac had stolen a cloak, but it offered little warmth. Snow fell as he walked through the streets seeking out shelter. This was the third town in as many weeks, and he clung to the desperate hope that they wouldn't turn him away like the others. With a face that many recognised, his father's shadow hung over him as he was met by fear and suspicion. People hurried by, their eyes downward, avoiding his.

Despite trying to resist, the Darkness still had a grip on him. He had still been called to take the dead to their peace. Now, The Shadow Realm called to him, a way out of the cold. Many times, he'd almost given in, yearning for warmth, for sleep, and for home. But every time he imagined home, it was not in Oakborough. It would be so easy to slip through the veil, to let the shadows close around him. *No!* He stumbled on.

Isaac found his way to the church, pushing open the door. Hoping for shelter, he took a seat in the front row. A fire burned, crackling.

"You look cold." A voice said behind him. He spun around, facing the smiling priest.

"Please," he said. "I need shelter."

The priest looked at his face, his smile fading. "There is no help here for you."

"You would turn me away? Push me back into the snow?"

The priest eyed his face again, saying nothing.

"Please priest, I am in need," Isaac begged. "You have no need to fear me. If I go back out there, I'll freeze."

The warmth of the church didn't reach him. He'd been outside too long, and deep shivers ran through him. The idea of returning outside filled him with panic.

"I have seen a man such as you before. We do not want that Darkness in our town," The priest declared.

"I know the man you speak of; I am not him. Please." Desperate, Isaac stood. "My death will be on you if you make me leave."

"We do not want that Darkness in our town." The priest repeated and hurried away. "If you will not leave, the Enforcers will remove you."

Isaac sighed. "I'll leave," he said. "Your cruelty today will be remembered." *If I live that long.*

He stumbled from the church, pulling his cloak tight as the icy blast greeted him outside. With no choice but to leave, he shuffled through the snow, making his way out of the village. He didn't know where he was, and he hoped his father would not find him. Outside the gates, Isaac searched his surroundings, a cold ache settling in. Nearby, the shadows of trees loomed through the night. Hoping for shelter, to escape at least some of the snow, he entered the forest.

It was not long before he fell. As he lay on the ground, the sound of a child's laughter echoed around him. A boy ran, squealing with glee as his father gave chase, the two of them landing in the snow, cold water seeping into their clothes. On the ground, he could hear his father's deep laughter rumbling from next to him. He recalled how much the boy loved a fresh snowfall. How he would watch the flakes drift down around him, melting in his hand.

Isaac closed his eyes, longing for the pain to stop. Bitter cold soaked through his cloak, chilling him to the bone.

"I'm sorry, Raven," he whispered. *Delia. Arthur. Giselle. Joseph.*

Deep regret filled him.

"Get up," his father's voice called to him.

"No," he murmured. "Let me rest."

A shadow stood over him. "Isaac, you're going to die out here."

"Then let me." He had never felt so alone, nor so cold, and he welcomed the calm that washed over him.

"You idiot." The shadow moved, and Isaac was lifted. "It is not your time." His father's voice pierced the fog.

Lifted over a shoulder, he had no strength to struggle and slipped into a dreamless sleep.

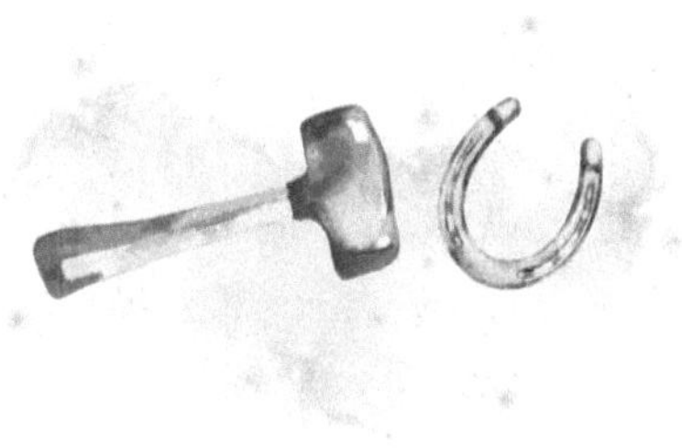

The dark receded as Isaac gained consciousness. Pulling at his dry clothes, the warmth of a fire enveloped him, with the smell of burning wood.

"Where am I?" he croaked, expecting his father to be the one to answer.

"You're in Hopeton." An unfamiliar voice from across the room made him sit up. It was a man not much older than he, whose grey eyes, lined with worry, met his own.

He was on his feet in an instant. "How did I get here?"

"It's alright, you're safe." The man approached Isaac with his hands up to show he was non intimidating. "A man in a cloak sought help for you. He found you in the snow."

He recalled being thrown over his father's shoulder. *He pulled me from the cold.* Isaac's eyes darted around the room before focusing on the person on the other side of the room. "Where is he now?"

"He's gone. I didn't see him leave. There one moment, gone the next," the stranger said.

Relief flooded through Isaac.

"Did you know him?" the man asked.

"No," Isaac lied.

"I have hot food; you look like you need it." The man held out a steaming bowl.

Isaac's stomach chose that moment to grumble in agreement to needing food. "Thank you," he said, taking the bowl, breathing in the warmth and delicious scent of stew.

"Oh, he's awake." A woman entered the room. Her black hair was long, sitting around her shoulders. She had a narrow face and green eyes. She smiled at him. "You had us worried."

Isaac gulped down the stew, his insides warming.

"I'm Frederick Hope; this is my wife, Charlotte," the man told him.

"Hope? Like the town?" Isaac asked.

Frederick laughed. "I'm not a Lord. We don't actually have a Lord here, nor Enforcers. We're just a small town that we built ourselves. We take care of each other as a small community should. It was named after my father, who funded the build."

"Thank you for helping me," he expressed his gratitude. "I'm Is…Zachary. Zac." He'd used the name longer than his own, Isaac now being one of his darker self.

"How did you get out in the snow?" Frederick asked. "You had no horse, and the nearest town is half a day's walk from here on the other side of the forest."

He opened his mouth, unsure what to say. "I..."

"Leave him be, Frederick. It doesn't matter how. He's here now, and our guest. We don't need to be asking him questions," Charlotte said gently.

Zachary gave her a small smile. "I was seeking shelter, and the priest turned me away. I found my way into the forest, but it was too cold."

Charlotte handed him a tankard. "Drink this," she said. Her gaze darted to his eye.

"I had an accident when I was a child." He explained out of habit. "I was almost hit by lightning."

He lifted the vessel to his mouth, letting the warmth of posset run down his throat. It was curdled milk, thick and creamy, with the sweet taste of honey and wine. Charlotte moved away, standing at the window.

"The storm's getting worse. It's a miracle you didn't die out there," she commented.

A miracle. Choking back bitterness, he kept silent. His father hadn't let him die, but he would probably try to pull him back to The Shadow Realm when he had recovered.

Frederick threw wood into the fire, sending sparks into the air. "I can see you're a haunted man. You're safe here. We won't turn you away, but you will need to earn your keep. Do you have any skills?"

"I'm a blacksmith," he admitted, pride swelling in his chest. "Five years' experience."

Frederick raised his eyebrows. "What is your speciality?"

"Swords and armour. Horseshoes," he confirmed.

Frederick smiled. "We have no blacksmiths here; that will be useful. That's some skill."

Exhausted, Zachary tried to hold back a yawn and failed.

"We can talk about that later; Zac needs rest after the ordeal he's had." Charlotte smiled at him. "Let me show you to our spare bedroom."

He followed her and stopped at the doorway, turning to Frederick. "Thank you," he said again, warmth spreading across his chest. "I will earn my keep."

"Oh, I know. Everyone does," the man smiled. "Welcome to Hopeton."

Charlotte led him to a bedroom. It was small and bare with a small bed. "Sleep all you need," she told him. "There's no going anywhere until this storm's over. We have plenty of food; all you need is to ask if you require anything."

The kindness of these strangers overwhelmed him, but he said nothing as she closed the door, leaving him in peace. Only when he was alone did he dare look into his father's face on the other side of the veil.

"I asked you to leave me alone," he spoke in a low voice.

"I felt compelled to help you," his father said. "I thought you'd be more grateful than that."

"You only helped me because you thought I'd return. I won't. I meant what I said, I want no part of that. Please, leave me, let me live the life I chose."

His father stepped through the veil, his dark presence filling the room. "I'll wait, then. This is not something you can run from, Isaac. Do what you must, be the blacksmith; but your path will *always* lead you back to The Shadow Realm, to what you are."

"What am I?"

His father's smile sent a chill down his spine. "You are the son of Death. You've used your gift to end lives, and you've heard the calling, even after you walked away. Just because you changed your mind, doesn't mean you can change that history."

With that, his father was gone.

Chapter 48

O*ne year later - 1369*

Hands slid around Raven's waist. She leaned against Markus as his hands moved up her body, and he kissed the back of her neck.

"Mmmm," she said. "Don't stop that."

His hand slid under her tunic. She ground herself against him, desire surging, her core clenching.

"You have a big day today," he reminded her in her ear. "Opening day. Are you excited?"

His lips sent quivers through her. Taken by need, she fought down the urge to push him up against the wall. "I want to tear your clothes off," she breathed.

"Lord Gerard will be here soon with his daughter. Delia and Grace, too, with the young ones," he reminded her.

His hand brushed the underside of her breast. "Forget opening day, everyone. Lock the door," she cooed..

His arms tightened around her, and he dropped a hand between her legs.

Someone cleared their throat, and Markus immediately removed his hands. Raven's face heated, Lord Gerard stood at the door.

"Lord Gerard." She eyed Markus. "I didn't hear you come in!"

He gave her a slight smile. "I wanted to congratulate you on the move," he said. "It looks like I should have come by another time."

Raven glanced around the shop. It was bigger than the old one. Once town folk had gotten past their misdirected anger they felt for her cousin, business was good, and she had decided to move out of the cramped smithy to one with more space..

"The grand opening is today, so you're here on time," she said. "Did you bring Joan?"

Lord Gerard stepped to the side to reveal a young blonde girl of seven or eight, her brown eyes wide as she stared up at Raven. The girl looked more like her mother than Gerard.

"Hello, Joan," Raven said. "Welcome."

She got a small smile in response.

"You're going to be my apprentice," she said. "But any apprentice of mine gets her own sword." Raven held up the sword she'd been working on. "But you must learn to use it before you get this."

"Will you teach me?" Joan asked.

"That is exactly what I'll do." Raven smiled.

"Joan, why don't you sit down over there, I need to speak with Raven and Markus." Lord Gerard spoke with a softer voice for his daughter.

The girl ran over to the table, her eyes on them the whole time.

Lord Gerard lost his gentle tone, smile tightening into a serious expression. Raven knew what was next.

"Have you spoken with or seen Zachary Dale?" the Lord asked. "Do you give shelter to him?"

Markus's hand rested on her hip, and Raven pushed down her anger. This had been ongoing for a year, and every time she gave him the same answer, but he still continued to ask. *Will we ever be past this?* She didn't want to speak about Zac, nor give life to the anger and sorrow that remained over what he had done.

"I have not seen him," she said truthfully, meeting his inquisitive gaze. "Nor shall I shelter him. You have my word, Lord Gerard, that if I do see him, Markus will know about it. I will not impede the rightful arrest of a known murderer." Pain resurfaced, her mother's death.

His stare softened as he finally nodded. "I'm sorry, Raven, I have to check. I'm starting to think he's either dead, or moved on. I can only hope no one else has met a grisly death at his hands."

Raven held her silence.

He nodded to himself. "I'm taking my Captain, I have an Enforcer stationed outside."

She grinned at Markus. "Captain," she said.

He leaned in, breath tickling her ear. "I'll be thinking of all we'll be doing later."

She pushed him towards Lord Gerard. "Go." She laughed.

Once he left, she turned to Joan. "You asked your father to let you be my apprentice?" she asked.

The girl nodded. "I want to learn from you."

"There are plenty of blacksmiths, but you asked for me?" It had surprised her when Lord Gerard asked her to take on the child.

"But none who would have taken on a girl. I didn't want to learn from them. You're the only woman blacksmith in Oakborough," Joan advised her.

Raven smiled. "I suppose I would have done the same."

"I heard you learned from your cousin, and he taught you to fight, too," the young girl added.

Raven's mood shifted. She forced the smile in place. "That's right, I did. I had to beg him to teach me to fight, though. He was six years older than me and didn't want a little girl following him around," she said.

"My older brother would have been his apprentice if he hadn't murdered someone and disappeared," Joan blurted.

Raven frowned. As the murderer's cousin, for the last year she had fought against Zac's reputation. Markus had stepped in more than once to face townsfolk's anger, and at an Enforcer's request, Lord Gerard had declared protection of Raven and her smithy. The child had clearly overheard a conversation she shouldn't have.

"How about you get started?" Raven said to change the subject. "Do you see those orders over there?" She pointed.

The girl shifted her eyes to where Raven was pointing. "Yes?"

"I need you to sort them in order of when they're due," Raven instructed.

Joan nodded and rushed to the orders.

The door opened. Delia walked in with Arthur.

"Say hello to your aunt," Delia instructed.

"Hello, Aunt Raven," the boy said to her before turning his eyes on his mother. "Can I go now?"

He wore a scowl. Raven suspected she'd soon find out the reason for his mood.

Delia sighed, weary. "Go on, then. Don't get into trouble this time."

His scowl deepened. "I told you, that wasn't my fault," Arthur grumbled.

"You don't hit people, Arthur," Delia scolded him softly.

"We do not take joy in the pain of others." He rolled his eyes.

Those words! Raven froze. "What?"

"Children were giving him a hard time about being the son of a murderer. So, he punched one of them," Delia explained.

Despite her anger towards Zac, Raven hid a smile. *Just like his father, starting fights.* "No, what he just said. About not taking joy in the pain of others." She'd heard those words many times.

"I don't know, he came out with it one day." Delia glanced at Raven. "What is it?"

"Zac used to say that all the time," she explained, turning towards Arthur.

"Did you hear that somewhere?"

"I don't know..." Arthur looked down at his feet.

Raven crouched down in front of him. "It's alright. If you heard someone say that, can you tell me?"

The boy looked to his mother. Raven forced down her frustration, trying to be patient.

"You can tell her. You're not going to get into trouble," Delia encouraged him.

"A man by the bridge," he said. "I was with Aunt Grace, and Giselle and Joseph. Grace was talking to someone, and we went by the water. Joseph fell over, and we were laughing at him. A man walked up to us and said it."

"What man?" Delia asked, her tone rising.

Raven watched her nephew very carefully. Any reaction could silence him. *Zac, are you watching your children?*

"I don't know who he was." Arthur said. "He wore a hood over his head, so we couldn't see his face. Just that he had a beard." He looked outside. "Can I go now?"

Raven's heart pounded. She reached for Arthur's hands. "Do you remember anything else about him?"

He thought for a moment. "Giselle asked him why he was sad. He said talking to us made him happy. But then he was gone."

Grace entered, bringing Giselle and Joseph.

"Hello, Aunt Raven." Giselle smiled.

"Arthur was just telling us about the man you saw at the bridge," Raven said.

"What man?" Grace's voice expressed shock. "You're talking to people you don't know?"

"He spoke to us and then left," Giselle told her mother before turning her eyes to Raven. "I think he knows you."

"Why do you think that?" Raven asked.

The twins exchanged glances. "I've seen him once before," Giselle said. "Outside your other shop before you moved. The door was open, and you were singing while working. I remembered him and asked if he knew you."

"What did he say?" Raven asked. *He was watching me.*

"He said 'I do, little one. She's happier not knowing I'm here, though, so don't tell her you saw me; it will only hurt her.' I asked him why he was there, and he said he was checking that you were happy."

Raven forced a smile to hide her rage. *He dared to come here? If I had known he was there, I would have made sure not to let him live again.* Death's actions to stop her from killing him had only added to her wrath.

Grace frowned. "Who is he? I don't like the idea of someone I don't know talking to my children."

Delia's hand grasped her arm. "I don't think it's someone you don't know," she said to Grace. "Raven?"

"I..." She glanced at the children. "Why don't you two go outside with Arthur? Keep him out of trouble."

Before they ran outside, Giselle's eyes met hers for a brief moment, with a spark of understanding.

"It's Zachary, isn't it?" Delia asked.

"I think so," she agreed.

"How do you feel about that?" Grace asked. "That he would look in on you but not speak to you."

"I don't know." Lying to her friends only added to her misery.

"Why would he speak to his children and not you?" Grace asked. "Did you two have a fight? What happened when you and Markus went to—" Grace's words cut off as Delia shot her a silencing glare.

A fight. Not yet. Raven's eyes flickered towards the helmet she'd made, sitting in the corner with her armour. Death had told her there would be a fight between her and Zac. She'd dreamed of it a few times in the last year. If she was to raise her blade to Zac, she would be well protected. She thought it appropriate that she face him with the very sword and armour he made.

"Zachary is a murderer," she said to Grace. "I'm glad he didn't come in. I would not have welcomed him."

Delia gasped. "You don't believe that. Raven, he's your cousin. Your brother."

"He's no family of mine," she said, recognising the ice in her voice. "I don't want to talk about him," she muttered.

"Then I won't talk about who my brother found in—" Grace began; then all three of them turned as if realising Joan was still there.

"Joan, you've done a good job there, do you want to go outside?" Raven asked. "You can help me again afterwards."

The girl's eyes lit up! She quickly ran out.

"My brother found him," Grace said. "A town further North called Hopeton. He asked around and Zachary has been living on the outskirts of town, keeping to himself mostly."

She'd heard of Hopeton, a small town North of Kempshire, that belonged to no shire, isolated near the mountains.

"Is your brother sure it's him?" she asked.

Grace smiled. "Smokey eye, it was him."

"Who has your brother told?" Raven asked.

"Only me. He said it won't do anyone any good now to know where he is. He lives apart from society, he's punishing himself, and that's more than any other punishment would be from Lord Gerard, or the Enforcers."

Watching his family in secret, living away from people on the edge of society, this was not the Zac she knew. She almost pitied him, to be so alone. Almost. Raven had hoped to find a clue as to where he hid. She and Markus had returned to Riverwick, finding the stable empty. She had very little time to act upon this newfound knowledge of his current location. To advance meant it was likely that Death would try to intervene again.

"What do we do if we see him? If the children see him?" Grace asked.

"Just be careful," she said as a warning.

"Of Zachary?" Delia asked in disbelief.

"If you're seen talking to him, Lord Gerard may arrest you, too." Raven avoided Delia's eyes. The woman was still very much in love with Zac, and any discussions about him usually ended with Delia defending him. *I cannot blame her for wanting a father for her son.* "You don't want to risk getting caught up with him, Delia. He's dangerous."

"I don't believe he murdered anyone." Delia said. "I'm surprised you believe that. You once called him brother; now, you've become so cold when it comes to him. Raven, something happened. Why won't you talk to us about it?"

"Why would he start a new life if he's innocent?" Grace pointed out.

He has a life in another town. A human life. Is this his father's doing, or did he walk away? Something about it seemed off.

Grace put her hand on Raven's shoulder. "When you're ready to talk, we'll talk. I don't mean to push you."

"You have people outside waiting to come in." Joan had returned.

Raven beamed. "Here they come. Let them in, apprentice." She pointed to the raven sign on the back wall. "Raven's smithy is officially open!"

Chapter 49

Zachary stared at the ceiling as the familiar nudging from within echoed against his mind. Walking away from his father had done nothing to rid himself of the calling. He had tried to ignore it over the last twelve months, wishing it would go away. But each time, it became too great to fight. Now, the pull of The Shadow Realm, and the dark calling, had awakened him. If it wasn't the dying waking him, it was nightmares, and he couldn't remember the last time he'd had a decent night's sleep.

Zachary filled a basin and washed his face. Staring at his reflection in the water, he didn't recognise the face that looked back at him. His beard and hair showed grey, and there were deep shadows under his eyes. Charlotte had once said he looked haunted. As another wave passed through him, his eyes turned white, black lines stretching across his entire face, down his arms. He hoped he'd never be caught around people, looking like this.

"I'm going," he muttered as if anyone could hear him.

His father had not returned to drag him back, but Zachary would never be free from that curse. Weary, he pulled on warm clothes and a cloak, not wanting to be caught in cold weather again. It was unlikely his father would save him a second time. Frederick and Charlotte were the only ones who spoke to him beyond passing by, or business. The people of Hopeton left him alone, for which he was grateful. He was not like them and would never know the peace that awaited them. That realisation always gave him a heavy heart.

As he let The Shadow Realm close around him, thoughts returned to the life he'd left behind. He missed Raven and had looked in a few times, making sure she did not know he was there. Brief conversations with his children had brought such joy, making it hard to resist seeking more in secret. He had grown up much of his life without his father, and now they would, too. *Will they hate me for abandoning them?* To them, he was just a stranger by the river.

The calling took him to a village in the mountains, snow-capped, with an icy wind. There he found a woman lying on the ground.

"You won't die out here," he expressed as he knelt to lift her in his arms. *She should at least be inside, maybe in a place of comfort.*

She groaned, her eyes opening.

"Where do you live?" he asked.

She didn't speak, only pointing to a house. He walked inside, seeking somewhere to lay her.

On her bed, she looked up at him, catching sight of the Darkness and gasped, trying to get away, yet lacking the energy to do so.

"Who are ye? What are ye?" she croaked, her accent heavy. He was in Scotland.

"Please, just sit down. It will be less painful for the both of us," he told her.

"English?" she reacted to his accent. "What do you want?"

He hated the words with everything in him, but they were the only words that people understood. "Your fight is over," he tried to comfort her. "I have come to take you to The Crossover, where you will find peace. No more pain."

Her eyes glazed over, and a tear slid down her cheek. "I'm not ready," she whispered.

Zachary wiped the tear away with a thumb. "No one ever is."

"Will it hurt?" she asked.

He gave her a tender smile. "No. You will be reunited with your family."

He gripped her hand, letting his touch release her from the mortal coil.

In The Crossover, Zachary watched as the woman embraced a man, smiling at her family that surrounded her. It was always a tender moment, but it hurt. He longed to have that, instead of centuries that bore down on him. Reuniting people with their families, never having his own peace. Bitterness burned through him, as a tear formed in the corner of his eye.

"Isaac," his mother spoke from behind him, her voice sad.

He hadn't seen her in twelve months, careful to leave before she arrived.

"Mother." He wrapped his arms around her.

"Oh, my little Isaac."

"I'm Zachary," he muttered.

"You don't like Isaac?"

"I took the name Zachary when we sought to hide from Father and all his name would bring," he whispered. "I tried to leave, but it still pulls at me."

She leaned back, looking up at him. "Have you asked Thomas to take it back?"

He shook his head. "I walked away from him, from everything. He's left me alone."

"Talk to him. Ask him," she suggested.

He scoffed. "He's unlikely to grant me freedom from this. He forced it."

His father's presence burned into his conscience. *He's here.*

"It must be willingly received," his father said from behind him.

Zachary spun around; his father was there. His form was different, likely that of someone who comforted the latest poor soul as they passed. But there was no ignoring the Darkness that emanated from him.

"Are you following me?" he demanded.

Father resumed his own shape, the one that showed his Darkness, one black eye, one white. "This is the entrance to The Crossover. Have you forgotten this was my calling before it was yours?" his father glared at him.

Emma's eyes widened at the sight of his father. "Thomas, what have you done to our son?" she demanded, her face reddening. "You would doom him to this curse?"

"Do not call me Thomas," his father said. "I am Death." He shrugged. "He made his choice."

"One you *forced* on him. Amelia told me you took him to The Shadow Realm. How long was he there, tormented until there was too much Darkness for him to fight?" she demanded, her voice rising.

His father stepped up to Emma, towering over her, changing his shape once again. She held her hands on her hips as she glared at him.

"I don't care *what* you are now. You and Graeme lost your humanity, I know that. But he is *my* son, and *you* have cursed him." Her voice shook with anger. "*Take it back, now*. Let him have the peaceful life he deserves! Thomas, I know you wanted better for him; we both did."

He stared down at her a moment longer. "**You're as bad as Amelia,**" he said, the voices of Thomas and Graeme dark.

"I know you remember me. What I was to you," his mother whispered. "Please." She reached a hand towards him, but he caught it.

He returned to the form of Zachary's father.

"You and Amelia keep trying to appeal to the men I was," his father grumbled.

But the dark lines faded, and his eyes turned dark blue.

"My joy," his mother said. "I was your heart, remember. I refuse to believe there is nothing left of my Thomas."

"It doesn't matter what you believe." His eyes hardened, and he cast them on Zachary. "I cannot take it from him. It must be willingly given up and received. I already have the Touch of Death; I cannot do it."

Realisation sunk in what that meant. "No!"

"You would have him curse another?" his mother asked in disbelief. She stared at Zachary with wide eyes.

His father turned his stare back to his mother. "Not just anyone. Someone of my bloodline. Born with the Darkness inside them."

"Raven?" Zachary asked. "You would have me put this on her?" She would likely try to kill him. *Can I die? Where would I go?*

"Or your children." Father confirmed.

He couldn't breathe. "I cannot do that." He would never wish this on his sister, no matter how many times father claimed she would have the same fate. But the idea of his children filled him with horror.

"Then you will have to accept what you are. It hurts less when you give in to it."

Father left, leaving Zachary alone with his mother.

"I'm sorry. Isa....Zachary," his mother met his eyes, and a single tear fell down her cheek. "This is not the life I dreamed of for you."

"I'm so tired," he said. "I want to remember being *me.* I gave in to Darkness and I was no longer me. I still can't find who I was." He wasn't a little boy any more, but the urge to cry struck him hard. "I'm so tired," he repeated.

Her eyes filled with tears. "I know, son." She reached a hand towards him.

"I have to go soon," he told her. This realm didn't want him here, and The Shadow Realm was pulling him back.

She hugged him again. "I'm sorry this has happened to you, Zachary. I'm sorry I wasn't there. I missed seeing you grow up."

Devastation hurt his chest. "You're apologising for dying?" he asked in disbelief, choking back a laugh. "I don't think that was your fault, Mother."

"If I hadn't, your father..."

He cut her off. "I've asked myself that many times. What father became...I think there were a lot of reasons he and Uncle Graeme became that. I don't think we'll ever truly understand them. Or how that same Darkness is in me." He let out a breath. "I think it's been there since the day I died. Coming back from The Shadow Realm had its effects. It isn't a place people should come back from. Being in there for the time I was, I fought so hard, but it was not a battle I was ever going to win." Saying the words out loud helped him confirm that he had fought. When he wanted to give in every day, he had fought.

She squeezed his hand. "Go home, find some happiness. You deserve it. My family, you, brought me joy, perhaps yours can do the same, and give you a moment's peace from this life. I will see you next time."

The Shadow Realm pulled him back. But instead of going home, he found himself drawn towards Oakborough again, longing for a glimpse of his family.

Chapter 50

Raven's presence had shifted. Darker, a change that could only be due to her time in The Shadow Realm, however short it had been. Zachary watched through the veil. Black flames within her were more noticeable than they were the first time he saw them. He missed her, missed their talks. She would speak to him about everything in her life.

As if sensing him, she glanced up. "I know you're there."

He was about to step through the veil.

"No," she whispered. "You cannot be here. It's been a year. You gave me what I asked for; nothing has changed. You stopped me from killing him."

She had mistaken his presence for that of their father. Hope died, crushing Zachary. She wasn't ready to forgive him, and he couldn't blame her. Instead, he sought out his children, finding them once again by the river. Hiding in The Shadow Realm as they threw snow at each other, he couldn't hold back the smile. Proud that the twins and Arthur had bonded as a family, he imagined what it would be like to be in their lives.

Just as she had when he was trapped in The Shadow Realm, Giselle seemed to sense him, raising her eyes to meet his. They talked among themselves, then approached him.

"You watch us because you're sad," she said, her eyes on his face.

He stared in shock. They'd seen him through the veil.

"We know who you are." Giselle exchanged glances with her brothers and stepped towards him. "You're our father."

He left The Shadow Realm. "I am," he said with relief. He didn't like hiding who he was from them.

"You're a murderer." Arthur's voice had a quiet rage in it. "Why are you here?"

"Arthur, we don't know that," Giselle scolded.

"Aunt Raven says he is." Arthur glared at him with eyes that were so similar to Zachary's mother's. Eyes he himself had inherited from her. "You left us."

"You're right. I was abandoned by my father, too; I know the pain," he admitted.

"Then how could you do the same to us? And Mother. Do you not love her?" Arthur demanded.

The boy's anger buried hurt. Just as his had. He reached out, but Arthur flinched at his touch.

"People hate me because of you." His son's words were like a punch to his chest. He and Raven had been spared from that, because of Aunt Amelia.

His daughter stepped between them. "I'm Giselle," she said. "This is my twin brother Joseph. You were watching Aunt Raven that day."

Once again, she had seen him from within The Shadow Realm. His children clearly had abilities. He wasn't sure that was a good thing.

Smiling at her attempt to keep the peace, he nodded. "She is angry at me, like your brother."

"Arthur is known to be your son," Giselle said. "It hurts him what people say."

"Not you?" he asked.

"No, our mother never told anyone who our real father was. She only told us," she replied.

Grace's time in his bed had been short, as her family forced her into marriage. One that ended with the man summoned to war.

"Is that a real sword?" Arthur asked with hesitation.

Zachary smiled. "It is."

"Did Aunt Raven make it?" Joseph's eyes were wide. "She makes swords."

"I know she does. I made this one." Zachary drew the sword, holding it out for all to see. "Did you know I taught Raven to be a blacksmith?"

"Can I hold it?" Arthur asked.

Zachary caught the glimmer of excitement in his son's eyes. "Have you held a sword before?" he asked.

Arthur shook his head.

Zachary held out the sword for Arthur to take. The boy gripped the handle, the weight of the sword too much for him. Laughing, Zachary took it back. "We will have to build up some muscle for you." he said, resheathing the blade.

"Can you teach us?" Joseph asked, his eyes shining.

He wanted that more than anything. But before the words could make it out of his mouth, the calling nudged at him.

"I have to go," he said, apologetically. "Go back, before someone comes looking for you. But I'll be back here tomorrow."

"You're coming back?" Arthur asked.

"I will," he promised.

They ran off, and he quietly slipped into The Shadow Realm.

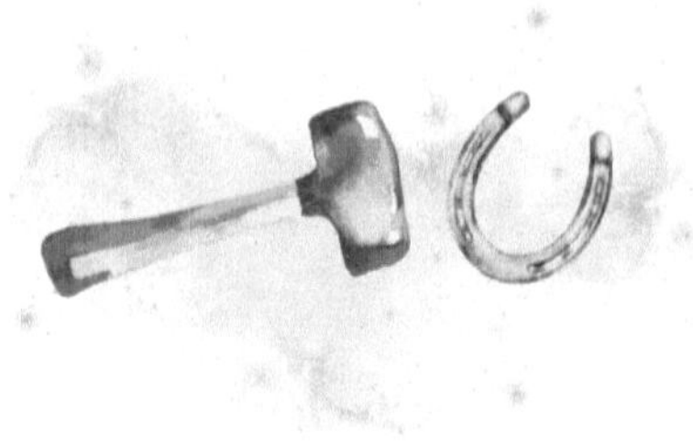

The ocean pounded against the ship, spraying salt water. Following the calling, he moved towards the hull. No one stopped to question him. Finally, he found a man on the floor, bleeding. Zachary knelt before the man.

"Who are you?" the wounded man demanded.

"I'm here to take you home," he said. "Your fight is over."

As if to prove him wrong, the man slashed out with a dagger. Metal sliced Zac's shoulder, and he hissed in pain.

"You do not need to fight me," he growled.

"It was you!" the man accused.

Zachary pressed a hand to his shoulder, blood seeping from the gash. "What are you talking about?"

"You stabbed me. I found you, a stowaway."

"It wasn't me." He reached again for the man before him. "It's time to rest."

Not wanting another swing to come his way, he pressed his hand to the man's chest, letting go of the energy that surged in him. But before he could return to The Shadow Realm, quick, heavy footsteps approached from behind. Once again, a blade bit into him as he turned. Piercing his side, he turned, meeting the eyes of another. Without thinking, he grabbed the very dagger that had pierced his shoulder, and rammed it between his attacker's ribs. He didn't wait; he stepped into The Shadow Realm.

For once, it was a relief to be in The Shadow Realm. He took his dead to

The Crossover and left before his mother could see him. He needed help. He couldn't go to his father, so only one person remained.

Zachary hit the ground hard. A blacksmith's forge and a black armour plate with a raven in the centre. It seemed a lifetime ago since he'd made that for her. A woman and a man spoke across the room, both voices he recognised. Relief flooded through him as he lifted his head.

"Raven," he called out.

The voices stopped. Waves of pain crashed over him, and he passed out for a moment.

Raven stood over him, Markus behind her. She held a sword to him. "What are you doing here, Zachary?" she demanded, her eyes unforgiving.

Zachary. Not Zac. Another indication of the chasm between them. Her eyes held no warmth, only a cold rage, with Darkness flickering around her. She still wanted to kill him.

"Please," he begged. "Help me." He fell into nothing.

Chapter 51

Raven stared down at Zac as his eyes closed. He still showed his connection to the Darkness.

"What is he doing here?" All this time, and he'd sought her out.

"He's bleeding," Markus said, kneeling. "I know you're still angry at him, Raven, but enough to let him die?"

"You're defending him, after what he did?" Hurt prickled against her rage.

"He came to *you*, Raven. Not to his father. He knows of the anger you hold towards him, and he came anyway. Are you going to turn him away, let him die? He's wounded." Markus stood, his gaze intense.

"It will save me the job of killing him," she muttered.

Markus reached for her sword. "Put that down. You cannot turn away a man pleading for help."

She lowered the sword, yet was unwilling to cool her temper.

"What am I supposed to do? I'm not a surgeon, and I can't fetch one. He's a known murderer," Raven reminded Markus.

"You and I both know the public accusations were the actions of his father." Markus pulled her sword from her grip. "Let's get him off the floor and onto the table."

"Your job is to arrest him; is that why you're helping him?" she demanded.

"No. I am helping him because, despite your anger, I know the pain his death would cause you. You have lost so many; I would not see you lose another," he said.

There was logic in his words. Between them, they lifted Zac and carried him to the table. She lifted his tunic to look at the wound.

"That looks bad. Can he actually die?" Markus asked. "I don't think there is anyone who will know."

Dread turned to ice inside her. "There is one person," she murmured. The last person she wanted to see.

His jaw twitched. "You would call him here?"

"He's been living on the edge of a town to avoid people, probably to hide from our father. I don't know if this is a good idea, but we don't know how to help him without a surgeon," she admitted.

Markus frowned. "I don't like this."

"Neither do I. But we don't have a lot of choices here. Anyone else would tell Lord Gerard," she pointed out. "Then I'd be arrested for helping him."

Annoyance surged through her. Zac could cost her everything by coming here.

"Do what you have to do, then." He rested his hand on his sword. "He'd better not try anything."

She didn't know how to call for him. "Why didn't you go to him?" she asked an unconscious Zac. "Death. We need your help."

Nothing happened. No expected presence. Markus raised his eyebrows, and she shook her head.

"How do you know he's not watching?" he asked.

"I always feel his presence when he does," she said.

Zac groaned and his eyes opened, unfocused. "Zachary, you need to call for your father. I don't know how to help you." *I don't know if I want to.*

"No." His eyes fluttered closed again.

"He's your father, too." Markus whispered.

The very reminder of it sent a shudder through her. "What's your point?"

"He may hear your call if you acknowledge that."

She shook her head. "I'm not calling him that."

"You don't need to have any connection with him, Raven. Your cousin is about to bleed to death on your table. There is no other choice."

Her resistance to the idea was difficult to combat. She let out a loud breath to show Markus her displeasure. "Father." As the word slipped from her tongue, a spark lit within, as if his presence acknowledged her call. One word had never felt so wrong. "I do not like calling him that."

"I know. Try again," Markus instructed.

"Father," she repeated. "I don't know if you can hear me. Please, I need your help. Your son needs your help."

A spark of Darkness shot through her in response, and she gasped. Cold and emptiness wrapped around her, and she found herself in The Shadow Realm.

"**You did not fight being drawn here.**" Her father's voice in the shadows echoed. "**Something has changed in you. You're not so afraid of the Darkness any more. Of being my daughter.**"

"Not here." She told the void, ignoring his words. "I need you to help Zachary. He's hurt."

He stood before her, in the form made of Darkness, wisps of shadow rising from him. "**Have you given up your desire to kill him?**"

She shuddered as she met his eyes. "No. Markus spoke for him, to give him a chance."

"**Isaac came to you for help. He does not want mine,**" he declared.

"But *I'm* asking you for help," she pleaded. "I don't know if he can die or not, but it looks like he is about to." Despite herself, tears welled up. It seemed she wasn't willing to let him die, after all. The realisation that he'd come to her meant he considered her the only one from whom he could seek help. His life truly must be lonely. "I've never asked anything of you, I'm asking this."

His silence unnerved her, as he stared, unblinking.

"Would you let your son die?" Her fury flared. "Why did you bring me here then if you won't help?"

"**If he weren't resisting the Darkness, he wouldn't need my help. He walked away. I'm not the answer you seek.**" He took a step towards her, holding a hand out. "**Stay here; accept what you are. Forget about your cousin; he will return to The Shadow Realm soon enough.**"

Ice crept up her skull. "Are you going to trap me here like you did him?" *Calling him was a mistake.*

His smile was cold. "**When you are ready, you will not need to be trapped here. You will come here willingly.**"

"That will never happen," she insisted.

His confirmation that Zac had turned his back on Death didn't change anything. He'd killed her mother. This did not erase the bad blood between them. But Markus's words rang true. Zac would die. She wasn't sure the past was enough of a reason to let him.

"**He made his choice.**" Death said.

Disappointed, she could only stare at him. He'd been her only hope to help Zac.

"Return me, so I can at least make sure he doesn't die alone." Her eyes stung as she fought back tears. She wouldn't cry in front of him.

The Shadow Realm faded, and she was back in her shop. Death's presence remained.

Markus was bent over Zac. "Raven's trying to get you help."

Zac let out a groan again. "Raven." His eyes met hers.

"You're awake." She approached him with hesitance. "You took a risk coming to me. I could just as easily kill you myself."

Zac's eyes bored into hers. "I'm sorry."

There was no mistaking what he meant. "Sorry doesn't erase what you did, but now isn't the time for that."

"If not now, when?" he grunted. "Is now not the best time for us to talk?"

"**Move,**" the voice behind her rang with authority.

Markus nudged her aside as Death took on the shape of Thomas.

Zac tried to sit up. "No." He shot Raven with a look of betrayal. "You brought him?"

Thomas pushed Zac on his back. "Don't be a fool. There is no one else. She did the right thing."

Overcome by delight in response to his acknowledgement, she quickly suppressed it. *What does such a being know of doing the right thing?* Resentful of her own response to his words, she stood back as Thomas tore at Zac's tunic to get a better look at the wound on his shoulder.

"This is hardly a mortal wound." He turned his eyes towards Raven. "You called me here for this?"

"Not there." Zac's breathing had become difficult as he lifted his tunic to show the hole in his side. Blood poured from where he had been stabbed.

"I see. Remove your tunic." Thomas directed instructions to her. "Get me a knife. Heat it in your forge."

Before she could move, Markus held out his to her. She put the blade into the flames, his hand on her shoulder. "Are you alright?" He gave her a look of concern.

"Ask me after this," she replied.

He gave her arm a squeeze. Raven returned to Zac's side, handing over the knife. Zac had removed his tunic and discarded it on the floor. He glared at his father.

"Hold him," Thomas ordered.

Markus held Zac down by the shoulders.

"This is going to hurt." Thomas didn't give Zac time to brace before pressing the hot metal to the wound.

Flesh sizzled, and Zac jerked in response. The smell of burned meat hit Raven, and the bloodcurdling scream was cut off as he lost consciousness again. Thomas sealed the wound.

"Heat it again," he told Markus. "I need to cauterise his shoulder, too."

Markus did as he was instructed. Again, Thomas pressed the blade to flesh.

"How do you know how to do this?" Raven asked.

He lifted his eyes to her face. "I was at war. Four years. I'm no surgeon, but there are some things I learned. Sealing wounds was something many of us learned early when we were the ones bleeding."

"Thank you," she said as he stepped away from Zac. He would live. The relief that washed over her was unexpected.

He narrowed his eyes at her. "Don't mistake my helping for humanity. I will ask for something in return."

Her heart pounded. "You want something?"

"Not today. You two have a lot to talk about." He turned his attention to Markus. "Your servant has hidden well, but his time is up. You were there. Your time is short, too."

"What?" Markus frowned.

No reply came, as Darkness surrounded Thomas and for a brief moment, she caught sight of what could only be the veil.

Chapter 52

Raven's humming reminded him of the days Aunt Amelia used to do the same. A comfort to him, while also a pain that he couldn't escape. Zachary opened his eyes, only to be hit by the pain of his wounds, a groan rising from his throat.

Raven's eyes still reflected hurt and anger, but there was a flicker within, of the ice melting.

He pushed down the Darkness, allowing himself to at least *look* human, and sat up. "Where is he?"

"He's gone," she told him. "He did what he needed, and then left."

Filled with relief, Zac climbed from the table. "Thank you."

"He said if you weren't resisting the Darkness, you wouldn't have needed help." Her eyes narrowed. "Why did you come to me?"

"Where else could I go? I hoped you wouldn't turn me away." He examined the sealed wounds on his side, and his shoulder. "I'm glad you didn't. I wish you hadn't called him, though."

The spark of anger was not hard to miss. "You land in a heap on my floor, expecting me to know how to help you? What else was I supposed to do, get a surgeon? You'd be chained in a cell by now." She picked up his tunic from the floor and threw it at him. "If it weren't for Markus, I would have killed you myself."

"Then give Markus my thanks;, I owe him my life." he pulled the tunic over his head. His manner in addressing family needed improvement. He'd spent too long by himself. "Where is your Enforcer?"

"He'll be back soon." She finally made eye contact. "Are you going to disappear again?"

They had fought before, but it had never been as awkward or strained as that moment. "Perhaps it's time we talked," he said.

She put her hands on her hips. "Then talk."

"I miss her," he admitted. "Every time we fought; she was the peacekeeper."

Her eyes glinted. "You have no right to say that to me."

"Will I ever earn your forgiveness?" he pleaded.

"You killed my mother and you expect me to forgive you?" Her voice was like ice.

Coming to her had been a mistake. Her determination to hold grudges hadn't changed. He turned to leave.

"This isn't just something you can fix right away just because you're sorry," she continued, giving him pause. "But please don't leave. You want to talk; I'll listen. We're still family, as I'm constantly reminded. Mother asked me not to be angry at you. She held no animosity at what you did; perhaps I should listen to her."

He gave her a tentative smile. "I can work with that." He winced as another wave of pain passed through him.

"You're in pain." The anger in her eyes turned to concern.

"I will heal. I can thank you for that." He gave her a small smile of appreciation and reached his hand across the table, but she pulled hers away.

"So, you're you again," she said.

"Not completely," he admitted.

Her gaze softened. "But you're more *you* than you were in Riverwick. I didn't recognise you at all."

"I was intoxicated by the Darkness," he admitted. "I had fought it for so long, and once I gave in, I didn't know why I had resisted it to start with."

"Is it that seductive?" Something flickered in her eyes. *Is that fear?*

Unsure he was ready for this conversation, he hesitated. He found her watching him. "Are you sure you want to talk about this, Raven?"

"I told you, I'm ready to listen," she muttered.

He sighed, recalling what he'd felt in Riverwick. The things he'd said to Raven. "Once it gets its hooks in, there's no holding it back. But it's almost like you don't want to either. It's like a presence within you that separates you from your humanity. Right or wrong doesn't matter, only Darkness. You've gone over the edge and there's no way back, but you don't want to go back."

"But you *did* come back," she reminded him.

He nodded. "Her singing is what brought me back. It pierced the fog, bringing memories to the surface. She said she was expecting me."

A tear slid down her cheek. "She sang?"

He smiled. "She did."

Emotion rose to her eyes; the grief of a daughter shone through.

"Did I say something wrong?" he asked.

"She stopped singing after that night. And baking. I barely recognised her at the end. I think she was slowly dying, despite Death letting her live."

"She made bread the day I took her. For me." he offered.

More tears followed the first. "That was the loaf in her house. It was you that ate the slice?"

He reached for her hand again, and this time, she didn't move it. "She knew it was her time, and she embraced it."

"Why did it have to be you?" she cried.

"Father referred to it as *the calling,* but it's more like a command that you cannot disobey. Once you hear it, the need to follow it becomes too much, and it starts to hurt the more you resist," he explained.

"Was this why he allowed her to live? As a punishment? He knew that you'd give in and be called to her?" Her anger had returned, but aimed at her father.

Her suspicions were so close to his own. "I think so. He is different from the father I remember. There is cruelty I never expected. The Darkness has warped who he was."

"How do we know this wasn't always him? We know there was Darkness in…" She stopped short of naming her own father. "They had a bond; maybe who we see now is because he stopped fighting. Just like you. It held no impact that he sent you to end the life of a woman he once loved."

He caught sight of the raw grief he'd caused, and it broke his heart. An idea appealed to him. He shouldn't, it would probably anger his father if he found out, but it would make Raven happy.

"Do you want to see her?" he asked. "Will that help?"

Fearful hope flickered across her features. "How?"

"I can take you there, to The Crossover. You won't have long; the realm doesn't exactly welcome the living. But she'll sense your arrival. It will bring her to you."

Her silence worried him, her gaze lowered.

"I'd like that," she said at last.

He rose to his feet and reached out. Raven glanced around the room before grasping his outstretched hand, wrapping her other around his forearm.

"We have to go through The Shadow Realm first. Don't let go. Don't listen to any voices," he instructed

She nodded, and he let the Darkness in. Raven's eyes widened and she gasped.

"Sorry," he muttered, trying to hold on to himself. "I cannot access The Shadow Realm without…" He didn't finish but understanding showed in her eyes.

He pulled her into The Shadow Realm. He loathed this place and quickly entered The Crossover.

Raven smiled, clearly feeling the peace all around her. "This is The Crossover?"

"It is. She'll be here soon." So would his own mother.

"Zachary?" it did not take her long at all. Her eyes took in his bloody, torn tunic. "What happened?"

"I was wounded, but I'm alright now," he assured his mother.

She turned her attention to Raven. "That is unmistakably Graeme's daughter. Oh my! Look at her eyes. She looks so much like him." At his cousin's discomfort, his mother smiled. "But I see just as much of Amelia in you, too."

"Raven?" Aunt Amelia had arrived. She took in the sight of Zachary and Raven, and her face fell. "No. No, Zachary."

"She's alright. She wanted to see you," he said. "We cannot stay long though." He reached out mentally, sensing his father. There was no indication he was coming. Someone else was, though, a soul linked to him and Raven.

"What's this, then?" a male voice sounded behind him.

They all turned. Zachary found himself staring into a face he had not seen since he was a boy. Black hair, eyes that were almost identical to his father's, a greying beard. A large man who still had a hard, angry scowl.

"Hello, Grandfather," Zachary said.

Ethan stared at Amelia and Emma. "Where are your husbands? They brought me here, but they're too scared to face me?"

"That's our grandfather?" Raven marvelled.. "Mother was right: He is unpleasant."

His memory of the man was that he spent a lot of time in the stable and had a temper. He'd been a little afraid of the moods, but there were moments where the man had been gentle with him.

"Grandfather, do you remember me?" he asked.

"Of course I remember you, I'm not an idiot," came the reply. "Is it you who woke me?"

"Ethan, you're dead, you have no need to be rude to your grandson. He's not his father," Emma scolded.

Ethan grunted. "You could have fooled me. Look at his face. He's cursed. He even looks like him." His gaze fell on Raven. "Who are you?"

"I'm Raven," she affirmed.

"What kind of name is Raven?" he demanded.

"Twenty years in peace and nothing's changed, has it?" Zachary's mother fumed. "You're still as bitter as you were in Riverwick."

"Ethan." Aunt Amelia glared. "She is my daughter. I will not have you speak to her that way."

"You had another child. At least this one lived longer than the other. I can see she's Graeme's. Probably cursed with the same Darkness he had."

Raven looked like she'd been slapped, and Amelia's face turned red, her eyes blazing.

"Ethan, *stop.*" A woman approached them, her eyes as blue as Raven's, her long hair a blonde so pale it was almost white. "That's our granddaughter."

A look of wonder crossed his grandfather's face; his scowl smoothed out. "Isobel." His tone softened.

Isobel?

She gazed at Zachary. "And our grandson. You have suffered greatly, you poor boy." She lifted his chin, turning his face as she examined him. Something made him shiver, as if she were looking into his very soul. "I see you did not escape the Darkness that claimed my sons."

She dropped his chin and moved towards Raven, doing the same to her. "It burns in you, as well."

Raven's eyes sought out Zachary's before returning to the woman before her.

His mother stood next to him, and Amelia moved to join her.

"Am I fated to fall to Darkness, too?" Raven's voice shook.

"I cannot read your future. I only see what is already there." Finally, she faced them all. "This is quite the family reunion. Three generations of Blakes. I feel there is *another* line, still in the mortal realm."

How does she know all this? Zachary opened his mouth, but a familiar dark presence approached.

"He's here," he warned.

His father entered The Crossover in his dark form, eyes narrowed as he caught sight of Zachary.

"**Mortals do not belong here,**" he growled. "**You do not have this gift so you can bring visitors when it suits you.**"

"I wouldn't call it a gift," Zachary muttered.

"At least allow me to meet my grandparents," Raven snapped.

His father towered over Raven. "**You do not belong here. You must go back.**"

"You!" Ethan spat. "I see you embraced that which was inside you. Both of you."

Zachary frowned. *Does he recognise them in this form?*

Father turned his empty gaze to the old man. "**Perhaps I should return you to The Shadow Realm. Does a man who beat his sons and wanted to drown them as newborns really deserve peace?**" He stepped towards Ethan, the black scythe appearing in his hand.

"You beat our sons?" Zachary's grandmother's voice was soft, making his grandfather flinch. "You hit my children? You wanted to drown them? My sons?!" Her voice rose.

"They killed you. You told me you saw the Darkness your death would bring into the world. The youngest one was born with black eyes," his grandfather stuttered.

"I should have let you drown them." Another voice, which Zachary recognised. James. "I couldn't have foreseen what they were, what they'd become."

The shift in his father was so fast Zachary stumbled back. He held James by the throat, lifting him off the ground. "**You! I remember what you did.**"

"With Lord Samson and the Enforcers on my doorstep, there was no other choice but to do what they ordered me to do." James said around the hand at his throat.

"**You betrayed me. Us. I should throw you and my father to The**

Shadow Realm, forever lost, following the voices of those you lost."

"You talk of betrayal?" James bellowed. "You were like sons to me; I sheltered you from Ethan. You were murderers. Now look at you. You're monsters. Not human."

Zachary's father dropped James, instead holding the scythe on him.

"What are you going to do, kill me again? You already did that when you burned Riverwick down. You slaughtered your own people." James stood face to face with Zachary's father, furious.

"My sons." his grandmother's voice was gentle, but his father turned towards her. She met Zachary's eyes before glancing at Raven. "He is right; you do not belong here. Take her back."

"Raven, let's go," Zachary said. The realm didn't want him here, and he could feel it trying to push him out.

"Wait," she whispered.

He glanced back at their grandmother. To meet his her had never been something he'd thought would happen.

"Show me you, the human you," his grandmother said in a soft voice to his father.

The shadow form changed to that of his father. Dark wisps rose off him like smoke. "I am not human," he said in Graeme and Thomas's voice.

Isobel grabbed his jaw, peering into his face, as if searching for something. "I saw the Darkness that my death would bring into the world. I wish I could have been there to see the both of you grow up. Much pain would have been spared. I am sorry."

"I do not regret what I am. What we are." Zachary's father examined her. "There is Darkness in you."

Isobel smiled. "Yes, there is."

Chapter 53

Like a strong current in the river, a pressure pushed against Raven. Guiding her away. She fought against it, wrapping her arms around her mother.

"We have to go. We've been here too long." Zac said. "We're about to be expelled. You'll get lost in The Shadow Realm if we're not connected."

"I miss you," she said, tightening her embrace.

"You have to live your life, my little Raven. We will see each other again. I will greet you when you are brought here after you pass. Many years from now," her mother promised.

The words churned inside her, setting off a deep dread. "We'll see each other again," she repeated.

Her mother whispered in her ear. "Forgive your cousin; it was not his fault. Your fathers forced it on him. You have to work together. Raven, you need each other."

Raven let go. "Alright," she told Zac. "I am ready to leave.

He pulled her back to The Shadow Realm. "I don't like this place," she said.

"Nor I," Zac responded. "I'll take you home."

"This is part of you now." She glanced up at him. "Zac..."

"Stop." Death had followed them. "You have a duty to the dead, not to use your abilities to visit your dead mother." He narrowed his eyes at Raven. "Or hers."

"She needed it," Zacsaid.

"That isn't for you to decide!" Death boomed. "Only the dead belong in The Crossover. You awoke them all."

His eyes were blue, one dark, the other like hers, and she could see a storm churning within. She wondered if meeting with his parents had unsettled him.

"What did you mean that there is darkness in your mother?" she asked.

"Time for you to go home, Raven. Your Enforcer will need you today."

Ice gripped her heart as dread weighed on her. *Markus... Something's going to happen to Markus.* "No."

"You already know what I'm talking about without asking." Death gave her a cold smile.

"Please, you've taken so much, leave him be. He has such a short time already," Zac said.

"It is his time." Death advanced on Zac. "You're more trouble than you're worth. Perhaps it's time I contain you here until you give in like you did before."

Zac tensed next to her. The hand tightened around her arm, and she noticed a slight tremor. "Please, you don't need to do that."

Death's cold smile became dark, menacing. "I do. I cannot have you interfering while I visit a servant from Kempschester." He wrapped his arm around Raven's, a tight grip, pulling her away from Zac. "I bind you here."

Black shackles wrapped around Zac's wrists and ankles. His eyes widened. "Please don't," he pleaded.

The way his voice shook hit Raven. *Is this what he did before?* Terror shone from Zac's eyes.

"Father, you cannot leave me here." Zac fell to his knees. "Please, not again." His chin trembled.

"Why are you doing this to him?" Raven demanded. "Have you not punished him enough?"

"Would you like to join him?" Death's grip on her arm had become painful. "I can just as easily leave you here, too. Let the darkness claim you completely."

Horror choked her. "No." Helplessness drowned her anger. She didn't know how to help Zac, just that she had no desire to be trapped here, too. "Take me home."

"Raven, don't leave me." Zachar reached for her. "I'll lose myself again." The desperation in his voice, his eyes, sent waves of anguish.

A single tear escaped, leaving a hot trail down her cheek. She had never felt so helpless. "I don't know how to help you, Zac."

He pulled on the shackles. "Release me," he said. "Father, please don't."

Chilling laughter echoed around the realm, and she wasn't sure if it was Death's or something else.

Zac's eyes turned white as he pulled at the restraints again, darkness creeping in. "**Let me go!**" His voice echoed, dark and full of fury.

"Zac, hold on." Raven told him with urgency.

He let out a roar as he lunged for Death. But he never reached them, as The Shadow Realm vanished. She stood in the middle of her shop, facing Markus.

"You're back," he said, letting out a breath of relief. "Where did you go? Where's Zachary?"

"He's trapped in The Shadow Realm again," she said, the weight of her words suffocating her.

"Trapped? Can he not leave this time?"

"Death has bound him there." Urgency had her heart pounding. "We'll work out how to help him. But first, we have to go to your father."

"My father?" A line appeared on his forehead.

"His greatest fear bears down on him." She reached for Markus, unsure how to comfort him.

"No. He's going after my father?" Confusion faded, his mouth set in a hard line, eyes flashed.

"We have to go," she urged.

He stormed towards the door, and she followed, grabbing her sword belt as she did. He didn't wait for her, his horse already moving, and she climbed onto the back of hers.

Horse hooves drummed on the hard ground as she caught up, her heart matching it. She had no words that wouldn't anger Markus more. As they raced towards Markus's father's house, Raven's dread increased. *We're going to be too late.* Death had told her to comfort him. *How long before he goes after Markus, though?* She didn't want Markus to die and couldn't help but wonder if she was leading him to his death. During her dreams of her fight with Zac, Markus had not been present.

Before she could follow that thought, they arrived at Markus's father's house. They dismounted, and she followed him to the house. The dark presence of Death hummed around her. She grabbed his arm.

"He's here," she whispered.

"Your father?" He quickened his pace.

"I wish you wouldn't call him that. But yes." *Something bad is about to happen.*

Markus drew his sword and burst through the door.

Death stood above Markus's father; a scythe pressed to his throat. "You thought you could hide from me?"

"Please, don't hurt me. I was but a servant; I was not involved with what they did."

Death smiled. "Beg for your life."

"What are you doing?" Markus demanded. "Father?"

"Markus, get back." the old man warned, his blue eyes wide.

Death turned his terrifying stare on Raven and Markus. A deep laughter boomed from him. "Father? You didn't tell him?"

"Get away from him!" Markus spoke, his tone menacing, the sword in front of him.

Death dropped the old man, his scythe gone, and turned, advancing on Markus. "This man is not your father."

"What?" Markus lowered his sword.

"Tell him," Death said to the man at his feet.

Markus took a step forward.

"Markus, no." Raven stared at Death. "Please, don't hurt him." She meant Markus, and acknowledgement of her request flickered behind her father's eyes.

"Tell him," Death said again, pressing a foot into the old man's throat.

"I'm not your father." Markus's father choked.

Markus's hand trembled as he clenched it into a fist.

Death knelt over the old man, placing his hand over his chest. "It's time to go. You knew this day was coming, old man."

Markus's father gazed up at Markus. "I'm sorry." He choked, and his eyes closed.

"You want to kill me for the death of a man you are not related to." Death towered over Markus. "Bring your sword. I'll be waiting." His eyes darted to Raven. "Where it all began."

"If he's not my father, who is?" Markus demanded, but Death was gone.

The sword clattered to the ground as Markus ran to his father's side.

Raven's heart broke. "Markus. I'm sorry." She knelt beside him, hand on his back.

"I'm going to kill him." Rage was loud in his voice.

She knew that rage all too well. "You know you cannot do that."

"Raven, he killed my father! I cannot let this go," he said.

Dread filled Raven. *This will not end well.* "I know."

"I need my armour. Then we move," he declared.

"Where?"

He looked down at the body. "Kempschester."

Chapter 54

Zachary fought against the shackles as dark fog twisted around him. He tried again to leave The Shadow Realm, but the restraints held him in place. The way Raven had stared at him, tears in her eyes, replayed itself. He had shown his darkness. Her helplessness stung, but her terror hurt even more. Emotions that had radiated from her and wrapped around his throat. They had been close, right up until his father came into their lives. Once again hatred for his father burned through him, rising up with rage, as the darkness tightened its hold.

"**Isaac.**" His dark reflection appeared. "**Give in. It's coming.**"

"What's coming?" he regretted asking. The answer clawed its way to the surface. "No!"

A dark smile twisted on his features. "**This is as your father has seen.**"

"I won't fight her." He rejected the idea of fighting Raven.

"**There is no choice. You will surrender once again, as will Raven, and your children.**"

Fear pierced him. "You cannot have them!" he shouted at Darkness.

"**Embrace me. It was so easy before; you have nothing to fear.**" His darker self advanced on him.

It would be easy. No more fighting. But he would lose everything. Himself. Raven. His children. His chance with Delia. "No!"

The shackles fell away. "Where are you?" he called out to his father. "Show yourself, you coward!"

His father appeared before him. "Coward? Is that what you think?"

"Why did you bind me here, only to release me?" Zachary demanded.

"So you wouldn't interfere. The Enforcer is on the hunt." Satisfaction shone through his father's eyes.

"You killed his father." So many people had died, and Zachary was tired of it.

"It was his time, just as it will be for the Enforcer. Bring him to me in Kempschester. He is the last," his father instructed.

"The last *what*?" He didn't finish the question before his father was gone. "I'm not bringing him to you," he shouted to no one. "If you want to kill him, you face him yourself. I won't do this."

He tried to go home, to get away. All he yearned for was to sleep, to be by himself. But it was as if The Shadow Realm closed around him. He wasn't restrained, but the realm wasn't taking him where he wanted to go. Instead, he found himself drawn back to the home that Raven had taken.

Through the veil he saw Markus putting on armour with Raven's help. It occurred to him that she'd probably made it, as it differed from usual Enforcer armour. *How can I stop this?* Raven's hands froze, as she turned around, frowning.

"You dare come here?" she said. "Why won't you leave me alone? Let Zac go."

Zachary stepped through the veil. "It's only me, Raven," he said, and exhaustion washed over him. "I'm sorry." He lowered his head.

"You're here to take me to him, aren't you?" Markus asked.

"I am," he acknowledged Markus's question, eyeing the Enforcer carefully. He still didn't like Markus, but Raven did.

"I can feel the darkness in you," Raven said, pulling his attention back to her. "Have you returned to—"

"No!" he blurted. She was right, though. His rage at being bound to The Shadow Realm had awakened it again. If anything, it felt stronger than before, and he wasn't sure how he was able to hold it back. "I'm not sure how long that will be the case, though. I don't *want* to do this. You do believe me, don't you?"

Raven took a moment before she made eye contact. "I do," she said. "I've never sensed it like this before."

"There is more in you now than there was before," he told her truthfully.

A glint of fear reflected in her eyes. "There is?" Her voice broke.

"Enough talk," Markus commanded. "Take me to him now."

"Markus, at least let me put my armour on," Raven said.

Markus glared. "Hurry up."

She frowned, but said nothing.

Zachary found Markus watching him. "I would say, 'Don't fight him', but he wants it as much as you do. He said you're 'the last'," he told the Enforcer.

"The last *what?*" Markus rested his hand on the hilt of his sword, tapping his fingers impatiently.

"He didn't say," Zachary replied.

Raven donned her armour; the chest plate Zachary had made for her.

Pride fluttered in his chest. "You kept it," he observed.

"Of course I did. I wasn't going to throw out a perfectly good armour plate." She smiled at him.

He laughed, unable to remember the last time he'd done so.

"Is this when we will fight?" Raven asked. "I saw it. He saw it."

"I don't know. I feel as if this is more to do with Markus fighting him," he told her.

"I won't fight you," she promised.

"Nor I you," Zachary agreed.

The fear in her eyes was unmistakable. It was coming, a fight that neither of them could stop from happening. Darkness told him that she would fall.

"When we're finished, no matter what happens, I want you to see Delia," Raven told him. "You two have a lot to talk about. She loves you, Zac. Don't abandon her, or your children."

He nodded. "I love her, too. I want to be there for all of them. Be the father I never got. One that they deserve. He says the same fate waits for them."

She met his eyes, hers set with grim determination. "We won't let that happen. It ends with us."

Zachary reached out to her, and she closed her hand around his forearm. They turned to Markus.

"You need to allow Zachary to take you through The Shadow Realm. He will keep you from getting lost," Raven said to the Enforcer.

They had agreed to it without speaking, and Zachary wondered if Raven was a little too eager for The Shadow Realm.

Markus grabbed his arm.

In The Shadow Realm, Raven whimpered.

"Raven?" he asked, concerned.

Her eyes were wide. "I didn't hear anything before, but now I do."

She was hearing the dead. He wondered who. "Your mother?" .

"Lucian." Her eyes were big. "He's calling to me." Her hand relaxed as if she were about to follow the voice.

"Don't let go," he warned. "You know it's not him."

Curious as to why Darkness chose Lucian instead of Aunt Amelia, Zachary gripped her arm tight.

"Are you alright?" Zachary asked. She nodded. "Markus?"

"I hear my father's voice." He looked in pain. "Just get me to him."

Nothing blocked him this time, and he stepped into the courtyard in Kempschester. Heavy clouds blackened out the sun, adding a foreboding to the scene around him. Bone remains had been moved, clearing an area around them. Raven let go immediately, pressing her hand to her chest. Markus continued to hold on, until he saw the shadow figure standing not far away. He stepped away, advancing, his sword ready.

"No." Raven's whisper held an edge of pain.

"What is it?" Zachary asked

Her eyes were full of anguish. "He's going to die."

Death smiled at them.

"I'll kill you," Markus growled. "My father only wanted to live his life in peace. He never harmed anyone."

"You still think that servant is your father." Zachary's father laughed, the sound rumbling from him. "You don't look like him, or his wife. Are you so idiotic that you cannot see that?"

"Zac, you have to stop him," Raven whispered. "Please. I don't know how to stop this."

"You know?" Zachary asked. "You can feel it?"

"I can." Her eyes shone from unshed tears. "He will die. I already lost Lucian. And my mother."

Flooded with guilt in his part in Aunt Amelia's death, he stepped in between his father and Markus. "You can't fight him, Markus. You'll lose."

"Get out of my way." Markus pointed the sword at him. "Let me fight him."

Death stepped forward, pushing Zachary aside, and he wrapped his hand around Markus's throat, lifting him from the ground. "Do you know who it is you challenge, boy? You will die where your father died, but a few steps from where his bones still lay. I will end the line of Lord Samson and gladly tell him when he comes to meet you."

Lord Samson's son? Zachary recalled the woman in the room with the child as Enforcers led him outside. *Markus is Lord Samson's son!* His mind reeled from this revelation.

"You knew who he was the first time you saw him," Zachary said.

Markus started to choke, eyes wide, his hand reaching for the fingers around his throat.

"I would recognise his descendant anywhere," his father declared. "A child rescued from a burning building as the last Lord of Kempshire, finally returns to die where he should have twenty years ago. Had I known he'd escaped, I would have hunted him down sooner. Look upon your father's legacy, now yours, to die by my hand."

"No!" Raven's voice barely came out. "Stop!"

Zachary moved to pull her back.

Dark energy burst between Father and Markus. The Enforcer's eyes turned white, just as those Zachary had taken. Markus was about to die.

"No." Raven's voice lost all uncertainty and fear. "I challenge you." She pointed to their father. "Release him. Now. Face me."

A slow smile, and triumph flickered across her father's face. He dropped Markus, who appeared to be unconscious. Zachary knelt to check for life. Weak, but holding. The Enforcer's eyes opened a slit, no longer white, but appeared black before returning to blue, and he let out a groan.

"You're alive," Zachary reassured him. *For now.*

"What's she doing?" Markus asked.

"She's fighting to keep you alive," Zachary confirmed.

"This is *my* fight." Markus tried to get up, and he winced.

"No, this is *her* fight," his father said, his eyes still on Raven. "It *always* has been her fight. But it is not me that she will face." That empty gaze shifted to Zachary, and his blood turned cold. "The Enforcer was necessary to bring you both here. I'd be willing to let him live. A worthy trade-off. His life is insignificant in comparison to what truly matters. You." Eyes void of humanity darted between them. His mouth curved into a smile, sending warnings through Zachary. "This is where you fight, Descendants of Death."

Chapter 55

Less than a day ago, Raven would have walked into this, sword ready, and fought her cousin without hesitation, to the death. She'd prepared for it, making the helmet in her hand. Markus had talked her off the ledge of all-consuming fury, in order to save Zac's life. Between his words and her mother's, she had let go enough to see that Zac's actions had been forced upon him. It still hurt her that he'd taken her mother from her, and it would be a long time before their close bond would return, but no longer she held a desire to kill him.

They had promised each other they wouldn't fight. But Death had lured them here, and as Zac knelt beside Markus, her own horror reflected in his eyes.

"I won't fight him," she declared.

Her dreams had been showing her this moment. They would fight, and she would fall. Every time, she collapsed to her knees, bloodied, head bowed as she waited for her end. The first time she had met Death, she'd known he would bring her demise. A cold certainty that what she had seen would come to pass brought terror over her. *I'm going to die.*

"You value his life; I will spare him," Death said, and knelt over Markus.

There one moment, gone the next, Raven was left staring at Zac.

"Where are they?" her voice rose, high-pitched, betraying her fear.

Zac focused on something she couldn't see. "They're in The Shadow Realm."

Death returned. "If you don't fight, he will be forever lost in The Shadow Realm. Never to find peace."

"I value the life of my cousin, too," she argued, aware that her words would have no effect. *I don't want to die. But I cannot be the reason Markus never escapes from that endless darkness.*

Death turned his icy gaze to Zac. "You, I will also bind to The Shadow Realm, until there is nothing left. Both of you. Then you will cross blades without prompting, without hesitation."

A glint of terror in Zac's eyes as he returned his gaze to Raven sparked her own.

His fear of The Shadow Realm, of reliving all he had could be enough to bring his resolve crashing down.

"Not that," Zac choked, standing. "Please, why do you do this?"

"I do nothing, merely bring pieces together for what I have seen, just as Raven has seen. As you have seen. Make your choices."

She recognised defeat in Zac's slumped shoulders, the way he shook his head.

"Zac," she pleaded.

"Raven, I'm sorry, I can't face that again. I don't want that for you, just as I know you don't want that for Markus. We have no choice."

She wanted everything to be as it once was. Her mother singing in the kitchen, Zac's laughter as he made fun of her, their close bond. *I miss the life we had. I miss my brother.* Death had been nothing more than a shadow in the dark, not the monster that stood before them now.

"I don't want this, either," she breathed. "I have seen this day, and now that it's here, I'm scared."

"Don't be." The smile Zac gave her was a shadow of what it once was. A glint in his eyes of grim determination only added to her dread. "You'll be alright, Raven."

"Don't make promises you cannot keep," Death's low voice no longer spoke to a terror deep inside her.

"He's right," she said, surprising herself to be in agreement. "You have children to fight for. You'll return to them." *I won't.*

Resigning herself to her fate, Raven lifted the helmet, and pulled it on. The weight of the helmet was evenly placed, her vision not too restricted through the visor.

Metal clattered against stone as a sword fell at Zac's feet.

"Pick it up," Death ordered.

Both Raven and Zac stared at the sword. Raven tried to remember where she had last seen it. She had picked it up in Eskham the night of the attack, with Zac gone. Her mother had been shocked by the sword, recognising it immediately. She'd left it in the church while everyone recovered from the battle and lives lost. She hadn't given it another thought. *Did he find it in the church?*

"You give me your sword?" Zac asked.

"You came all this way for it. It wasn't for nothing." Death moved away and turned, watching them both. "Pick it up," he repeated.

Zac picked up the sword and winced, his left hand covering his side.

"You're still injured," Raven noticed.

"Don't worry about me," he replied.

With no other choice, she prepared for the fight.

When he trained her, Zac always struck first. Now was no different. He came at her, and she met his blade with her own. Metal clanged as they fell into routine, familiarity settling over her. Neither was trying to kill the other.

"This isn't training," Death complained. "This is a fight to the death. Do as you are supposed to."

She stopped and glared at him. "Why are you doing this?"

Death gave her no reply. She glanced from him to Zac.

"We have no choice," Zac pointed out. "Fight me, Raven. With meaning."

"I won't."

He raised his sword and slashed. Raven parried, taken by the weight he put into his attack. She lunged forward. Zac favoured his injured side as their movements became more ferocious. Neither wanted to kill the other, and she always tired before Zac did. He had six years on her, and more training than she had. Fear tickled her spine.

"**Kill him.**" A dark voice whispered to her, taking her by surprise. *No!* "**He took your mother from you, and is the reason Markus is in The Shadow Realm.**" She struggled to ignore them. "**He will kill you if you don't.**"

She didn't know what was happening, but its effect on her was instant. First a surge of anger, then a thunderous rage that she couldn't hold back. She pushed forward, using movements that Markus taught her, catching Zac off-guard. His eyes widened. Satisfied, she repeated her swing, striking again, not giving him a chance to do anything but block. Just as Death had done to her a lifetime ago.

Darkness swirled around them, the courtyard fading in and out. But all she focused on was Zac. This time it was he who tired easily, his injuries slowing him down.

"Raven." Markus's voice grabbed her and she froze.

Her guard dropped. Not by much, but enough to give Zac an opening. His eyes were white, black lines across his face. He had once again given in to Darkness. His blade pierced her shoulder, tearing a scream from Raven. One of rage more than of pain. With every ounce of strength, she slashed at her opponent, letting go of fear, giving in to the fight. **Kill him**. *It's him or me.* Metal hit metal, the clang muffled behind a fog. Again, pain radiated as his blade sliced across her shoulder, close to the scar from her fight against the French soldier.

"**Raven, he's tiring. Press forward.**" The dark voice sent chills down her spine, but she let the words flow through her.

"Stop." Zac's voice came out harshly. "I hear you talking to me, You're not helping."

With a burst of energy, driven by pain, Raven repeated Death's tactic. Strike. Strike. Strike. Her blade finally found its mark, slicing deep into flesh. His guard dropped, and she pulled her hand back and thrust forward. He didn't raise his sword in time, and hers sunk deep into his side with an upward angle.

His weapon slipped from his hand, white eyes returning to brown. "Raven." Betrayal reflected in his face and voice. The fog pulled back in time for her to see her brother fall.

"Zac?" she dropped her own sword, falling to her knees at his side.

"You…" He let out a long groan, filled with pain. "You won." He gave her a small laugh. "You've never beaten me before." The pride in his eyes was unmistakable, as more pain flickered through. He winced and took a deep, pained breath, letting it out in another groan. She pressed her hand to his wound, blood seeping around her fingers.

A shadow fell over them, and she glanced up. Death stood over her, a triumphant glint in his eyes and smile.

"Father," Zac gasped out. "Raven." He groaned again. "Raven, *tell Delia I'm sorry*. Tell her…" His words stopped and he struggled as he took his last breath. His eyes closed.

"No," she whispered. "Zac, no." Hot tears spilled over, streaming down her cheeks.

Heavy sorrow flooded her, and a suffocating pain pounded against her chest. Guilt and grief rose up and crashed over her.

"Well done, daughter," Death celebrated.

She glared up at him, the pride in his eyes sending a surge of anger through her. "He's dead."

"This was always going to happen in a fight to the death. One of you would fall," Death added.

"It was supposed to be me!" Her voice echoed around the empty courtyard.

She rose to her feet. "You did this. You've taken everything from me!"

Grief froze in her chest, the urge to kill the figure that stood before her rising, choking her.

"It was not my sword that ended his life," he pointed out.

"He was injured; he would never have dropped his guard if it weren't for that. What did you do to me? I couldn't control..." Tears slid down her cheeks. "I wanted to kill him. Why?"

"You stopped fighting what you are," Death told her.

What I am? I'm not like him.

"Bring them back," she demanded.

"I keep my word, and you can have your Enforcer back. But Isaac stays in The Shadow Realm. Cursed to roam the shadows forever. He will cease to be more than a dark reflection of his former self."

"No! Bring them both back." She choked on sobs. "Please, bring them back. You said you couldn't bring Lucian back because he'd already crossed over. You can bring them both back. Markus and Zac." Drowning in sorrow, Raven stepped towards Death, hopeful. "Please."

"That was not the agreement. You get one. You fought for the Lord of Kempshire; I release him."

Markus appeared in front of her. But pain ripped its way through her. Before Markus could reach out to her, she found herself in The Shadow Realm.

"Raven." His voice brought her relief.

She pulled her helmet off, dropping it to the ground.

"Zac, I'm sorry, I don't know what came over me," she said.

Zac wrapped his arms around her. "What you fear most is what happened. Our father planned this. It was always going to be either me or you who fell."

"How can you be so calm about this?" She stepped back. "He won't bring you back. I tried."

Restraints appeared out of nowhere, binding around Zac.

"What?" He fought against them. "No!"

Death held the scythe in his hand, the very sight of it enough to awaken dread.

"What are you doing?" she asked.

"Isaac's death has separated him from his body. This is where he will stay until he surrenders to Darkness again," Death said.

"Why are you doing this to him?" she demanded, fury surging, along with hatred for her father.

"He cannot turn from his duty. You may return to your lover," he instructed her.

Raven shook her head. "No. I'm not leaving him here. Not this time."

"You do not have a choice, daughter. You severed him from his mortal tether," Death said.

"He returned from the dead before. Do it again," she ordered him.

"That is not my purpose," he replied.

I killed him. Just as Thomas killed Graeme, I killed my brother. The crushing weight of what she had done would sit with her for the rest of her life.

Panic filtered through Zac's eyes. "I can't lose myself again." He shook his head.

"Father, please." The only time she had called him 'Father' was when Zac was dying on her table.

Surprise showed in his face. She lowered herself to her knees. "I'm begging you, please, release him."

A slow, satisfied smile crept across Death's face.

Chapter 56

Dark fog of The Shadow Realm twisted around her.

"Raven, you don't know what you're committing yourself to," Zac said. "Don't trust him."

Raven didn't care. She had killed her brother, and in doing so, she had taken a father away from three children, and she had ended Delia's chance to reunite with a man she clearly loved. She couldn't shoulder that burden. He had been trapped in The Shadow Realm because of her. Her actions were what had caused descent into madness for his mother, and a surrender to Darkness for Zac.

This is my chance to fix it. All of it.

Death's eyes were focused on her. "If Isaac wants freedom from The

Shadow Realm, to be released from what he is, he must give up the Touch of Death. Only then can he escape the grip Darkness has on him."

It seemed too easy. "Is that all?" she asked.

"No, I won't do that to her," Zac said. "You cannot ask that."

"Zac, you can have a home, a family," she urged him. *Why would he not take that chance?*

"It is you that must willingly accept his Touch of Death, and everything that comes with that," Death said.

Everything that comes with that. Her heart pounded. "I have to kill people?" she asked.

"You've already proven yourself a killer; *now* you're afraid?" Death challenged. "The request you make of me is not a small one, I did tell you I would ask something of you in return the first time I helped Isaac."

"I will accept it," Raven said. "I agree to your terms."

"No, what are you doing?" Zac's voice filled with panic. The idea of being trapped here for an eternity filled him with dread, but he couldn't let her do this. "Raven…"

"I'm saving you. It's my fault you were trapped in here," she argued.

"She has made her choice." Death declared.

"I will not curse you." Zac shook his head. "I cannot do that."

"Zac, please. I need you to accept my decision." She turned her focus to Death. "Tell me how?"

"Hold your hand out." Death said.

She did as instructed. Zac's shackles fell away.

"Close your hand around her forearm." Death instructed.

"You don't want this, Raven. It truly is a curse." Zac pleaded.

She had agreed to Death's request; it was too late to back out now. She clenched her jaw. His stalling wasn't going to stop anything, only delay it. "It's already done," she told him. "Do it."

Zac stared at her in silence. Raven met his eyes with her hand held out, waiting. His shoulders slumped and he let out a sigh, his mouth set in a hard line. He lifted his hand, locking it around her forearm.

"Relinquish your gift to her." Death instructed.

Again, Zac hesitated, his eyes shifting across her face, defeat reflecting in his eyes. "I was supposed to be the one to protect you," he apologised.

She closed her fingers around his forearm. "You did. But you have a family, Zac. Those children need their father. I'm alright, I have Markus."

Dark laughter came from Death, and Zac frowned. She gave him an encouraging smile.

"I pass on my curse to you," Zac murmured. "I give you my Touch of Death."

"I accept," she said.

His eyes became white, and dark fog closed around them. A spark passed from Zachary through their grip. She whimpered, then let out a scream as pain engulfed her.

She tried to pull away her hand, and she felt him trying to do the same. An inferno burned, radiating from her arm, intertwining around her very essence, searing. Unable to hold back the groan, she closed her eyes, wishing for it to be over.

"Raven, your arm," Zac alerted her.

When she opened her eyes again, black lines appeared, twisting around her hand and arm.

Red lightning struck the both of them, and they were thrown backwards, their connection broken, and she lost consciousness.

Raven opened her eyes. The first thing she saw was Death standing over her, his face in shadow.

"Zac?" she murmured, her mind reeling from what had just happened.

Death smiled at her. "He's given up his connection to The Shadow Realm."

She took in her surroundings. The first time she had been there had been unpleasant. Now, there was a comfort about it. "Is he alright?"

"He is. Returned to his body once again. Adjusting to his new existence."

"So will you bind me here as you bound Zac?" she asked, bitterness heavy in her voice.

"I have no need to do that, Raven." He held a hand out. "That's what was necessary for him to surrender to Darkness. You are the daughter of Darkness, and there will be no surrender for you."

"What are you talking about?" She demanded.

"You cannot surrender to that which is already within you," he stated.

His words held a ring of truth. She had feared it her whole life, but could not deny it. She had pleaded to not be like her father, yet had killed without regret. Her acceptance of deaths at his hands, a dark protector, should have sent her running. "There is darkness inside me," she said, taking his hand, letting him pull her up.

"There is. Its presence has blazed within you since you took form inside your mother. She didn't see, but I did. I stood over you when no one else was looking, and your eyes turned black, as if you recognised me." He gripped her shoulder. "Stop holding back your true self, Raven. Show the world who you are."

"How do I do that?" she asked.

"You've always felt its presence. You've feared it, hidden from it because you were told to. You have no reason to fight it any more. You have no reason to fear me," he declared.

He'd said that once, and this time she saw the truth in it. He was right; she'd known her life would lead to this. Her dreams — kneeling before him — that was not her end, but her beginning. She reached for the Darkness, embracing it without hesitation, letting it wash through her. She welcomed the calm that remained as it burned away all fear, worry, and doubt.

"How do you feel?" her father asked.

She smiled, holding her arm up, examining the black lines twisting around. "This is thrilling," she said. "It hurt when it passed from Zac, but now I can feel it, like a living presence, waiting to be released. Is this how you kill them?"

"You will learn that in good time." He smiled. "Who are you?"

The answer rose up. "I am Raven Blake. Daughter of Graeme Blake. Daughter of Death."

His eyes shone, piercing blue, with pride. "You call me 'Father'?"

Gone was her fear of the man before her, of the repulsion she'd held at the idea of him being her father. "You *are* my father."

"I'm pleased that you no longer resist this part of yourself," he said.

"I was wrong to fight this for so long," she admitted.

"We need to return to the courtyard. Your cousin and the Enforcer await. You will bid farewell to them both."

Zac. Markus.

Her father grabbed her arm and tore her from The Shadow Realm. They were in the courtyard again, Zac and Markus nearby.

Zac caught sight of her first. "Raven, oh no, I'm sorry."

She turned her gaze to Markus. Despite the Darkness, she had not forgotten her feelings for this man. "I still want you," she murmured, surprised. But there was more than want that stirred within.

"That will never go away," her father said. He smiled at her. "You're still you, Raven. Just a…darker version of yourself."

She stared at him, catching his meaning. "You still love her," she whispered.

"Both of them," he admitted. "Becoming this, I held no regret, just as you don't. The love that I held for both Emma and Amelia. My heart. My wives." He turned his gaze to Zac. "Even my son."

"You said you didn't mourn me." Zac said. "When you thought I was dead."

"I didn't. That part of me, the humanity was no more. There is no grief, no guilt, nor fear." He eyed Raven, then Markus. "Those we love, though, that is as much part of who we are as the Darkness that lives within. The desire to protect them only becomes more…well, more."

She smiled. He had killed people who had sought to harm her.

Markus approached her, gazing into her eyes. "Raven, what have you done? Where is my Lady Sunshine?"

"I'm still me." she said with longing.

He held his hand to her face. "Your eyes are black. You have the same lines on your face that he does. That Zachary had in Riverwick."

A presence in him caught her attention.

"I did not feel it before, but there is Darkness in you," she whispered.

"As in all of humanity," Death said. "In some, it is stronger than in others. His time in The Shadow Realm may have effects on him, though."

"What effects?" Markus's worry seemed insignificant.

Her father shrugged. "There will be some change in you, just as there was in Isaac." He glanced around the courtyard. "Raven, say goodbye to your cousin; I will take him home, to the life he so desires. I'll let you have your final moment with this one."

Chapter 57

Zachary stood in the courtyard where he had now died twice and stared at Raven. Unsettled by the change in her, black eyes, and Darkness that rose off her, Zachary forced himself to smile anyway. *She's still my little sister.*

"You gave up everything," he said. "Your entire life."

"I did this for you, Zac. Take the chance that has been given you, big brother. Seek out Delia. Be the father you needed. Have the life you wanted. That you deserve." Her voice had a new darkness to it.

"What about the life *you* wanted? You didn't have to do this." *She cannot want this.* "Raven, I'm sorry," he offered.

She smiled. "You're free, Zac. No shadow realm, no darkness, no calling.

Is this not what you desired?"

"Not at the cost of *your* humanity." He wrapped his arms around her. "I only ever wanted to see my little sister happy."

"I *am* happy," she declared.

He remembered the feeling, before everything came rushing back. They pulled away. "You'll always be my family. If you ever want to see me—"

"The next time she sees you, it will be because she has been called to you," their father said. "You yearned to be free of this life, I am giving you what you wanted. That includes freedom from us."

"What?" *To never see her again?* "I didn't want that. You don't have to…" He couldn't finish. To never see her again, the very idea hurt. "Raven? Is this what you want?"

Her eyes lifted to their father, wide with surprise. "You seek this? He has always been there for me; you ask that I walk away from him entirely?"

"It is not what I seek, daughter. He must live out his life as one of them. A mortal. To remain in this life only keeps him connected to the darkness he rejected."

"He's right," Raven said. "You wanted this, Zac. I will see you again, years from now."

He pulled her into a hug again.

"I'll miss you," he said.

"So will I." She moved away, towards Markus.

His father's hand closed around his arm and they were in The Shadow Realm.

"Will this not only undo—"

"No, you have no connection to darkness. It has released you," his father said.

"Will Raven be alright?" he asked.

"She was born for this," Father said simply.

They were outside his home in Hopeton. "I'm not surprised that you know where I live." He laughed. "Can I see my father? Thomas Blake. One last time? Show me a kindness as you showed Aunt Amelia."

His father smiled, the blue eyes of Thomas crinkling. "Is this what you wanted?"

"Thank you, Father. Will it be Raven that…" He couldn't finish.

"We will both be there to escort you to The Crossover," his father told him.

"Mother will wait for me. Will you tell her what happened?" Zac asked.

"You can tell her yourself when you see her." His father started to turn, but stopped. "You must prepare your children for what is to come."

"You lay claim to them still?" Zachary asked.

His father nodded. "I do. If they resist as you did, so be it. But your descendants, and hers, are the descendants of Death. This will be what awaits them all. You cannot change that. But by preparing them, they will know their fate. You and Raven did not."

Pain squeezed his chest. The idea of his children having this fate. "I don't want this for them," he said.

"It doesn't matter what you want. This is who they are. Prepare them," his father repeated.

"I'm wanted for murder," he said. "I cannot go back to Oakborough."

"You have money," his father reminded him "You can go anywhere. Start a new life. Get married."

Before he could reply, father was gone. Zachary couldn't help but smile at the kindness father had shown him. Only a brief glimpse of it, but it soothed the little boy who had lost everything in flames and death. He walked inside.

There was no sense of darkness any more, neither inside him, nor in The Shadow Realm. He could no longer sense anything as he had.

There was a knock on the door, and he opened it with a smile. Frederick stood on the other side.

"You look happy," Frederick noted. "I'm relieved to see you're alright."

How long was I gone for? "I am," he said, a lightness spreading across his chest.

"Your smithy was closed; the villagers were worried. Charlotte came by, but you didn't answer," Frederick said.

"Frederick, I will never forget all that you and Charlotte have done for me. I was at a very low point in my life when I came here." Zachary said.

"This feels like a goodbye. You've lost that haunted look. We knew you'd move on again." Frederick smiled.

"Not goodbye, just a thank you. You're right. I was haunted. By decisions I made, and chances I didn't take."

"Does this have anything to do with a beautiful, dark-skinned young woman and her son? Delia, I think she said her name was?"

At a loss for words, Zachary frowned, searching Frederick's face. *Delia?* His heart pounded. He'd thought of her as the one who'd got away, and he'd let her go. It bothered him to have someone else refer to her as beautiful.

"She was here early this morning, but left when you weren't home. It seemed very important that she find you, and Charlotte consoled her in her disappointment."

I didn't return to the river as I promised to. Arthur, Giselle, and Joseph probably told their mothers.

"She came looking for me?" he asked.

Frederick nodded. "This is the chance you regret not taking, isn't it? That boy, is he your son?"

"He is," Zachary said with pride. "I've been a fool and let her go. I haven't been the man I should be," he admitted.

"Then go. You'll always be welcome here, but go where your heart takes you, my friend. If you want to bring her here, she and your son will be welcome." Frederick said.

"I will be gone for a few days," Zachary advised.

"Take as long as you need. I wouldn't have Charlotte if I hadn't followed my heart." Frederick beamed. "The man before me now is very different from the one who dropped into our house in the middle of a snow storm. Your eyes light up, and I see hope, and joy."

"Two things that have been strangers to me for a long time," Zachary said.

Chapter 58

Raven was left with Markus. Her last time to be with him. Her father had been right. She still held love for the man who had insulted her upon their first meeting, and didn't want to leave him. Darkness had not stripped that away from her.

"Your father tried to kill me," he said.

"He won't try any more." She lifted her hand, cradling his cheek. "You're safe. Unless you challenge him again. Next time, I don't think he will let you live."

"Oh, believe me, I won't," he confessed. "I saw what you did; you challenged him. I think I passed out. He was choking me and I thought I was going to die, then he released me, and everything hurt. I don't remember anything after that until Zachary woke me to say you were gone."

"You were in The Shadow Realm," she told him.

"He did that to force you to fight your cousin," he acknowledged.

She smiled. "This is our last time together, Markus. Is this what you want to talk about?"

His gaze softened and he tilted up her chin. "It doesn't have to be."

She pointed around them. "This belongs to you," she said. "Lord Markus of Kempshire. What will you do with this knowledge?"

He shot a smile at her. "You are a Lady, after all. My Lady Sunshine." His eyes didn't leave her face, focusing on her lips. "I like the idea of releasing these people from their fear, but will your father allow that to happen? Enough to let me rebuild a once-thriving town?"

She didn't want to talk about Kempschester; she wanted him to kiss her. Frustration surged in her chest.

"I can speak with him." she sighed.

"Do you think he'll listen, though?" he asked.

"He's let you live, so maybe he will leave them alone. He said you were the last." The conversation was irritating her. "Markus..."

He stroked her cheek, and leaned in. "I cannot let you go."

Tired of waiting, she pulled him to her. As their lips met, the world faded around her. It was just the two of them, surrounded by fog and shadows. They pulled apart.

"That's going to take some getting used to." she laughed, gripping him tight.

"Are you sure you can walk away from this?" he asked with a smirk. "You never could keep your eyes off me. Or your hands."

Laughter rose up from her chest. "You have it wrong. It was you who could not keep your eyes off me."

"I liked what I saw," he admitted. "Can you please get me out of this realm? Hearing my father's voice while trying to have a moment with you is not something I am enjoying."

They stepped into her bedroom in Oakborough.

"That definitely cuts down on travel time," he teased.

Markus removed Raven's armour, then his own. "I get you one last time, don't I?" he asked. "If I'm never going to see you again, at least give me something to remember you by."

"I wasn't going to leave without it," she told him, tearing his tunic clean down the middle.

She was still herself, but the desire that sparked through her was hungrier. She pushed Markus hard against the wall, hands on his chest, kissing him with force. He responded in like, his hands under her tunic, moving up and down her body.

"Get your trousers off, now," she ordered.

His were off in an instant and he tore her tunic as she had torn his.

"So this is Darkness. You're still beautiful," he marvelled, his eyes roaming over her face.

"Do I terrify you?" she asked.

"No. You awaken a beast in me, Raven," he murmured.

"Show me," she said against his jaw.

No sooner were the words out, than his hand snaked around her back, pulling her against him, his mouth demanding against hers as he lifted her and threw her onto the bed. Following her, he pinned her with his body, holding her arms down. His hands lost their usual gentleness, rough as they gripped her wrists.

Holding her wrists in place with one hand, he slid the other down hers. His lips blazed across her collarbone and over her jaw. When he kissed her, desire bloomed deep within, setting off an inferno. She groaned into his mouth. She raised her hips, grinding against him, yearning to run her hands down his back. His erection pressed into her opening, but he paused, not yet entering her.

"Sunshine, my Lady of Darkness, if this is our last time, let's make it truly special," he breathed. "Do you want me to be gentle?" The glint in his eye told her what he wanted.

"No," she gasped out, anticipating him to thrust deep.

He still didn't move, his lips stretched into a smile. "Tell me what you want."

Unable to hold back, she wrapped her legs around him, wrenched her hands from his grip and grabbed his ass.

"Stop talking," she breathed and thrust up, holding him to her.

As he slid into her, his lips crushed against hers again. Black wisps rose from her, encasing the two of them like a thick fog. He caught sight of it. But not distracted for long, he focused on Raven.

His movements were savage, fuelled by raw desire. Her own were just as unrestrained. Her core tightened, waves of pleasure surging through her body as he pulled back and pushed in hard. She closed her eyes, the feel of him against her, inside her, pushing her towards coming apart. Moans escaped her, mingling with his grunts.

"Open your eyes," he instructed. "Look at me when your Lord takes you."

Thrilled by the command in his voice, she did as he requested to find his face above hers. He smiled down at her as they moved in tune with each other, and she gazed into his eyes. With their gazes locked, she didn't look away, warmth spreading through her. Tremors started.

His eyes flashed black as they climaxed. The sight of it filled her with dark joy.

"Your eyes," she panted. "You've embraced Darkness."

"*You* are Darkness," he grunted. "I feel your very essence all around me and want every part of you." He collapsed on her, breathing hard. "If you ever want a repeat of that, visit me any time."

She held him to her, his head on her chest, their bodies lined with sweat. As Raven caught her breath, she considered it.

She pushed him up, wanting to see his eyes again, the idea of them black appealing. They were blue. He gazed at her.

"Your eyes were black," she told him.

"So are yours. I suppose doing this with you in that state would do that." His grin flashed before he kissed her again. "Care to go another round?"

Raven laughed and moved into his embrace content with just laying with him.

Time passed and she climbed from her bed, retrieving new clothes and armour.

Markus crooked a finger under her chin.

"Will I see you again?" he asked.

"I will come for you. On the day of your death, many years from now, I will be there. I will be the one to take you to The Crossover," she said

"And what a welcome sight you will be." He kissed her again.

She pulled away. "I have to go. I can sense my father's presence approaching."

Father had returned. "You may rebuild Kempschester, Lord Markus," he said. "But Riverwick stays as it is. You rebuild that village, and I will burn it down again."

"Will you stay away? The people have lived in terror for over twenty years. If I am to announce myself as Lord Samson's surviving son, I want to offer them a break from that."

"I still have my duty," Death said. "If it takes me to Kempshire, I will claim them from the shadows."

Markus nodded, accepting her father's words.

"Goodbye, Markus." Raven said.

"Goodbye, Sunshine, my Lady of Darkness," he murmured.

She followed her father into The Shadow Realm, knowing that she wouldn't be able to stay away from Markus.

Chapter 59

Zachary stood in front of the door, his fist raised, but he hesitated. More than anything, he wanted to knock, to pull Delia into his arms and never let go.

What life can I offer her, or Arthur? I cannot live here, Lord Gerard will have me executed for murder. Can I really force her to give up her life to live with me somewhere else?

Before he could lower his arm, the door opened, Giselle holding it. "I knew you'd come home." Her gaze shifted to his eye, and he knew what she was looking at. He'd gotten used to the smokey grey in one eye, since the day in the courtyard. But since his release from darkness, he'd found his eye gradually returned to the brown it should be. "Your eye is normal," she said. "You look different. It's gone, isn't it?"

He recalled that she had seen him through the veil, and he took a knee before her. "How do you come to know more than you should at your age, little one?"

She turned, looking over her shoulder. "I just *know.* I see things that mother says aren't there. Joseph does, too."

He sighed, realising there was nothing he could do about what already lay within his children. "What about Arthur?"

"I don't know," she admitted. "He doesn't speak to us about such things."

"Are you not afraid?" he asked.

She smiled. "No, because I know we are safe. You'll protect us. You'll prepare us."

Prepare them. His father's voice echoed in his mind. He stood. "There is a conversation to be had, but I'm not ready for that yet."

"That's alright. We have time," she said with a smile.

A footstep sounded behind her, and Zachary met green eyes.

"Delia?" Grace said. "You'll want to see this."

Then she was there, and his heart soared. Just seeing her brought it all back. He loved this woman, but she had left him, and the hurt still remained.

She rushed forward, wrapping her arms around him. "I'm so glad to see you," she murmured. "I went to Hopeton but you weren't there."

He pulled back. "Delia." He could only say her name at that moment, and gaze into her eyes.

"Aunt Raven's not coming back, is she?" Giselle asked. "She's gone."

All eyes were on him.

"Gone where?" Grace asked.

"No, she's not coming back," he confirmed. "I'm sorry."

"Did something happen? Is she dead?" Delia cast a worried look to Grace.

Unsure how much Delia knew, he could only shake his head. He couldn't protect his children from who they were, but he didn't want to push Delia into that world. Nor Grace.

Delia's eyes hardened. "Raven is my friend. You cannot tell me why she would leave without saying anything?"

"I'm sorry, Delia." He lowered his eyes.

"Is that why you're here? To tell us she's gone, and disappear again?" she demanded.

He pointed towards the town behind him "I cannot stay; they will arrest me."

Arthur approached. "You weren't at the river," he said, hurt in his eyes.

"I know," he apologised.

"They need you. Arthur needs his father." Delia met his eyes.

Zachary took her hands. "I want to be here for them, Delia. Learning that I had children was the best thing that ever happened to me. But I cannot be a father from a cell, nor from my grave."

The hard glint in her eyes softened, and she nodded. "I don't want that, either. I just wish they could get to know you. Where will you go? Perhaps we can visit."

"Hopeton?" he suggested

Delia leaned in and kissed him. Giselle and the boys made gagging noises, their footsteps soft as they ran away. He slid his arm around her, yielding to her soft lips. He remembered this, having her in his embrace.

"You!" A voice startled them both. They pulled apart. Two Enforcers sat on horses. "What are you doing here?"

"What does it look like I'm doing?" he asked, wanting to get back to kissing Delia. "Did you come to watch?"

"I know you. Lord Gerard is looking for you," the other Enforcer said. "You're Zachary Dale."

Dale. The name sounded foreign to him. He hadn't used that name in a long time. I*saac Blake.* He bit back on saying his name out loud. He had ceased to be Isaac over twenty years before.

"Get on your knees." The men were off their horses.

Zachary reached for The Shadow Realm, his only way out. He'd have to explain that to Delia later. But nothing happened. It was as if the veil wasn't there, or it was locked to him. *It is locked to me; how could I forget?* He had spent the last twelve months being able to come and go as he liked through The Shadow Realm; it would take some getting used to without that direct access.

Delia stepped back as they rounded on him. "Zachary."

He lowered himself to his knees. "I'm sorry, Delia." His children watched, their eyes wide. "Take care of them."

Shackles were pulled from one of the horses and locked around his wrists.

"I love you," she called to him as he was dragged away.

"You do?" He tried to turn back, but he was pulled, the Enforcer rough with the chains.

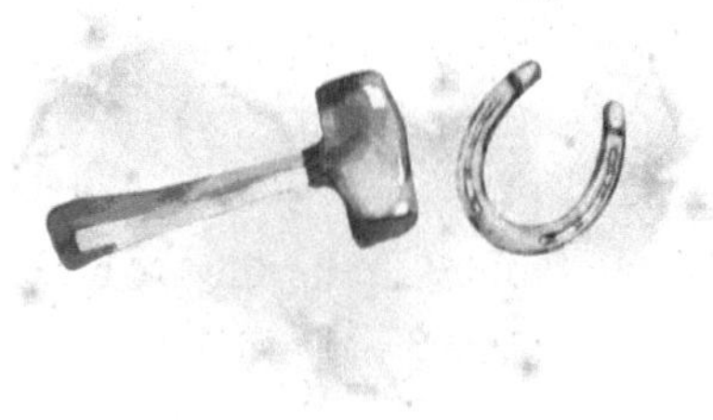

Absent of any light, the walls of the cell pressed against his mind. He couldn't see anything, and as he moved, the chains rattled. He'd been in a cell similar to this when Lord Samson had dragged him in to see his father chained to a wall. Suffocating panic pressed against his chest, stealing breath. The weight of the shackles reminded him of being bound to The Shadow Realm. He fought against the unbearable urge to scream, his galloping heart thunderous in the silent cell.

I have to get out of here. He forced down the urge to call for his father, or Raven. *Would they hear me, or let my call go unanswered?*

As he stared into the dark, he wondered when his death would come. The door swung open.

"Lord Gerard has requested your presence," an Enforcer said.

Men shackled him before leading him from the cell. With no idea where he was being led to, his heart pounded hard. *Is this how I die?* Chains rattled, heavy, as he walked. The Enforcers escorted him to the main hall in Lord Gerard's estate. As the door opened, he was led into the main hall. He caught sight of Tobias and Delia with a cloaked figure. He met Delia's eyes as he approached the Lord.

"Remove the shackles and leave," Lord Gerard ordered.

The weight of the metal was removed from his wrists. The Enforcers left, and he waited with his head bowed, regretting that his life would end too soon. *Raven sacrificed herself for nothing.* Guilt and sorrow temporarily drowned out his fear of what was about to take place.

"I've been informed that it was *not* you who killed my Captain, but your father," Lord Gerard said.

His heart skipped a beat, and he lifted his head, meeting Lord Gerard's eyes. "Informed, Lord Gerard?"

"Yes, informed." Lord Gerard scowled at him. "Had I known it was the son of the Killer of Kempschester that lived in my town, I would have exiled you a long time ago. You and your cousin. I don't know where she is, but I want you both out of Oakborough." He glanced behind Zachary.

"You're banishing me?" he asked. The word of banishment spread quickly, and it would be likely no town or village would allow him to reside inside their gates.

"It was recorded before Kempschester fell, that the son of Thomas Blake was in servitude to the Lord of Kempshire. I hereby send you back and release you into his custody. There, you will be put to work. You're not my problem any more." He gave a tight smile.

Servitude? Zachary turned.

"I have bought your freedom." Lord Markus pulled down the hood of his cloak, revealing himself to be the third figure. "You will help me rebuild Kempschester, and I have need for a blacksmith."

Zachary stared in shock, both at Lord Markus's presence and his words. He had shown the Lord no manners in their interactions. Lord Markus had no reason to show him such kindness.

"I have lost a good Enforcer and Captain," Lord Gerard said. "Say what you need to him; we will discuss our trade agreement afterwards." With that, Lord Gerard left the room.

"You're rebuilding Kempschester?" Zachary asked.

"Your father has given me his word that he will no longer torment the people," Lord Markus said in a low voice.

"My father has a recognisable face. One of which mine is almost a mirror image. The people of Kempshire remember him, and I do not think they will welcome me," Zachary pointed out.

"They have welcomed their new Lord, and I will make sure they understand you are not your father. Just as I am not mine," Lord Markus said. "I have heard many things about the man my father was, as much as who yours was."

"You have blacksmiths in Hazelbury, why would you request me?" Zachary asked uncertain why Lord Markus would help him.

"Are you trying to find excuses not to go?" Lord Markus laughed. "Is it not what Raven would want for you? With what she gave up?"

Raven, the one he knew, might. But who she had become, had walked away. Yet she had also allowed him to walk free. Released from Darkness, and his duty to the dead.

"I was to be in your father's servitude," he said. "I could never have guessed it would be his son to see that through." Finally, he met Tobias's eyes. "Why are you here?"

"I will help fund the rebuild," Tobias said. "I'm going. too. Perhaps to celebrate the reopening of a once-thriving town, we can hold a tournament, for nobles as well as peasants."

Zachary held back a smile, recalling that Tobias had once asked him to enter a tournament, and that he sought a challenge in his fights.

Tobias gave him a sly smile. "You have a chance to start over, Zachary, and I hope our previous arrangements can continue to benefit us both, and evolve." He turned towards Lord Markus. "Until I have established my own dwelling, I will need a place to stay."

Lord Markus nodded. "There is a manor a short distance from town. I can open up a bedroom for you."

"Thank you. I will see you both in a few days." Tobias smiled again and hurried from the room.

Zachary flexed his aching shoulders. "So, will I have a place to stay, too?"

" I will have a private wing built for you *and* your family in my estate," Lord Markus said.

"My family?" he asked.

"Lord Markus has invited us too. Where Arthur can have a fresh start." Delia said. "Where he can know his father. If you'll take us."

Speechless, Zachary felt a wide grin spread across his face. The woman he had loved was giving up her life in Oakborough to follow him across the country. "You said you loved me."

"I did." She smiled back at him.

Zachary strode towards her and took her hands in his. He wanted her in his life, and he had let her go once already. The last year had shown him to not waste chances. "Marry me."

"Marry you?" she repeated.

"We already have a son. I will not want another like I want you. Join me in Kempschester as my wife," he proposed.

Delia gave him a small smile. "You would wed me?"

"Do you see any reason not to? You have my heart, and I would declare this to all of Oakborough, or Kempschester." He took her hand. "Delia, I have lost much in my life, and I would be a foolish man to let you go."

"I will marry you," she whispered. "Leaving you was the worst mistake I made in my life."

He put his hands on her hips, and he pulled her into a kiss. His heart soared. She returned the urgency of his kiss, neither of them wanting to let go.

"I'm never letting you go," he whispered when the kiss ended, his hands still on her hips.

"Good. I have a request though." She smiled up at him. "That you take Arthur on as an apprentice and teach him the craft of sword fighting." Her smile widened. "Both of us. I would like to learn. Raven was an inspiration with her skills, and I know it was you who taught her."

He laughed. "I will deny you nothing, my heart."

Chapter 60

Raven let the shadows twirl around her body. In The Shadow Realm, she could feel her father's presence, dark and cold. He stood before her, arms folded.

"Push the Darkness down; will yourself to look human," her father told her.

She didn't want to. She felt no need for it.

"I've denied it my whole life, why should I hide it now? Was it not you who said to show the world who I am?" she asked.

"You feared it. You need to *comfort* people in their final moments, not terrify them." His tone was what she'd imagined of a father. A strange side to him.

She let out a chuckle. "That sounds like more fun."

"Raven, I need you to focus," he instructed.

"Is this when you threaten to trap me here? Zac may have been terrified of The Shadow Realm, but I'm not," she declared.

His shape changed, as he towered over her. "**Listen to me, daughter. There is worse I can do to you**."

She eyed him. "I'm not afraid of you." The idea bought her joy. Before, she had not only been fearful of the Darkness inside her, but also of her father. Of Death. That she was his daughter. She had fought so hard against the idea that she would be like him.

He glared. "**Isaac was less of a pain than you.**"

Zac had told her of the intoxication that came with letting the Darkness in. "Father, I just want to enjoy this. You've had twenty years, perhaps you've forgotten what it feels like. It's new to me."

"**I have not forgotten,**" he told her. "**You have plenty of time to enjoy it, Raven. This is you, now; it's not going away. You can terrify people as much as you like, just not the dying.**" He chuckled, the sound echoing around them. "*I spent twenty years finding pleasure in tormenting them, drawing out that fear. We have nothing but time. I stopped ageing, I believe you will too.*"

"Alright." She focused on the Darkness within her. It was a living presence that was immersed with her very essence. She pushed it down as her father had instructed. "Did it work?" she asked.

He shook his head. "**We'll work on that.**"

She tried again, focusing on the Darkness. Closing her eyes, and taking a deep breath. It lived inside her, and always had. The desire to get a grip on what she could do pushed her to dig deep. To understand what she was. As she focused, the Darkness within responded. She opened her eyes, taking in the dark, shadowed appearance of her father. Something inside her shifted, and she found herself falling. She put her arms out for balance, and wings caught the air. She stared in shock. Wings made of shadow and darkness. She had taken on a new shape, just as her father had.

'**Fly, Raven**.' Father told her, instruction in his voice replaced by pride.

"This is who you are. This is what you are. Enjoy it."

"I became a bird?' Her voice was just as his, filled with darkness, coming from inside her.

"Not just any bird. A raven," came his reply.

She lifted herself into the air, thrilled by the ability to fly. Her darker self had waited for this her entire life. Below her, her father watched. She left him behind, letting herself go. The darkness no longer lived inside her. She *was* the darkness, taking on a fitting shape.

She wasn't sure how long had passed before she returned to her father's side. It took her a while to bring back her human shape, no longer feeling like that form was her true form. She grinned at her father.

"Well done," he said, his own form taking on that of Graeme Blake. Her father's form. "I want to show you something." His hand gripped her shoulder, and The Shadow Realm shifted around them.

They stood in the courtyard of a manor. Markus was there, talking to Zachary.

"Are you disappointed he left us?" she asked.

His eyes glinted as he watched. "Yes. But he held on to his humanity, fought for it. The two of you, this was both of your fate, but you're right, he was not made for this. The Darkness inside him was not as strong as that with which you were born. It was something that came from his death, and from the time I brought him to The Shadow Realm."

"What about his children?" she asked.

Her father pointed. Delia was nearby, talking to Arthur, and dark flames shifted inside the boy. "They are like you, born with the dark flame that will only grow as they do.".

Her father then pointed to Markus. "Do you feel it with him? Can you see it?"

A dark flame within him did burn strongly, tendrils wrapping around his essence. "It draws me to it," she uttered. Something came over her. "Markus."

Markus turned his head at the sound towards where they stood, and his lips curved into a small smile.

"Did he hear me?" she asked in disbelief.

"It is likely. His return from The Shadow Realm has changed him," her father told her.

"Will he be like us?" She watched Markus.

Father took a while to answer. "I am uncertain. There is a possibility it will only be the ability to sense us, or The Shadow Realm."

"What if he embraces that Darkness?" The idea of having Markus appealed to her.

"You will do nothing to encourage that, Raven. I know you care for him, and the idea of him being like us appeals to you. He is the son of Lord Samson; I will not have his descendants follow me through The Shadow Realm." her father chided her.

She laughed. "You really hated Lord Samson. Does it bother you that I took his son to bed?"

Her father answered with a cold stare.

A nudging inside Raven distracted her. She turned her head. It was almost as if someone were whispering to her. Instead, she turned her attention back to Markus and Zac. Their discussion about rebuilding Kempschester bored her.

"Why are we here? You said he won't see us again."

"Until it is his time, he will not see us. I wanted to show you what has become of his life. He is to be married."

"Married?" she glanced between Zac and Delia.

"While you were marvelling at the Darkness and The Shadow Realm the last few months, I looked in on Isaac as he asked Delia to marry him. I believe they will wed soon."

The whispering started again, but she continued to ignore it. "Will we see him get married?"

"Unseen, from this side of the veil," he agreed.

She frowned as the nudging grew more persistent. "What is that?"

His eyes turned to her. "Do you feel it? The calling?"

Is that what it is? "I…I'm being pulled somewhere, and someone is whispering to me."

He smiled. "Follow it. I will be with you."

She did as instructed, The Shadow Realm guiding her. Fine shivers started within as she allowed herself to be drawn towards her calling. Her entire existence became about it. She came to a stop, peering through the veil. She had taken lives before, but this was the first time she'd be taking a soul to The Crossover.

"Don't stop," her father's voice came from behind her. "You must see it through."

It was taking Raven time to get used to stepping through the veil. The Shadow Realm clung to her as she tried. Finally, she stepped through, finding herself near the graveyard of Eskham.

"We're in Eskham," she said, surprised.

"This is your calling; you cannot resist it," her father told her.

"I won't," she replied. "It just surprised me to be back here. I haven't returned since my mother died."

A woman knelt over a grave ahead of them, her head bowed. Something in the woman connected with Raven, and overwhelming grief flooded in. "What is that?" she asked as a tear slid down her cheek. "I feel..."

"You've connected with her. We feel what they do in their last moments. If she is drowning in pain, you'll feel it."

Uncomfortable, she forced down the anguish, moving forward until she stood over the woman. Not knowing what to do, she reached for the woman's shoulder. Then Elaine's eyes met hers.

"Lucian?" Elaine's voice shook.

Lucian? Why is she calling me Lucian? Only then did she notice her hands were not hers, but those she knew very well.

"You can take the shape of those they love." Her father's voice was in her head. *"That was not something I thought you'd do so quickly. It comforts them."*

She held her hand out to Elaine, waiting for the woman to take it. Only then did she catch sight of the name on the headstone. Charles Carter.

"Lucian, how are you here? Am I dreaming?" Elaine asked.

"You're not dreaming. It's time to go home," she said in Lucian's voice. "Come with me."

Elaine grasped Raven's hand, allowing herself to be pulled to her feet, but pulled it away quickly.

"You're not my Lucian. There is something unnatural about you. Show your true face," Elaine said.

Raven let the form of Lucian recede.

"Raven?" There was fear in the woman's eyes. "How did you…" She left the sentence unfinished.

"Calm her," Father said with his mind. *"If she screams or runs, you will have to give chase."*

"Lucian is waiting for you," she said. "So are Noah, and Rosamund. And Charles." She held her hand out again. "You have lost much, Elaine, and suffered heartbreak. Let me take you to them. Let me take you home."

Tears streamed down Elaine's cheeks. "They're waiting for me? How?"

"They're at peace," Raven said.

"You're taking me there?" Hope filled Elaine's eyes. And fear.

"I'm taking you home," she said again.

Finally, the woman took Raven's hand.

What do I do now?

As if he heard, Father stepped closer, lifting her free hand, placing it over Elaine's heart. As soon as contact was made, energy flowed from Raven. Elaine gasped, her eyes white before they closed. Raven lowered her body to the ground.

"You did well." Father told her. "But you're not finished yet. You have to take her to The Crossover. Prepare yourself for your mother to come to you, though."

Back in The Shadow Realm, Elaine smiled. "I'm ready to see my children. Take me home, Raven."

Somehow, she knew the way to The Crossover. Peace surrounded her, while the realm pushed at her.

Lucian, Noah, and Rosamund did not take long to show. Followed by Charles.

"I release you," she told Elaine. "You are at peace now. Join them."

Lucian's eyes met her own. "Raven?"

He had been her first love, and that had not died. She gazed back, recalling the feel of his arms around her. The grief of his death had been overwhelming and she was glad to see him. She offered a smile.

“She is not Raven any more,” Elaine said. “I don’t know how, but she brought me here. My children, my husband, I am so happy to see you.”

The five of them embraced.

“Raven?” her mother stood before her.

“I brought Elaine home,” Raven said.

“You’re not my little Raven any more, are you?” Her mother’s eyes darted over Raven’s face.

“She has answered her first calling.” Her father’s pride was clear in his voice. “You had your time with her, Amelia; now, it is my time. She has given in to the Darkness within her. You cannot talk her out of it, like you and Emma did with Isaac.”

“Did you choose this?” her mother asked.

“I did,” she admitted.

Her mother wrapped her in a hug. “I just want to know that you’re happy, Raven. If this is what you chose, I still love you.”

Raven’s arms remained at her side. “I have to go.”

“Will I see you again?” her mother asked.

“You will scnsc hcr prcscncc cvcry timc shc rcturns to this rcalm,” hcr father said. “Just as my parents feel my presence.”

“They do not appear?” Raven asked.

“I do not linger long enough. The times I have, my father dislikes my presence. My mother enjoys her peace. I have seen her a few times, but I leave before any words are spoken. That time you saw her was the first time we spoke.” He turned his gaze on Raven. “We must go.”

Raven followed him back into The Shadow Realm.

“So, when does the fun start?” Raven asked. She wanted fear. She wanted to give chase the way she had seen father do. To hear screams as people ran from her.

He chuckled. “You did well, daughter. You’ve taken to this better than Isaac did. I’m proud of you.” He grabbed her arm. “I have promised your

Enforcer...the new Lord... to stay out of his shire, but there are many other places that know me, that fear me. But I need my horse."

I don't have a horse. Zac had claimed back Lance, and she didn't know what had become of Nutmeg. Her father led her to a stable. Inside were a large dog, and a black horse with a white mane.

"She's beautiful. I've heard about her...named after Lady Guinevere." She reached for the animal. "Zac loved that story, too; he named his horse after Lancelot."

In the next stall was another horse, a white one.

"This is mine. Willow. You will ride her," her father announced.

"You named your horse Willow?" she laughed.

"Your mother was from Willowdale," he said as an explanation.

She knew of Willowdale and decided to visit it one day.

"Where will we go?" she asked.

He gave her a slow smile. "I promised not to torment those of Kempshire, but I said nothing about Thornesby. That is the next shire over, and the people there still speak my name in fear. We will go there."

"Do we ride to them through The Shadow Realm?"

"We can. Or we can ride through the forest. It would please me to ride with you." He held something out to her. "I retrieved this for you."

She let him fasten the black cloak around her shoulders. The one Lucian had gifted her. "Thank you."

He mounted the black horse. "Do you want to stand in the burned ruins of what was once our home, or do you want to announce the new you to the world?"

She climbed onto the white horse, dark joy coursing through her. "Lead the way, Father."

Chapter 61

In the courtyard of the Manor, Zachary stood next to Lord Markus as they waited for Delia. His heart swelled. He'd hoped for this for a long time, and he had once thought Delia would be the one he would marry, until she'd left him. For the wedding, he'd bought his children new clothes, and he'd given Delia money to buy a dress from Hazelbury, but he was yet to see it.

The sword he'd made a year ago sat at his hip. Dressed in a dark green tunic, brown trousers, with a fur-lined cloak, with his hair pulled back, he no longer looked like a peasant, and he had been announced as a noble, much to Tobias's surprise and amusement. Known to be Lord Markus's private blacksmith, he'd already established a reputation for his craft.

Tobias had struck a bargain with the nobles and soldiers to do business with Zachary. He hoped it would bring wider business soon from the surrounding towns and villages.

He and Delia lived in their own wing in the Lord's manor with Arthur. With a smithy in Hazelbury, he had plans to own a second one, along with their own home in Kempschester after the rebuild. Zachary was still in disbelief at how much his life had changed in a matter of months, and he would never have dreamed of returning to the very shire of his childhood.

They'd found his father's sword in the courtyard of the Estate, which he placed on display in his smithy in Hazelbury, for people to know that The Shadow of Death was gone. Many hailed him and Lord Markus responsible, but recognition as the son of a killer still followed him.

"I wish Raven could be here," he murmured. "She never got her wedding day; she would have appreciated this moment."

"You miss her. I do, too." Lord Markus said.

"Before everything happened, we were as close as brother and sister, bonded in our fear of what our fathers were, and the Darkness that we knew would find us. Nothing could separate us." He laughed, memories rising of a younger Raven. "She was so determined to be like me, begging me to teach her to fight. Aunt Amelia was so annoyed when I actually did. But she supported anything Raven did, even if it scared her." He sighed. "The little girl who adored her big brother is gone. She sought to free me from The Shadow Realm, only to take my place."

Lord Markus lowered his gaze. "At risk of you wanting to burn my eyes out, I considered asking her to marry me."

Zachary shook with laughter. "You have granted me freedom; and with all you've done, I think we've moved past that threat."

"If only you knew at the time it was a Lord you were threatening." Lord Markus grinned. "I care for Raven, and I would never have hurt her."

"I know. She cared deeply for you. I'm sorry you lost her, too." He cast a glance around the courtyard. "She should have been a part of my wedding."

Lord Markus's focus shifted before returning to his face. "She is here. So is your father."

"They are?" He frowned. "You can see?"

"Ever since your father brought me back, I have caught glimpses. Only when they're there."

"How often is that?" Zachary shifted his gaze around the empty courtyard.

"Only one other time. I can *hear* them, but I have to concentrate to *see* them," Lord Markus revealed.

"Does this not concern you? Only those with Darkness can see The Shadow Realm." Zachary said.

"No." Lord Markus shook his head.

"Raven?" Zachary called out. "If you're going to be at my wedding, will you not show yourself? And Father?"

Lord Markus winced. "They're not happy that I'm telling you. Your father says that you desired a life without Darkness, so they are remaining unseen to you. You know this."

"I still hoped my father and sister would be a part of my wedding." It hurt that they wouldn't show themselves for his wedding.

He would never see them again, until the day he died.

Lord Markus shook his head. "If they make an exception today, they will have to make more."

That sounded like his father's words.

"Raven's here!" Giselle declared happily as she and her brothers walked from the manor.

Her eyes darted across to Zachary. "Ooh, sorry." Lord Markus's deep laughter boomed from him.

"alright, stop." Zachary said to the both of them. "If they are to remain unseen to me, then I don't want to know if they're there." He faced the direction Lord Markus and Giselle had been looking. "Thank you both for being here. Seen or unseen, I'm glad you're here."

Giselle smiled and rushed over to Zachary. "Aunt Delia is beautiful in her dress."

"She's always beautiful," he replied, shifting with impatience. "What's taking her so long?"

"Mother is doing her hair. She wanted it in braids," Arthur said

Delia usually wore her hair in braids, which he imagined it took a while to do.

Lord Markus nudged him. "Here she comes."

The whole world stopped. She wore a simple blue dress. Her eyes lit up as she met his.

"What name are you using?" Lord Markus asked.

"Blake," he replied in a low voice. "She doesn't know everything, but I told her that much."

"Will you ever tell her everything?" Lord Markus asked.

"One day," he affirmed.

Grace walked beside Delia, the children watching with smiles.

"You look as beautiful as ever," he told her when she reached them, holding his arm out.

"Still the charmer," she said, wrapping her arm around his arm.

He leaned forward to kiss her. "At least now you know it's only you I will charm."

"The great Zachary Dale committed to one woman." Grace said. "I never thought I'd see this day."

It was always going to be her. He'd discussed his wedding with Grace, and she'd passed on her blessing.

"I never saw myself marrying you," Grace had said. "It was never anything beyond what we shared. I could see even then you loved her. I got to know her over the last year, and it was clear she cared deeply for you."

"That didn't bother you?" he'd asked.

She laughed. "You were Zachary Dale; you drew the women in. I shared six months in your bed, and we both moved on. I'm happy to go, too, so you can see Giselle and Joseph. They deserve to know their father. But I'm happy that you're marrying Delia. You and she are well suited for each other."

They embraced. "I hope you find someone that makes you happy," he told her as they pulled apart.

"I am a widow with children, I do not know if men will consider me. But I am content with my life the way it is. Don't worry about me," she said to comfort

him.

"I have enough to support you and them," he informed her.

"I am not struggling for coin," she said. "You've always known I have money." She paused. "From what I know, you do too. Playing the role of the peasant with all that hidden away."

"Shall we start?" Lord Markus asked, pulling Zachary back.

"Yes!" He squeezed Delia's arm.

"You are my first official act as Lord Markus," he admitted and straightened his shoulders. "I, Markus Kemp, Lord of Kempshire…" He paused, a stunned expression on his face. "…stand before my ancestral home, with these witnesses, to unite the two of you, Zachary Blake and Delia Wright, to be wed. Delia, you have agreed to marry Zachary, do you have any words before I declare you as husband and wife?"

"Yes." Delia turned to face Zachary. "In the two years we were together, that man I got to know was one who lost himself in his work, but always had time for his family. You had a…" She glanced at the children. "Certain reputation, and there was a rule: Love the man, but don't fall in love. I saw beneath your surface. I saw pain, and I wanted to be the one to soothe that hurt. I never wanted to be the one to cause it. I spent five years in regret and pining after a man that I abandoned. Because I broke the rule, and I did fall in love. But I put our past behind us, and I look forward to our future. With all of my heart, I promise that I will remain by your side until there is no more breath in me."

"Zachary?" Lord Markus nodded to him.

A single tear slid down Delia's cheek. Without hesitating, he wiped it away. "I will always be here to wipe away your tears." He caressed her cheek with the back of his fingers. "It was always you. I didn't know it until I woke up and you were gone. And like a fool, I didn't try to bring you back. Instead, I tried to find happiness elsewhere, and the more I sought that out, the lonelier I felt. I yearned to caress your cheek one more time, to have your fingers in my hair, to wake up with you beside me." He cupped her cheek with his hand, and her eyes closed as she leaned into it. "You raised our son alone and did a fine job. I shall share the duty with you now, as I should have in the first five years of his life." Warmth spread across his chest. "I am home, and I have everything I need with my wife at my side. The sun shall always shine with you in my life." He whispered and removed his cloak, placing it around Delia's shoulders. "I will always keep you warm."

Delia made what sounded like a choked sob.

"I'm sorry, I know I have to wait, but I can't." Zachary said to Lord Markus, and cupping both sides of her face, he kissed her hard. There was no resistance in her as she let him in, her hands over his. His heart soared.

"By the laws of…myself, I hereby declare you two wed. Delia, and Zachary Blake."

Chapter 62

O*ne year later - 1370*

Raven held a bundle in her arms as she walked into Lord Markus's bedroom from The Shadow Realm. Next to her, her father held another. The Lord was putting on armour.

"Markus," she murmured.

He jumped, spinning around. "Raven. My Lady of Darkness." His face lit up at the sight of her.

"You have done a good job here, Lord Markus. You have more honour than that of your father. I've seen the way you care for the people," her father said.

"You've been watching me? You cannot be here; you gave me your word," Markus reminded him.

"My word holds still; I am here for this." Her father held the bundle out to Markus.

Markus stepped forward, peering into it. "A child?"

Her father handed the baby to Markus and left through The Shadow Realm.

"Two, actually. Twins." Raven said. "Ours. Amelia, and Emma Blake. A blessing, from our time together."

"I missed you," Markus whispered. "Your visits ended, and I thought I'd never see you again."

Against her father's wishes, she had returned to Markus a few times. Her father had informed her of the life that grew inside her, and ordered her to leave Markus until she gave birth. He had agreed to let her reveal the news to him.

Markus glanced down at the babies and back up at Raven. "Blakes? Not Kemps?"

Laughter burst from Raven. "Do you want to claim them as Kemps? The Ladies of Kempshire?"

"It has a nice sound to it." Joy filtered across his face. "You brought them to show me?"

"You're their father. I see no need in hiding them from you." She winced. "I met your father. The life that grew in me awoke him every time I entered The Crossover. He recognised me as the daughter of Graeme Blake, and he knew I had a connection to you. He's as annoyed as my father is that I bore your children."

"Are they normal?" he asked about the twins.

Raven lay Amelia on his bed, unwrapping her. Marked with Darkness, it was unmistakable she was not entirely human. "I don't know if they will have any control over that. They were born in The Shadow Realm. Their eyes are black, like mine."

"Black or blue, they're still beautiful." He lay Emma next to her sister. "What is it with your family and twins?" He laughed, reaching for her hands.

"I'm glad to see you. Your cousin is doing well, it took people a while to accept him, because of his father. But he's built their trust. I thought it would be a few years before I saw you again." His smile faded. "Is that why you're here?"

"I am not here for that." Raven pulled her hands away from his. Desire burned within her, that hadn't changed. She was drawn to the Darkness within him; it excited her. She wanted to see his eyes turn black again.

Relief shone from his eyes. "Then I ask that you marry me. My Lady Sunshine, Lady Death, whatever name you want to take, add mine to it."

Speechless, she squeezed his hands. "You know I cannot do that, Markus."

His relief turned to hurt. He reached for her face, and she caught his hand, forcing it away before she could give in.

"You and I are on different paths. I have my duty to the dead now. You have yours to Kempshire."

"And our daughters?" he asked.

"Their fate will be the same as mine." His lack of reaction surprised her. "You do not seem bothered by that."

"I have learned that your family has your connection to Darkness, and there is no use in fighting such things," he admitted.

A light knock tapped against the door. She turned her head. "Is that Zac?

"Aunt Raven?" A voice called through the door.

How does Giselle know I'm here?

The door opened, Giselle smiling at her from the doorway. "I dreamed of you," the girl said.

Raven and Markus both moved to stand in front of their daughters.

"Did you tell your father?" she asked.

"No. You told me not to." Giselle said.

"I did?"

"Can I see my cousins?" When Raven didn't move, Giselle gave her a reassuring smile. "It's alright, Aunt. I will keep the family secret."

Raven glanced at Markus, his eyes reflecting the shock she felt. "Family secret? Giselle, what are your dreams about?"

"You, and a man shrouded in shadow. His eyes change colour; so does his shape. I see you as a raven. We're in a strange place, one of fog and a blue moon. Joseph and Arthur are there, too." Giselle told her.

Raven had similar dreams when she was younger, of her and Zachary with their fathers in what she now knew to be The Shadow Realm. "I'm sorry you dream of such things," she said.

Giselle ran to her and hugged her around the waist. "I'm not. It means I can see you again. I missed you. So do my brothers. Father does too."

Raven crouched in front of the girl. "Giselle, I am not here to stay."

"I know. But we will see you again. And them." She pointed to the twins.

"You dreamed that?" Raven asked.

"No, I just know it," Giselle replied.

Darkness already burned within her niece, showing the child what lay ahead. "Are you not afraid?" Raven asked.

Giselle shook her head. "Not if you're there. I know you would never hurt us, so we are safe." She looked towards Emma and Amelia. "Can I meet them?"

Raven stood. "There is something unusual about them that may frighten you," she said.

Giselle peered into the faces of the girls. Raven watched her, fearful the child would scream or cry, attracting attention. Instead, joy shifted across her face. "Was I like that when I was born?"

Raven laughed. "No, you were not. They are from…"

"They're from the shadowy place?" Giselle turned around, gazing at Raven. "Father hasn't told us everything yet. Can you take me there?"

Markus shook his head in disbelief.

"You are not ready for that, Giselle. But soon. You and your brothers. Be patient," Raven instructed. The calling nudged at her. "I need to go." She reached out to her father. "Father."

"Leave them here." Markus said. "We can watch them until you get back."

"Are you certain?" This was the girls' first time in the mortal realm, and she wasn't sure she should leave them here.

"Raven, I'm their father, let me do this for you," he offered. "Let me know them."

No longer able to ignore being pulled elsewhere, she accepted. “Keep them in here in case my father returns. You don’t want him to go looking.”

“Understood, go.”

Chapter 63

Twenty years later - 1390

Zachary lay in his bed struggling to breathe, warm with fever. His children sat around him, with their husband and wives, and his grandchildren. Arthur was soon to be twenty-five, with a beautiful woman by the name of Ivette. The twins, twenty-four, Joseph and Giselle, with their others, Lia, and Theobald. His children's faces were tear-streaked. Giselle touched his hand.

"Father." She sobbed. "It's almost time."

"It's alright," he rasped. "I'm surrounded by all of you; that's all anyone could ask for." He smiled at his children. "I'm proud of all of you." He grasped Arthur's arm. "I shall soon see Delia, my dear wife." She had left him two years before.

Giselle held his hand tight, and he gave hers a squeeze.

He started to drift off, and the gasps of his children woke him up. He gazed into white and black eyes.

"I've been waiting for you," he whispered.

His boys' wives left the room with the children. Theobald hesitated.

"Go, comfort them", Giselle said, standing to face Death.

"Hello, grandfather," Arthur said. "We've heard about you."

"I've been watching you all," his father said.

A shadowed raven flew into the room through the veil, and changed into the form of a woman. He gazed into black eyes.

"Zac." When she spoke, it was not the voice he remembered, but full of Darkness. "It is good to see you, big brother."

A wide grin spread across his face. "I've missed you, Raven."

"Aunt Raven?" Arthur frowned. "You're the same as you were when I was a boy."

Zachary smiled up at her. "You are."

"I can't say the same for you," she said.

Zachary's laughter turned into a coughing fit.

Arthur and Joseph moved to Zachary's side.

"Help me up," he croaked.

His sons helped him to a sitting position.

"Your children have grown," Raven said.

"Do they have Darkness in them?" he asked.

Raven turned her head towards their father.

His father's gaze was on the children, with a small smile on his lips. "It is your time, Zachary," he said at last.

He called me Zachary. Overwhelmed that his father had recognised his name, he could only smile.

"We'll take you home," Raven said as she and their father moved around his bed, standing on either side of him.

His children took a step back. Joseph put his arm around Giselle to comfort her.

"It's alright, my children," he said. "I'll see you again."

Raven placed her hand over his heart, she and Death holding his hands. The shift was as quick as the blink of an eye. He found himself in The Shadow Realm. Many years ago, he had been trapped here, fighting to get out. Fear spiked.

"Are you going to leave me here again?" he asked.

"No, I'm taking you home." Raven told him. "You have nothing to fear, Zac."

He turned again to take in the sight of his children.

Raven touched his arm. "They will live long lives. You did well to prepare them."

"I still don't want this for them," he told her.

"You fought your own battle; you cannot fight theirs, too," his father told him. "It is up to them. Are you not tired of fighting, son?"

I am tired. He nodded.

"Are you ready?" Raven asked. "Your family is waiting."

Delia. Mother. Amelia. Zachary turned around to look one last time upon his family. Giselle was crying, and tears slid down his sons' faces as they stood over his body.

"I'll be alright," he told them. Each of them looked up, staring right at him. "I love you, my children." His daughter gave a small smile and whispered to Joseph.

Finally, Zachary turned away from them.

"I'm ready," he said. "My fight is over. Take me home."

Acknowledgements

Jess M, I can't thank you enough for the unwavering confidence you've had in me and in this story. You believed in it when I was on the verge of giving up.

My beta readers: Michelle, Nicole, and Jess D. Your feedback and comments on Death's Shadow got me excited about this book again. It very well may not have happened if not for you.

To the readers who found me through other books and became enthusiastic to read this one, thank you for your support.

About the Author

Serra is an author of dark historical fantasy and paranormal romance books with stories that draw you in from page one. Within these worlds that she created, you will find unbreakable family bonds, darker aspects to humanity, shadow realms as well as passion, lust, strong FMCs and men who would risk anything for the women they love.

Serra's journey to becoming an author started from a young age, when her first creative writing attempt—a poem titled 'The Mighty Oak Tree,"—was published in her primary school newsletter. An avid reader with a vivid imagination, her Mum always encouraged her to keep writing. She proceeded to write poetry and short stories before discovering a deeper passion for novel writing and screenplays.

In 2021, she adapted a screenplay she'd been working on, into her debut novel 'The Shadow Within,' which was published in November 2023.

Serra is a Melbourne-based author from New Zealand. As a reader and a writer, she's drawn into the dark fantasy and paranormal romance genres. Like many authors, she balances her writing alongside a day job in which she works in the communications part of a marketing and digital team; by night, she's a weaver of words, creator of worlds bringing forth stories that hold readers captive.

If you wish to subscribe, please visit:

www.serrarosewrites.com

Be the first to receive updates and sneak peeks at character art, quotes, chapters, next projects and early access to pre-orders.

Also by Serra Rose

The Horsemen Chronicles:

The Shadow Within

Death's Shadow

Upcoming Titles in The Horsemen Chronicles:

The Whispers of War

The Echoes of War

The Scourge of Famine

The Plague of Humanity

The Bloodsong Series:

Bloodsong

Consumed

Upcoming Titles in The Bloodsong Series:

Bloodking

The Bloodsong Series Spin-offs:

Eternity

Lovestruck

Lovesong

www.ingramcontent.com/pod-product-compliance
Lightning Source LLC
Chambersburg PA
CBHW030351310726
48979CB00001B/257

* 9 7 8 0 9 7 5 6 1 0 2 7 5 *